THREE LITTLE GIRLS

By

JANE BADROCK

?

Question Mark Press

I, Jane Badrock, hereby assert and give notice of my rights under section 77 of the Copyright, Design and Patents Act, 1988 to be identified as the author of this work.

All rights reserved. No part of this publication may be reproduced, stored in a retrieval system or transmitted at any time by any means electronic, mechanical, photocopying, recording or otherwise, without prior permission.

All characters in this publication are fictitious and any resemblance to real persons, living or dead, is purely coincidental

First published in 2021 by Question Mark Press

Cover art by Elli Toney

1

Saturday 2 November 2013

Detective Sergeant Karen Thorpe, outside, in the dark of a cold evening, flattened her slender frame against the brick wall and edged towards the corner. Holding her breath so as not to give herself away, she risked a quick peek. *They're there*. She gently held her charged pistol close to her side. Timing was everything.

She counted to herself. *One...two...three...* she pounced.

'Hold it right there!' she shouted. 'Hands up!'

Her prey, looking terrified, did as they were told.

'Back there!' Karen nodded her head the way she had just come and watched as her subjects obeyed her command.

'Pick it up now, or I shoot!'

'You're mad,' the little girl said.

'Shush.' The boy replied as he picked up the sweet wrapper and put it in the litter bin. 'We'll get her later,' he whispered.

'What did you say?' Karen stepped forward, holding her water pistol with menace. She fired. 'Take that you little beasts, and don't let me see you around here again.'

The children ran off giving her finger gestures as they went. Karen smiled at her success and went back into her apartment building. At least she'd had a tiny bit of action.

Earlier that day she'd been to visit Stella Cary, which was nice, but it also reminded her of the most exciting case she had ever managed. And still, the trial date had not been set. That was an irritation she and Stella had in common.

In the intervening months, try as hard as she could, there had been nothing happening in the day job to get her pulse racing. Yes, work was always busy, but it was all footwork and paperwork. Even her sometime boyfriend John had seemingly abandoned her to spend more time with his parents. His mother had recently had a hysterectomy and seemed to be taking the longest recovery time in history.

Settling down in her flat, she began knocking back the wine while watching the latest talent show. Unfortunately for her, it was at that stage where more of the show was about the contestants' background than their performing ability. She preferred the thrill of the voting and especially the more vicious comments from the judges.

Ignoring the inevitable *It's my dream* gush, Karen looked behind the bum-fluffed teenage lad to see some rather lovely background scenery. It reminded her that there was something that she had been putting off for far too long. She had inherited her late father's house and had no idea what to do with it. Could she sell it and find something nicer?

Her fingers scrabbled towards her tablet – a new feature in her life and a present from John.

Finding the website 'Homes4U' she typed in *rural* and began to browse. Almost immediately one particular house caught her eye. It was newish-looking in a so-called desirable semi-rural location in Lincoln. The Robin Estate.

A flickering of the lights alerted her to a small power surge. When she looked back at her tablet it was on screen saver mode, but pressing the button an image appeared.

'Blimey,' she said out loud. 'How cute'. On the screen, she saw a country lane, and standing in the middle was a little girl wearing a pretty layered party dress. She was waving as if she'd seen the camera coming. Karen rarely had time for children much but this girl looked so happy. *And very old-fashioned. Must take a screenshot. I could put it on Wonder Web in the morning.*

She pressed the buttons and went back to watching the programme. It was nearly finishing; the votes were in, and she reckoned that the old geezer was about to be knocked out.

'You were shite!' she shouted at the television as she polished off the bottle. An enormous yawn escaped her mouth, and she realised she was tired. She brushed her teeth and clambered into bed in her onesie. She slept easily and snored like an ancient sow, careless as to whether anybody was there to hear her or not.

Sunday 3 November

Karen woke up and rubbed her head. *No more cheap wine for you* she thought as she trudged to the kitchen to make herself some coffee – a procedure which in John's absence required the removal of the previous week's takeaways and ready meal remains.

She put the kettle on and gathered her thoughts. Gradually she realised it was Sunday, still the weekend and nobody – other than absolute geeks – would be in work that day. Guiltily she smuggled the unwashed foil containers, bags, and cardboard into a black bag and merely nodded at the unwashed cutlery and glasses before going into her living room. *Later* she decided.

Slouched on the sofa, she reached for the remote and turned the television on. She quite liked *The Moral Debate* but the TV was still tuned to the channel she'd been watching the night before. It was a rerun, on the exact same point when Lincoln came up. *Why does that happen? If I watch a programme in a series twice, it's always the same episode.*

It reminded her of the little girl and she reached for her tablet. She looked through the photos. There was no sign of the little girl. *Did I imagine it?* Pop-up ad, she decided as she answered the call of her grumbling stomach and hauled herself into the kitchen to make some toast.

Damn, need to do the washing. The washing mountain in her bedroom had reached the wardrobe doorknob meaning that if she left it any longer she would have to buy new clothes. She bundled a shirtful of laundry from the floor into the kitchen tripping over the rubbish bag as she went.

Her flat gradually took on the appearance of a very poor Chinese laundry. By the evening she was looking forward to the week ahead. *Something's got to happen someday*.

2

Monday 4 November

Karen's police station was a short drive away. This morning, instead of arguing with the news channel presenter and his guests, she sang. There was a certain song in the back of her mind, something about little girls in blue dresses. But she couldn't remember all the words so she bellowed what she could, interspersed with 'um's and nods all the way to the car park. She stopped only when she went into the station. 'Morning Bill.' She greeted the desk sergeant.

'Nice to see you looking so cheery, Karen.'

'Good weekend. You?' She didn't wait for his reply, instead she went into the main office, her eye catching something on her desk as she hung up her coat. Approaching her desk, she was immediately flummoxed to see a thick bundle of papers in a grey cardboard cover. She knew by its colour it was a cold case file. *Like Dad used to get.*

'What's this?' She yelled into the office.

'You asked for it,' came the reply from a young woman already walking away.

'No, I didn't,' said Karen, now apparently talking to herself.

'Check your emails,' came a fading reply as the admin assistant disappeared down the stairs.

Karen turned on her PC leaving it chugging into wakefulness while she walked to the coffee machine for hot chocolate. When she returned, she sat down and began to leaf through the file. It consisted of photocopied old records about a little girl who had gone missing in 1964. *Not my thing at all*. Karen thought. *This isn't even a murder. There's no way I asked for this.*

When the login screen appeared, she signed in to her emails and clicked on her 'sent' mail. What she saw made her sit back in her chair in astonishment. In the subject matter, she saw a name. No request, nothing else, only **Katherine Engles**.

Karen rested her head on her hand and tapped her cheek. But her logic kicked in, and she quickly concluded it was a mix-up. As her earworm awakened, it reminded her of the contestant's song on the show. And that reminded her that she'd seen another little girl, or thought she had, on that Saturday night. But even if she had wanted to put two and two together, this girl was from Yorkshire, not Lincoln – if that's where it was.

Before she had time to think any more about it, her phone rang and her curiosity was drowned out by necessity. Another Road Traffic Accident, straightforward from what she'd heard, so she wasn't especially engaged with it but there were lots of forms to fill in and a few people to interview so the day passed swiftly enough.

While she tidied her desk, Karen saw the admin assistant, in a thick coat crossing the floor on her way out, and it jogged her memory. She peered at the slim red-haired woman as if she hadn't seen her before. *Younger than me* she guessed. *Gap year?* 'Hi, it's Sasha, isn't it? How long have you been here?'

She rolled her eyes and said 'Saskia. And it's been eight weeks.'

'Sorry, yes, Sachia. Sar-she-ah,' Karen repeated. 'About that file this morning. I know I sent the email, but I didn't actually send it.' Saskia stared back at her. 'It must be a blip on the system. I never ask for cold cases like this.'

'No, Sergeant,' Saskia replied ambiguously as she walked out of the door, leaving Karen taken aback.

***

By the time Karen was home and inside with her takeaway supper, she was strangely very tired and irritated to find that some of her clothes were still damp. She put the next day's selection on the dryer cycle and spaced the rest out on the rack to hasten their drying.

When Tuesday's outfit was retrieved from the dryer and hung up in her bedroom she flopped in front of the telly and plugged into the usual Monday soaps. She finished off the last dregs of Sunday's wine while munching through the reheated kebab.

Constitution of an ox she thought to herself as she ate the last morsels. *Just like Dad*. But this time she was wrong.

In bed, Karen couldn't sleep at all. Her stomach was churning, necessitating several visits to the toilet. At the fourth venture out, she was shivering with the cold and before getting back into bed, put on her onesie. By then, even though extremely tired, she slept fitfully. Her stomach was still grinding when she was woken by a bumping noise.

Hauling herself to a sitting position, she concentrated and listened. She heard it again.

Undaunted, she went into her living room, her eyes widening at what she saw. The clothes rack had fallen over and all her clothes had been scattered around the flat.

'What the actual...' she began. 'Damn.' She shivered as the coldness in the room began to penetrate her onesie, and remembered that she had left the bathroom window open after her last visit. *Must've been windy outside as well*.

After closing the window, she picked up the clothes, folded the dry ones, and left them in a pile on the sofa. She picked up the rack and spread the remaining clothes over the rails before crawling back into bed.

She warmed up a little and at last, she began to sleep properly and deeply, but this time she dreamed. She was somewhere in the countryside, there was an abandoned bike in the road and she was scared. Too scared to move.

3

Tuesday 5 November

Karen woke, instantly looking at her alarm clock. *Two minutes to go.* She turned it off. *No snoozing today*. Rubbing her stomach, she still felt uncomfortable, but it was the dream that worried her the most. *I never dream. No, that's silly, I did. Stella's accident. But I'm not on a case now.* In her rush to leave for work, she didn't look further than the sofa.

Today she was in a particularly bad mood and that meant shouting at the radio. Some politician or other was being interviewed about police corruption. 'Moron' she shouted out. 'Arsehole!'

She was still grumpy when she arrived in the office, and her mood was about to get worse. She hung up her coat and turned to look at her desk. Sitting in the middle was a cold case file.

'What the hell?' Karen walked to her desk. *Yesterday's file back again by mistake, or even out of mischief?* It wasn't. It was another file. Another missing child. Karen was both rattled and angry. She switched on her computer.

'OK!' she shouted out. 'Who's having a laugh?' Heads turned away as one. She stomped to the coffee machine, almost knocking into her partner, Detective Constable Macy Dodds on her way in. Macy got a full-on Karen glare.

'What?' Macy said.

'Another file. Like yesterday.'

'I wasn't here,' Macy said, an edge in her voice.

Karen frowned. 'Someone's winding me up.'

'Tell me,' Macy said as she hung up her coat.

'Cold case files,' Karen snapped. 'And emails.'

'But you like those. And emails are always annoying.' Macy stood and wiggled a little, cupping her hatless black bob with her hands.

'Hmm.' Karen replied. She stared at her immaculately suited colleague. Her black, green, and gold neck scarf was a proud reminder of her Jamaican heritage. 'You look different, Mace.'

'Uh-huh.' She gave a little twirl.

'What?'

Macy sighed, her shoulders drooping a little. 'D' she said. 'I've got a D now.'

'D'oh!' Karen slapped her head. 'Your first day as a detective, isn't it?' She beamed. 'We'll have to celebrate. Later.'

Still smiling, Karen went over to her desk and logged on to her emails. There it was, in her outbox just as before. Her frown returned. 'Damn.' The email subject matter was **Amy Warren**, the name on the case file. This time Karen noticed that the email was sent at 00:00 - the exact stroke of midnight. *It can't have been me, even if I sleepwalked, I was at home on the toilet then.*

She scrolled back to find the previous email. This had also been sent at 00:00. *That's very odd. Must be a blip in the IT system. I bet someone's been looking these cases up but it's going into the ether and being thrown out in my direction.*

Just to be sure, she checked every detail, having been humiliated by the IT department in the past for missing a blind copy. PICNIC they used to say to her. She had been furious when she found out what it meant. 'Well, this is definitely a Problem In the Computer, Not In Chair,' she muttered as she punched in the phone number. She tried not to let the electronic version of some music she'd played on her recorder at school wind her up even more. At last, she heard a voice.

'I want someone to look into this. Someone or something is sending out phantom emails.'

'Sure,' said the voice. 'And you are?' Karen strained her ears to detect any sign of a sneer or a mocking tone.

'DS Karen Thorpe.'

'Forward them on to info@picnic so I know what I'm looking at,' said the impassive voice adding, 'By the way, there's no such thing,' before ending the call.

Furiously Karen forwarded both emails and hit the return button with an audible *thwack*. Then she looked at the file. Her curiosity about the contents remained unaroused.

But who would do it? She looked at her overflowing inbox. *Nope. I'm not going there.* She put the file back in the outbox pigeonhole and carried on with her work.

***

At lunchtime, Karen summoned Macy with a nod of her head. They didn't lunch often. Karen was almost devoid of small talk. But today was an exception. She led all the way to the little cafe and when they went in, ordered for both of them.

'On me,' Karen smiled. 'Good to have you with us properly. You were wasted in uniform. I'm only surprised Harris didn't try to nab you.'

'Oh, he did. I resisted.' Karen chinked coffee cups with Macy. 'But he did ask me out for a drink.'

Karen raised her eyebrows. 'Did he indeed. And what did you do?'

'I resisted that too, of course. He's such a knob.' Karen grinned. 'What was all that with the emails this morning?'

Karen explained succinctly about the appearance of the files.

'That sounds very odd,' Macy said. 'Even a bit spooky.'

Karen sat up straight in her *I'm your superior* manner. 'Don't be ridiculous. It'll be wires crossed on the system,' she said. 'Let's change the subject.' As usual, Karen led the conversation, but Macy listened with renewed enthusiasm.

Later in the afternoon, Karen had a call back from the IT department. 'OK, there *was* a blip on your account. It came at exactly the time we do our backup. I've put in a couple more lines on your securities so it should be fine now.'

Until she heard these words, Karen didn't realise how relieved she was. 'Thanks,' she said, simply.

***

That evening Karen followed her usual routine but ducked the kebab shop and went to the Indian instead. *Much safer. Freshly made and all those spices kill off all the germs.* She'd been working her way up the *hot* scale, much to the amusement of the restaurant owner, and was comfortably on *Madras*.

Back home, she opted for a hot bath and a glass of red wine before dinner. She emerged bright pink, tired but calm, wrapped in her comforting thick brown bear onesie.

Going into the kitchen to reheat her supper, she had a flash of seeing something not quite right in the living room. She turned around and froze; there was a pair of pants on the television. Walking further she saw her clothes strewn all over the floor. *Jesus Christ.* If it had just been the ones on the rail, she would have managed to find an explanation, but even the ones she had folded were messed up.

'Fuck this!' she said out loud. Defiantly, she began to pick up the clothes. Glaring around at invisible onlookers, she took everything into the bedroom and furiously put them away as if to make sure they couldn't escape.

After a second glass of wine with her meal, her brain engaged. Someone's playing tricks. *Someone who knows how to get into a flat without a key.* 'Shit.' There were loads of her colleagues capable of that. But how to catch them out? *A camera. And I know who will do it for me. No one messes with me.*

4

Wednesday 6 November.

By morning, Karen, already a one hundred percent *and* twenty-four-seven detective, was raring to go. A recent RTA necessitated a visit to the lab that morning, and the lab was the place she would find the only person she was absolutely certain she could trust. John Steele.

John Steele, the thirty-two-year-old head of forensics was, in the most important sense of the word, Karen's boyfriend, but the walls in her head stopped her from getting too emotionally involved. He always came second to the job. But more recently she, too, had come second to his mother. John adored her and took whatever crumbs she threw at him – a lesser man would have given up on her a long time ago. Actually, most men wouldn't have bothered. Her facial expressions ranged from intense to scowl, and her attire screamed out *nothing doing here*.

As she drove to the lab, Karen was neither singing nor shouting in the car. Instead, she was having a conversation with whoever it was who had been playing tricks on her.

'OK, you may think you're very clever, but I am sure as hell that I will find you out, and then you just wait and see what I do to you.'

She went through the office personnel one by one. Macy was the obvious one, she knew Karen better than almost anyone, but it wasn't her style. Besides, in the last few years, Karen had dragged many a colleague over to her flat, solely to discuss whatever case she was working on. So, except for Macy, it could have been almost any of them. Most of them seemed to be pranksters from time to time. It was a by-product of the stress that inevitably arose on a daily basis. And no one liked her.

Karen pulled up in the lab car park, illicitly parked in a space reserved for senior personnel and made her way to the modern but unremarkable red brick building. They knew her well and the receptionist was almost a fan.

'Good morning, DS Thorpe.'

'And you.'

Karen made her way to John's office. John was tall and slim and, as he had noted himself, was not that far in dress and appearance from being a male version of Karen. His face broke into a smile as soon as she walked in.

'Hello my love,' he began.

'Cut the crap, this is serious,' Karen replied. 'Can't stop, just picking up the results from the RTA. But there's something else.'

'Go on.' John was always interested in Karen, but he picked up her mood and tuned into it.

'Someone's playing silly buggers. Playing tricks on *me*,' Karen began.

John's eyebrows raised with a hint of *who would dare to pick on you?* 'Are you sure?' he said.

'No time to talk now. Come round tonight, dinner on me. Seven sharp. But get me a camera, will you? One of those snake ones would do. I'll tell you about it tonight.'

'Of course,' John could barely stop himself grinning.

'And wipe that smile off your face. This is serious' Karen replied, smiling as she turned away from him.

'Haven't you forgotten something precious?' John teased.

Karen stopped in her tracks. *If he thinks I'm going to engage in soppy talk anywhere, never mind at the office*... She turned to face him; her smile evaporated. 'How is your mother?'

John gaped. 'She's fine. That's not what I meant.' Karen frowned, confused. 'The results,' John said, now smiling at her. 'Don't you want these?' He patted the brown envelope on his desk.

'Ha!' Karen grabbed the package and swept out without another word. Now she had something else to think about. They both knew the rules about their evenings together, and it wasn't quite all Karen's way. John was expected to provide dinner but 'on me,' meant that she might reimburse him. More often than not she forgot and he never ever reminded her. She also had to clean her flat. John was allergic to untidiness and a passionate recycler. And the alternative was John's tiny bedsit which made her claustrophobic. It was almost too small to get undressed in without banging her arm on the wardrobe door.

***

The day was uneventful. No random files on her desk; certainly, no hints of mischief from the rest of the team. Karen returned home to her flat tensing a little as she turned the key in her door.

When she stood in her small entrance hall, she breathed in just a little heavily as she slowly opened and looked round the door of her living room. Nothing. Nothing untoward at all. 'I've got you, you bastard!' she said to the ceiling. 'You won't get me again!'

She hung up her coat and surveyed the room properly. *This isn't too bad. Well, it's OK. But no, it's not up to John's standards. But wait till he sees the kitchen...'*

All she had left to do was clear the last couple of days' detritus. And John had given her ample instruction, even demonstrations. *Rinse and stack the foil trays. Tear the cardboard. Rinse the bottles and black bag anything else.*

She looked at the clock. Ten past seven. He was late. He was *never* late. She tried not to see the accumulated grime over her stainless-steel sink. *Stupid name. Mine's always stained.* Reaching under the sink, she pulled out an old scourer. *Give it a go. You can do this.* 'Shit. This just makes the rest look bad.'

At last the buzzer sounded. *Too late now*, Karen grinned and pressed the entry button waiting for John to appear at her door.

While she waited she picked up the newspaper and junk mail. Still no John. Her heart began to beat faster. *What's keeping him?* 'JOHN!' She grabbed her phone and hurtled down the stairs in a panic.

5

Karen stood at the main entrance looking this way and that. 'Where the hell are you?' She was now in a tizzy. She punched his number into her phone. No response. Leaning against the brick wall, Karen tried to rationalise the situation. *There's bound to be a good reason* but her nerves wouldn't stop jangling.

She still had her hands over her eyes when she heard a familiar voice.

'You're keen,' John said. 'Nice welcome,' his lips brushed hers.

Karen regrouped in a second. 'I thought I heard a buzz and decided to take the rubbish out,' Karen said, shaking her head.

'Oh,' John's shoulders drooped a little. 'I did see a little girl running this way,' John looked back to the road. 'She looked a bit old-fashioned.'

'And you know even less about fashion than me,' Karen smiled, her relief kept to herself. 'I'm always ticking kids off around here. Was it a girl on her own or with a boy?'

'On her own. Why?'

'Oh, just some kids I caught the other day. She was probably playing Knock Down Ginger.'

'Do kids do that anymore?' John asked.

Before Karen could answer they both heard a whoosh followed by a loud BANG.

'Bonfire night every night,' she said. 'Maybe chancing a penny for the guy.'

'I've not seen any kids doing that in years.'

'No,' said Karen thinking. 'Neither have I. Come on, what have you got for us?' Karen looked at his bag and sniffed the air. 'It'll get cold out here.'

'I had a better idea. I thought we could sort out your camera first, then go to the park. I saw a fireworks display notice...' He paused to check her facial expression which didn't reflect her words.

The camera? That's why he was late. 'The fifth was yesterday. Why can't people get the dates right?'

'Probably the only day they could do it. And don't forget it's Diwali too. We could eat out properly for a change. Your choice. On me.' Karen was silent. 'What do you think?' he ventured carefully.

'I think,' Karen said slowly, 'it's a bloody brilliant idea.'

'Which means the flat is in a mess,' John smiled.

'Not at all.'

'So there'll be no problem siting the camera?'

'None whatsoever.'

Suppressing his urge to check out the kitchen, John went straight into the living room. He had the perfect eye for this sort of thing having studied angles for years and knew exactly how to get maximum vision. Karen's walls were sparse, but courtesy of the previous owner there was a fussy pair of curtains on her window, with a big fabric pelmet.

'Perfect,' John approved as he looked at it. 'This is a fisheye lens, too, so it will get almost the whole room.'

He moved the coffee table over to the curtains and stood on it so that he could reach the pelmet. Then he wriggled the small device into place.

'Where's your tablet?' he asked. Karen handed it over in complete trust. 'It's a wireless signal, transmits here...' he pointed to the camera, 'and records on this disk in here...'

He sat down, took a small hard drive device out of his pocket, and plugged it into the tablet. Karen watched, understanding the output if not the technicalities.

When he was done, John patted the tablet in satisfaction. 'All set up. I've just got to check the connections to the....' he fiddled a bit more. 'Here. Have a look. Not much to see yet. It takes pictures every ten seconds, so it'll pick up almost anything.'

Karen peered at the screen; there was almost her entire living room squashed into a round picture. 'That's great.' She said. 'Gotya!' She looked up to the ceiling. 'Now for the bait.'

John watched in admiration as Karen redeployed the sorted recycling to become her experiment. She went into her bedroom, leaving the door wide open since it was tidy. She came out with assorted underwear which she piled up neatly on the sofa. She

15

checked the camera view to make sure everything was clearly visible. 'Perfect. Let's go,' she said.

***

Karen had forgotten how much she loved fireworks and it was a lovely evening; cold, but still with an exceptionally clear sky. She gazed up at the stars as John pointed out some constellations. They joined the happy throng of families with small children holding sparklers, older children waving neon bands, and teenage lovers holding hands.

John paid the small entrance fee while Karen breathed in the wafting bonfire fumes. *Do you remember taking me, Dad? Seems like a lifetime ago.*

There was a small lake in the park and the display was arranged along the back so that when the giant Catherine wheels were lit, the reflections in the lake doubled up the spectacle. It was all done in sometimes perfect timing with the assorted music bursting out and accompanied by 'Ooohs' and 'Ahhhs' especially when the big rockets went up at the end. When it was all over, Karen stood a little spellbound for a minute.

'Not bad for a local do,' John nudged her. They turned homeward, arm in arm.

'Yes, I actually enjoyed that,' said Karen. Quickly adding 'I fancy Thai tonight. How about you?'

'Good choice,' he said. 'We haven't had Thai for a while. Since...'

'Yes. Since then.'

In the restaurant the service was good and the food delicious. Karen mentioned her spat with the IT department then they chatted happily about Karen's current caseload, even a little bit about John's.

'And are you still in touch with Stella?'

'Yes. I think she's happy now. She's been very forgiving. I'm not sure I could be.'

'But she wanted another baby, didn't she?' 'Yes,' Karen replied as if it was an unnatural desire. But she did have a desire for company. 'Are you staying tonight? I've still got all those towels.'

John blushed ever so slightly. 'Er, sorry, not tonight.'

'So that's why you're holding back on the wine. How come?'

'I promised Mum I'd go over. Dad's away overnight and she's worried. One of the neighbours got broken into the other day and she's a bit scared on her own. You know how it is. After the op...'

Karen knew exactly how that was, but she would never have admitted it. 'Fine,' she said dispassionately. 'Another time.'

'I'll come back with you, just to check there's been no movement.'

'No point. No one will get up to anything tonight. It'll be during the day if at all. And I know what to do now.'

Their meal ended in silence: Karen, irritated – but unable to express it, John sensing something was wrong but unable to put it right. After he paid the bill, they walked back to Karen's block together stopping when they reached John's car.

'See you soon,' John said. 'In fact, I'll come over tomorrow, if you like. I'd like to see that recording.'

'Fine,' she said. *Phew,* she thought. They kissed goodnight and she watched John go to his car.

What's that? 'Hello, puss,' she bent down to stroke a little ginger and white cat that was walking towards her but it ran off before she could reach it. When she went indoors, she was relieved to see she was right. Nothing had moved.

6

Thursday 7 November

Karen woke to the alarm almost forgetting about the camera. Once she was washed and had eaten breakfast, she checked her phone. The calendar reminded her of a scheduled routine visit. She generally loathed this part of her job, but her attitude was improving.

Today was going to be good. The door she knocked on remained unanswered. With a small fist-pump, she got back in the car and drove to the station. Maybe there'll be a new, big case today.

When she walked into the office, she hung up her coat then peered at her desk with some apprehension. But the surface was clear, apart from her usual full in-tray. It wasn't until she was ready to sit down and pulled out her chair, she froze. There on the seat was another cold case file. This was definitely not the adventure she was seeking.

'Who the fuck did this?' she yelled. 'Do you think it's funny or something?' She picked up the file and waved it in the air so that everyone could see. Macy came towards her, almost running.

'Karen, calm down. You're making a show of yourself. Let's talk.'

'I've got to check something first,' Karen growled. She threw the file on the floor without looking at it and turned on her computer, drumming her fingers on the keyboard until the *Welcome* screen appeared. Macy hovered by Karen's desk, looking out in case the boss, DCI Winter, appeared.

Karen keyed straight into her email outbox; there was no email. She frowned. *Is this a good or a bad thing?* But it calmed her a little.

'It *must* be someone here playing a prank this time,' she surmised, looking around the room.

'Come on. Coffee on me now.' Macy ordered, bravely. She picked up the file and put it on her own desk while Karen got her coat.

They went to the local coffee shop. 'Espresso and chocolate muffin,' Macy declared. 'Sorts everything.'

'Thanks,' Karen muttered.

'So tell me from the beginning. What's been going on?'

'Somebody's playing tricks on me,' Karen said, scanning Macy's face for any signs of guilt. *No. Not her.* She opened up a little and told Macy about the washing.

'That is really weird. Like it's a – what is it? Poltergeist?'

'I don't believe in that crap,' Karen replied. 'It's someone mucking around. I'll catch them.'

'OK. You know how I love paperwork,' Macy said, Karen raised a *Did I?* eyebrow. 'Leave the file business with me. I'll find out where it came from. Somebody must know.'

'Thanks Macy. I'd appreciate that.'

Macy gave one of her whole-body smiles in response.

***

The rest of Karen's day passed as usual. Nothing harrowing and as always, lots of admin. John had cancelled but she was still calm when she got home clutching her takeaway fish supper. The recycling and underwear piles were unmoved. Nothing had changed. *Good.* The only odd thing, and she didn't see it until she turned around, was that a note had been pushed under her front door. She picked it up and read it with surprise.

'Please turn your TV down during the day. Some of us are on night shifts. Flat 32.'

Karen looked upwards; it was the flat directly above hers. She looked at her TV; it was off. *Must be a mistake,* she thought. *Or the prankster* she added. *Anyone could push something under the door.*

She checked the disk to see if anything had been recorded from the camera. 'Nothing, nothing, nothing...' she clicked through the fast forward. 'Nothing... what the fuck?' She stopped the film and rewound it. It looked like a light was passing through

19

the room. She looked at the wall where the light had appeared. It was difficult to imagine in November, but yes, in the summer, the sun did come in that way. She whizzed through the rest of the disk and didn't see anything else suspicious at all.

She looked at the note again, the aroma from her wrapped supper permeating her nostrils. *I should go and see them. But that smells so good.* Instead, she sat down and began to eat with her fingers.

After eating, Karen couldn't settle. There was nothing she wanted to watch on TV, and she quickly ran out of lives on her tablet game. She wavered on Wonder Web until she realised she'd been unfriended by even more people. She recalled some rather acerbic comments she'd made on a post. *Can't take it, don't dish it out.*

At bedtime, once again she found it difficult to sleep. She tossed and turned seemingly all night. The more she tried not to think about the files the more she did. The first two were both young girls? Was there a pattern? Even if someone was doing it for a joke, should she be looking into it?

Finally giving up she sat up and rubbed her eyes. There was a fine strip of light under her bedroom door. Moving darkness broke the line.

SHIT

Get up and look, you silly cow.

Karen grabbed her baton and got up silently, cursing the one creaking floorboard she always seemed to tread on. She opened the door oh so slowly.

WHAT?

The light was off and there was no one there. Nobody.

Where's the light coming from? A brighter beam of light escaped under the living room door. She flung it open.

There! She looked down to see her tablet was screen side down on the floor but emitting a powerful light.

Did I leave that on?

No, I didn't.

Or did I?

Karen picked up the tablet and looked at the screen, blinking The whole screen was as bright as a fluorescent bulb. In an instant, her regular screensaver appeared.

She sighed with relief. *OK, so it's faulty. John can sort it.* She sat down on the sofa thinking. *What was that first girl's name?* She called up her email account. Engles. Katherine Engles. She entered it in the search field and almost immediately the screen changed. No bright lights this time, but a pink and red swirling mass encompassed the screen.

What the fuck is that? Karen stared as the image transformed into something. *What?* It was the face of a girl. But it wasn't a normal picture. The girl's face was distorted into a silent but terrifying scream.

'FUCKING HELL!' Karen flung the tablet across the room It landed under the radiator.

When she was able to move again, she went into the kitchen and pulled out a bottle of brandy from a wall cupboard. She took a large swig then returned to the room.

Pacing around, her eyes fell on the visible bit of the tablet. She tapped it with her bare toe. There was no light. Holding her breath she picked it up with her thumb and forefinger, squinting at it sideways to see if the image was still there.

Where's that bloody idiot John when you need him?
Should I ring him?
Don't you dare, you wuss. It's a bit of kit. Deal with it.

With a deep sigh, she turned the device round and looked at it full on.

Phew. The screen was blank again. *Probably hit some keys in the fall.*

Tentatively she sat down on the sofa and turned the tablet off then on again. She could feel her heart racing as she waited for it to reboot.

After what seemed to be a lifetime, she was back on the home screen, and once again she typed **Katherine Engles** into the search box, holding the tablet as far away as she could and squinting at the screen.

There were no horrible faces, just her normal screen and a few references. Relieved, but now extremely tired, she turned it off and vowed to do some more research in the morning.

7

Friday 8 November

Karen jumped out of bed the second after she woke. *I must look at those links.*

There was nothing significant, only a few snippets of information – mainly from journalists reviving the story of the missing girl over the years. She looked at the *image* option and dared herself to click. It was a full ten sweaty seconds before she did, but there was nothing upsetting.

She scoured the random selection of images, presumably of assorted Katherines but none were, as far as she could tell, of Katherine Engles. There were many completely unrelated items – including pictures of bits of naked women. She wondered, not for the first time, why they appeared in nearly every search she did.

She looked more closely at the stories behind the links. There were clearly people in Katherine's community still trying to keep her case alive but nothing of any recent interest.

Who was the other girl? Amy Warren?

Once again, all she saw were odd scraps and incomplete pieces, but this time something did catch her eye.

She lived in Lincoln? Shit! She dared herself to click on the images.

Oh my God. Karen shivered as she looked at the aged black and white image of a little girl in a layered party dress waving at the camera. *Enough already*. She turned the tablet off and got ready for the relative safety of work.

By the time she got to the office, Karen had rationalised the whole thing. Images get corrupted all the time. It was probably a virus. She'd often seen strange things on the Wonder Web, and it was highly likely that somehow an image of a girl from Lincoln had got into street view, or at least onto her tablet.

The first person she saw was Macy. It looked like she'd been waiting for her. And she was looking more serious than Karen had ever seen her. 'What is it? A murder?'

Macy shook her head and held up the file she'd commandeered the previous day. 'This file,' she said. 'It's not our file. It's a Scottish case. Edinburgh to be precise. Nobody even knows how it got here. I've spoken to the mailroom and everything. I've even checked the recycling for the envelope.'

'What the fuck?' Karen visibly blanched. 'Ring the Edinburgh office. They won't have let go of it without instruction.'

'Something interesting, Karen?' DCI Winter, who had a knack of appearing when least expected, approached the two women from the direction of the water dispenser. Macy tactfully sidled away. 'I heard about the file waving the other day. Is this another episode about to start?'

'No guv, it's...'

'My office. Now.' He ordered.

Karen followed him into his office, looking back at Macy with a little shrug.

DCI Winter looked sternly at Karen. 'Sit.'

'But...' Karen sat while he remained standing.

'I've been looking at your holiday card; you are well overdue for a break.'

What is he on about? The last thing I need is a break. What would I do with one? Before she had time to respond, her boss cut in.

'That wasn't a question, Karen. You've had an extremely difficult case to handle. You've had a large caseload to manage and you're now displaying symptoms of what the quacks would call stress. Your colleagues have expressed concern. I expect you to take at least a week off with immediate effect.'

Karen gulped. 'Now? This second? I have to sort some things out guv. And what about Macy?'

'I'll deal with DC Dodds. But no. Not this second. End of play today will be fine. And Karen?'

'Yes, guv?'

'Go away, somewhere nice. Try and have some fun for a change.'

Fun? 'Yes, guv.'

***

Karen trudged out of DCI Winter's office deep in thought. *Does he mean a holiday? There's far too much to sort out.*

Still stunned, she sat at her desk, ignoring Macy's worried looks and rang John. 'I've been ordered to take a holiday,' she said. 'Are you doing anything tomorrow?'

Like a shot John replied. 'I can be. I can be off all next week if you like. Two weeks actually. I'm owed time too.'

'Are you actually allowed to come over this time?'

'My mother is better, if that's what you mean. I'll be there but not until around nine?' he said. 'Things to do.'

'OK. See you then.'

Karen needed to get some facts and logic back into her train of thought. She'd spent a guilty couple of hours researching paranormal activity but concluded that it was always entirely explicable. *Now for the paperwork.* She saw Macy heading over. 'Any news?'

'I've rung Scotland; they say they had an interoffice email at 12:00 pm exactly on Tuesday night. No specified names, it was the general office email. They sent the file by DX. The messenger probably handed it straight in at reception here.'

'And somebody there assumed it was for me?' Karen said.

'Oh, and DI Wallace sends his regards.'

'Davie?' Karen smiled. 'I hadn't realised it was from his station.'

'And you know your father had a reputation for cold cases. Other people think that, too.'

'Like our desk sergeant Bill?' Macy shrugged. 'OK. Do you still have it?'

'I do.'

'Bring it over. I might just take a look.'

'I knew you would,'

'Oh, did you?' Karen said. 'Well guess what? I'm going on holiday from today. Just for a week.'

Macy's mouth dropped open. 'You? Holiday? I don't think I've ever...' Her expression began to change from surprised to knowing. 'You're not going to investigate those cases, are you?'

Damn, she's getting good. Karen had to acknowledge that Macy was a step ahead of her. Investigate was too strong, but taking a good look? *Hell yes.*

She smiled at Macy with such genuine delight that Macy was taken aback. 'How could you even think that Mace? Anyway, you will have the pleasure of being directed by the guv himself, or so he tells me. It'll be good for you to work with him.'

Macy drew back as if she wasn't sure that it would be so good.

'If you get better it makes me get better too,' Karen said.

'You're right,' Macy replied. 'As usual.' Karen grinned.

8

Karen went back to her paperwork, but when she looked at her emails, something odd came up. It was a pop-up box advertising psychic services. *Strange. Must've been when I was searching earlier. What does it say? '£1 a minute to speak to our best psychics. Results guaranteed.' What a load of tosh.* Fascinated, she clicked the link and started reading.

The woman, if the picture was accurate, looked perfectly normal, and her testimonials were extraordinary. 'I have helped the police with their murder investigations on several occasions thanks to my intuition and psychic powers.' *Blimey. It's about time I spent my expense allowance.*

She picked up the phone to speak to the operator. 'I need to make an investigative call, but it's one of those premium numbers.' She waited for the operator to acknowledge her and gave her the number. 'If I haven't finished in five minutes, please cut me off,' Karen instructed the woman. 'I'm expecting to be drawn into a long conversation and my watch isn't that precise.'

She listened to the tinny notes played as the operator dialled the number. Almost immediately a female Scottish voice answered.

'Good morning.'

It was a caring, comforting voice. Picked precisely, Karen cynically decided, to keep you talking, let out your innermost secrets for later exploitation.

There was some preamble about who she was, how the organisation worked, and what the listener could expect to get from the service. Karen, already impatient, was about to interrupt when the woman began to question her.

'Now, my dear, I'd like to have a little information about you too, to help me tune in. You don't have to give me your name, but your date and time of birth – if you have it, would be good. Then I will summon up my guide who will surely be able to tell you what you want to know...'

'First August 1986,' Karen said while looking at her watch. *OK, that's two minutes gone, and I've got nothing yet.*

'I sense that you are a very solitary person with an important job...'

Can she see the incoming number somewhere? Probably not difficult with the right technology to spot a police station number. How much do they invest in this stuff? How much do they make?

'...and there is somebody out there for you ...'

Oh shit, I forgot they would be doing that. She listened for another second before jumping in. 'I'm not looking for love advice, I want to know what's going to happen about something...' she said as obscurely as she could. *Over three minutes gone now.*

'You're going on holiday soon aren't you?' *Hmm. Everybody is probably going on holiday at some point.*

'Aren't you?' the voice insisted.

'Yes, I am as it happens'

'And you're going North?'

'Might be.' Karen was still looking at her watch; four minutes. 'I want to know about a mystery,' she said, trying to direct the woman a little but giving nothing away. 'Something strange that happened to me recently.'

'Ah, yes I see it now,' said the voice. 'I'm getting something through.' Karen rolled her eyes. 'Yes, I can see something. It's about three little girls...' The phone went dead.

'Shit shit SHIT!' Karen yelled.

The operator came on the line. 'That was your five minutes. Is that OK?'

'No,' said Karen, hastily adding 'Not your fault. Can you try to reconnect me?'

'Will do,' said the operator. 'Put the phone down, and I'll ring you when I've got it.'

Karen waited and waited but no call came. After ten minutes she rang the operator.

'I'm sorry, Sergeant Thorpe. I've tried over and over; the number seems to be unobtainable.'

27

'Damn.' Karen kicked the desk leg. She put the phone down and scratched her head. She made a note of the number anyway. *I'll try again when I get home.*

***

It was getting late and Karen had been tied up with seemingly endless telephone calls and interruptions from colleagues. Even Bill had popped in to wish her a nice holiday. *Holiday? That's a laugh. It'll take a week to sort this lot out. At least I've got those emails out to the locals.* She looked up to see Macy approaching her desk.

'You should be gone by now. Anything specific?

'No. Just stuff.'

'Leave it. If anyone calls, I'll cover you.'

You're much too kind for your own good, Mace. I might just do that.'

'Go then. Try and have a bit of a holiday, you need a break. Are you going with John?'

'Might be,' Karen said, tight-lipped. 'I hope you have a good week, too.'

'It'll be fine. Bye,' Macy turned to go.

'Night, Mace.' She looked at her watch. *She's right. Get your arse in gear, it's time.*

Karen got up and made her way down to the basement storage area. It was dark but not horror-film scary. She flipped on the light switch filling the filing room with orangey light. *Now, where do I start?* She noticed the assistant's desk was clear of files and walked around the room looking at the indices on the ends of the filing racks. *Cold case files. Do they even keep them here? Wouldn't they send them back? No. They're digitised copies. Where are they? At the back, I suppose. Ah, this looks promising.*

As Karen bent down to look at a name, she heard light footsteps somewhere. She jumped up a little too quickly and caught her hand on a shelf bracket, scratching the skin. 'Ow! She said loudly. 'Who's there?' She heard a faint giggle.

Sod this for a laugh. I'll call in tomorrow on my way to...Where the hell are we going, anyway?

As she walked out of the room, she heard the approaching footsteps of the admin assistant coming down the stairs. *Thank god. It's Sachia.* She tried to erase the giggle from her mind until the feet and legs gradually appeared, and she realised it was the head of administration, Phil. Karen composed herself. *Mustn't let the juniors see you're scared.*

'You know those files I supposedly took out then sent back?'

Phil nodded. 'I heard. They're filed away now, just in case,' he said.

'I'd like to...' Karen watched as he went to his desk seeing the two files a moment before he did. *What? Where did they come from?*

'That's odd,' Phil said as he looked at them. 'I'm sure I put these away.'

Karen didn't know whether to laugh or cry. She was very senior to this young man. She laughed. 'You couldn't have done. Never mind, we all make mistakes.'

Phil was insistent. 'I put them back, Sergeant.'

'Oh, that was me,' Saskia appeared from the darkness. 'Macy said you'd need them.'

Disguising her relief but unable to concede she was wrong, Karen turned to Phil and held her hands out to take the files.

'I told you,' he said, irritated.

Karen went upstairs talking to herself. *Since when were police stations spooky, you silly mare?*

9

John was running late. Karen spread the files open on her coffee table. All three young girls, all three missing, presumed dead. Bodies were never discovered. *Is there a link? What could it be?* 'Dad, where are you when I need you? No, that's silly. I know exactly what you would do.'

A good speed reader with an eye for detail, she worked through the first file from cover to cover. Katherine Engles from York, abducted on the twenty-sixth of July 1964 somewhere between one o'clock, just after lunch and six o'clock when she was called for her tea. She'd been on her way to play with her friends just a short walk away but had never arrived. She was wearing a white T-shirt and blue shorts. There were reports on the searches that had been organised and records of interviews with all connected parties. *And I bet a few kiddie fiddlers had their collars felt. Nearly fifty years ago though. Who'd even be around then? Where would I start on this? When were The Moors Murders? Wasn't that 1964?*

She turned to the next file, Amy Warren, and shivered slightly when she again saw the photo of the little girl in the party dress. Amy from Lincoln was on her way to a friend's party on the eighteenth of June 1964. It was only a five-minute walk away. Neither family had a telephone connected. She never arrived, so she must have been abducted soon after she left the house at four o'clock.

Now your turn. Karen had just opened the third file when the door buzzer sounded. *John.* She picked up the receiver. 'Did you get dinner?' *Oh, it's too early. Didn't he say nine?* 'Who's there?' Karen froze, remembering the previous incident. Then she heard a little squeaky sigh down the phone. 'Come on up.'

She went to the kitchen and got out glasses, plates and cutlery ready for the meal before going back to look at the third file. *Where is he?*

The buzzer sounded again. 'It's those bloody kids.' *No, I'm not getting up.*

But when the buzzer sounded yet again, she began to get angry. 'What the fuck are you playing at?' *Was that someone laughing?* 'I'm coming down you little beasts.'

Karen wedged her front door open and stormed downstairs just in time to see John walking up to the door.

'What?' He looked surprised.

It couldn't have been him. 'Did you see kids again?' Karen asked.

'Let me get in first. The food's getting cold,' said John with a brown takeaway bag in one hand and a rucksack in the other. When they got into her flat, he realised something was up. 'Hey, what's happened?'

'I asked you if you saw a kid again, ringing the doorbell,' Karen repeated as she went into the kitchen.

'Karen, what's up? I can see you're upset.'

'Don't be stupid. I'm not upset. It's just...' As she unpacked their dinner it all came spilling out. The files, the mysterious images, the clothes. But like a true copper, every incident, however small was relayed in strict chronological order. John listened patiently only half remembering the takeaways now cooling in their foil trays.

'Oh, Karen. That's some story,' he said, grabbing the bottle of wine from the carrier bag. He unscrewed the cap and poured her a glass of red wine, which she gratefully gulped.

'What do you think?' she said, her voice a tiny bit unsure.

'Like you, I don't believe in ghosts but there's definitely something strange going on. Maybe someone's conscience is playing up. Have you thought of that?'

'Yes,' Karen replied. 'I have. But I can't work out how they could have done it.' She took another swig of wine.

'Feeling better?

'I'm fine.'

'Can we hurry up and eat then? It'll be stone cold by now.'

Their takeaway was reheated in seconds and, in Karen's case, devoured in not much longer. John savoured his meal. 'It's bad for the digestion to eat too fast,' he scolded.

'Being a snob is worse.' Karen poked him in the gut. While she waited for him to finish, she thought about what had happened and like John, agreed it was definitely weird but not out of this world. She gulped on her wine. 'I forgot about the psychic.'

It made John splutter. 'The what? Karen, for God's sake. I'll pretend I didn't hear that.'

'Don't worry. It's not important.' But it was important that she planned her week off. *OK, I'm not chasing criminals this time, it needs a whole new approach. He's not ...surely?*

'John, what are you doing? That can wait.'

'A job's not finished...' John replied as he took the remains into the kitchen and began the washing up. 'What about the camera? Have you checked it today?' Karen shook her head. 'Set it up and we'll look at it together when I've finished.'

'Yes, sir,' said Karen waiting until he joined her. She picked up her tablet and handed it to him. 'I did think I saw something last night, but I'm pretty sure it was a trick of the light. And nothing was moved at all.'

'Let's see then.'

John patiently went through the disk frame by frame, much more closely than Karen had. He, too, stopped the disk at the strange light effect. 'Any more wine?' Karen nodded and topped up his glass. She watched as John peered at the image. He captured it with a screenshot and opened it in another programme, blowing up the image.

'What? What did you see John? It looked like the face of a little girl, didn't it?'

'Only if you've got a good imagination. You're right, it was just a light effect.'

Karen grunted. 'We need to plan where we're going tomorrow. Can we look at the files now?'

'Seriously?'

'You bet.'

'I'll need more wine.

10

'This is Katherine Engles from York; she was playing on Sunday afternoon, the twenty-sixth of July 1964. This one, Amy Warren, lived in Lincoln; went to a party at a house down the road on June the eighteenth also 1964.'

'Lincoln,' John muttered.

'Now this one,' Karen paused to leaf through the file. 'I haven't read through yet I was just looking at it when you...' she pulled out a photo. John nearly spat out his mouthful of wine. 'What?' Karen said, perturbed.

'Nothing. Just went down the wrong hole.'

'You're lying, John. Tell me.'

'OK but don't freak. It looks a little like the girl I saw ringing your door the other day.'

'Jesus. You're getting as bad as me. It's Caitlin McFee. Edinburgh. Disappeared 8th September also 1964. Out playing on her bike after school. Wearing a skirt and cardigan. You did say that, didn't you? Is it the same?'

John shook his head. 'I can't say for sure. So they all disappeared in the same year. Did they have anything else in common?'

'Amy was six and blonde, Katherine also six, dark-haired but Caitlin was just seven and had red hair. All lived in rural but close-knit communities where it was normal for them to walk alone, and all were abducted within a four-month period at a time when The Moors Murderers were doing their stuff.'

'Are you suggesting anything by that,' John frowned.

'No, just throwing it in the mix. That would have pulled out massive resources. Maybe they didn't get the attention they needed at the time?'

'Surely it would have been front-page news everywhere?'

'Who knows? In each region, one missing girl may not have been so significant. And they were younger than the moors victims. It's only if you put all three together – and we don't know they *are* linked – except for the fact that all three files were pulled out of police systems. And if they *are*, I'd guess they'd keep it quiet so as not to panic people.'

'Do you think that somebody very high up could have been keeping a lid on it?' John frowned.

'Possible,' Karen nodded. 'But there's nothing to suggest these three forces knew about each other's cases. I don't know how proficient information sharing was back then, but it would have been more difficult I'd guess. There may have been others suppressed at the time. I doubt we'll ever find out.'

'There is a possible pattern.' John said. 'Not just the similarities of the girls, also the direction. He, and I'm assuming it's a he, is travelling almost in a line north. It's not just his local area.'

'Yes, but if there are more, they could be spread around all over the bloody country. How would we ever find out?'

John turned to look at Karen, his mouth lagging a bit behind his brain. 'OK. Well putting aside all the things we know can't be happening,' he peered down his nose at Karen, 'if this is something like a confession, or even a mix up with somebody else's investigation, it's fair to say that these are the only three.'

'Yes, said Karen. 'Then there's what the psychic...' John shook his head.

'No. We must stick to the possible, or even the probable, or whatever the damned saying is.'

'OK. You're right.'

'So we're agreeing?' John smiled.

'We both want to investigate, don't we?'

'It sounds like a road trip to me,' he replied.

Karen grinned. 'Road trip it is. But whose car?'

'Mine of course. Do you think I'd trust your driving after what you did to your last car? Joking!' John added hastily.

'Mine's newer, stronger.'

'Insurance?'

'Yes, you can take your turn, too. If you're good.'

'I'm more than good. Wanna see?' He leaned forward and kissed Karen on the lips. 'So that's sorted,' he said, 'now bedtime.'

***

Saturday 9 November

Karen woke to find John sitting hunched over his laptop in a very tidy living room. She could even see the sparkling kitchen through the open door. *How could I ever think it was haunted?*

'John? You were up early.'

'I'm always up early. I've been doing some research. Can you manage breakfast?'

'Of course. Full English? I never bother for myself but I stocked up just for you.'

'That's nice of you.'

Karen started the cooking, wondering for a microsecond if this was what married life was like. 'Another coffee?'

'Please.'

Karen took it to him and peered over his shoulder. 'Routes?'

'Yes.'

'I hope you're booking some accommodation,' Karen said

'What? No. It's in the rucksack,' John replied.

'What is?'

'My tent of course.' He waited for her reaction then laughed. 'Your face. There are plenty of B&Bs and it's off-season, so we'll easily find a place. Are you packed?'

'Like I've had time.'

Karen wondered what to pack. She'd rarely been away. She started by filling her bag for life with her purse and credit cards, leaving enough room for the files. She packed a toothbrush, toothpaste, two clean pairs of pants and a jumper in another carrier bag.

'Is that it?' John stared at her meagre efforts. 'I've never met a woman like you before.'

'I'm being practical. It's cold, we're not going disco dancing. What else do I need?'

'At least seven days' worth, just in case.'

Karen grunted. 'Bloody hell. If you insist.'

'And haven't you got a proper bag? I'm sure Bill gave you something.'

'This is a proper bag,' she held it up. 'OK, I agree there's more room in that.' She went into the bedroom returning with her messenger bag, several more pairs of pants, and a bra.

'I'm going to buy you a suitcase for your birthday. When is it?'

'First of August.' She replied.

'Hey, you never told me.'

'You never asked before. Anyway, you bought me that tablet. I assumed you knew. Didn't you look me up?'

John frowned. 'Of course not. Did I give it to you on the first of August?'

'Close enough. Let's get going.'

'Don't ask when mine is then, will you?'

'I won't.'

'You've got exactly three weeks.'

***

Once John's rucksack was put in the boot, Karen sat in the driver's seat with her bag while John, beside her, looked at his notebook.

'You've got all the addresses and locations?'

'I have,' John said. 'Except that they don't exist anymore.'

'What? None of them? Let me look for Katherine Engles' house,' Karen took out her tablet and went on the 'Houses 4 U' website.

John peered over. 'That won't help. I think the house must have been demolished.'

'Just looking…' She called up the address. Nothing there. She stuffed the tablet back into her messenger bag and slung it onto the back seat. 'Lincoln first?'

'Yes, it's logical.'

Karen turned the key in the ignition. 'I wonder what's left after all this time. Any police officers from back then will be long retired, if they're alive. And witnesses. But I've got a list of names we can ask about. A few journalists covered the stories recently.'

'Are they expecting us at the police station?'

'I emailed a warning yesterday. Are you ready?'

'Just need a minute. There's something about the locations I can't quite fathom.'

'Can't you look while I drive?'
'Good grief, no. I get car sick.'
'What?' Karen was astounded. 'How old are you?'
'OK, let's get going.' John put the notebook down and Karen pulled out.

11

It was a bright, sunny day and the traffic was light. John had brought some CDs along and Karen discovered that there was nothing she violently objected to. There were even a few opportunities for duets, and as they both had shockingly bad voices, they were happy to belt them out together.

'OK, left in about one hundred metres.'

He's not bad at this, Karen acknowledged. *He hasn't even criticised my driving yet. But we seem to be taking a lot of scenic routes.*

'Was that your phone or mine?' John said.

'Either way, you have to look. I'm driving, remember?'

John reached around for Karen's bag not daring to actually look inside. 'It's yours. Shall I?'

'Go for it,' Karen replied. She knew it certainly wasn't going to be another boyfriend.

'Hello?' John answered her phone. 'There's a message.' He clicked off the phone. 'It was your father. He said he'd be in touch.'

Karen slammed the brakes on so hard it nearly activated the airbag.

'What are you doing?' he shouted, first searching ahead for potential reasons for her actions. Puzzled, he looked at her face which was even paler than usual and waited while she pulled over on the verge. When she put the handbrake on, she was taking in deep breaths. 'What's the matter?'

'My father died last year.' When her heart stopped trying to crash through her ribcage, she spoke again. 'Give me the phone.' She looked at the device, hands shaking. The recent call display read **MISSED CALL FROM DAD**

'What did it...he say?'

'You've got to find them for me.'

Karen sat rigidly for a good few seconds, then her relief was obvious. She burst into nervous, slightly hysterical laughter.

'What's going on?' John asked.

When Karen finally recovered enough to talk, she turned to John, smiling. 'It's an old message,' she said. 'From when he lost his gloves or something. Yes, his driving gloves. I didn't delete it at the time, I liked hearing his voice. It must've got thrown up somehow.'

'Jesus, Karen. You never told me your father died? When did that happen? If you had...'

'What?' said Karen. 'If you'd known he'd died would you have lied about the message? It's technology. I'm sure it's happened before. Delete it. In fact, delete the contact, too. I won't be needing it.'

'But when did he die? That wasn't when you did your disappearing acts was it?'

'No. Do we have to do this now?'

'Yes. I'm curious now,' John replied.

'I had to lay his ashes.'

'And you couldn't think to tell me that?'

'None of your business, John. You never knew him.'

John paused for a moment. 'Don't delete the contact,' he said. 'I don't believe in the inexplicable, but if someone is hacking your phone, we need to find them. Like whoever sent those files. We should leave all channels open in case I can get them traced.'

Karen looked at him in amazement. *Is he kidding me? No, he's deadly serious.* 'OK. Delete the message but leave the contact.'

'Do you want me to take over the driving?' John asked carefully.

'Good god, no! How the hell would I find your route? I'm fine. Let's go. Where next?' she said firmly.

'Keep on this road for another ten miles,' John replied. 'But please tell me about your father, if you don't mind.'

Karen sighed as she pulled out. 'I think I told you he was a copper. He drank too much. Anyway, I'm very like him, I'm told, except he was much nicer and everybody loved him.'

'And your mother?'

'Died when I was ten. Lung cancer. Ironic isn't it? She never smoked. Someone said passive smoking from Dad, but he was hardly around, and I can't remember him ever smoking in the house. One of those things, I suppose. So there we were, Dad and me, except he couldn't really manage – not without help from friends. Uncle Jack and Auntie Sal – except I've dropped the titles now.'

'You mentioned an uncle once. How was it? I can't imagine living without a mother.'

'I was mature for my age and I coped. I loved hearing his work stories. That's what got me hooked – the passion in him when he talked about his job. I loved him so much when he was in full flow. I overlooked the drunkenness, the late nights or not even coming home sometimes.'

John couldn't resist a '*hmm*'.

'I was on his side, you see? I was always waiting for the end of the case when the villain had been banged up and he was all fun and full of stories again.' She looked sideways to John. 'You're quiet.'

'It must have been so hard for you. I know you don't see it because that's all you've ever known. But it's not right...'

'Butt out John. OK, so it was different, but it's who I am now. And I'm Dad's daughter. No doubt you had a lovey-dovey namby-pamby life with Mummy and Daddy.'

'I wouldn't say that. Well, not quite. What happened to him?'

'Heart attack. Apparently, he was an accident waiting to happen. He was still working, stubborn like that. Many coppers retire at fifty, he was fifty-five. I think they kept him on out of pity really. It was his whole life – apart from me. He was a desk sergeant too, like Bill is now, but not at my station. And he was very into his cold cases. He helped out old mates all over the place.'

'And did he turn the house into an incident room?'

'Oh, often. Where do you think I got that from?'

'So what happened? When...'

'Someone came into reception one day just to ask something silly, like directions, and he collapsed.'

'That's awful,' said John.

'Nope. Quick, relatively painless, and on the job. Perfect for him; a shock to me of course.'

'But very young.'

'Better that than dying of boredom at home. I do miss him though. He was such a good sounding board.'

'I'm sure he was.' John said.

'Jack is, too. Go on, tell me about your folks,' Karen said, more cheerfully now.

'My mummy and daddy are very lovey-dovey and absolutely namby-pamby,' John mocked. 'I had a fabulous middle-class childhood, spoilt rotten, an only child, too. It nearly broke Mum's heart when I moved down South.'

'Oh,' said Karen, now interested. 'Where did you used to live?'

'Near Lincoln,' John smiled. 'We'll be meeting them soon. And we can stay over.'

'What?' Karen turned her head to look at him. 'Why the fuck didn't you tell me that? Is this what this bloody route is all about?'

'Watch the road, Karen!' Karen looked ahead.

'Partly,' John continued. 'There's something else I need to do on the way too, though. And Mum's only just confirmed it's OK with them.'

'What do you need to do? You know I hate surprises.'

'Oh, there's a little bookshop I want to visit. I used to go there a lot. I love it; it's full of wonderful things. You'll love it, too.'

'Books?' snorted Karen. 'I don't do books. Except for real-life crime.'

'These you will,' John replied. 'And for the record, my parents are really looking forward to meeting you.'

'Oh, bloody great.'

'And there's something else.'

'What?' snapped Karen.

'Mummy makes wonderful namby-pamby food,' said John, trying not to laugh.

41

12

Karen was paying attention to the driving instructions and not the scenery when John spoke.

'This is it; pull up over on the left.'

Karen looked around. It was an unremarkable little village high street. They had stopped by an ancient thatched building next to a large red brick house.

'What the hell?' Karen said. She had been expecting to see a state-of-the-art techy sort of shop; this looked like it came from another century, probably the sixteenth. 'Binks' Books?'

John got out of the car and stretched his shoulders back. 'Isn't it wonderful?' he turned to look at Karen, also stretching as she emerged.

'Very nice,' she said flatly. 'What is so special about it?'

'Walk this way.' John crossed the pavement to the entrance where a hanging sign on the inside of the glass-panelled door was turned to 'OPEN'

'Well, well, well,' said a hearty sort of voice audible over the sound of the tinny bell set off by the opening of the door.

'If it isn't young John and his young lady friend.'

Karen watched as a smiling rotund man of below-average height stepped forward. His face was lined, and his baldness was balanced by bushy side-whiskers. He wore an old-fashioned waistcoat which housed a pocket watch on a chain. *Like something out of Dickens,* Karen thought. The smell of old leather and musty old books hit her straightaway.

Mr Binks looked sad. 'John, much as I would love to offer you some tea, I'm afraid I have to pop out for a while. Could you possibly return in,' he looked at his watch, 'say, an hour?'

'Of course,' John replied. 'I haven't been home yet. We'll see you soon.'

***

It can't be far, Karen thought, *especially by car. But judging from the sweat on his upper lip, he's nervous.*

When they arrived outside John's parents' house, the door opened before they'd even got out of the car. She surveyed the house in a manner somewhere between crime scene investigator and house buyer. *Tidy garden; the epitome of the comfortable middle class. He wasn't joking.*

'John-boy,' said his mother without a hint of an accent. The slim, bottle-blonde woman with bright blue eyes hugged him, her head to his chest, for several seconds too long. She turned to Karen; they were eye to eye. 'And you must be Karen. I'm pleased to meet you. You'll be in the guest room. I'm Daphne.'

Whoa! That told me. Karen reached out straight away and shook Mrs Steele's hand more firmly than usual.

'Pleased to meet you, too.'

Inside, everything Karen saw confirmed her initial impressions. The colours were tasteful with coordinated colour patterns everywhere. Not modern, not old fashioned, something indistinct and in between. John led the way into the living room where his father, a tall man with a long nose, turned round to greet them with a big smile. Karen's eyes were drawn to the big patio doors, noting the manicured garden full of autumn colours.

'Delighted,' he said as he bent slightly to shake Karen's hand.

Karen looked at John, then back at his father. 'You're the spitting image...'

'I know,' John sighed. 'Everybody says so.'

Daphne appeared at the door behind them. 'The kettle has just boiled. Would you like a cup of tea?'

'Yes please, Mum. Tea for me. Karen?'

I could kill for some wine. Better not. 'Tea, too please Mrs...'

'Call me Daphne dear, and John's father is Big John. Well, that's what we call him. You can call him just John,' she tittered. 'I don't mean call him 'Just John', I mean just call him John if you like.' She giggled as she went to the kitchen to make tea.

'That would be too confusing. Big John and John-boy? Really?'

Big John smiled. 'It wasn't my idea; it's been passed down in my family for generations. I didn't care, but Daph is one for tradition.'

43

Karen smiled wistfully. 'I have no idea where *Karen* came from. But I do rather like John-boy,' she stuck her tongue out at a cringing John.

'How is she?' John whispered to his dad.

'Getting there,' came the equally quiet reply.

'We're off to the bookshop and the police station soon,' John half-shouted so that his mother could hear. A moment later she came in with a laden tea-tray. Karen's mouth watered at the sight of the chocolate biscuits.

'That's fine dear. Dinner is at seven. You haven't told me what you're doing here, John-boy. Or is it secret?'

John looked at Karen and she picked up the cue. 'I'm investigating some old cases; what they call cold cases.'

'Oh, I think I know what those are,' Daphne said. 'Unsolved murders. I've seen it on the television.'

'Yes, well, it's all unsolved crimes really. But often murders, that's true.'

'Isn't that rather horrible?' Daphne wrinkled her nose.

'And this is how you spend all your holidays, Karen?' said Big John, sounding perturbed.

'No, not at all,' Karen replied reassuringly.

'I'm glad to hear it,' Big John said. 'We all need a break from our work, and I imagine yours is more stressful than most.'

'Actually, I never normally have holidays at all,' Karen announced. Big John frowned.

'She's very dedicated, Dad,' John explained.

'She'll think differently when she wants to settle down.' Daphne poured the tea. 'Not that I'm suggesting anything... sugar, Karen?' she added hastily.

'Four please,' Karen said.

'Four? Yes of course.'

John made a horrible spluttering noise.

13

'That went well,' said John sarcastically.

Karen turned to look at him as they got into the car.

'I was on my best behaviour.'

'*Four* spoonfuls of sugar and *four* chocolate biscuits? That's a world record in our house. Mum's never had to replenish the plate before.'

'There are limits? How am I supposed to know that? And what's this about the guest room? What century are we in?'

'She's old-fashioned, Karen. We've always got my tent.'

Karen laughed. 'So what's so special about this book shop?'

'You'll love it. Wait and see. You only saw a tiny bit last time. Next left... and we're here.'

Mr Binks was waiting at the door for them.

'May I offer you some tea?'

John answered quickly for both of them. 'Yes, please, Mr Binks. That would be lovely.'

'Come along.' They followed him into the shop.

As she got further in, Karen could see the shelves stuffed with books, but nothing seemingly special. She looked at John, he nodded towards Mr Binks who was pulling aside what looked like a whole shelf of books.

'A secret room?' Karen, eyes wide, walked into the little room which had wall to ceiling shelves crammed full of books. But these were not just ordinary books. Here were almanacs, charts, maps, timetables, logbooks, and every esoteric publication you could possibly think of. *I bet he's even got some books of spells.*

'This is wonderful,' she said, turning to the man, whose face creased into even more lines. *How on earth does he make a living?*

'Please, sit,' Mr Binks gestured to the small table and chairs and disappeared through yet another door.

'This is why we have tea,' John said.

'You obviously know him very well.'

'He's a dear old man, and he has the most wonderful ginger biscuits. Or at least he used to.'

'*Mmm*. Ginger.' Karen sat at the table. 'Is this where he clinches his deals?'

John laughed. 'Or entertains his lady friends. I've always suspected he's a bit of a rascal.'

'OK. So he sells old maps and things. Is that why we're here? So we can see what the places looked like in 1964?'

'Yes. Lincoln, like all cities, has expanded outwards. Could you find Amy's address on the internet?' Karen shook her head. 'It's most likely that they were all redeveloped years ago during the tail end of the post-war regeneration. It's impossible to tell what it all looked like back then.'

'How come he's got all this?'

'He inherited a fair bit of money from his aunt.' John paused as the back door opened. 'Mr Binks will explain.'

Mr Binks backed in. Karen's eyes widened as she saw what he was carrying. It was a much more impressive – and better laden – tray than Daphne's had been.

'Yes, my dear? Your young man hasn't told me your name?'

'It's Karen,' she smiled.

'As John says, but not just money. I inherited an absolute treasure trove. It would never have occurred to me not to keep it. I'd already begun my own collection. In fact, it was my Aunt Hermione who started me off. She knew we were kindred spirits. Looking back, I suspect she was preparing me from the very beginning.' He put the tray on the table and sat down. 'She was the most wonderful hoarder and not just maps and guides. She picked up anything unusual that caught her eye. She bequeathed me her house, too, you see, the one next door. Five big bedrooms and each one was full of her wonderful acquisitions. She slept on the sofa. Can you imagine? With all that room?'

'She must have been very committed to her stuff,' Karen said, eyeing the biscuits.

'Indeed. And this delightful old building came attached. She left me enough money to live on for the rest of my life. I am quite well off now, you see. I've always loved old books, and I thought I'm sure there are hundreds of people who would like to look up old things. It's been a lifetime's achievement. I've sorted it all out and picked out the ones most likely to be requested to put on the shelves. There is a great deal more back in the house; this is just the tip of the iceberg. I've even got the complete set of the Radio Times going right back to 1923.'

Blimey. 'Really?' Karen said. 'That's amazing. Do you sell very much?'

'Oh, my dear, no. That's not how it works at all. I will have to explain it to you.' He poured her some tea. 'Help yourself to sugar and biscuits.'

John threw her a look as she added three highly heaped spoonfuls to her cup and took a biscuit.

After he had poured the rest of the tea, Mr Binks sat down. 'I keep it for very special people.'

Karen smiled. 'Like who?'

'Lots of people. People who want to remember what was on the television when their child was born. People who want to relive their childhood and walk down a memory lane that has been destroyed by the war or the even worse damage done since the war. People sometimes even like young detectives.'

Karen laughed. 'And how do they find you?'

'Oh, now that is very interesting. They just do. People come to me from all over the world. I don't advertise, and I'm hardly in the most easily identifiable place, but still, they come.'

'That's amazing,' Karen said. 'How many people do you get here in a year?'

'Ah, not so many nowadays, my dear. Times are changing now and, thanks in part to this young man of yours, I am becoming, what do they say, a silver surfer? I am very nearly computer literate. As people of my age die off there will be fewer and fewer people with memories of the old days that need to be rekindled. But there will always be some people who just want to know *things*.'

'So you're putting all this on the internet?' Karen asked.

'That is my ambition, with John's help. Would you believe that I now even have an email address?'

Karen nodded, her smile disguising her incredulity.

Mr Binks continued. 'But the website will be tucked away as carefully as the shop so only the most informed people with the very most need will ever find it.'

Karen looked around the walls. 'He is quite good,' She gave John a glance. 'But that's going to take forever, isn't it?'

'Indeed,' Mr Binks nodded. 'But you have to start somewhere. Obviously, in some cases, there is already a digital record of things, but you'd be surprised how often there isn't. Much of the literature produced by small organisations and old county councils was destroyed and replaced by newer versions. In many cases, I have the only known original.'

'You sound like my perfect solution. It would have taken weeks to access this from local council archives.'

'So I believe, my dear. What is it you think you need?'

What an extraordinary and lovely old man, Karen thought. *He's practically Father Christmas.* 'Do you believe in ghosts?'

'I believe in all sorts of unbelievable things,' he replied. 'Tell me why you ask.'

'It's like this...' Karen relayed with her usual attention to detail, the files, all the strange happenings, all the half-seen or imagined things, even the recorded message from her father.

Mr Binks listened patiently 'I think, my dear, that whatever you have experienced thus far, however strange, you must put it all to one side and do what you are best at. Investigate those cases. You will be doing a huge service to somebody whether it be putting minds at rest, or souls. Another cup?'

'Yes, please,' said Karen. *I feel like a weight has lifted*. 'And I think we'll be needing to borrow some of your maps.'

'Of course, my dear,' Mr Binks said as he poured the tea.

14

When tea was over, and there was one gingernut left, Karen took her notebook from her pocket.

'As we're nearly in Lincoln,' she began, 'what's the oldest road map you have? We're looking for 1964.'

'Let me see...' said Mr Binks, going straight to a shelf. 'I have Lincoln in 1959 and 1968. Will that help?'

'Perfect,' said John. 'Do you mind if we look at it here?'

'Of course not,' Mr Binks replied. 'I'll clear the table.'

'Let me guess, these are the digitised ones?' Karen pointed to a very tidy section.

'You have a very good eye for detail. Quite right.'

When he had gone, Karen whispered to John. 'How did you find him?'

'I got lost on my bike once,' John said, 'when I was eight. I'd been riding for miles. I took a wrong turn and kept getting further away from home. I found myself here, and came in.'

'I can imagine that,' Karen grinned. 'What happened?'

'He told me how to get home, in fact, told me about some cycle paths I never even knew existed which went quite close to my home. Then he lectured me a bit about road safety. I had to go, as it was late and I didn't want Mum to worry, but he said I could come back anytime. So I did. Apparently, I wasn't like *other* boys.'

'Oh?' Karen raised an eyebrow.

'Good grief, nothing like that. I was serious and interested, so he just took a shine to me; well, that's what he told me much later anyway.'

'I bet he has books of spells and stuff. He's not a witch, or do I mean warlock?'

John laughed. 'No, I don't think so, but he certainly has an interest in all sorts of things. Not so much the magic, more the geography that goes with it. Hidden landmarks, old worship sites, ancient pathways. He's always nagging me to look out for anything like that in my work or wherever I go. He's got a list of books that his aunt saw, or heard of, and he's been trying to track them down for years. So I do. I find the oldest tattiest bookshops and have a browse. I've found him a few things over the years. He'll expect you to look out for him as well now.'

'Oh, that would be fun,' Karen smiled. 'Now let's look at these maps.'

John spread out the map of Lincoln dated 1959. 'This should be post-war regeneration so we ought to be able to find Amy's house on here.'

'There,' Karen pointed at the tiny index and followed the reference on the map with her finger. 'Great. Now we have to find the same location on the modern map. But let's just check the 1968 version.'

Karen pored over the map looking from one to the other. John looked at the index.

'It's not here,' they said together.

'This looks like some sort of industrial area,' John said, pointing at the newer map. They must have demolished all the old houses and built a factory or something over the top of it.'

'Or farm buildings?' Karen was remembering the image of the little girl in the lane. She took out her tablet and went to her history. 'Look, see? This is the house I was looking at. It's meant to be new. And in a village location.'

'Fifty years is a long time, John said. 'Maybe the usage changed more than once. Pan out on the map; let's see exactly where it is.'

Karen clicked the arrows on the screen and the area expanded.

John saw it first. 'There's the lane. I'm sure it is by the shape. They must've renamed it.'

'That means...' began Karen.

'Yes. You saw something pretty much at the location where Amy Warren lived fifty years ago.'

Karen took in a long deep breath. *I will not be spooked.* 'Yes. Let's go there first. And what about York and Edinburgh? Should we find out if there are maps for those too?'

John slapped his head with his hand. 'Yes. I'll go and ask him.'

While John was gone, Karen took the opportunity to have a snoop around. On the wall in a gap between two shelves was a small cork notice board on which a crusty, yellowed piece of paper was pinned with an old-fashioned drawing pin. It was headed **TO FIND**, and there were thirty items listed. Number one read **The Witches' Pathway** Karen shivered a little as she read the description. ***Only three copies made; author unknown, handwritten in gold ink on leather bound/human skin.*** *Hmm. Maybe not so nice Mr Binks.* She jumped when John came back carrying more maps.

'I didn't get modern maps for York or Edinburgh. Idiot,' he said, oblivious to what Karen was looking at.

'We can trace the old addresses and take pictures. It'll be easy enough to buy them when we're there,' Karen said.

'True. And we have got 1957 and 1967 for York and 1958 and 1969 for Edinburgh.'

'Then let's have a look.'

They spread each map out in turn and located both addresses on the oldest maps Mr Binks had. For both York in 1967 and Edinburgh in 1969, the maps showed considerable development of the areas since the girls were abducted. Satisfied they had captured enough information, they returned the map to Mr Binks who was snoozing in his chair in the back room. John restored the maps carefully to their correct location.

'Just leave him,' John said, 'The one thing he really doesn't like is being disturbed while he's sleeping.'

'OK,' Karen said but as they left the building, she turned back to look at him. *Did he just wink at me? What a rogue.* 'Bye Mr Binks. Thanks so much.' *He's far too naughty to be bad.* 'What next?'

'Police station.'

51

15

When they arrived at the local station Karen marched straight up to the front desk. 'I'm here to see Sergeant Floyd Cannon,' she said to the woman on reception.

'I'm sorry, it's Saturday. Was he expecting you?'

'I emailed him, yes.'

'And you are...?' said the woman, the irritation in her voice unmistakable.

'Detective Sergeant Karen Thorpe.'

'Ah, I see. Sergeant Cannon tends to stick to normal hours here. Unless there's a major incident.'

'What? Is he in tomorrow?'

'Sunday? I doubt that...'

Karen turned to John. 'Come on, we're done here. Where's the local rag office?'

The woman gave her a strange look. 'Do you mean the local newspaper?'

'Yes. What else?''

'That's closed today.'

'We'll have a look for ourselves,' Karen said curtly, turning round to leave.

'She's probably right,' John said when they were outside. 'It's that way, just up there,' he pointed.

When they arrived at the little building Karen sounded hopeful. 'There's a light on.' They were disappointed. The cleaner was the only one in. 'I should have checked, ' Karen pouted.

'Let's go home.'

'No, it's too early. Have you sussed where the house is? Have we got time to go there now?'

John looked at his watch. 'No chance.'

'Tell me,' Karen said as they got in the car. 'Why did you get into forensics?'

'Well originally, when I was little, I wanted to join the police. But...'

'You got in trouble with them?' Karen guessed.

'No, of course not.'

'You got lost even more times than that time on your bike and people kept taking you there?'

'No.'

'OK, I give up. What?'

'I did actually start to train as a cadet.'

Now Karen was interested. 'Really? Why did you give up? No, I know this, don't I? You preferred the research and the forensic details to the people, didn't you?'

'Spot on,' John agreed. 'But I did do some work there, too, as part of my degree. Nice station. Nice people. I like police officers. Especially ones called Karen.'

'You Muppet. John-boy indeed. Let's get going.'

***

'Damn,' Karen said as they walked up to the house. 'I should have bought a bottle or something.'

'Ah,' said John meaningfully. 'They gave up drinking. At least Mum did after her operation. I know Dad still has the odd pint when he's feeling brave, but there's none in the house at all.'

'Shit! That's terrible.'

'We can nip out to the pub after dinner if you like.' John held out his door key but Daphne appeared before he could use it. She looked the perfect hostess in her pearls and ruffled apron.

'Hello. May I go up to my room?' Karen said. 'I need to freshen up a bit.'

'Upstairs, second on the right. There's an *en suite*.'

Of course there is. 'Thanks.'

Karen's room was nice enough, simply furnished with a well-designed shower room. She didn't need long but as she left, she stopped at the top of the stairs when she heard voices.

'She's very intense isn't she?' said Daphne. 'Four sugars! What self-respecting girl has sugar in her tea these days, not to mention *four* biscuits. Think of the calories. And did you see her face?'

Big John spoke. 'Quite pretty I thought.'

'But not a scrap of makeup. Can you imagine? You don't think she's... you know, that way inclined do you?'

Big John laughed. 'I expect she's got more important things on her mind. She is a sergeant you know, and John-boy thinks she'll make inspector soon.'

'Oh no,' said Daphne. 'I hope our John isn't wasting his time on her. Career women are no good. He should be looking to settle down. He's already thirty-two. Older than you were when...'

'It's different today Daph. They'll do what they want when they want.'

If she's hoping I put some slap on, she'll be very disappointed. Karen shut the door of her room with enough noise to alert John's parents. *Interesting about John though. Telling them about my career.* Two minutes later she registered Daphne's sour expression as she walked down the stairs.

Dinner was served precisely at seven. *This is the best food I've had in years. Shame about the conversation. She's only interested in appearance. How things look. God, I need a drink. Hell, it's Sunday tomorrow. And I've got to get going on things. So much to do. Damn, is she talking to me?*

'Sorry, I was just thinking. John? You said we could go to the pub. There's so much we need to plan, and I'm sure we don't want to bore your parents to death.'

John frowned. 'Later Karen. We haven't had pudding yet.'

Daphne looked down at Karen's feet. 'I couldn't help noticing your shoes, Karen. I suppose that being a policewoman means you can't wear fashion on duty. But I assume you have others?'

What the actual fuck? 'I have others, yes. All flats.'

'Would you like to see my shoe collection? I have some lovely Guccis, and I do so love Diane von Furstenberg. Of course, I have some of her dresses too...'

Karen stood up so suddenly, her chair fell over making a terrible clatter on the parquet flooring. 'Sorry,' she muttered, trying to pick the chair up but only managing to drop it again. John picked it up while Karen went into the hallway. On the top of the radiator cupboard, she saw some old black leather driving gloves and a light went on in her head.

John appeared. 'What is it?'

'I just can't do this.'

'I guessed that,' John said. 'Let's go to the pub.'

'No,' Karen said firmly. 'I have to go back. Something I have to do. You stay here with your parents. I will probably be back tomorrow.'

'You have to be. I haven't got my car here.'

'Hmm. Can't you borrow your dad's? I was hoping you could get an appointment to see that house. Have a good look around the area; look at the maps. There's a clue there, I'm positive.'

'I'll do my best. You will say goodbye, won't you?'

'Of course.' Karen went back into the dining room having recovered her polite personality. 'I'm very sorry Mr and Mrs Steele. I've left something at home, and I have to go back to collect it. We need to go to Scotland soon, and it's better to go back from here before we're too far north.'

Big John nodded sympathetically. *He understands,* Karen thought. Daphne sat transfixed without saying a word. *She's pleased I'm going.*

John followed her to the door.

'I will be back. Promise.' She gave him a kiss which told him she would be.

16

Karen drove off as fast as she dared. Her tried and tested way to deal with unfamiliar terrain was to drive around in ever-increasing circles until she hit a main road sign. There were going to be no scenic routes for her, besides it was dark. *Thank God I didn't have a drink. I'd be climbing Daphne's coordinated pastel walls by now. There. A1. Perfect.* Even as she drove, she wasn't at all sure if there was a point to it. *Does it add anything? Maybe not, but I can't be worrying about it in Scotland.*

By the time she got home, she was exhausted. She hauled herself up the stairs to her flat and flung her front door open as if she were challenging anyone or anything that might be lurking there. 'Now where the fuck are you?' she said out loud. 'And the bloody wine'

Wine is essential, she decided. *Even if I have to go out and buy some. Hey, you'll do.* She grabbed a screw-top bottle of cabernet sauvignon with just enough in it to anaesthetise her, if not to knock her out completely. Taking the first receptacle she found, she poured herself a large mug of the stuff and took a long gulp. *Wait for it...* The soothing and weighty sensation in her legs commenced. When the tingling numbness in her brain kicked in, she breathed deeply as if reinvigorated and sat on the sofa. *Now where the fuck are they?*

Gradually her memory clicked into action. *Really? Didn't I sort it out before?* Standing on a chair, with one hand she began to pull a large green bag out of the top of her cupboard, holding back the inevitable fallout with the other hand. She was almost successful and only a few things tumbled out.

Now, who's calling? John. Wait for it... John rang off. *He still thinks I'm driving; I've made such good time. He'll ring again in a minute.* She flopped down again on the sofa and dragged the bag to her.

First, she pulled out her father's old black driving gloves and put them carefully beside her on the sofa. Next, she pulled out his notebook. 'Now, Dad, you'd better have been trying to tell me something or I'll have had a long and wasted journey.'

Her mobile rang again. 'Just this second got in,' she lied.

'That was good timing,' John sounded concerned. 'Are you OK? What was it all about?'

'I'm fine. I'm not telling you yet, because you'll think I'm mad.' She paused. 'I mean really deeply mad; I know you think I'm mad already.' John laughed. 'How are your parents after…?'

'Karen-struck,' John laughed. 'Dad really likes you but Mum, well let's say it'll take her a while.'

'She's a nice lady, in her own way, it's just…'

'Don't incriminate yourself, Sergeant. Leave it there. Are you really all right though?'

'I'm fine. No strewn underwear, no screaming kids, nobody ringing any bells. It's OK. And I'll be up with you tomorrow. What about you?'

'I've found something really interesting,' John said.

'What?'

'You'll just have to wait. See you tomorrow.'

'Night, John,' said Karen. 'I mean, night, John-boy.'

Karen went back to her father's notebook. She turned each page one by one looking for anything meaningful. *What's that? A Yorkshire number.* She checked her phone contacts. *It's the police station. Why Dad? And when? June 2012. Five months before… Why would you go that far afield? I thought you were strictly armchair.*

She looked at her watch; it was nearly midnight. *Too late to do anything now*. She drained the mug of its wine and carried on with the notebook. After about ten pages, she read something that made her heart stop. **Katherine Engles**.

'What were you doing? That's way off your patch.'

Karen's mind raced. *The files, the emails. Could they have been meant for him? Another Sergeant Thorpe?* She flicked through the notebook looking to see if the other names were there, but no.

She saw nothing of interest until she got to the very last page on which there was some scribbled writing. Undated, but it could have been written on the day he died. Then she saw two words that shook her. **Binks' Books.** 'What the hell?' *Did he know you Dad? Was he involved?* And w*hat did he have to do with Katherine Engles?*

G*radually her rational side came to the fore. It's just a name. One of the last things he wrote, but maybe completely unconnected. Maybe he wanted a map? And as Mr Binks had said, people who needed him managed to find him.*

'OK, Dad, if I wasn't hooked before, I am now. You were clearly investigating something to do with Katherine Engles, and maybe that was a message from beyond the grave even if you didn't intend it like that. I will find them for you, Dad. I promise.'

Now calmer, Karen's tiredness began to take over and she yawned so hard she nearly hurt her jaw. She stripped off her outer layers and climbed into bed exhausted, falling into a deep but troubled sleep. She dreamt of the three girls. Mr Binks was in there somewhere, even Daphne made an appearance dressed as a witch, and she heard her father humming one of his favourite songs. She knew the tune but didn't know the words. Something about a Scottish soldier.

As she began to rouse, she smiled at the silhouette of the shape lying next to her.

Ah John, such a good...

Hang on. He's not here.

As her eyes adjusted to the dark, the shape moved away. She could just make out the balding head and fuzzy grey hairs of Mr Binks. He began to turn towards her, talking. 'Find the way,' he said. Immobilised, she knew she didn't want to see. She knew it would be horrible, but his head kept turning towards her. She could almost see his face then WHAM! She woke up.

17

Sunday 10 November

The weak, autumn sunshine was permeating Karen's bedroom blinds and she saw, of course, there was nobody in the room. But she was still shaking and drenched in cold sweat. She jumped up and went straight into the living room for a swig of brandy. *No, that's disgusting this early. Have coffee. A strong one.*

When she emerged from the kitchen, mug in hand, her mobile beeped from the sofa. **Missed call from John**. *What do I tell him? I really don't want to see Daphne again. I'm clearly not the daughter-in-law of choice.* She laughed out loud. 'Marriage? Me? No way.' *I'm never going to get married. Anyway, I'm too young. I wonder what he thinks? He's past thirty. Is that the time you... enough. You've got too much to do. But he is handy to have around.* Before she'd quite finished speculating, John rang again.

'Morning,' she said as noncommittally as she could.

'Am I allowed to say how much I've missed you?' John replied.

Karen laughed. 'Why? It's not as if we spend every night together.'

'This was meant to be my holiday,' John said plaintively. 'And I wanted to spend time with you. And the ear-bashing is getting worse.'

'What?' *What does he mean? Not his mother... OK Level with him.* 'It's not you.' *Damn. What a dreadful cliché! Explain it.* 'The investigation I mean, getting complicated. I think my father's involved somehow.'

'Are you sure?' John sounded far too enthusiastic.

'No, but I found some things in his notebook. What ear-bashing?'

'Erm, I shouldn't have said that.'

'It's your mother, isn't it?' *If she hates me that much....* 'Sorry. I can't come up there again.'

'I know, but 'there' is a big place. Why not meet up in York? I'll get the train and I'll tell the folks I'm off home.'

Karen's enthusiasm returned in a blink. 'Good idea. I'm really curious about York now. Let me get my act together; I may need to see an old friend of Dad's. Get some background info.'

'York's good for me, too. I can start testing my location theory.'

'Just one thing, John.'

'Yes Karen?'

'Get a B&B with a double room.' John smiled so loudly Karen could hear it.

'It's the first thing I'll do today. Talk soon.'

Karen showered away the sweat and the bad dreams and got dressed all while her brain ticked over the new plan of action. *Jack.* Her father's friend and now hers. *He'll know something.*

'Jack? It's Karen here.'

'Hi, love. What have you been up to? Inspector's exams yet?'

Karen laughed. 'No, not yet. I haven't quite had the guv's finger pointed at me yet.'

'It won't be long, I'm sure. What can I do you for?'

'I wanted a chat about Dad, actually.'

'Anything in particular?'

'Yes. Did you know he was looking at a cold case in York?'

'Oh dear. I'll have to get my brain in gear for that one. There was something odd. Pop round. I'll have a think.'

***

Jack's wife, Sal, opened the door. 'Hello love, come in and take the weight off. Not that you've got much weight. Are you looking after yourself?'

'Yes, Sal, I am.' Karen gave the cuddly blonde woman a big hug.

'Go in. I'll put the kettle on. He's just having a rummage.'

'That sounds good.' Karen went into the living room.

'Hi love. It's not very good,' Jack said, holding a laptop. 'I'm not sure what I think if I'm honest. Maybe you should see it; but first, sit down and tell me what you wanted to know.'

Karen, now curious, reached in her bag for her father's notebook. 'Don't ask why, but I've been looking into a couple of cold cases. Three to be precise, and I've just discovered the name of one of them in here. Katherine Engles in York. Do you know anything about it?'

Jack sighed. 'Just a little. Tommy told me that one of his old mates from Hendon days had asked him to help clear up a case. I think that was Yorkshire somewhere. It'd preyed on his mind. Happens to all of us. Young girl abducted, never found the body. The lass's mother was sick, and this friend wanted your dad to take it up, help him out. He was in a wheelchair apparently, so couldn't get about so easily.'

Karen flicked through the notebook. 'Brian Appleby?' she asked. 'I've got that name and number here, it's a Yorkshire number.'

'I don't know the name; not someone I knew. It could well be. You haven't rung it yet, then?'

'No, I thought I'd talk to you first.'

'He mentioned it to me in the pub one day; didn't seem particularly exercised about it, not like he would have done in the old days. More a case of helping out an old mate if he could. I think he preferred the paper cases, not the chase.'

Karen nodded. 'That's what I thought. Somebody in the York station may be able to tell me more. Did he ever mention a shop called Binks' Books?'

Jack scratched his head. 'It's got a ring to it, but I can't place it. Why?' She showed him the page. 'No number or anything.' Jack said. 'Maybe someone just mentioned it to him. Just before...'

'Just before what?' Karen pressed.

Jack looked thoughtfully at Karen, she felt him sizing her up for something. Her father had that look, too. Maybe she had it, or was beginning to learn it. There was no point hurrying him or pushing him; he would have to decide for himself.

'Just before he died,' Jack said. He fell silent for a moment. 'That thing I wanted to show you, it's footage of your dad,' Jack said finally. 'It's the CCTV from the station. When he had the heart attack.'

Karen sat up, shocked. 'What?' *Footage? Do I really want to...?*

'It doesn't show him dying or anything grim like that,' Jack paused again.

Karen frowned. 'OK, why do you think I should see it? I mean, I will, but I was told it was just someone asking for directions.'

'That's true,' said Jack. 'But apparently, they asked to speak to him by name. And there's just something odd about it all.'

'What do you mean?' said Karen, now unnerved. 'He wasn't murdered; the post-mortem was very precise.'

'Just have a look. There's no sound, just pictures.'

When Sal appeared with the tea, Karen resisted the urge to ask for something stronger.

18

Karen watched as the black and white film opened with the view over the reception desk, the camera behind her dad showing him sideways on. He appeared to be looking through some papers rather than sitting on the desk. A young woman sat looking straight ahead of her.

A tall man with a long beard came in. Not quite a homeless type but clearly no middle-class suburbanite either. He looked straight up at the camera, then spoke to the woman.

'Who is it?' Karen asked, her heart beating faster.

'We don't know,' said Jack. 'I've done some preliminary stuff; no facial recognition match but that beard could mask all sorts.'

'Rewind, can you? I want to see what he said.' Karen squinted to watch the man's lips. 'Tom Thorpe,' she said. 'I can make that much out.' As her on-screen father turned to speak to the man, Jack stopped the film.

'Yes,' Jack agreed. 'I got that bit, and the girl said as much. It's the next bit.'

'Go on.'

Jack restarted the film. The man spoke some more words then put both his hands on the desk and leaned forward as if to whisper in her father's ear. Her father leaned forward to hear, then he suddenly began to clutch his chest and stepped back out of view.

'Shit!' *I shouldn't have watched this. Professional Karen. Steel yourself.* 'What happened to the man?'

'We don't know,' Jack replied. 'Everybody was helping Tommy. No one bothered about him. You OK, love?'

Don't you dare cry. 'Yes of course I am,' she swallowed hard. *Dad would want me to do this*. 'Let me see it again.'

Jack rewound the film and played it again at half speed. Karen watched, glued to every tiny movement of the man's mouth. Nothing.

'I can't make out any words at all, but I'm glad you showed me. Do you know of any lip-readers?'

'I expect there'll be someone we can find.'

Karen sat back, contemplating. 'Why do you even have this video? What made you look at it?'

'Well now, love, that's the strangest thing of all.'

'What?'

'Somebody emailed it to me. It came from the IT department but nobody remembered doing it. It was at midnight. Last Sunday night.'

'Bloody hell!'

Sal, who had remained quiet up to now, was concerned. 'Karen, love. What's wrong? It's more than just seeing your dad, isn't it?'

Karen sat for such a long time without speaking that both Jack and Sal looked worried.

'Karen?' Jack ventured.

When Karen replied she told them about the files she had been sent, including the email on Sunday night.

'Sorry, Karen, but it has to be said, ' Sal commented. 'That is all damned spooky.'

And you only know the half of it, thought Karen. 'It's got to be a blip on the system. The files that came to me were probably meant for Dad last year. It's about the right sort of time and we're both Sergeant Thorpe. He was authorised to get cold case files. I think something slipped on the system. I got the files, you got the film. Ghosts don't do IT.'

'Yes, love. I have to agree with you there,' said Jack. 'That makes perfect sense to me.'

Sal was unrepentant. 'That thing, that man was saying, just before Tommy died. Supposing it was some sort of curse?'

Sal had now said out loud the one thing Karen was trying to stop herself from thinking. Instead of admitting it, she overreacted 'That's just ridiculous Sal. Surely you can't believe that bloody nonsense?'

'Sorry I spoke.' Sal retreated. 'There are more things in heaven and earth,' she muttered. 'More tea? At least I can have some use.'

'Sorry Sal,' Karen shouted as Sal went into the kitchen. 'It's just that the last few days have been really hard.' She turned to Jack. 'What do you think?'

'I'm with you. I don't believe in all that mumbo jumbo business. But it could be somebody playing with both of us, someone who knows all about IT. A hacker perhaps?'

Karen nodded her head vigorously. 'Yes, that's what I was thinking. Has to be. Someone connected with the cases, trying to lead us on. Can you email the film to me? I really better get going. I've got a long journey ahead of me.'

'Of course I can. And if I think of anything else...' Jack reached out to put his hand on Karen's hand.

'Thanks. I'll keep you posted. Now I'd better make my peace with Sal.'

Karen went into the kitchen where Sal was tensed up, furiously filling the kettle to make more unnecessary tea. 'I'm sorry Sal, I didn't mean to upset you.'

Sal's shoulders relaxed and she turned round. 'It's not you, it's him.' Karen looked at her curiously. 'Oh, you won't know. I do believe in that so-called *mumbo jumbo* but he's so pig-headed...'

Karen laughed at the unintended joke. Sal looked surprised for a second then realised what she'd said. 'Oh not that sort of pig,' she giggled. 'But I've been to see psychics lots of times, and I agree, sometimes it's a con. They seem to be making it up as they go along. But I tell you, Karen, I've heard some really detailed things which no one but me could possibly know.'

'Really?' said Karen, trying to sound interested but looking at her watch. Sal took the hint.

'Another time,' she said. 'But you mark my words, there's a lot of stuff that no one can understand, not even the cleverest scientists.'

Karen went up to Sal and gave her a big hug. 'Thanks so much. I really will bear that in mind. I must be going now. I'm meeting up with John in York.'

'That's nice.' Sal smiled. 'Have you thought about Tommy's house yet?'

'I just can't decide what to do.'

65

'When you're ready then, I'll be here for you. And remember what I said.'

Karen poked her head into the living room to say goodbye to Jack. 'Thanks again, Jack. I'll let you know what happens – if I get anywhere.' *If there's anywhere to get,* she added to herself. 'I'll see myself out.'

Driving home, Karen began to think about her dad's possessions again. What else was in that hospital bag?

This time the bag was easy to find having been abandoned in her bedroom. She tipped the contents out onto the floor. *His phone. Damn, do I have a charger? And here's his wallet.* She looked through it and found a few notes, some old receipts and in the back compartment, a folded piece of paper. She spread it out. It was a pencil drawing; like a map but with very few positions marked on it. **House. Oak tree. Old path.** An **X** and a crudely drawn arrow pointing North. Karen pinned the edges down with coffee mugs and took a photo of it.

Finding nothing else of interest, Karen picked up her own notebook and flicked through it. Her eyes rested on the phone number of the psychic she had rung a couple of days before. *Sal seemed to think they were worth a go...* She pressed the numbers and was surprised to hear the ringing tone. She wondered whether last time the psychic service had recognised and blocked the police number.

'Good morning,' came the welcoming Scottish voice.

'It's me again.' Karen immediately realised how stupid that sounded.

'The policewoman? The tone was no longer friendly.

Karen sat bold upright. 'How did you know...'

The woman cut her off. 'There is great danger in the path you take.'

'What do you mean?' said Karen, now rattled.

'Stay away, or you will meet the same fate as your father.'

The line went dead. Karen shouted helplessly at the phone.

'WHAT THE FUCK DO YOU MEAN BY THAT?!!!'

She threw the mobile on the floor and cried. Tears for her father and tears for the nervous wreck that she had become.

19

A long swig of brandy and Karen regrouped. *Sort out your life time. Decision time. John decision time.*

How much did Karen need John? Probably more than she'd ever needed anybody and that was the problem. She regarded herself as a solo artist, not a member of a duet. This stuff was getting too personal. He'd be hurt, sure. But she could say she'd had a tipoff to go to Scotland and... Her phone rang. *It's him.*

'Hi, Karen. How did it go with your dad's friend?'

'Not good. No good. No, I mean it was good and not good.'

'I see,' said John, not sounding convinced. 'I'm at the station now, the train's due in five. Where are you?'

'Still at the flat.' Karen paused. *Make or break time.* 'If I didn't come up there today...'

'You'd better.' John replied. 'I think I'm on to something up here. I'm going anyway. I want to get to the bottom of it.'

Karen was floored. *What happened to the steady, slow, thorough forensic scientist? He was beginning to sound like a copper.* 'You'd go without me?' she said, incredulous.

'You betcha. Obviously, we'd need to hook up soon.'

What? This was definitely a duet of sorts – a crime partnership. *I can do that.* If he's on to something then I have to find out what. *And this is work. And I do like him.* 'OK, OK, I get it. I was thinking... no never mind. I'll come up to you, then we've got the car and can go wherever. There's just one thing,' she paused. 'You're not telling me what to do are you?'

'Would I dare, Karen? Seriously, this is important stuff. See you at the B&B.'

'What about...' too late. *He's cut me off!* She'd been thinking about dropping in on Mr Binks. *He's not a player, he has maps. He can wait.* Karen threw everything she needed into a carrier bag and took a last look around the flat.

***

The drive to York was straightforward. The traffic was light but her dicky tummy, which she put down to Daphne's good wholesome food necessitated a couple of comfort stops. On the third stop, she rang John who answered immediately. 'I need directions. Where's the B&B?'

'I've checked in, but there's a problem. Unfortunately, there's no WIFI. I looked around but can't find anywhere else at such short notice, except hotels.'

'And they cost,' Karen said. 'No problem, we got lots to talk about. What's the postcode?' John reeled it off.

Before setting off, Karen checked her tablet for emails. *Great. Jack's sent the video.* She saved it to her files then reluctantly picked up the Satnav and punched the details in.

The roads got ever more empty the closer Karen got to her destination. But in the dark, her headlights gave her only glimpses of the wild rugged beauty she was passing through

At last, she pulled up outside an old stone cottage with a B&B sign creaking in the wind and hanging from a wrought iron post. *Brr.* As she got out of the car, the noticeably colder wind whipped round her legs. *Might need some thicker jeans. Who's that?* She could see a face peering out of the window surrounded by a triangle of light. It disappeared and a few seconds later, John was standing at the door. He gave her a tight hug and a big kiss on the lips.

'I almost thought you weren't coming. You sounded so weird.'

'Something and nothing,' Karen waffled. 'Anyway, I'm here now.' *And it feels right.* John grabbed her bags and took them inside as a cheerful looking woman welcomed her in.

'Hello, lass. You must be starving. We've got meat and tater pie and gravy on special offer. Three pounds fifty tonight if you're interested.'

Food? 'Oh, yes, please, I'm starving.' Karen said as her nose picked up the heavenly aroma drifting from the pie. 'That smells wonderful.'

'We're up here,' John said leading her upstairs. 'Down in five, Mrs Townend.'

'Right you are, Mr Steele.' Mrs Townend went into the kitchen.

'This is lovely,' said Karen. 'So old fashioned and homely.' The room was furnished with big old wood furniture, a sink in the corner, and a colourful quilt on the bed. Nothing matched at all. *Not a bit like Daphne's spare room.*

'There's a little shower room in here,' John opened a door that looked like a cupboard. Karen peeked inside; it was small but sufficient, and there were big fluffy towels on the radiator. She took off her coat, kicked off her shoes, and flopped down on the bed just to savour it all. Nothing whatsoever could be spooky about this place; it was a little heaven.

John laughed at her. 'I've never seen you so relaxed without alcohol,' he laughed. 'But come on K. I'm hungry, I thought you were.'

'Ravenous.' Karen sprang up. 'Yes, let's eat.'

Downstairs in the front room a table was set for two. Mrs Townend came in with a tray holding two platefuls of pie and a jug of hot gravy.

'Now what would you like to drink?' She bent down and whispered. 'We're not licensed, but I can let you have a bottle of wine for seven pounds if you promise not to tell the bobbies.'

Karen laughed out loud. 'As if! ' she said. 'Of course we won't'

Mrs Townend smiled. 'White or red?'

'Red, please,' said John. He waited for her to go out.

'Karen, you mustn't tell her.'

'I won't.' Karen filled her fork with pie. *'Mmm.* This is real comfort food. I feel better already.'

'I knew something was up.'

'Just a bad tummy,' She replied. 'Oh, and a couple of other things, but that was what I meant. Are you going to tell me what you've found?'

'Nope,' said John. 'Not until we've eaten. And I think there's spotted dick for pudding,' he gave her a funny look and tapped his nose.

Karen shrieked with laughter. *He is good for me and so disciplined.*

'Nice to see you in such good spirits.' John said.

'Oh, hell. Why did you have to mention spirits?'

'What?'

'Nothing. Tell you later. You're right, let's enjoy the meal first. How was your journey?'

***

It was late, and Mrs Townend's bustling around prompted them to realise she wanted to close up for the night.

'Telly's on in the lounge,' she said. 'Now what about breakfast? It's a proper Yorkshire breakfast here. Nowt of that continental rubbish.'

'What time?' John answered for both of them

'No later than ten tomorrow; I've things to do.'

'That's fine,' said Karen. 'And thank you, that was lovely.'

Mrs Townend nodded. 'You haven't told me how long you're stopping yet. It's no worry, I just like to know.'

'At least another night,' John said looking at Karen.

'What's your business up here, if you don't mind me asking.'

'We're investigating the disappearance of Katherine Engles in 1964,' Karen said.

'You're not the police, are you? Mrs Townend frowned.

'Yes, but don't worry about the wine,' Karen tapped her nose.

Mrs Townend relaxed. 'I remember something about that poor lass in the paper a year or two back. I'll have a word with Mr T. See if he remembers anything.'

'Thank you. We need all the help we can get.' Mrs Townend beamed all the way to the kitchen.

'Shall we?' said John. Karen nodded, and they left the table to go straight up to bed.

'You don't want to know then...?' John began, perplexed.

'No,' Karen replied. 'And you don't either. I'm knackered. I need to sleep. Just for once, it can all wait till morning.'

Karen fell asleep almost as soon as her head hit the pillow, but it was after John wrapped his arms around her.

20

Monday 11 November

Karen pulled back the curtains. Outside it was windy and drizzly.

'A day to spend indoors looking at the fire,' John said.

Karen laughed and got back into bed. 'Nutter. Now tell me, what have you found?'

'Well, a rather nice woman in my bed for one thing,' John pulled her towards him.

'That is the very best way to start the morning.' John smiled while Karen sprang out of bed with almost indecent haste.

'Let's get going,' she ordered.

Fifteen minutes later they were ready and waiting at the breakfast table.

'Tell me what you've got,' Karen said.

'I've found some old photos. I'm not sure when they were taken, there are no dates or names on them, but they are aerial shots covering a large area of the county.'

Karen sat up. 'And?'

'They must have been taken when there was a drought or something because the land's parched and it shows some old routes. They look like they could be old pathways.'

'Lincoln?'

'Yes. And what makes them of interest is that one path seems to go right through where Amy Warren used to live.'

'Like footpaths or something?' she said.

'Older than that,' John replied. 'Mr Binks says...'

'You've talked to Mr Binks?' Karen said, astonished.

'Yes. Why not?'

Karen hesitated for a moment. 'No reason. Go on.'

'He thinks it could be a really ancient pathway. He says that some of them just became normal footpaths, but some of them go back centuries. To pagan times even.'

Karen's mind was sorting through her personal database. 'The Witches' Pathway,' she said suddenly.

'What? The book? How did you know about that?' John gaped.

'Never mind. What's the connection?'

'Apparently, interfering with a path protected by old magic was a very serious thing. It would have demanded a high price.'

Karen's eyes widened. 'You don't mean sacrifice?'

John looked up. 'Shush! Our breakfast's coming.'

They waited just smiling at each other until Mrs Townend had deposited two plates on the table. Karen stared at hers – an enormous Yorkshire pudding, nearly covering the plate, and containing fried egg, sausages, bacon, mushrooms and tomatoes.

'It's like a work of art,' said Karen, tucking in.

John nodded his agreement. 'There's evidence that it happened,' he said, between mouthfuls. 'Sacrifice, yes, but centuries ago.'

'But not nowadays. Who would care enough to do that?'

'Maybe our murderer cared,' said John.

'That's insane. And we don't know they were murdered yet. But I agree, it's worth looking to see if there was a path there.'

'I know. Not because it's black magic or anything, but because some misguided idiot might think it was.'

'Yes. Fair point,' Karen nodded.

'But first we've got to try to pin down the other areas in the photos.'

'Hang on,' Karen frowned. 'How did you identify the first one? Mr Binks?'

'Yes. He recognised the area straight away. And it fits with the old lane. He got quite excited about it.'

Karen grunted. *Now is probably not the best time to mention my dream.* 'He's a bit odd, isn't he. Do you trust him?' she asked

'Trust him? Of course I do. I've known him for years. Yes, he'd love to find *that* book, but that's not very likely, is it? We might end up digging up places, but we'll be looking for bodies, not books.'

'True.'

'Anyway, what about you?'

'I've told you about Jack, an old friend of my father's.' John nodded. 'He showed me some CCTV footage. It's of someone talking to my dad, just before he died.'

'That sounds horrible. Why would that be relevant?'

'Because I think Dad was investigating the Katherine Engles case. It even explains why the files were sent to me by mistake. This isn't just a road trip now, John. It's a proper investigation. It's serious now, and I have to get to the bottom of it for his sake and now mine.'

'We haven't got long, Karen. How far can we get?'

'We'll see. Oh, and talking of black magic, that psychic...'

John listened patiently. 'I'm really sorry, Karen. That must have been terrible to see, and I'm absolutely with you all the way. But the psychic, that's just guesswork, isn't it?'

'I don't know. Based on what? She didn't know who I was. If it's a random guess, it's a very good one. All this stuff is so very odd.'

They finished their breakfasts at the same time.

'I can't believe I ate all that,' said Karen. 'Especially after last night's meal.'

'I can't believe you ate it all, either,' laughed John. 'I don't know where you put it. Thanks, Mrs Townend.' He shouted towards the kitchen, so she'd know they had finished.

'Let's go through to the lounge.'

They sat down on a comfy sofa and turned to each other, speaking at the same time.

'You first,' said John. 'It's your show.'

Karen gave a little cough. 'OK. First, I need to ring this Brian Appleby; see what he knows. Can you start looking at the photos?'

'Yes. If I can spread out on the table here. I'd better ask. Oh, hello.'

Karen turned to see Mrs Townend standing at the door.

'I'm off out, but I did speak to Mr T. He says Stanley Briggs, on th'newspaper in the village, knows all about it. He's been doing some digging, or he did a while back.'

Karen flicked through her notebook. 'Yes, I have that name. Excellent. Thank you, Mrs Townend.'

'Do you mind if I use the table?' John asked.

'So long as you put everything back where you found it,' she replied.

While John cleared the table, Karen looked up the telephone number and rang it.

'Hello,' said a female voice.

'Can I speak to Brian Appleby, please?'

'You can but you'll not get much sense out of him.'

'Who is this?' Karen asked.

'It's his wife. He's in a home now. He doesn't even know me nowadays.'

Karen visibly slumped; this was not what she wanted to hear. 'I'm very sorry, Mrs Appleby.'

'Who are you? What did you want with him?'

'I'm DS Karen Thorpe. Tommy Thorpe's daughter...'

'Oh. Aye, lass, we knew him. My Brian thought he were champion. What brings you our way?'

'The Katherine Engles case.' Silence. 'Mrs Appleby?'

'Sorry, lass. Just brought some things back. '

'Can I come and see you?' Karen asked.

'I don't know about that. I reckon it were that case that did for my poor Brian. But he'd want it sorting if it were possible.'

'I'm sure he would. When can I come?'

'Better make it soon. I've got to visit him later.'

'Of course,' said Karen. 'And your address?' She wrote it down. 'See you later.'

Karen joined John who was poring over the outspread photos.

'Hang on,' she said. 'I think I've seen that somewhere before.' She ran upstairs to fetch her tablet and returned puffing. 'Look at this,' she showed him the photo of the pencil map. Could it fit?'

John peered at it. 'Maybe,' he said. 'Can you send it to me so I can look at it properly?'

'I have to go now to see Mrs Appleby. I'll send it to you when I get some WIFI again. OK?' She gave John a kiss on the forehead and left.

21

Karen pulled up outside a pretty stone cottage and parked the car. *WIFI? Damn. Maybe in the nearest village?*

Mrs Appleby, a thin, grey-haired, and sad-looking woman opened the door as Karen walked up the path.

'Well I never. You're the spitting image,' she said, a smile lighting up her face. 'Come in and sit. Tea?'

'No, thanks. Just had some. It's nice to meet you,' Karen shook her hand. 'I'm not sure where to start. This investigation has sort of come my way so if anything has already been uncovered, it would be really helpful to hear how far it got.'

'Ey, I don't know much, love. Just bits and pieces I picked up.'

'Anything, however unimportant it sounds, might be useful.'

'I'll do my best.' Mrs Appleby sat down. When she spoke it was very slowly and carefully.

'It were when my Brian retired. Old Mrs Engles came to see him worried that he'd given up on th'case. He hadn't, but he was already poorly. He'd had a stroke, you see. Lost the use of his left side. He could talk all right, and there was nowt wrong with his mind. That's when he called your dad in. They were old pals.' Karen nodded. 'Well, your dad were right pleased to be asked.'

'Is there a file?' Karen jumped in.

'Ee. I never thought of that. Let me go look.'

After what seemed like an hour, Mrs Appleby came back holding a big brown envelope marked 'Engles'. She passed it to Karen then glanced at the clock.

'I'd better get a move on now, love. But don't forget to talk to Stanley Briggs at th'paper. You follow my road till you get to th'post box, then turn right and go past the old mill, then left into High Street and it's about halfway down. You can't miss it and Stanley's always there.'

'Thanks. I'll let you know how I get on.'

'Ey, it'd be grand to know it was sorted. Won't help poor Brian now though. He had another stroke, and that did for him. Happen Mrs Engles is still alive. See, you talk to Stanley. He'll know.'

As Karen got into her car, she saw Mrs Appleby pointing the way before getting into her own car. Karen waved at her before checking her phone. **MISSED CALL. MACY DODDS**.

She'll have to wait.

***

Karen arrived at the local paper office with only one wrong turn. *Call that a high street?* The door wasn't locked so she pushed her way in. A middle-aged man, late forties she guessed, was sitting at a desk typing away.

'Stanley Briggs?' she asked.

'Aye. Who wants to know?' The man didn't look up.

'Karen Thorpe. Tommy's daughter.'

Stanley's head jerked up. He pushed his glasses up onto his forehead. 'Well, I'll be blowed. What brings you here? Not Katherine Engles surely?'

'Got it in one,' Karen replied. She relayed her involvement to the incredulous Stanley Briggs.

'We never got too far. Sadly, Brian had another stroke, and then we heard about your dad. Was that a stroke, too?'

'Heart attack.'

Brian sighed. 'He weren't that much older than me. I tried to get some other lads at the station interested, but you know what youngsters are,' he looked at Karen. 'Well, some of them.'

'Did you make any progress?'

'Not much. Old Charlie Worthington reckoned it were all to do with the old witches' path.' Karen blinked at the mention. 'But no one paid him any heed. They began developing the site not long before the young lass were taken. But nobody made a complaint about it being built over.'

'You said the old witches' path, is that the same as the witches' pathway? Where was the path?'

'Aye, like as not, and that's a good question. T'was only old Charlie who even knew back then. Apart from mebbe one man.'

'Who?'

'There were a man out walking. He found Katherine's sister Elsie out walking. Told her the witch would get her if she ran away from home. He were right bothered when he heard about Katherine. He were a kind man, Mrs Engles said. He spent hours helping with the search.'

'Is he still around?'

'Nay. He moved on after. It were Elsie who remembered after all these years. She was proper scared, that lass.'

'What did he look like?' Karen asked with some trepidation.

'Typical beardy man he were. Tall, carrying his house on his back like a snail, Elsie said.'

Tall, bearded like the man in the clip. But this was fifty years earlier. 'Is she still around?' Karen asked. 'Elsie, I mean?'

'Nay. She moved away some years ago. It just happened she were visiting when Brian and your dad were here. She's in Australia or New Zealand now. Her mum will know.'

'And Charlie Worthington?'

'Aye. Happen you'll find him in the Old Nag's Head. He's there most nights. Shall I tell him if I see him?'

'Please.' Karen remembered Caitlin. 'What was Katherine like? Was she naughty? Did they search straight away?'

Stanley grinned. 'Aye, her mother told me she had a thing about washing. Pulling things off people's lines. Brian told her off, and she stopped. And yes. They were on th'case as soon as.'

Karen felt a chill run down her spine. She looked at her watch. *What's John up to? Better check on Macy, too.* 'I'd better be getting back. I've got lots to look at now. Can I come again?'

'Any time. There are lots of us want to know what happened.'

***

Six missed calls now? Karen rang Macy. 'What's up?'

'At last,' Macy huffed. 'The IT department came back to me. I asked them about all this file business. They had a really good look around the system, just to see if they could uncover anything. And buried deep in all their security files they found some encrypted stuff; don't ask me what it all means, but they think they found out who had been sending the emails.'

'Go on' said Karen, her pulse beginning to quicken. 'Who?'

'You're not going to like this Karen...'

Karen felt herself stiffening. 'Tell me.'

'John Steele,' Macy replied. 'They found it was all done on his ID.'

22

Karen picked the phone up from the car foot well. She felt like she'd been kicked in the stomach *and* punched in the face. Now her head was spinning. *My lovely, sweet John. How could he? Is this why he tried to get close to me? What does he want? What does it all mean?*

What do I do? I need to get my head in order.
OK.
First, I have to complete the investigation; for my own sanity if nothing else and that means getting all the papers at the B&B.
Second. I can't trust John, so I have to ditch him.

Looking round, Karen saw a small garage just up the road. It gave her an idea. Holding her phone until her hands stopped shaking, she breathed in deeply a few times before ringing John.

'Karen. How's it going? You've been ages.'

'Fucking car's broken down. I'm at the garage. It's Mike's Motors on the high street. It'll be a couple of hours. Get a cab over here, and we'll have a bit of lunch. I'll tell you what I've got.'

'And you said your car was in better nick than mine,' John laughed. 'OK. Lunch sounds good. I've seen some flyers in the hall, I'll be there as soon as.'

'Give me a call when you're on your way. I'll get the drinks in.'
'Will do.'

Karen clicked off the phone and waited patiently for ten minutes. *Now, I came this way, but would a taxi? No, I got lost.*

She moved off following the route she had just come and waited when she got as far as Mrs Appleby's house.

John rang seconds later. 'OK. Taxi's here, see you soon.'

Karen drove up to the B&B looking around as she went. A surprised Mrs Townend opened the door.

'Hello love, you've just missed him. He's gone into town by cab.'

'Oh, really?' said Karen, trying to sound surprised. 'Did he say why?'

'No, just something about meeting you for lunch.'

'Crossed wires,' Karen smiled. 'I just need to pick up my things. I'll catch up with him later.' She ran upstairs and packed all the files and accumulated paperwork back into the carrier bags and stuffed her dirty clothes in her bag. It took her two trips to get it all into the car.

Mrs Townend watched suspiciously. 'Are you leaving?'

'I am. John will be back though; he's left all his stuff upstairs.'

Mrs Townend frowned. 'Well so long as bill's paid.'

'Sorry. How much do we owe you?' Karen reached for her bag.

'It's all right,' She replied, reassured by the offer. 'As long as yon man is back to settle up it's fine by me.'

'Thanks.'

'Where to now then?' Mrs Townend asked.

Good point. Where? 'Newcastle. I've had a lead to follow that way.'

'Well, I'll go to the foot of our stairs,' Mrs Townend said. 'Whoever would've thought that. Safe journey then.'

Karen sat in the car just long enough to come up with a plan. *The Scottish case. Edinburgh,* she decided. *Davie will be pleased to see me. Let's go.*

***

John arrived at the garage, paid the cab driver and thanked him. But when he went inside, he soon saw how small it was. A mechanic was under the only car in sight. *That's not Karen's.* He walked around a little. *No sign of it.* He rang her. *No answer.*

John was perplexed. *Where could she have got to? Maybe she had no signal.* He could make out a couple of pub signs farther up the street, so he walked up to the first one. Still no car. *Damn. Maybe it'd been towed away somewhere else.* He walked back to the garage.

'Excuse me,' he said to the prostrate mechanic.

'Aye,' came the response from underneath a car.

'My girlfriend's car broke down. She said she'd brought it here this morning.'

'Nowt else in today,' said the man, half pulling himself out.

John was alarmed. He walked back to the pub and stuck his head round the door; it was small enough to see all around. There was no sign of Karen. He checked outside in the car park. Nothing. He ran up the street to the other pub and checked inside and out. No car, no Karen. *What the hell happened? Have you been kidnapped? No, the car would be here. Have you broken down somewhere? Must be that.*

John walked back towards the garage, but this time he noticed the local paper's office and walked in.

'Hello. Sorry to trouble you. I'm looking for my friend. Karen Thorpe. I think she might have come to see you. I'm sorry, I can't remember your name.'

'Stanley Briggs. Aye, she did come by here about an hour or so ago. Gone now though; drove off up the high street.'

'What?' said John, now even more shocked. 'She told me the car broke down.'

'Nowt wrong with it that I saw,' Stanley replied. 'She were off like a rocket'.

'Bloody hell,' said John. 'What did I do?'

23

Karen put her foot down but discovered the farther it got, the harder the journey became. Three lanes became two, became one, and ever-larger slow vehicles appeared in front of her. The weather was atrocious. The drizzle soon turned into rain which became torrential. Her substantial breakfast was keeping her hunger pangs at bay, but petrol was running low and she was beginning to need the toilet.

The occasional update from the Satnav and the radio were the only things to keep her company. But each national station, in turn, lost its reach so she had to keep tuning in to local stations. *Karen, you're knackered. You have to stop soon or your bladder will explode. Hey, I know that tune.* Shit. *It's Dad's song. A Scottish Soldier. That's it.* It energised her briefly, a small question in a universe of puzzles now answered.

By the time she crossed the border into Scotland, the weather was so bad she could hardly see where she was going. *I've seen too many car crashes to risk this*, she decided. Carrying on slowly, she scoured what few visible landmarks she could see for welcoming lights, but there were none. *I can't believe this rain's getting worse. Bloody hell, it's gone nine. I should've been in Edinburgh an hour ago, latest.*

She struggled on for a while, but all traffic on the road came to a standstill. When it started to move again, she found an entrance of sorts and pulled off the road. *It's a field. No one's going to come out here in this weather, it'll have to do. Damn. How do I get to the boot? Even more importantly...* Fighting her way out of the car, she emptied her dirty clothes bag in the boot and held it over her head as she squatted behind the car. *Ahh.*

Now for the bedding. Pulling her emergency blankets and pillow from the boot, she dragged herself back inside the car and pulled the door shut. *Not too wet,* she felt the blankets before throwing them to the back seat and followed them. She locked herself in and pulled the blankets over her, falling asleep a few minutes later.

***

Where are you, Karen? What's happened? John had absolutely no idea what to do. He was used to analysing data, cold hard facts, not following trails. Realising he could do nothing without transport, he trudged back to the pub and called a taxi. It was the same taxi driver that had picked him up.

'If you'd told me you were going to be that quick, I'd have waited,' the man laughed.

Oh, ha ha to you, too. 'Back to where you picked me up, please.'

When they pulled up outside the B&B there was no sign of Karen's car. John settled up and went to the door.

'You're back then,' said Mrs Townend. 'Did you not catch your girlfriend?' She gave him a knowing look. 'Row, was it?'

'No, it was not. I don't know what's happened to her.'

'She said summat about going to Newcastle...'

John was flabbergasted. 'What? She came back here?'

'Aye. Took all her things and went. Said something about a lead. She mebbe tried to call you. Reception's shocking here.'

John leant back on the closed front door. *Could it be that simple?* He wondered. *This is Karen. She's done this before.*

Mrs Townend looked concerned. 'I'll put the kettle on.'

John went into the front room and flopped into a chair. *What was she playing at this time?* he asked himself. Nothing made sense. *Did she leave a note?* He charged upstairs to the room. There was no note but all Karen's things had gone and all the papers – including the photos he'd been working on. 'Damn!' He said, slamming the bedroom door as he left. 'What do I do now?'

He went down to see Mrs Townend holding a big mug of tea.

'Here,' she said. 'Tea helps everything.'

'Thanks,' he said, taking the mug from her. 'I think I'll have to go after her,' he said. 'Are you sure she said Newcastle?'

'It was.'

'I need a car...'

'Yes, dear,' said Mrs Townend, giving him a strange look. 'You'll be leaving then?'

'Yes. Sorry to muck you around. I'd better get back to the station. I'll call another cab.'

'I'll get your bill,' she replied and left the room.

John gulped at his tea and settled the bill in a daze. When he'd packed his rucksack, he waited outside for the taxi to come.

'Station please.' He stared at the cabbie. 'You again? Are you the only cabbie in town?

'You'll not be leaving, will you? Business will halve once you've gone,' the cabbie grinned.

***

On the train home, John tried to work out what had happened. The journey passed by as if he were in a dream. It wasn't until he got a taxi at the station he realised he'd have some explaining to do.

'John? We weren't expecting to see you so soon.' A surprised Daphne answered the door.

'Sorry, Mum. Should've phoned ahead. I'm not stopping.' *Was she looking smug?*

Big John appeared in the hall. 'Hello, son. What brings you back so soon?'

'Come and sit down love. Do you want some tea?'

'No, Mum. I can't stop. Dad, I need to ask a big favour.'

'There's always time for tea.' Daphne went into the kitchen.

'Go on, son.'

'Can I borrow the car for a few days?'

'Sit down lad. Tell me what's going on.' They went into the living room and sat down. 'It's trouble with that lass again, isn't it? She's a lively one, I'll give you that.'

'Sort of,' John began. 'No not really. We're just investigating separate lines of enquiry.'

'You don't fool me, lad. Or your mum, I'm sure. But I can't let you take the car anyhow. I've to take your mother to see Auntie Nellie tomorrow. Besides, we need it all the time these days, and I know you young people.'

John sighed. 'OK. I'll go home and get my own then. No problem.'

'You'll do no such thing John-boy,' said Daphne, coming in with a tray of tea. 'You look exhausted, and that girl will just have to wait. I knew she was trouble the moment I set eyes on her.'

The two Johns exchanged glances.

'I'll tell you what I'll do, lad,' Big John said with a wink. 'How about I take you down to Peterborough first thing tomorrow. You can get the fast train from there. Can't say fairer than that.'

John was tired and very fed up. 'I'll sleep on it. Thanks Dad. She might ring me before then.'

'Have you eaten, love?' said Daphne, about to play her trump card. 'I've got some stew left over.'

Stew? It had to be, didn't it? If he'd had any resistance left before, it was all gone now. 'Yes, please, Mum. I'm starving.

That night as he curled up in the warmth and comfort of his childhood bed with a satisfyingly full stomach, John wondered where Karen was sleeping and tried hard to believe that she was safe and well.

24

Tuesday 12 November

Karen woke bleary-eyed just before dawn to a knocking sound. She blinked and saw a face staring in the window at her. A little girl with red hair, the spitting image of Caitlin McFee.

Shit! She sat up petrified. *Not in my car! Surely not in broad daylight?* The girl stuck her tongue out. *You moron. Ghosts don't do that.* Karen stuck her own tongue out in return, and the girl's face broke into a big, freckly smile. Karen heard the comforting voice of an adult calling her away.

'Leave it, Maggie. We'll be late for school.'

Karen waved at the girl who waved back then ran off down the road to catch her mother's hand. She sat up and properly looked around. *No rain, thank God.* The air was still a bit misty but much clearer. *Where am I?* She shook her head remembering the events of the day before. *This looks like a B road. Did I take a wrong turning?*

She moved to the front seat and set up her Satnav. *Thank God again. It's got reception. Now, where are the nearest services?*

She set off purposefully, and after a few miles, she was pulling into a drive and parking in a very small but adequate service station. Reorganising her carrier bag, Karen headed straight for the ladies'. There were no showers in the toilets, but having no shame and encouraged by the fact there were very few people around, she gave herself as good a wash as she could at the sink and changed into fresh underwear in the cubicle.

When she emerged, she looked almost respectable, but her tummy was rumbling. There was a small restaurant attached to the services area, and she went in looking for the biggest, fattiest breakfast she could find. *Nearly nine. Better get a move on. Mmm. This is so good. Better let him know I'm on my way.*

Karen composed and sent an email to Davie while she finished the dregs of her coffee. Then she checked the map.

Refreshed and refuelled, Karen found the local police station she was aiming for. She parked and went straight into the reception area. *He'll be there. He wouldn't miss me for anything.*

'I've come to see Davie Wallace,' she said. The man at the desk nodded towards the chairs opposite and picked up the phone. Karen went to sit down at last feeling safe; this was home territory, not hers, but still home.

***

By the time Karen had reached the service station, John had been up for hours. He'd hardly slept at all and was wide awake well before his father knocked on his bedroom door. Neither of them talked in the car on the way. When they got to the train station, there was a muted farewell.

'I hope you sort it, John-boy.'

'Me, too,' John replied as he got out of the car.

The train was on time and busy, packed with commuters. John managed to find a seat and sat down looking out of the window thinking about what had happened. *Why did she do it? Has she dumped me? Again? No. It has to be something to do with the investigation.*

He took out his phone, and oblivious to a couple of pained expressions in the carriage, rang Karen's mobile, getting the 'unavailable' voice message. *I don't even know what to say.* 'Call me.' *He hung up.* His mind went round and round in circles trying to think who else he could call. Macy. What was her surname? He started muttering out loud. 'Grey. No, don't be silly. Biggs. Boggs. Diggs... DODDS!' he said as his fellow passengers began to rustle newspapers and dip their heads into books.

John looked at his watch. *Nearly nine.* They'll all be at their desks. He dialled the office number. 'Can you put me through to Macy Dodds, please?' he asked.

'Who may I say is calling?'

'Personal call.' He waited for a response.

'Hello? Who is this?' It was Macy's voice.

'Macy, it's John. John Steele.'

'Oh,' said Macy.

John knew from her tone something was up. 'What's wrong? Have you heard from Karen? She's gone off somewhere without telling me where. Do you know anything about it?'

There was a short silence then 'You know perfectly well, you bastard.' *Whoa! Is that Karen or Macy talking?* 'How the fuck could you do all that? Scare her like that?'

John was stunned. 'Macy, I have no idea what you mean.'

'Liar,' Macy hissed. 'They found your ID on the system. It was you who sent those emails, wasn't it? Did you think it was funny?'

John was beyond shocked. 'I really don't know what on earth you are talking about, Macy. I haven't sent Karen any emails. What is going on?' Silence. 'Macy? Please talk to me, you know I'm not like that. Macy?'

'The IT guy was very sure of his facts, John.'

John smacked himself on the forehead much to the amusement of his fellow travellers; he had remembered something. 'Macy, listen. I ran a few search programmes. Just to see if I could find anything out. That's probably what they've found. Tell them to check. Please.' *She's gone. Did she even hear me?* He stamped on the floor in anger, and his earwigging fellow passengers pulled their newspapers and books back up.

25

Karen didn't have to wait long. Davie, a tall muscular man with reddish-brown hair, strolled out grinning from ear to ear. There was clear chemistry between them, but it was of the cerebral kind. He spoke with a tempered accent.

'Hello Karen. Good to see you. Come through.' They shook hands vigorously. 'We can go in there,' he said, indicating an interview room. 'Coffee?'

'Please,' said Karen, getting up with her bag. *I hope I don't smell too much.*

'And I'll get my DC to bring our file in. I've been doing a wee bit of digging myself.'

'Great,' said Karen. *This is more like it.* She remembered why she both liked and disliked him so much. They thought in the same way, were equally dismissive of anything they disagreed with, and both unable to take criticism without getting all wound up. But both managed to hide it sometimes. *Even the training games. We had to play opposites because we went about things in exactly the same way.*

A young woman came in and deposited a file on the table. 'These are for your meeting.'

Karen couldn't resist looking. It had exactly the same contents as the copy file she had, but it was interesting to see the documents in their original form.

When Davie returned, he was carrying coffee and a whole pack of chocolate biscuits under his arm. 'I remembered you like these.'

'Do you know who sent the copy file to me?'

Davie shook his head. 'I've asked around but no one remembers doing it. How about telling me where you are?'

Karen began by outlining the Amy Warren and Katherine Engles cases then she was happy to munch biscuits and listen to what Davie had to say about Caitlin McFee.

'As you know, I've no interest in this personally, but it is intriguing. Ah do know the original copper on the case.'

'Hamish Broad?'

'Aye. He's a bit of a local hero. He's knocking on a bit but he's as sharp as a pin and happy to speak to you. The girl's mother is still alive, and her brother, too. I've sounded them out, and the journalist who covered the reopening of the case. They're all up for a meeting too.'

Karen helped herself to the biscuits and drank her coffee – which was fine – while Davie went on to outline the case, most of which she knew by heart. For the first time, she was getting a glimpse of what other people saw when they worked with her. She wasn't completely sure she liked it, but she certainly appreciated it. Her mind had wandered slightly when she heard...

'...and the brother remembers talking to this rambler chappie.'

She sat upright. 'That wasn't in the original file,' she said, pulling out the file she had been sent. 'I'd have remembered.'

'Och, let's see.' He began leafing through. 'You're right, as always. This is an original. I expect it turned up and someone couldn't be bothered to send it to archives.'

'Was he very tall? Mrs Engles daughter also mentioned a tall man with his whole house on his back.'

Davie read from the file. 'Aye. A tall man with a large backpack. They didn't talk to the kiddies at the time. This came out on the poor wee lass's twentieth anniversary. Some of the team got really into it at the time from what I can tell. They didn't get very far, but they did keep a decent set of notes.'

'Then that could be our man,' said Karen excitedly. 'All we need is confirmation in the Amy Warren case, and we've got ourselves not only a link, but a prime suspect.'

'Aye, what have you got in the files for Amy then?'

Karen's face fell. *What do I tell him? There's no way I can go back to Lincoln yet...* 'Not much yet. Logistics. It made more sense at the time to come here via York first. But in York, there was also a journalist who did some research on the Katherine Engles case. Also on an anniversary '

'Och, we have video links here.' Davie said. 'We even have telephones,' he winked at her. 'Shall we give it a go?'

'Yes. Let's do it. DS Floyd Cannon.'

Davie made a call to one of the admin people to organise the meeting and asked for some more coffee to be brought in. 'Now. While we're waiting, tell me what you've been up to Karen.'

'Oh, quite a bit,' she reached for the biscuits. How *much* shall I tell him? She wondered. Withdrawing her hand she did a full retreat. 'Just popping to the Ladies.' She left the room and returned, having decided what to say, gave him a John-free account of her most important cases since she had last seen him. This time the timing and circumstances of her father's death did come up; it was clearly going to be relevant.

26

Karen was both astonished and impressed when the equipment was quickly set up and seemed to actually work. 'I can't imagine our office being so efficient,' she began.

'That's because you don't have our weather,' Davie grinned. 'We can't always make house calls.'

Minutes later, DS Floyd Cannon, a clean-shaven man in his early forties, she guessed, was sitting talking to them both through a monitor.

'Nice to see you, Floyd.' Karen began. 'I did call in on Saturday... '

He smiled and spoke clearly but with a discernible Midlands accent. 'Had to go shopping then interview a steak dinner with the wife.'

Karen, who never had early nights, suppressed her slight irritation. She smiled back. *Must keep him on side.* 'That's nice. I'd like to bring you up to speed. I assume you received my email?' She paused for his nod in response. 'There are three cold cases I'm looking into, including Amy Warren. All are abductions of young girls in 1964. And it looks like we may have found a connection to them all.'

'What sort of connection?' Floyd asked.

'In the other two cases, one in York, one here in Edinburgh, siblings of each of the abducted girls remember talking to a tall, bearded man.'

'A walker? Like a rambler, you say? Floyd looked pensive. 'Not that I recall.'

Damn. Karen couldn't help frowning. 'OK, we also think there may be a very old, ancient even, route which could connect all the abductions. The timings fit, assuming the man was on foot. June, July and September 1964.' Floyd shook his head.

Karen continued. 'In the other two cases, this man talked to some of the children, the ones who were with their parents waiting to join the search party. The children weren't interviewed at the time. This only came out when both cases were reopened on the anniversaries of their disappearances.'

Floyd Cannon looked straight at the camera. 'I'm sorry, I'd only just joined the force then. Farnsworth was the investigating officer before me. And it was twenty years ago when they did that here. I don't remember much at all. I'll need to check the paperwork.'

He began to leaf through a file which looked much thicker than the file Karen had. *Maybe they didn't digitise the whole thing?* She couldn't help but compare Floyd's approach to Davie's*. He's old school,* she concluded.

'I've got a note here about two children who were at the original scene of the abduction when the search party was put together.'

'Names?' Karen asked.

'Sorry. There's definitely no record of an interview on the original file. Let me look at the reopening.' He looked through a smaller file while Karen and Davie exchanged impatient glances.

'No,' Floyd said. 'I've got nothing here. In the original file, there was a list of the searchers, I can give you that if you like. But in the new file... I'm sure it mentioned something... Let me have another look.'

Davie intervened looking at Karen. 'Aye, please send the list.' Karen nodded. They waited for Floyd to continue his search, both checking their watches every few seconds.

'Ah, here it is. A note referring to the reporter who instigated the reopening. It says he'd interviewed several people who were children at the time.'

'I have the name Matthew Warren but...' Karen said.

'Of course!' Floyd sprang to life. He flipped to the front of the file and ran his finger down the page. He was Amy's little brother. This is what inspired him to become a reporter.'

Karen looked at Davie, both pairs of eyes gleaming. Karen went first. 'That's excellent. He's a first-hand witness.

'Aye. Can we have his details, Sergeant?' Davie reminded him.

'Sorry, yes. He'll be in the book somewhere. Just give me a minute.' Floyd walked out of the room while Karen and Davie exchanged rolled eyes. Karen went to speak, but Davie put his finger up. Floyd reappeared holding a local telephone book.

'We could have done that,' Karen whispered as he looked through it.

'Och, I know, ' Davie whispered back. That reminds me. Have you booked in anywhere tonight Karen?'

'Here,' Floyd said and read out the number while Karen wrote it down.

'There's someone else we may need to identify,' Karen said. It's a man who may have something to do with the cases, but we're not sure yet. He came into a police station and spoke to...' she hesitated, 'an officer. As I said, he may have nothing to do with it, but we need to identify him just to rule him out.' She turned to Davie. 'If I do a screenshot on my tablet, can you email it?'

'Easy,' said Davie.

'Did you get that Floyd?' Karen said. 'I might as well send you the video, too.'

'Yes, I'll look out for it,' he replied.

'Thanks Floyd, and don't forget the list of searchers,' Karen said. 'Talk soon.' She nodded to Davie, and he closed the link.

'I'm impressed with your system. Not so much with Floyd.'

'Och you're a hard woman, Karen,' Davie replied. 'It's hard to pick up something from so long ago, especially if you had no involvement. Now what about you?'

Karen looked confused. *What did he ask me? Ah.*

'I haven't got anything booked yet. Can you recommend somewhere?'

Davie smiled. 'Better than that, you can stay at mine. I've got a spare room. You can make it your base.'

'That's fantastic,' said Karen. 'Dinner on me then. Unless...' She peered at him a little.

'Och, there's no girlie on tow if that's what you're thinking,' Davie grinned. 'I'll take you there and you can settle in. I have to get back to the day job now.'

'Of course.' Karen was beaming at him. 'Let's just get this screenshot out of the way first. But I have to say, I am so sick of men with beards.'

Davie instinctively rubbed his chin while Karen pulled out her tablet.

'Damn,' she said. 'Flat battery.' *Bloody weather.*

Davie nodded. 'You can do that at mine.'

27

Macy had not been idle that morning. She'd got straight on to the IT department to check out John's story. 'It's very important,' she told them. 'Vital. An officer's life may be at risk. He said he'd only run a search program. Can you check it out?'

'OK,' came the response. 'We'll get back to you.

'I need the answer now,' Macy barked, crossing her fingers. *Damn. That's on-hold music.* She looked at her watch while she hung on the phone. Three minutes and ten seconds later she heard the voice again.

'Yes, it's a search type program.'

'Oh, what a relief.' Said Macy. 'That's great. Thanks.'

'Not so fast,' the voice said to her. 'I need to check this out thoroughly. I'll get back to you ASAP'

'Shit!' Macy drummed her fingers on the desk. *Should I ring Karen?* She tried but the line was still unavailable. *No mobile reception,* Macy guessed correctly.

Frustrated, she looked at the pile of paperwork on her desk, then got up to get a hot chocolate before getting stuck into it. She nearly jumped out of her seat when the phone finally rang. 'Yes? Have you got something?'

It was a different voice. A slow, deliberate, and rather condescending one.

'Miss Dodds, I have checked into what your colleague told you he had done and it's not quite what he said.'

Oh hell.

'In layman's terms, the program your colleague ran is like a 'search and destroy' program. Yes, it seeks out information, it even transmits it.'

And?

'But then it tries to destroy all the evidence of its existence.'

'What?' Macy was confused.

'Basically, it's a baad program,' The voice now talking to a small child. 'It interferes with the data on the system, tries to suppress access records, and hides illicit activity.'

'That doesn't sound good.'

There was an audible sigh at the other end. 'It's not. It's the sort of thing a hacker might do – but not a very good one in this case.'

Oh shit. 'It's very bad then. Is there any way it could be a mistake?'

'I couldn't rule it out, Miss Dodds. But the degree of skill it takes to run the program in the first place would make me conclude that your colleague knew exactly what he was doing.'

Macy took in a deep breath. 'So just to be absolutely clear about this, could he have sent those files to DS Thorpe then tried to hide it?'

'I would say on the balance of probability, yes.'

'Thank you,' said Macy, clunking the receiver down on its cradle. *This is out of my pay grade. Better tell the boss. Is he there?* She looked round and could see movement through the half-drawn blinds. She got up and knocked on his open door.

'Can I have a word, sir?' she said. 'About Karen?' His face fell immediately. 'Sorry,' she added.

He sighed. 'Come in Dodds. Tell me what she's done now.'

Macy explained about the mysterious emails which had called up the files sent to Karen and that John Steele, the head of forensics, had probably sent them. DCI Winter sat back and put his hands behind his head.

'So, are you telling me that Karen is investigating some cold cases when she's meant to be on holiday?'

Macy paled. 'She's not in trouble, is she?'

DCI Winter exhaled. 'It's a grey area. All sorts of cold cases get opened for all sorts of reasons. Often, it's the family getting onto journalists. But if she's talking to other offices, that alone should have an official seal.'

'And will you give it?'

DCI Winter gave a half-smile. 'Her father was exactly the same. Runs in the family. Find out precisely what she's up to, and I'll get the record straight.'

'Thanks, sir.'

'This guy John, how is he a risk? OK, he needs a rap on the knuckles for interfering with the IT system, but what actual damage has he done other than sending Karen on a wild goose chase. And we both know she likes nothing better.'

'But she's in danger, sir.' Macy remonstrated.

'Dodds. Present me a clear case explaining precisely how she is in danger, and I promise you I will do whatever it takes to sort it. But quite frankly, I think you're overreacting. If it's the guy I think you mean, he wouldn't say boo to a goose. Even a wild one. I think that is all.'

'Yes, sir. If you put it like that.' Macy left DCI Winter's office feeling a little silly. She sat back at her desk and tried to get on with her work, but she was worried. *I have to speak to Karen.* She tried one more time. There was no answer, but this time there was a message option.

'It's Macy. Ring me, Karen, as soon as you get this.'

28

Karen followed Davie as he drove from the station. It seemed a very short while before they were out into the countryside to his little cottage. They drove along a newish road, judging from its straightness, before joining a much more winding rural lane. *And no bloody annoying Satnav,* Karen thought. *Better memorise the route.*

Davie turned the car into a small gravel lane and pulled up outside a tiny stone cottage almost hidden from the road. Karen pulled up behind him and got out.

'Wow, this is lovely, Davie. How did you get this place?' She pulled her things from the car.

'Och, I bought it for a snip a few years ago. Horrible wreck of a place. I've worked hard on it, with some help of course.' He opened the front door, and they walked straight into a stone-floored, open living/dining area.

'Lovely.' Karen couldn't help repeating. *It's small, simply decorated and furnished, one large table in the middle, and not an ornament in sight. I couldn't have done better myself.*

'Bathroom's downstairs I'm afraid,' Davie said, opening one of two doors on either side of the almost vertical staircase at the far end of the room. There was a tiny lobby followed by another door, opening into a stark white and chrome shower room and toilet.

'No lock, you'll have to sing loudly.'

Karen laughed. 'I'm sure you've heard my voice and know how terrible it is.'

'Aye. I remember all that glass shattering on the last night of our course.' He put his hands to his ears. 'Kitchen's here,' he said as he opened the other door. Another white and chrome fitted room, small but well equipped. And absolutely filthy; stacked with dirty plates and empty takeaway boxes. Davie gave a little cough. 'I'd have cleared up if I'd known...'

'No, I'm impressed. That you actually get takeaways out here.'

Davie grinned. 'Och, we're not that isolated. The bedroom's upstairs.'

Karen followed him. There were two rooms, one on each side of the staircase, both reached by two small steps off a landing.

'This is yours,' he opened the right-hand door. 'It's not much I'm afraid.'

Karen went in and took in the rather shabby room with a clothes rack and a sofa bed.

'It's perfect,' she said appreciatively. 'Thanks so much for putting up with me. I mean putting me up.'

'No bother,' said Davie, beaming. 'We're going to get on a treat. Come down and I'll give you a key.' He turned to walk downstairs again. 'Then I'd better be getting back to work. Can you remember the way back to the station?'

'Of course. OK to use the table?'

'Karen, you make yourself at home. There's WIFI when your tablet's up and running, code's on the fridge. But no landline and reception's a bit dodgy.' Karen nodded. 'If you walk outside to that tree there,' Davie pointed through the window, 'you get a strong signal. No idea why, but it always works.'

'That's great. Now I'd better work out what I'm doing for the rest of my day.'

'I'll be off then.' Davie took a set of keys from a hook by the front door and handed them to Karen.

'You OK with Chinese?' he asked. 'I'll pick some up on my way home. Back about six-thirty.'

'Perfect,' Karen smiled. 'But on me. See you later.'

Within a few minutes, Karen was sorted and ready to go. Her tablet was charging and connected, so while she was waiting she went outside to check her phone. *Macy called.*

Karen rang her.

'Oh thank heavens I got you...' Everything came out in a tumbled rush. Karen listened intently.'...then I spoke to the boss.'

'What? Macy, why did you involve him for fuck's sake? Macy? Are you still there?' *Damn. No point winding her up.* 'Sorry, Mace, what did he say?'

'Actually it was quite useful. First, did you know that you should have got some sort of authority to do what you're doing?'

'Tosh,' Karen replied. 'Dad did it all the time.'

'Well, it doesn't really matter because he said it's OK. But you need to tell me who you're liaising with. Just to be on the safe side.'

Karen sighed. 'Fair enough. I'll text you as and when. Any other pearls of wisdom?'

'Yes. He said that John was too wimpy to say boo to a goose and couldn't have put you in any danger even if he did send you those files. And I was thinking, why would he anyway? I mean none of it makes sense.'

It really doesn't, Karen thought. *Unless he's been playing me for over a year. And he's not that capable of deceit.*

'We don't know, Mace. I haven't known John that long. I agree with you. When did he run the so-called search programme? Can you find out? I can't think of anything yet, but I'm going to keep my distance until I'm sure.'

'OK. That does make sense. I'll let you know if the IT department comes up with anything else.'

'Thanks. And Mace?'

'Yes Karen?'

'Send the guv my love and tell him I'm fine, will you?'

Macy snorted down the phone. Karen smiled as she clicked the call off.

'Must send that screenshot and video clip,' she said to herself. 'Bloody John,' she added.

29

Back in his bedsit, John finally understood Karen's reaction. *But how could she believe I'd do it? What does she think my motive could possibly be? All this running away again. It's so childish. Then again, she's usually incredibly logical, and her intuition is amazing. There's something there, I just can't see it. Better call IT*

'Hello? John Steele here. Apparently, there's a problem with a search I ran on the sixth of November. Can I talk to someone about it please?'

What about my emails. Nope. No reprimands. Nothing but the usual. What do I do? Go into work and wait for her to get in touch or follow her?

'We're running some tests. Someone will get back to you.'

'OK. Thanks.' *Damn.*

While he reorganised his rucksack, he made a decision. *Let's go back to Lincoln. Have a word with that sergeant. What was his name? Cannon. Floyd Cannon. See if there's a Newcastle connection. Then maybe pop in on Mr Binks.*

Just before he left, he rang Macy but her line was busy. *Just get going. It's a two-hour drive, don't waste time.*

John drove straight to the local police station. As soon as he walked in, the woman at the desk recognised him.

'Hello. You came up to see DS Cannon, didn't you?' She picked up the phone. 'Shall I try him for you?'

'Yes.' *That's handy. No explanations needed.*

Floyd Cannon appeared moments later. 'What can I do for you?'

'This is the man who was with that pushy female DS; they came in to talk to you on Saturday,' the woman said.

'John Steele,' John leaned to shake his hand. 'Forensics'

'Ah yes,' Floyd replied. 'I was talking to DS Thorpe earlier today as it happens. She's just sent me a video clip to look at. Very odd it is too.'

She did what? Don't panic. He heard Karen's voice in his head. *Wing it, moron.*

'The clip?' he said. 'So I understand. I haven't seen it yet. She had a problem with her tablet I think.'

'If she did, she sorted it. Come in. I'll show you.'

John followed Floyd into the room where a few hours before he had been talking to Karen.

'You two split up then?' He asked.

What? Does he know about us? Of course not. Karen wouldn't...'Yes. We're looking at different areas. There's broader coverage that way. She's in Newcastle.'

'Not now she isn't,' Floyd replied, the surprise evident in his voice. 'Edinburgh way now.'

What? Quick. 'Of course. Caitlin McFee. Edinburgh after Newcastle. She's making better progress than me, then.'

Floyd peered at him. 'What can I help you with, John?'

John hesitated, pretending to be deep in thought which he was, but not in the way that Cannon supposed. 'If you've spoken to her, she's got what she needs. But if you can send me the clip that would be really helpful.'

'I can do that. What's your email?'

Thank God for my ID. John casually took out a business card and handed it over.

Floyd reached for the keyboard and tapped in. 'All done.'

'Thanks so much. I'd better be on my way.' said John.

'Good luck to both of you. I wish I'd had time to help out more when they reopened the Warren case before. Such a shame for the family when Sam died.'

Sam? Who's Sam? Do I ask or do I get going?

He found his courage. 'Sam?' He asked

'Sam Farnsworth. He was the investigating officer when they reopened the case.'

'But it's your name on the papers.'

'The file was passed to me when he died. But I had my own caseload to manage, too.'

'What happened to him?' John asked.

'Sam? We don't rightly know. He was found out on a path somewhere. Heart attack. He wasn't the fittest bloke in the world, and it was a tough route to walk.'

John felt a rush of excitement. 'You didn't mention this to DS Thorpe then?'

'No,' said Floyd. 'Never thought about it. She was mainly concerned about the rambler.'

Karen's going to love me for this. 'Do you have the precise location of his death,' he asked. 'It might be really important.'

'It'll be on his file. I'll get it back from archives for you. You'll have to remind me though.'

'That's really helpful.' John shook Floyd's hand. 'I'd better get going.

Two minutes later John was sitting outside in his car, beads of perspiration on his brow and feeling like a criminal. But he'd got away with it. 'Bloody hell Karen. The things you make me do,' he said out loud. He tried to ring her again, but once again got the *unavailable* message.

What about this video clip? He pulled out his laptop and saw he had just enough battery to have a quick look. *What on earth am I looking at?* He remembered something Karen had said about someone asking for directions. *Is that your father? What is that man up to?'* He played it until the end and was shocked. Was that when he died? *Karen, my poor love. How awful. I have to help you.*

John played the clip again and studied the man's mouth as he spoke.

'He's saying something,' John said out loud. 'Not English. I bet Mr Binks will know.'

30

'Hello again, dear boy.' Mr Binks looked up as John entered the shop. 'What's wrong?' he added when he saw John's worried expression.

'Everything,' said John. 'But mainly this. Can I show you something?'

Mr Binks nodded. 'Of course. A book? Have you found something special for me?'

'Not a book. It's this. This man's speaking in what looks like a foreign language. I think it may have brought on a heart attack. Can you have a look and see what you think?'

'Of course,' said Mr Binks, flipping the shop sign to CLOSED. 'Come to the back room.'

John set up his laptop while Mr Binks went to retrieve his special glasses, the ones he kept for looking at important manuscripts. When he sat down, John played the clip. Mr Binks put his head close to the screen and stared at the images.

'My dear boy,' he said. 'That is terrible. Awful.'

'What is it? What did he say?'

'I would not venture even to say it out loud,' Mr Binks said, looking around. 'It is a curse. A terrible curse.' He looked at John strangely.

What's up with him? 'What are you saying?'

'Who is the man? Did he die?'

'I think it's Karen's father. He died after someone came into his police station asking for directions. And then somehow Karen got this video clip.'

'Then dear boy, she may be in very great danger. If this man tried to kill her father, he may very well want to do the same to your young lady.'

John was horrified. 'I must go to her – if I can find her...'

'No,' said Mr Binks so firmly John was taken aback. 'All in good time. Nearly everything is founded on preparation, and there is much we can do to prepare first.'

'We?' John said.

105

'Yes, we,' Mr Binks replied. 'You are not remotely equipped to deal with this. I will have to come with you.'

But you're too old for this. 'No, I can't ask you...'

'I'm fitter than you think,' Mr Binks said, looking at John as if he'd read his thoughts. 'And I assure you, you will need me with you. Now first things first; there's something I need to look up. Something tapping away at my memory. We'll need somewhere to stay. You organise that and make us both a nice cup of tea. I'll put my thinking cap on.' He disappeared out to the back room and was gone for ages.

'Mr Binks? Where are you?' Having booked some accommodation and watched the tea go cold, John was tired of waiting. In the back room, he was astonished to see yet another secret door. This one leading to a small passageway. 'Mr Binks?' He looked around in amazement as he entered another room full of books even more extraordinary than the room he'd just left. 'Mr Binks?' He looked up to see the little man perched on a bookshelf ladder.

'I won't be a moment. It's just that I've forgotten my indexing system. I'm having to look at every copy with a red leather back.'

'Can I help?'

'Oh, my goodness, no. Most of these books have hardly ever been touched by human hand.'

'What?' John walked around the room but couldn't even read the titles of most of the books.

'At last!' Mr Binks waved a rather small, thin, red book in his hand. He handed it to John when he reached floor level. It was called **Ancient Lowlands Footpaths** by Fergus Anderson. John looked at it in bemusement.

'Look inside the back cover,' Mr Binks said with relish.

John opened it, and below the blurb, at the bottom of the creased and torn flyleaf, was a small grainy photograph. He peered at it. 'It looks a bit like the man in the film,' he exclaimed. 'But it can't be. It's too old.' He looked inside the front cover. 'Nineteen sixty-five.'

'It is all rather unsettling,' said Mr Binks. 'But there is a bookshop in Edinburgh which might be able to help. Have you sorted accommodation?'

'I've found a B&B near the city centre. I don't know where Karen is though. From memory, the police station is near where the third child was abducted, but I can't remember the details.'

'The city centre is a good start for me,' said Mr Binks. 'And I have a feeling young Miss Thorpe will be asking for your help before long.'

John looked at Mr Binks in surprise. 'How did you know her name was Thorpe?' he asked.

'She told me, of course. Are we gathered? Can we embark on the journey? I must find some boiled sweets. I get terribly car sick. I think I have a tin somewhere. By the way, does your electronic thing have a camera?' he asked. John nodded. 'Take a picture of the book, will you? All of it? I don't want to take it away with us, it's far too precious.'

John took perfect shots of the cover and the book itself while Mr Binks found his barley sugars and packed his ancient old suitcase.

'I am prepared,' he announced. 'Come along, John. No time to lose.' He put a new sign on the door. **Closed until further notice**, and when they were both outside, pulled it shut and locked it.

31

Karen was fed up. She'd already tried to call Matthew Warren, Peggy McFee, and Hamish Broad from the spot under the tree, and none had picked up. Now her tablet was fully charged but her phone battery was on red. *Bloody tech*.

Stuffing the charger connector into the phone, she plugged it in. With her tablet, she called up the image she wanted from the video of her father at the station, took a screenshot, then sent it with the complete clip to Floyd Cannon.

She collected all her things from the car, leaving the paperwork on the sofa and taking her clothes upstairs which she sorted into two piles: clean and worn. When her phone had a bit of green in the bar, she went to the magic reception tree, but her messages remained unanswered.

It was cold and she went back inside to make herself a cup of coffee – which necessitated clearing up the kitchen. *Now I know how John feels.* She looked at Davie's washing machine and was delighted to see it was a washer/dryer with a quick wash function. Bundling in a small load from upstairs, she set it off then sat down at the table with her coffee.

The first thing she wanted to look at was the aerial photographs that John had discovered. *Why would he go to all this trouble if he was being devious? Was he connected with the cases in some way? Were there connections to Lincoln?* But then she thought of some of the things he'd done to help her. *Maybe he was just a bit of a prat.*

Karen first picked out all the photos with single trees and compared them to the image of the hand-drawn map in her father's wallet. Nothing seemed to fit. *Why should they? The photos were thirty years old, who knew how old the map her father had was.* 'Not enough information,' she said to herself as she put them all in a big pile. *What about Mrs Appleby's envelope?*

Before she could look at it, Karen noticed her tablet was showing two new email notifications. One was from Macy. The subject matter read. **Search report run 6 November at 12:00**

Strangely economical for Macy. The other alarmed her. It was from Floyd Cannon. *What's this? It's addressed to John, just copied to me. Why the fuck would he do that?*

Shit. Does John know I'm here then?

Double shit! Well, he'll never find me here.

Seeing Cannon's name reminded her of Matthew Warren. He still hadn't answered her phone calls – as far as she knew – but checking her notes, she found an email address for him. *Worth a shot.*

Karen composed an introductory email referencing Floyd Cannon, explaining who she was and what she was doing, and specifically asking him whether he remembered a tall man. She gave her mobile number too, with a warning about poor reception then clicked the send button.

She next looked at Macy's email and read it with interest. *So John, Macy says you ran the report on 6th November. That's the night you went back home. Or did you?*

A few seconds later, the envelope icon appeared again. *Now what? DCI Winter?*

Karen, I assume you are OK, please respond to confirm.

'Ha!' she said to herself before typing a response.

Having a lovely time wish you were here. XX

As soon as she clicked the *send* button another email dropped in. This time it was a reply from Matthew Warren. She felt her pulse start to quicken as she read his reply.

Yes, happy to talk/ring ASAP. I do remember a tall bearded rambler.

She sat up, excited. *A tall, bearded rambler was involved after each abduction. There has to be a connection.* She replied and attached the screenshot for him to look at.

Will call ASAP when the phone is charged. Probably nothing but do you by chance recognise the man in front of the desk?

Karen paced around the room. Her instincts were screaming at her that it was relevant, but there was absolutely no reason he should recognise the man at all. This man was late forties/early

109

fifties. The rambler Matthew saw would be in his late seventies/eighties by now.

The envelope icon appeared.

Ring me. Urgent. Matthew.

Karen unplugged her mobile and ran out to the tree.

'Matthew Warren? It's Karen Thorpe. What is it?'

'That man,' Matthew was stuttering. *With cold or fear?* 'It made my blood run cold. I'm sure he's the man I saw.'

'But he can't be. It's a recent video. That man is too young The man you saw back then must be at least eighty by now.'

'Then it's a doppelganger,' said Matthew. 'Or a ghost. I swear that's the man I saw when my sister disappeared.'

'Jesus Christ!' *He said ghost.*

32

Karen was still standing by the tree contemplating ghosts when her mobile rang.

'Is that DS Thorpe? '

'Yes,' Karen replied taking in the frail, heavily accented, but defiant voice.

'It's Hamish Broad. I gather ye want tae see me?' he began. 'I'm sure there's nothing I can tell ye that you dinnae already ken.'

Ken? Know! Flatter don't batter. 'Maybe. But it would be really helpful if you could give me personally the benefit of your knowledge and experience.'

The voice was calmer. 'Well if ye want to drop by now, I could give ye a wee bit o' insight. No much mind. I still dinnae know it all.'

'That would be great,' Karen enthused. *Finally, progress.* 'I have your address, I'll be there as soon as I can.'

Karen ended the call and saw that there was a message waiting for her; from Peggy McFee, Caitlin's mother. She listened to the voicemail and a very shrill voice began.

'Aye, I'm Caitlin McFee's mother. Ye can come and see me by all means if you want but only if you are going tae dae something this time. I've had my fill o' half measures and wayward journos. And I'm warning you, I've nae time for useless police either. I'll be in from about four this afternoon. Catch me then.' *Well, Caitlin. You're just my kind of person.*

Karen looked at her watch. *Time to do both.* After a quick review of her notes, she set off to see Hamish Broad. She found the house easily enough, a rundown mid terraced house some ten minutes' drive from Davie's cottage. A thin gnarled old man opened it.

'Ye'll be DS Thorpe.'

'At your service,' said Karen ingratiatingly.

'Ye'd better come in.'

Karen tried hard not to reel from the smell of the old man's house. *Is this what my flat smells like after a curry?* Parking that thought, she went into the old man's kitchen where he gestured for her to sit down.

'I've nae time for tea.'

'That's fine,' said Karen taking in his appearance. *Another victim of this job. I know many get thrown out after a screwup. But there's something worse here.*

She let him talk without interruption. He was clearly well-rehearsed in what he said. *Better needle him a little. Probe the hidden disappointments, the self-imposed innocence, break down those ancient defences.*

When Hamish paused, Karen pounced. 'So why was it a full twenty-six hours before you took any action? Caitlin went missing at around four-thirty. Her mother reported it at six pm but the search didn't start until the next morning.'

Clearly surprised at her reaction, Hamish shook his head. 'Och, ye dinnae understand. That lassie was a wee devil. She got up to all sorts. If we'd dropped everything each time she got an idea in her head, we'd have done nothing else.'

'So a seven-year-old girl goes missing and nobody does anything because she is naughty. Is that right?'

'Och, ye're no understanding.' Hamish was getting agitated.

'She'd gone missing before then?' asked Karen.

'I didnae say that,' Hamish replied.

'So why was it left so late?'

Karen systematically picked over every inch of the investigation. It was sloppy, to say the least. *But would it have made any difference?* She pitched her main question carefully, not to draw undue attention to it. '...and do you remember a tall, bearded rambler helping with the search party?'

'Nae. I cannae say I do.'

'I'd like to show you something.' She took out her tablet and played a few seconds of the bearded man, watching Hamish's expression like an owl watches a mouse. His body remained rigid but his eyes gave him away.

'Nae. I dinnae know him.'

'Thank you. Is there anything further that you can tell me?'

Hamish shook his head.

He's holding something back. 'What about the reopening of the case? Did Donald McTear, the sergeant get anywhere further? There's nothing in the file I have.'

Hamish suddenly sprang into life. 'Who, yon eejit? Nae, he gave up after the journalist was taken off the case.'

At last. 'What happened?'

'Och, it's always the same with these things. Anniversaries spark off interest and folks get worked up but it never gets anywhere. It was yon journalist, cannae remember his name, who pushed, along with Peggy, to get the case reopened. I reckon Peggy drove him mad with her constant nagging at him and he took off.'

'Took off? Where?' Hamish shrugged. 'Why was he interested in the case?' Karen pressed. 'Was he local?'

'Nae. He was trying tae find a link with the moors murderers. I told him that was rubbish. I think he realised that for himself and buggered off. There was nae glory in our wee story. He was after a big one.'

That's plausible.

'I only have a first name here. Mick.' Karen said. 'I'd better do some searching. I may need to talk to you again if that's all right.'

Hamish sat stony-faced. 'We'll see.'

'I'm off to see Peggy McFee now.' Karen added. This time there was a very definite response.

'Aye, the woman's a vixen. Never satisfied, Always blamed us instead of her daughter. Us police have a duty tae stick together missy and don't you ever forget it. Peggy's daughter was the devil incarnate. She was...' he stopped.

Asking for it. Karen finished the sentence in her head. 'Seven. She was only just seven. Thank you, Hamish.' *What's he hiding? A cock-up? Certainly, the delay in searching was unforgivable. But why pretend he didn't recognise the rambler?* 'I'll see myself out.'

33

It was just past four. Perfect timing. Karen checked the map. *Not far at all.*

She arrived a few minutes later outside a small end-of-terrace house – simple but cared for.

The door was opened by a haggard stony-faced old lady with tiny piercing eyes. Karen recognised her from her file; much older than in the photos but she'd have recognised her anywhere.

'Good afternoon Mrs McFee. Can I start by saying that I am not a useless copper but I cannot work miracles either.'

Mrs McFee's eyes seemingly glared at Karen who stood firm. Then Peggy burst into loud and hearty laughter. 'Awa wi' ye. We'll get on just fine young lady. And my name's Peggy. Come in. I'll put the kettle on.'

Thank God for that. Karen went in and sat on the proffered chair. Inside as out, in marked contrast to Hamish Broad's house, it was clean and tidy and odour free. It was almost completely free of ornaments but the walls were crammed full of photos of, she presumed, Caitlin and a boy, youth and man she assumed was her son.

Peggy returned with the tea and talked, unprompted, about her daughter. 'Caitlin was full o' mischief. She drove us all mad with her nonsense, but for all that, she was a good bairn and she was kind. She gave her favourite dolly tae the wee lassie next door when the head fell off hers, and when the dog got sick, she nursed it day and night.'

'What else did she do?' Karen asked.

'Och, her favourite wis Chap door run,' said Peggy smiling.

'What's that?'

'It's when you knock on doors and run away,' Peggy replied. 'She'd do it over and over.

'Knockdown ginger we used to call it.' *Didn't that happen to me?*

'The wee ones are too wrapped up with their computer games noo.'

'Yes. You're right.' *What? Surely not. That's too close. Did Caitlin knock on the wrong door?*

Peggy mistook Karen's expression for disapproval. 'She wasnae a bad kid. Nowadays there'd be a fancy title for the poor bairn, some condition or other and folks would be sorry. But they just saw her as a wee tyke.'

'Is that why they didn't begin the search straight away?'

Peggy looked Karen sternly in the face. 'There's nae doubt at all in my mind. The bastards telled old Hamish not tae bother, she'd like as not be up tae more mischief.'

'What happened when they started the search?'

'Och, all the neighbours came oot then. I was telled tae stay home in case Caitlin come back. It was awful just waiting there. And she never did.'

'So you weren't involved with the search at all.' Karen said rhetorically. She frowned. 'You mentioned a journalist, too,' said Karen. 'Do you mean Mick? What happened to him?'

'Och he was full o' shite,' Peggy said. 'He telled me he'd find oot something. Said he had a real lead, but the bugger disappeared on me. I never found out what he knew.'

'Why did they reopen the case?' *What was the trigger?* I saw an article in the local paper...'

'It was twenty years after the disappearance.' Peggy began wearily. 'I'd been on at Hamish for years to keep going, but then this journo comes a-knocking on my door. Mick said he might have an idea what happened tae Caitlin, so together we went back to press Hamish tae dae something.'

'But it wasn't Hamish who took on the case,' Karen started flicking through her notebook. 'It was Donald McTear, wasn't it?'

'Aye. Hamish was a high and mighty Chief Inspector then. He wasnae interested in me or the poor bairn. And that Donald was useless.'

'Peggy, would you show me where you lived and where you last saw Caitlin?'

'It's all gone noo. There's a new estate on top o' our old place. But I'm happy to take you where it was. You got a motor?' Peggy got up in readiness.

'I do,' Karen said. *How disgusting is it?* 'It's a bit untidy though'

115

'Nae bother,' came the reply. 'And we can call in on my son on the way back. He should be back from work noo.'

'You wer'nae kidding.' Peggy gave a little laugh as she saw the accumulated mess in Karen's car.

Karen quickly cleared the passenger seat by throwing the detritus into the back. 'Where are we going then?'

'Go right at the end o' the lane...'

Karen followed her directions until she came to some very familiar territory. 'I'm staying near here,' she said as they turned into the newish straight road en route to Davie's cottage.

'Keep going, keep going,' said Peggy. Karen drove on for a few minutes. 'Stop here.'

Karen stopped in the road. They were facing the entrance of a new housing estate. Peggy struggled to open the car door, so Karen ran round the front to help her. They walked together.

'My wee house would have been somewhere in there,' she pointed to the middle of the development but tears started to form.

Oh no, she's cracking up. 'Thank you, Peggy. Let's go back now. Does your son Stuart live nearby?'

'He's the other side o' me.' said Peggy, regaining her composure. 'I'll show you.' Karen helped Peggy back to the car and they were soon on their way again to Stuart's house.

34

Stuart McFee was a stout red-faced man with a broad smile. Karen could just make out some traces of red in his very receding hairline.

'Come in,' he said cheerily. 'Ma maw rang me. It's about time we found out what happened tae Caitlin.'

In the comfort of his living room, Karen listened to everything that he said, making notes – but more for show than use.

Nothing new here at all. 'I want to show you someone,' she said. 'You, too, Peggy. I'm not sure if there's a connection but there may be.' She took out her tablet.

Their reactions were shocking and different.

Stuart's face froze. 'Aye, that's the bloke that spoke tae me.'

'That's that bloke that got Hamish's sister pregnant,' said Peggy.

'Please tell me more,' Karen said, but Peggy had clammed up. She sat on the sofa, rocking backwards and forwards, and wouldn't say anymore. Stuart led Karen to his front door.

'That was a shocker. Seein' that man again.'

'I'm sorry.' Karen said. 'I had no idea it would have such an impact. I can tell you it can't be the man you saw, it's a recent video – only a year old, but at least it gives us an idea what the man you saw looked like.' Stuart nodded. 'Is your mother OK?'

'She has her moments. It's probably best left for noo; she's a wee bit fragile these days and this has upset her, bringin' it all up again.'

'But what about Hamish's sister...' Karen began.

Stuart interrupted her. 'I've heard her say this before but it's not true. I've nae idea where it came from, but I know there was nae bairn. Gracie Broad lived and deid a spinster.'

'Thanks.' said Karen sympathetically. 'I've told Peggy I'll do what I can, but it will be really hard after all this time.'

Stuart looked at her, tilting his head on one side. 'Can I ask what got you ontae the case?'

Heck. *What do I say?* Suddenly the words came tripping out. 'My father began to investigate a similar case a while back. He died, and I thought I would pick up where he got up to.'

'Och that's grand,' Stuart beamed. 'Really fine. I hope for all our sakes you find her. It'd mean the world to my mother tae put wee Caitlin to rest before she goes herself.'

'I'll do what I can, I promise.' *And I mean it.*

***

Karen was tired, and it was dark and very cold. *Get back to Davie's* she told herself. *You can research online. Now, where was that little shop?*

She parked outside and picked up a bottle of red and a bottle of white, just in case, and several packets of smoky bacon crisps. There was a fog forming as she drove back to Davie's cottage. *It will be nice to have some company.*

She pulled up outside the cottage and sat for a moment taking in the atmosphere. Suddenly she heard a giggle.

What? She put the headlights on full beam, opened the car door, and looked around.

Nothing. Everything outside the light was pitch black.

Tutting to herself she closed up the car then walked to the front door. The cottage was in darkness. As she reached in to turn on the porch light she heard the giggle again. Looking round she saw a small child dressed in white. As she got closer she saw she also had red hair. But this was no ghost; it couldn't be.

'Hello,' she said. 'Who are you?'

There was another giggle and the girl ran across the field disappearing into the fog. Karen followed a little way but tripped over an old tree stump. By the time she got up and looked again, the girl had gone.

Karen rubbed her ankle and looked back towards the cottage deciding that the welcoming light over the door was too good to ignore. As she walked towards the cottage a tall shadowy figure stepped out from behind the tree. Suddenly the thick fog was lit up by headlights. The figure disappeared.

Davie pulled up behind Karen's car. 'Are you checking my garden at this time of night?' he asked her.

'No, I thought I saw something,' Karen replied.

'In this fog? You're joking,' Davie said opening the front door.

'Are there any children round here?' She asked as she went inside the cottage.

'Not for miles,' he replied. 'Now don't tell me you've seen the little lassie?' Davie said.

Karen was shocked. 'You mean she's real?'

'Och, one of the reasons I got this place so cheap was the owners said it was haunted. I've never seen her in the five years I've been here. It's a load of rubbish; people imagining things.'

'You think I imagined it?' said Karen, slightly irritated.

'Aye,' Davie replied. 'Your head's so full of missing wee lasses you're seeing them now.'

'But did you know Caitlin McFee lived not too far from here?' Karen said.

'Now that I did not,' Davie replied, sounding slightly less sure of himself. 'I should have seen that in the file.'

'Has anyone ever rung your doorbell and there's been no one there when you've opened the door?'

Davie looked thoughtful for a moment then shook his head. 'Pure rubbish,' he began. 'I'm hungry and I've a meal enough for two.' He waved a big brown takeaway bag.

'And I've brought wine enough for me,' Karen added, glad to change the subject. 'But I need a bath first. Is there hot water?'

'Aye, and a hot laddie to scrub your back if you like.' Davie laughed. Karen glared at him. 'Only kidding,' he added. 'But don't forget to sing.'

'Do you have spare towels?' Karen asked.

'Aye. What sort of a mank do you think I am, Karen? There's a cupboard in the bathroom, help yourself.'

Less of one than me, clearly, thought Karen, remembering John having to use hers once. She went upstairs to get changed and came down in her onesie.

'Help yourself to wine,' she shouted at Davie in the kitchen. 'I won't be long.'

35

Karen had a nice long soak in the tub, submerging her head and borrowing Davie's shampoo. *What did he say? Sing?* Um um um soldier, a Scottish soldier, dum dum dum dum de dum.... She carried on until she was out, dried, and in her navy onesie.

As she passed the kitchen door she looked in on Davie.

'Why were you singing that?' he asked. 'Although I wouldn't describe it as singing.'

'You said I had to.'

'Aye, but why that song?'

'It was one of Dad's favourites,' she said. 'No idea why.' They sat at the table where Davie had put out plates and opened the takeaway containers. 'I was thinking. When I first drove up here, I slept in the car, and I also saw a little girl like the one I saw just now and she was definitely real. I'm rubbish at directions, but it may well have been somewhere around here. Are you positive about there being no children around?'

'Let's get the map and see where you were.' Davie retrieved a map from a bookcase and opened it out on the table. 'Now I'm here. And that's the nearest house...aw wait a sec. Where were you?'

Karen pored over the map. 'I'd gone off the 'A' road, must've been somewhere around here,' she pointed. 'It was a mum taking her daughter to school.'

'Och, a wee traveller group have settled around here recently. I've not seen them but...'

'You were wrong,' Karen finished. 'I win.'

Over dinner, they turned back to the case. Karen summarised her progress. 'In each case, there is a child who saw a tall, bearded walker. Now, what are the odds of that?'

'In three rural communities? I should say very high.' Davie replied. 'They're all bearded in the country.'

'No, you don't understand.' Karen mumbled through her mouthful. 'Two of them identified the man who spoke to my dad.'

'Aye, but we know it can't be him, and as I say, all walkers have beards. How likely is it that these kids could remember the detail? Are you sure they're not just remembering the overall persona? Did you try with other pictures of tall, bearded men?'

Damn. He's right, but then again... 'I know what I saw. Their reactions were very similar.'

'Is this really how you're going to spend your holiday?'

'Mmm.' Karen nodded. 'My dad was clearly involved, and he died before he could solve it. I owe it to him and those poor little girls and their families.'

'Good on you. I'd have done exactly the same.'

They chinked glasses.

***

It was very late when John and Mr Binks arrived in Edinburgh. The journey had not been helped by Mr Binks' incessant chatter and frequent comfort stops. He had also insisted that they find somewhere respectable en route so that they could have a decent evening meal.

'My dear boy, one must feed the inner man,' he'd said. 'An army marches on its stomach, and we have much marching to do.'

John was already regretting bringing him along, but here they were at last, parked outside a small hotel on the edge of the city. Mr Binks marched up to the reception leaving his suitcase behind, but he did hold the door open for the struggling John.

'Binks and Steele,' Mr Binks announced, taking the young receptionist by surprise. 'And I'll want a road map of the city. Nothing older than 2012 if you please.'

The young woman shuffled off her stool and came to the desk.

'Yes, I have two single rooms booked. Room number three and room number seven. They're adjacent.'

Mr Binks shook his head. 'No that won't do at all. Are there any others?'

The receptionist was astonished. 'I have number six?' Mr Binks shook his head. 'Eight?'

'Eight will be fine,' said Mr Binks.

'I don't care.' John was tired and confused. *So long as I get a break from this man.*

The woman handed over the keys. 'Down the corridor, through the double doors. Breakfast is from seven in the restaurant through there.' She pointed to some glass doors opposite the reception.

'Thank you,' John said. He turned to Mr Binks.

'I'm off to bed now. See you at breakfast.'

'Oh, I doubt that very much,' Mr Binks replied. 'I shall be on my way very early, as long as this young lady provides me with a map.'

'Whatever.' *Thank God for that.* 'Fine. I'll be going down at...'

Mr Binks interrupted him. 'Dear boy, do as you must. We will no doubt meet up precisely when we need to. Not a moment sooner not a moment later. I bid you a good night.' He picked up his suitcase and minced away.

'Night then,' John, now completely bemused, watched him go. He picked up his rucksack and went to find his room. Once inside he took off his shoes and flung himself down on the bed in relief. A few moments later he pulled his mobile from his pocket; it was eleven o'clock. *Too late to ring Karen? Don't be silly. Success! I can leave a message.*

'Um, er Karen, it's John. I'm here. I mean I'm in Edinburgh. I've got things to tell you. Talk tomorrow. Er. Bye then.' Shaking his head at his own ineptitude, John ended the call. *She'll either talk to me or not.*

36

Wednesday 13 November.

Karen woke up organised and raring to go but Davie was already on his way out. 'Can you let me know if Donald McTear's working today? I may need to speak to him about this Mick character.'

'Aye. He should be but I'll double-check for you. See you later.'

She walked up to the tree to look at her phone and saw the message. *John. He's turning into quite the detective. I'm weakening, but not just yet. Things to do.*

'Mick' she said out loud as she walked back. 'What the devil happened to you?'

She began searching the internet over a second large cup of coffee but couldn't find anything at all. *He's either dead or changed career.* She checked her emails. There was one from Davie. *He is coming in. But in the afternoon. Damn. What else can I do?*

As time wore on Karen found it increasingly difficult to access central databases from the cottage. The remote links kept breaking, making her irritated and frustrated. *I'm going to have to go in and blag a desk.*

She was in luck. Davie arranged a desk and a PC for the day in a little alcove just behind reception. She settled in nicely until her concentration was interrupted by a familiar-sounding voice.

'I've come to see DS Karen Thorpe,' John said.

'Och, we've no one of that name here,' the woman on the desk said.

'Medium height, cropped dark brown hair, English, and mouthy,' John said.

The woman laughed. 'Och, yes, she's... '

Karen stood up and stepped out from behind her spot. 'Right here, John. What do you want?'

John's jaw dropped. When he'd recovered he spoke. 'We can't talk here.'

123

Davie suddenly appeared behind Karen. 'And you are?' he asked. The woman at the desk turned her chair sideways to watch.

'I'm her boyfriend,' John snapped, pointing at Karen.

'Are you?' Davie looked at Karen who half shrugged, half nodded. 'Better come through then.' He nodded his head back. 'She hasn't mentioned you to me and she's been staying at mine.' Davie said bluntly. He glared at the woman who quickly swivelled her chair to face the front again.

It was John's turn to be shocked. He gave Karen a *what the heck?* look and followed the pair of them to the back office.

'Who is this eejit Karen?' said Davie. 'Is he really your boyfriend?'

Karen looked at John who was as angry as he was confused. *He looks quite cool when he's angry.* 'Right. Introductions. Davie, this is John. We sort of began this investigation together.'

John harrumphed.

'But something weird happened, and we went our separate ways.' Davie eyed John with suspicion.

Karen turned to John. 'Davie and I have known each other for years. We were on a training course together. And he's very kindly letting me stay at his cottage.'

Davie grunted. *Is he jealous?* Karen wondered. She looked from one to the other. 'It's customary to shake hands.'

Davie reached for John's proffered hand and shook it fleetingly.

'Davie, are you staying? John and I have lots to discuss.'

'You're putting me out of my own office, Karen?' He replied. 'Am I not part of the investigation too?'

'Yes, if you're not tied up with other things.'

'Och, I can always spend a wee bit of time on yours, too.'

'But anyway, John and I need to have a few words.' Davie looked at her strangely. 'In private.'

'Aye. Gotcha. I'll be right outside if you need me.' Davie backed away and went out of the room.

John let rip – in so far as he ever did. 'Karen, what's going on? I've spoken to Macy. I have no idea what the IT people are going on about, but I swear I did nothing until after you told me about the files. The data must have got corrupted or something. You know it was all looking very odd before I got involved. And anyway, what possible reason would I have for doing it?'

Karen had more or less reached the same conclusion, but her trust in him had been damaged. 'I think I know that, John. Can we just stick to the investigation? If you still want to, I mean. I'm sure you might have other things you want to do on your holiday.'

'There's nothing I'd rather be doing, Karen. Just tell me honestly. Davie. Is there something between you two?'

Karen laughed. 'Don't be ridiculous. He's a mate, that's all. Look, John. I don't understand what's happened. But if you mean what you say, let's just see how it goes. Where are you staying? I could have a word with Davie, but it'd be a bit cramped.'

'Oh, no worries there. Mr Binks and I are staying in a hotel in Edinburgh.'

'Mr Binks is with you?' Karen was shocked, but she didn't quite know why.

'He's being very helpful,' John said.

'How?'

'How about a coffee?'

37

Mr Binks had been up before the restaurant had opened. *Hmm. It's foggy outside.* He knew precisely where he needed to go, in theory, but things changed so much and not everything of importance was transcribed into each new version of his maps. The demolition of a couple of ordinarily unimportant – but to him, key – buildings could completely throw them.

The people he needed to seek out did not inhabit the modern twenty-first-century city of Edinburgh, they existed in hidden niches. Small courtyards, basements, cellars and occasionally crypts. Knowing precisely where he needed to go didn't necessarily mean knowing the actual location. First, he had to find a gatekeeper – the man or woman who knew the deepest darkest secrets of the people of the city, town, or village he was in. Sometimes gatekeepers died without nominating a successor. Without one, the only option was to summon the medium Magda – but she could only be approached as a last resort. She was, legend had it, notoriously difficult to engage with and would not entertain speculation. You had to know precisely what to ask of her for even the slightest chance of getting information from her.

Mr Binks took out his map and compared it with the one the receptionist had provided. He'd consulted this gatekeeper some twenty years ago. *He might still be in the bookshop. There. I think that's it. It's not too far away. I wonder?* He put a cross on the new map then thought out loud. 'Breakfast first.' He went downstairs and looked around. *No sign of John, I see. Poor lad must have been exhausted after all that driving.*

He ate a hearty full Scottish breakfast washed down with a whole pot of English tea. He looked out of the window. *Fog's lifted but still dark and dingy. Perfect.*

Handing in his key with a cheery 'Good morning, miss,' Mr Binks set off at his purposeful pace. In exactly the right number of footsteps, he arrived at the passage, a tiny cobbled alley just off a secondary road. Twelve paces later he stood outside an old, shabby building, the sort that most people would have hurried past. *Eight o'clock precisely*. He rapped three times on the door, paused, then rapped again. The door opened slowly.

'Mr Binks,' said a quiet and very old voice. 'How pleasant to see you again. I have the documents you require.'

'Excellent. And anything on the Reticulum?'

'Yes, again. We have news about the person you seek. I can give you a name and a location.'

'Splendid,' said Mr Binks rubbing his hands together. 'I'd better come in.' Ten minutes later, Mr Binks had left the bookshop to hail a taxi.

***

Karen was still interrogating John. 'I'll get you a coffee if you explain what you mean.'

John sighed; he'd bought himself time. 'Mr Binks has been very helpful. He's got a contact up here, too, who might know something.'

'Why would he? What is his interest in all this?'

'I've honestly no idea,' John replied, secretly crossing his fingers. 'Other than he wants to help.'

'OK. I'll get you a coffee,' Karen said, 'and you can tell me what you've found out.' She left the room and returned with one word. 'Spill. I know you've seen Floyd Cannon and for some reason he sent you the video clip. Why?'

John took out his notebook and began to explain his thinking. Karen's irritation gradually dissipated. *He is trying.*

'...and then there's Sam Farnsworth,' he said.

Karen frowned, her mind whirring. 'Amy Warren reopening?'

John nodded. 'Unfit, died of a heart attack whilst walking a footpath.'

Karen sat up. 'Very interesting. Like my father. Maybe there's another connection. Someone wanted both of them out of the way. But when did Sam die?'

John looked at his notebook. '1993. Soon after the case was reopened.'

'Then Floyd took over, but without much enthusiasm apparently.' Karen added.

'I've found something even better than that,' John said, sensing Karen's growing excitement.

'What?' said Karen.

'I think I know who the tall bearded rambler is.'

'Shit. Really? Who?'

'His name is Fergus Anderson. He wrote books about footpaths.'

'John I could almost...' Karen began. 'Get you another coffee' she added hastily. 'I assume there's no ISBN. Is there a publisher? Were the footpaths local to Lincoln or nationwide?'

John took out his phone. 'No. It was a local press I assume. But the paths were nationwide. There's the picture of him.' He showed Karen the photo he had taken in Binks' Books. She blanched.

'I know,' John said. 'It does look like the man in the film. But he's tall, bearded, and wearing a rucksack. If you stripped that away, would the faces match?'

'Three people thought they recognised him when I showed them the clip.

'Who?' John asked.

'Caitlin McFee's brother and mother. And Amy Warren's brother, Matthew. They recognised him – or thought they did – immediately.'

'Have we found our connection?'

'We've found more than that,' said Karen. 'I'm willing to bet this is our murderer.'

'What? A rambler?' said John, shocked.

'Why not? Or someone posing to be one. Look at that rucksack,' she said. 'Elsie Engles remembered a man like a snail with his house on his back. Are you telling me you couldn't get a small child in there?'

John shuddered. 'That is one horrible thought,' he said.

'Email me the picture, John. Donald McTear was on the reopening, and Hamish Broad handled the original investigation. And it's possible that he had a child. With Hamish's sister. I'll see if I can't shake something more out of them.'

'What about you?' said John. 'Do you have anything else?'

'Yes, dammit, of course. The map,' Karen said. She leafed through her pile of papers and pulled out the drawing. 'I'm assuming it relates to the Engles case,' she said. 'Which reminds me, we should find out what precisely happened to the copper there, too. Brian Appleby....'

At that precise moment, Mr Binks came bustling into the room followed by the receptionist. Karen and John looked at him in amazement; Karen more in shock, John because he had never seen him so agitated.

'John. We must go to York straight away. No time to lose.'

The receptionist looked at all three people in the room and sighed. 'Ah suppose ye know what ye're doing,' she said and left them to it.

Karen looked at Mr Binks suspiciously. 'York? It wouldn't have anything to do with Katherine Engles would it?'

'Most certainly not, my dear. I have some information about a book I have been seeking for a long time. But I assure you that if there is any possible connection to the case of that poor child, I will assuredly let you know.' He gave her his best smile then glanced at the map spread out on the table.

'May I borrow this?' he said looking at Karen intensely. Karen nodded without a second thought. Mr Binks took the piece of paper in the blink of an eye.

He turned to John. 'John, dear boy, I can't go without you. Quick march!'

'Karen? Are you OK with this?'

'I'd like to know why it's so urgent.'

'It may be nothing,' Mr Binks said. 'But my senses are rarely wrong and they are telling me to seize the moment. Can you manage without your young man for a few hours? '

'I suppose...'

John with a backwards look at Karen and a shrug of his shoulders followed Mr Binks out of the station like a well-trained dog.

38

'What was that about?' Davie stuck his nose round the door. 'The wee old man and yon John bloke.'

'A lead in York,' Karen explained. 'He's very persuasive that *wee* man. And there's plenty to do here.'

'Whatever suits.' Davie withdrew, shutting the door behind him.

'Fergus Anderson,' Karen said. 'I'd better start trying to find you. You could be mixed up with all of them.' She gazed at the empty walls of the room. *God, I miss my whiteboards.*

Putting her nose to the computer she began searching. Nothing online. *What about Cannon's list? The searchers in Lincoln? Where's the email*?

There were thirty names but not one of them was Fergus Anderson. *He'd have given a false name anyway if he was the murderer* she thought. *But he published a book. Why would he need to lie? I now know that Sam Farnsworth, the investigating officer of the reopening, died. But who was the original officer?*

A cursory glance at the file told her all she needed to know. The officer in charge had retired at the time the case was closed. He would be long dead now.

Parking that thought, she began searching for the missing reporter Mick. *Surely his name would come up in the police database?* Her persistence paid off. She finally found the name Mick Chatterton at the end of a list taken for fire regulation purposes. The Daily News? Let's have a look…

When her search came good, Karen was put through to the former editor of the paper. There was a grunt at the other end of the phone.

'Hello? This is Detective Sergeant Thorpe. I'm investigating a case that one of your fellow workers reported on twenty years ago.'

'You what?'

'Mick. I'm trying to trace Mick Chatterton,' she said.

'Blimey.' There was a pause. 'That's when he disappeared – twenty years ago or thereabouts. He never came back to the paper – yes, must be twenty years.'

'Tell me more,' she said.

'He was a freelancer. Only got paid if we accepted his stories. He'd done a good one on that missing girl...'

'Caitlin McFee?'

'That's it. Caitlin McFee. Yes, he did a nice piece on that, but he was obsessed with The Moors Murders. Wanted to prove a link. Now I agree, that would have been a real story, but everybody knew they stayed local to Manchester. We assumed he got bored with the case and buggered off somewhere else. It was like that in those days. Lots just went back to the day job, too.'

'So you never tried to contact him?'

'God, no. These blokes contacted you. It was almost impossible for them to be contacted; always moving around, always chasing a story. We didn't all have mobile phones back then, you know.'

'Yes, I understand,' said Karen. 'But what about his family?'

'Sorry, Sergeant. I've no idea. I'd forgotten all about him until you mentioned his name.'

'Thanks.' Karen put the phone down. *Another dead end. I need a researcher. Hmm.* She picked up the phone again. 'Macy. You busy?'

'Hello, Karen. How's it going and what are you after?'

'You read my mind. Are you up for some research? I'm not best placed here.'

'Fire away.'

'Fergus Anderson. Born circa 1934. Rambler and author. He might have been a soldier.' *Where the hell did that come from?* 'And possible suspect.'

'OK, got that.' said Macy.

'Missing person, Mick Chatterton. Journalist. Last seen 1994 in the Yorkshire area.'

'OK. That, too. Anything else?'

'Yes,' said Karen. 'This might be more difficult. Gracie Broad. Sister of a copper, Hamish Broad, so if you find him, you'll get her. May have had a baby circa 1965. Get what you can.'

'OK. And how're things with John? Is he with you now?'

'Sort of,' Karen clunked the phone down. She looked at her watch. Donald McTear should be arriving at the station any minute. She walked out to the reception desk and asked the woman there.

'Och, he's just rung in sick,' she said.

And it was going so well... 'Can you ring him and see if he's up to a visit from me?'

'I'll have a go. I'll ring you in the room.'

'OK. I'll grab a coffee. It's actually drinkable here, isn't it?'

The second she sat down again the phone rang. 'Karen Thorpe.'

'Och, it's Donald. He says he's in bed with the flu.' *Damn. Guess I'll have to make do with Hamish for now.*

Karen settled down to a bit more reading when Davie popped his head in. 'Tell me, what's going on in York?'

'What do you do for lunch around here?' Karen replied. 'And I'll tell you.'

'Deal,' said Davie. 'There's a nice wee cafe round the corner.'

'Perfect.'

The cafe was very basic but friendly and extremely cheap.

'I recommend the Edinburgh Bacon Roll,' Davie said.

'Sounds good to me.' When the waitress appeared Karen ordered for both of them. 'Least I could do.'

'Och, no,' said Davie 'I love having you around. I never...' he stopped. *Please don't tell me...* There was a brief pause before Davie spoke again. 'About this John bloke then.'

'Oh,' Karen replied. 'He's the...' she struggled for the word. 'Best fit I've ever found. I've never been one for relationships, but we sort of fit together. His mind works in such a different way.'

'Aye, that's work, but what about after work,'

'It's always about the work,' Karen explained. 'We'll sit up in bed discussing cases sometimes. That's how it is, and I love it.' *Damn. Did I say love?*

'Aye, you're in love then,' Davie said. 'He definitely loves you.'

'Oh.'

After a slightly embarrassing pause, Davie spoke. 'Where are you on the case? Do you know what John's found out?'

'Lots,' Karen replied. 'I even have a name for the hiker.'

'You do?' said Davie 'And you haven't told me?'

'Only just,' Karen smiled. 'Fergus Anderson. Mean anything?'

'Och, no. But I can ask around.'

'Please. I'm going to have another go at Hamish Broad. Some stuff I need to flush out.' She hesitated. 'What if I want to find out things like birth and adoption records? Things that might not be online?'

'There's an adoption agency in the centre. But my best guess is going online.'

The bacon rolls arrived and talking gave way to eating.

'Mmm. You're absolutely right,' said Karen between mouthfuls.

Davie texted Karen the information about adoption agencies and made a call to the office to ask about Fergus Anderson.

'Och, they can't find anything relevant. It could be a false name.'

'That's what I thought,' Karen said. 'Don't worry, I've got someone good on the case.'

Just then the phone rang; Karen picked it up. 'Hi Macy,' she looked at Davie and pointed at the phone.

'I have to go,' he got up.

Karen nodded. 'See you later.'

39

John and Mr Binks were making exceptionally good progress back down to York. This time there were no stops for food or any other reason, and the endless chatter never began. John was happy to concentrate on driving. But as each mile passed, he sensed the atmosphere, like the day, was getting darker. *I'm feeling very strange.*

The road signs seemed to whoosh past; there seemed to be hardly any traffic and they arrived in York in no time at all. It had taken them an incredible three hours.

As they approached their destination, Mr Binks finally spoke to him. He jumped. Surprised to hear a voice after so much silence.

'Please take the road on the left. Now the first right, up the road,' he paused. 'That's right, now left into the car park.'

John parked the car then followed the bustling Mr Binks into The Black Cat pub.

'I'll deal with this, John,' Mr Binks instructed. John followed him meekly through the side door and into the pub. 'Sit there,' he pointed to a small table in the corner. John sat where he was told, rubbed his eyes and yawned. *Why am I so tired?*

***

Mr Binks looked around the pub, his eyes finally resting on a small and aged man with a flat cap and a wonky eye.

'Charlie Worthington, my good man. Delighted to meet you,' said Mr Binks, holding out his hand which was ignored.

'I knew someone would come,' said Charlie. 'Omens were there.' He nodded over to the bar where a woman watched expectantly. 'Mine's a pint of Black Sheep. Since you're buying.'

Mr Binks squinted at Charlie who sat rigidly at the table, arms folded, and made his decision. He went to the bar and ordered the pint adding 'and a dry sherry for me, thank you.' He looked over at John who was gazing out of the window. 'Would you please take a lemonade to that young chap sitting over there, too?'

'Of course, sir.'

When the beer was drawn, Mr Binks turned to look at Charlie who immediately jumped to his feet to take the pint.

'Sorry, wasn't thinking. 'Happen this is all rather queer to me.' He went to sit down again nursing his pint.

'That'll be five pounds fifty-three pence, please,' said the barwoman. Mr Binks took out his wallet and handed her a five-pound note, then twiddled his fingers in his pocket for the loose change.

'Thank you, miss,' he said, placing the coins in her outstretched hand. He picked up his sherry and joined Charlie at the table, looking back to make sure that John was handed his lemonade. 'I am seeking someone, Charlie. Someone who may have chosen the dark side.'

Charlie nodded. 'Aye, I've heard there's someone whose power is waning.'

Mr Binks nodded. 'The man I seek has used the name Fergus Anderson. Is this the man of whom you talk? You may know him by another name.' He took a sip of his sherry.

Charlie thought for a moment then nodded. 'I think it likely,' he replied.

'Then what can you tell me?' said Mr Binks.

'In his father's footsteps.' Charlie picked up his beer and took a long swig.

'Ah!' said Mr Binks. He smiled, pleased at the answer. 'I know what you mean. But where?'

'That I don't rightly know,' Charlie replied. 'But there's been contact between father and son. Find one...'

'Thank you,' Mr Binks interrupted. 'Now kindly tell me about the Crossway.'

'That's tricky.' Charlie took another swig. 'It all got messed up when that copper Farnsworth started digging things up.'

'Not literally?' said Mr Binks, his eyes wide open.

'Ah, no.' Charlie shook his head. 'Not that, no. Come closer. Too many ears in here.'

Mr Binks shuffled forward and listened.

John was still looking out of the window when Mr Binks came back towards him smiling.

'We have to go, John. Back to Edinburgh. Are you ready?'

John nodded. 'Whatever you say, Mr Binks'.

***

Macy had spent several hours on the internet and the police intranet. She'd drawn a complete blank with Fergus Anderson and found nothing more on Mick Chatterton than she guessed Karen already had. *How about Gracie Broad? Jo might be able to trace her.* She picked up the phone.

'Jo Smith speaking.'

'Hi, Jo. It's Macy here. Remember me?'

Jo laughed. 'Silly cow. Yes, it's been at least a week since I saw you last. How many notches on your bedpost now?'

'You're so jealous,' Macy grinned. 'Tell you later. Meanwhile, I need a favour. Possibly a big one.'

'Go on.'

'One of my sergeants is following up on some cold cases, and she's hit a brick wall with this one. She thinks there was a baby but is being told different things.'

'What's the name and district?' Jo said.

'Gracie Broad. Birth circa 1965; Edinburgh.'

'You're right,' said Jo.

'Eh? That was quick.'

'No. It's a big favour. Half the records don't exist anymore. I'll do what I can, but it's drinks on you, you bloody mare.'

Macy laughed. 'Deal.' *There's someone behind me.* She turned to see DCI Winter. *Oh shit.*

'I don't remember you needing to research adoption records, Dodds?' Macy turned round to face her boss unable to disguise her guilty look. 'I hope you're not doing work for DS Thorpe,' he said, not waiting for an answer. He bent down a little and looked her in the eyes. 'How's that report coming on?'

Macy gave a little cough and said 'fine,' in a very small voice.

40

Karen was getting impatient. *Where are you, Macy? You should have been back to me by now about the baby.* She stared at her mobile and looked at her watch. OK, let's try to blag it out of Hamish. She set off just as dusk began to fall. It was already dark when she arrived at Hamish's house There were two cars parked outside. *Damn. Don't say he's got a visitor. Should have rung first.*

Karen marched up to the door but stopped before her hand reached the doorbell. *Who's talking?* Carefully she opened the flap of the letter box and listened. *That's Hamish. And what did he say? Donald? Donald who's meant to be at home with the flu?*

'She's like a dog with a bone that one. You'd best get yir story straight before ye talk to her.' *Interesting.*

'But you said you'd destroyed all the records. There's nothing linking me to him is there?' *Who's that?*

The voices dropped. *Damn! Speak up. I can't hear you. What was that? Something about a half-wit brother.* She peered through the letter box. *They've moved.* She put her ear to the front window. *That's better.*

'Och ye know as well as I, he's been getting madder and madder, ever since he found out who his daddy was. But Fergus hasnae been seen for years ye said. I heard he'd died in whatever hell hole he came from.'

'Aye. I've not seen hide nor hair of him since we reopened the case.' *That's definitely Donald.*

'You saw him then? I didnae know that. I've not seen him since I ran him out for messin' with Gracie. We had nothing on him; I just wanted rid.'

'He came to see me one night. Och, it was when I took on the case. I knew he was my daddy after what you told me. He swore he had nothing to do with the bairn, but didn't want to be discovered since he did his runner. He was afeared he'd be court-martialled or something if he was discovered. He was very convincing. I believed him.'

'So where is yir man? Has he seen him d'ye know?'

Who's he talking about now?

'Och I never know what he's up to. He comes and goes in his own wee world. He goes out after dark and stays out till morning. I dread to think what he does.'

Karen could wait no longer. Stepping back onto the doorstep she rang the doorbell. The curtain in the front window was pulled back, and Hamish's face peered out briefly. *What's that noise? Someone leaving out the back?*

She looked up and down the terrace wondering where the back doors opened into, but before she'd thought it through, the front door opened and Hamish stood there staring at her.

'Ye'd better come in,' he said.

Karen wasted no time at all. 'I know about the baby, Hamish. He was given up for adoption, wasn't he? I know everything except his name.'

'Ye know shite,' came the reply. Hamish tried to stare her down but Karen was on a roll.

'I know it all, Hamish. What happened? Was your sister a bit of a slag? Did she like older men or what?'

Hamish stopped, looking furious. He raised his fist as if to hit her and turned red with rage, but she stood firm and he dropped his arm.

Thank fuck for that.

He blinked and his whole demeanour changed. No longer the aggressor, now he was the victim.

'I didnae know what to do,' he said. I was supposed to protect my sister. She loved him. She said she'd do anything. And I wasnae allowed to question him. Och I never believed he was capable of taking the wee lassie. I just thought he was one of those... those, hippies aye hippies. Free love and all that shite. There was nothing at all tae link him to Caitlin McFee. Nothing. I let him go, I had tae.'

Karen listened. Now was the time for gentle persuasion. 'I understand. And I don't know whether he did anything either, but someone who looked like him killed my father. You understand, don't you? I have to find out what happened. It's personal now.'

'Aye. I'm sorry, Karen, is it? I don't know any more. When Gracie found out she was with child, she denied it all. Said he'd bewitched her. Said she didnae want anything to do with the bairn and made me promise to deal with it. She stayed inside, wouldnae go out at all and it came early. A wee sickly thing. She left it at the hospital as soon as she was fit to go. She never spoke to me of it again.'

Karen took all this in. *Sounds plausible.* Certainly the 'bewitching' bit seemed to fit. Momentarily forgetting about Donald, she spoke softly to Hamish.

'Thank you Hamish. I'll be getting off now, but I might be back. I need to find out what happened to the baby.'

'I understand,' said Hamish.

Karen let herself out and drove back to Davie's cottage. *Damn. Donald. What happened to him? She pulled over, thinking. Too late to go to the office and I can't go back to Hamish's now, without looking very silly. Go home, Karen. Damn this fog.*

She parked up as usual, then automatically looked towards the tree. *What the hell?*

She saw in the fog, the ghostly figure of a little girl. The child stood still. Whatever it was, this wasn't what she'd seen before. She got out of the car and walked slowly towards the girl.

'Caitlin? Is it Caitlin?' The figure disappeared. She got as far as the tree and looked around to get her bearings. The next thing she felt was a presence behind her and a hand smothering her mouth. *Shit! Who's that?* She struggled with all her strength then succumbed to the chloroform. And everything went black.

41

John and Mr Binks arrived back in Edinburgh just after dusk. 'Drop me here,' Mr Binks commanded. 'I shall see you later.' John obeyed. He pulled in and stopped to let Mr Binks out. He shook his head. *Are we home already? Where have we been?* Everything was such a blur. *I remember going to a pub.* He blinked his eyes and looked at his watch. *Gone six. Where's Karen?* He looked around to see where he was, then drove off slowly looking for somewhere he recognised.

There. He spotted a small computer shop that he recognised. *Good. I'm close now.* He headed off to the station. When he arrived, Davie was pacing. The two men squared up to each other.

'Where's Karen?' said John.

'I was going to ask you the same thing,' Davie replied. 'She's not answering her phone. I have no idea where she could be.'

'What was she doing when you left her? She's probably just out of range.'

'She said she was going to see Hamish Broad. Reception's poor out that way. But it's on my way, I can check easily enough. Or she might have gone to see the adoption agency in town.'

'This late?' John said.

Davie looked at his watch and shook his head. 'No.'

'I'd better have your mobile number,' John added awkwardly. 'Damn. Flat battery. Write it down for me, I'll get back to the hotel and get it charged up. There's someone else who might know.'

'OK.' Davie handed him a business card. 'It's all there.'

***

John arrived back at the hotel. There was no sign of Mr Binks. He went to his room and plugged in his phone. Immediately a message popped up. From Macy. **JOHN, RING ME. URGENT**. Crouching on the bed to avoid pulling out the charger, John rang her.

'Hi, John. Thanks. It's this research I'm doing for Karen. She's not answering her phone. Do you know where she is?'

'No, Macy, we've lost her for the minute. Reception round here is very hit and miss. Davie thought she might be checking out the adoption agency. I'm sure I'll catch up with her soon.'

'I've got someone working on that as a favour for me. Tell her, will you?'

'I will. Is that all you wanted to say?'

'No. I wanted to know whether she had anything else on Fergus Anderson. I can't find anything at all.'

'Ah,' said John. 'I can help you there. I have a photo. Any use?'

'Only if his mug's on the web somewhere,' Macy replied. 'But it's worth a shot.'

'I'll send it.' John paused. 'I've got another similar face, too. It's a still from some CCTV. Karen may have already searched for it, but I'll send it anyway.'

'Cheers, John.'

'Oh, and Macy?'

'Yes?'

'Don't work too late. She's meant to be on holiday, you know.'

'Holiday? Is that actually a word?'

***

Macy got up to stretch her legs while she waited for John to email the images. A few minutes later the email dropped in her in-box. The first one was from the book cover. She didn't study the other but printed both out.

'So, you might be a soldier? Let's have a look for you then.'

She ran every search programme she could find. She was on the point of giving up when she spotted something obscure but in the right date range. *The Suez Crisis. Let's have a look.*

She peered at the grainy images. *OK, let's take a copy of you, Mr Soldier man, and run it through our ID software.*

To her astonishment, there was a match. *But that's not the name. It's pretty close though. Andrew Ferguson. Are you really Fergus Anderson?* I think you are. 'Bingo!' she yelled out to no one. From there it was easy to find a record of Andrew Ferguson, but unfortunately it led very disappointingly to a dead end. 'Missing in Action in Aden. Presumed dead. Damn.'

Macy's phone rang. It was Jo. 'Hi, Macy, this is all very suspicious. It looks as though someone has been trying to mess around with the files. It'd have to be someone senior with that level of access.'

'Do tell.'

'There were actually a few missing. But someone had the forethought to keep a separate record; not much, just a list.'

'And?' said Macy, now excited again.

'Gracie Broad did have a baby boy. It was adopted by Mr and Mrs Logan. And according to this, he put in a request for a search for his real father in 1983, on his eighteenth birthday. But then he withdrew it. There's no record why.'

'What was his name?' asked Macy.

'Logan of course. Ah, you mean...' there was a pause. 'Archibald. Archibald Logan was his name.'

'Thanks so much, Jo. That's an amazing help.'

'It's fine. Dare I ask what this is all about? It doesn't seem like your usual job.'

'Like you, I'm doing someone a favour.'

'Not that Karen one again? Promise me...'

'I can't help it. She gets under my skin.'

'Serves you right then. Ciao.'

Macy looked at her watch. *I really should be on my way. Hell, I'm turning into Karen. One more search.* Unfortunately, it was not an uncommon name. *Who'd have thought there were so many? Let's look at deaths.*

Patiently she waded through the records until *There. It's him. 1955, when he was just twenty-three. Gotya. And your date of birth.*

By the time she had finished she had a marriage in 1954, to a Susan Harrison, and a baby christened Donald Anderson.

'OK. Fergus Anderson aka Andrew Ferguson has two children. A legitimate one, Donald Anderson *and* Archibald Logan by Gracie Broad. Archibald Logan asks to find out who his real parents were, then gives up. Why? Change of heart? Or did he find out anyway?'

'Talking to yourself again, Macy?' Bill the desk sergeant passed by. 'And so late. What happened to the party girl I used to know?'

'Karen happened. That's what.'

She tried to ring Karen again. *Still no reception. Better try John.*

'Hi, Macy. Not still working, surely?'

Macy laughed sarcastically. 'I'm just about to knock off, but I've found out some interesting stuff. Have you got a notebook handy?'

'Fire away.'

'Fergus Anderson was actually born Andrew Ferguson. He fought in the Suez crisis and went AWOL in the Aden Emergency, presumed killed in action 1967.'

'Really? That's fascinating. Go on.'

'He had two children that I could find, there may be more. Gracie Broad did have his baby in 1965, or at least it fits with what Karen told me, it was a boy, adopted at birth, and was called Archibald Logan.' She paused. 'But before that, he had a child with his wife, a boy called Donald Anderson born in 1954.'

'That's great. Karen will be delighted with that.'

'Good. I owe someone a good few drinks for this, and now Karen owes me.'

42

Davie's first decision was to check whether Karen had gone home. It was only a small detour to Hamish's place and would make his evening a lot better if she was already home. He was delighted as he drove up. *Her car. But no lights on in the cottage? Not another power cut?*

He jumped out of the car and opened the front door. 'Karen?' The coat that had been there on the bannister that morning was not there now. *I bet she's at the tree. Bloody fog.*

He marched outside. 'KAREN!'. He went as far as the tree, still calling, but there was no sign of her. 'KAREN! WHERE THE FUCK ARE YOU?!' He walked back to the car. The only other thing he could think of was that someone had come to pick her up after she got home. *But who would do that? John? No, he couldn't have made it here in time, and he didn't know the way. I'm going to have to phone the nerd.* He walked to the tree again and his phone rang.

'Hi. Davie?' John's voice sounded. 'Have you seen anything of Karen yet?'

'No.'

'Have you tried ringing her?'

'Of course I have you stupid bastard,' Davie spat.

'Where is she then?'

Davie bit his tongue. *Don't lose your head now.* 'I'm going to see Hamish Broad. The old copper on the Caitlin McFee case. See if he's seen her.'

'Broad? Apparently he lied about the baby,' John said. 'Gracie, his sister did have one. It was adopted and named Archibald Logan.'

'Thanks. How does that help?'

'I don't know. But it means he's dishonest if nothing else.'

'Aye. Anything else you've got for me?

'Maybe,' John said. 'Fergus Anderson had another son, called Donald Anderson.'

Davie frowned. Thinking. 'Right. I'll be off now and let you know what I find.'

Davie was feeling unsettled. Going inside the cottage, he pulled out a small metal box from the cupboard under the stairs. Inside was a small old army pistol. He wasn't sure where it came from, but it had belonged to somebody in the family. His grandfather had given it to him as a souvenir. He'd cleaned and oiled it but had only fired it once to check. Now loaded, he put the safety catch on and tucked it into his pocket.

On the way to his car, something caught his eye. He saw the small white figure. 'Hey, lassie, what are you doing out here?' He walked towards her. The next thing he felt was a blow on the side of his head. He was knocked out cold.

***

His phone now fully charged, John went down to reception bumping into Mr Binks.

'Ah, dear boy. I trust you have had a successful mission? I certainly have.'

'No. Karen's gone missing.'

Mr Binks looked at him. 'John, this is your young lady, Karen, we are talking about.' John nodded. 'Then I have rarely met a more capable young lady. Yes, she *may* be in danger as I myself suspected. But you haven't eaten since breakfast. I am going to freshen up a little and I suggest you do the same. We shall have dinner, then we will think about what we need to do.'

'Yes. That's a good idea.' *He's right of course, Karen is extremely capable, and I am exceptionally hungry.*

'And I wouldn't be surprised in the slightest if your young lady is in touch before we finish our meal. Now, I'll meet you in the restaurant here in, say ten minutes?'

Precisely ten minutes later, John was sitting at a table when Mr Binks walked in wearing an added woollen waistcoat and carrying his tweed jacket over his shoulder. He tutted and shook his head before moving to table number twenty-four.

John followed behind. As he sat down he asked, 'Did we really go to York and back today? I must have been very tired. I don't remember anything about it.'

'Fatigue, dear boy. From driving.' Mr Binks replied picking up a menu from the stand in the middle of the table. 'And I found out everything I needed to know.'

'You did?'

'Do you not even remember the pub and the lemonade?' Mr Binks hid a smile.

John looked down, then up. 'Yes, of course I remember the pub,' he frowned.

'You young people are all the same. You look at things but you don't *see* anything.' John shook his head in frustration at that. 'I wonder if you're going down with something?' He leaned over and placed the back of his hand on John's forehead. 'You do feel rather hot. A hot toddy and an early night for you, I think.'

The waitress came over and Mr Binks ordered first. 'I'll have the grilled salmon, my good lady.'

John thought for a moment. 'The same for me, please.'

'Thank you,' said the waitress, taking back the menus. 'And what would you like to drink?'

'A jug of filtered tap water, please.' Mr Binks said immediately.

'But...' *I really need a drink*

Mr Binks gave John one of his stern looks. 'We will need clear heads later,' he said mysteriously. 'And you will need to drive.'

'What?' said John, surprised. 'Please explain.'

'All in good time,' said Mr Binks. 'All in good time.'

While they were waiting for their order to arrive, Mr Binks regaled John with descriptions of his walks around the city. *Please, no more road names or buildings. My brain can't cope.*

'...and news of Archibald.' *What did he say?* 'Does that name mean anything to you?'

John sat up straight as if something in his brain had pinged. 'Well, yes, maybe,' He said. 'Nearly. Fergus Anderson was the author of the book that you found. And I've just found out that Gracie Broad had a son who was adopted and is now called Archibald Logan.

While he sat trying to force his tired brain to work properly, the waitress came over with their meals, and Mr Binks' upheld hand meant that talking was now forbidden.

John tried to keep pace with Mr Binks but he was too unbearably slow, savouring every mouthful and dabbing his mouth with his napkin after nearly every swallow. John sat in silence, waiting for him to finish. *At least I'm not having trouble eating.*

Finally, Mr Binks put down his napkin and addressed John. 'Yes. You are right. I am certain that Archibald Logan is the son of Fergus Anderson, the man Karen is seeking. It is also possible, assuming a filial likeness, that Archibald was the man who spoke to her father.'

'That makes a lot of sense,' John was reanimated. 'But how do we find him?'

'Oh, it moves us forward a great deal,' Mr Binks agreed. 'We will need to ask your Scottish detective friend for some help though.'

'You know Davie?' John was surprised.

'I know *of* him, John. A mutual acquaintance.'

John shook his head a little. *What? How does that make sense? Although nothing Mr Binks says seems to make much sense.* He tried to get back to the main issue. He looked at his watch, it was nearly nine o'clock. *Where did the evening go?*

'When do we start looking?'

Mr Binks took a long sip of water and turned to John.

'I think we should set off now,' he said.

43

Karen was beginning to come round. Her mouth had been tightly tied with a scarf, and her hands were tied behind her back. Her eyes were at ground level, she was lying on her side on a dirt floor. She heaved herself upright and shuffled her bottom back until she reached something solid. She blinked as her eyes first became accustomed to vision, then looked around in the black emptiness of the place she was being held. She wrinkled her nose at the dank air. *This is like a cave.*

Peering towards what looked like the lightest area, she began to make out a figure coming towards her. As it got closer, she began to shiver uncontrollably. She was locked into the eyes of a creature so old and gnarled it bore little resemblance to a human. Its eyes were deep-set and piercing, almost burning into her brain. She stared back at it, transfixed.

Its voice, when it began, was deep and throaty. He – she was sure it was male – spoke with a heavy accent but like nothing she had ever heard before.

'I bid you welcome to my humble abode, Karen Thorpe.' She shuddered. 'I have already been on a very interesting journey, and you are about to make it so much more so.'

So you are human. You just wait. Karen, more reassured than scared by the voice, began slowly easing her wrists against the rope tying them.

'I was summoned. Like priests say they are called,' his mouth spread into a black toothless smile.

That's disgusting. Karen kept wriggling her hands.

'But I was called by someone oh so much better than *him*.' The creature made a phlegmy gurgling noise then spat on the ground. 'You have many questions. I will let you speak.'

As he came closer, repulsed as she was, Karen examined him closely with her copper's eye. He was badly hunched but she could see from the length of his limbs that he was very tall. His muscles had wasted, but the remnants of his clothes indicated a much broader, stronger body once inhabited them.

Oh my God he stinks. His stench made her gag, but swallowing it down, she could see past the encrusted grime and the deep wrinkles. *I know that face.* She held her breath as the man untied the scarf around her mouth.

'Fergus Anderson. You're meant to be dead.'

'Am I?' he said as he lumbered back a few paces and sat cross-legged on the floor. 'Or am I Andrew Ferguson?' He gave a croaky deep laugh and made a strange noise. She caught the words *a Scottish soldier...*

'Don't,' said Karen. 'That was...'

'Oh yes, your father knew it, too. It was a popular song back in the day.' He carried on singing...'

'What do you mean?' Karen shouted. 'What the hell do you know about my father?'

'He met a close relative of mine once upon a time,' Anderson cackled. 'Almost at the same time as he met the biggest father of them all.' He paused. 'Death.'

Karen now openly struggled with her ties. 'Who was it? Your bastard son? He looked like you.'

Anderson cackled again. 'Would you like to meet him? He's just over there waiting.' His tone changed. 'Such a dear, obedient boy.'

That reminds me of... 'Why have you brought me here?' She shouted. 'You know they'll be looking for me. Let me go.'

'Did you know,' he said to her in a very matter of fact way, 'that army body bags are so strong that they can disguise any smell? Even that of rotting flesh. It was very useful. Especially in hot climes.'

Karen squirmed. 'You monster. We're on to you,' she spat. 'We know you did it.'

'Then prove it. But first, you'll have to find me.'

'Oh, we will. Whatever you want to do with me, there'll be others behind me.'

Anderson laughed a cynical sneering laugh. 'Will there, young lady? Like this one?' He pointed, and Karen's gaze followed his arm. Her eyes, now accustomed to the dark, could just make out another body on the other side. There was no mistaking that physique. *Davie.* Tied like her, he wasn't moving.

149

'What have you done?' she shouted. 'Have you killed him?'

'Death will surely come, but not at my hand.' Ferguson said. 'And talking of hands, the other one is in the capable hands of a friend of mine.'

'The other one?' She said flatly. *Does he mean John?*

'Your companion betrayed you. Not so much him, more the unsavoury company that he keeps.'

'Mr Binks?' she said despondently.

'Do you mean the map keeper? Aye, I think you do. He wants something from me. He doesn't know me but I want something from him.' He turned to look at her again. 'Everyone has a price,' he hissed.

'And what do you want from him?' Karen said. 'He can give you nothing. He has nothing, just an old shop full of maps.'

'Oh, my dear girl,' he said in a definite parody of Mr Binks. 'He has already delivered two of you to me. You who would try to stop me. I'd say that is quite a bargain, don't you think?'

Karen's heart sank. *Was this the plan all along? All to stop Dad's investigation?*

'No, you are not nice pretty little virgins,' he looked at her in disgust. 'But you are three people who think you are good. You have goodness in your heart. You seek the truth. And sometimes, my dear,' he smiled at her and her blood ran cold. 'Sometimes truth is the most powerful weapon in the world. And when it is applied correctly, when the lives of truthful people are taken, it can make some very serious magic.'

'What are you going to do? You'll never get away with it, you know that don't you?'

'Oh, I think I will,' he sneered.

Karen, summoning up all her courage growled at him. 'That's funny. How are you going to kill three of us? John isn't even here.'

'No my dear. Not yet. But he will be. Timing. It's all timing. You see that fool there,' he looked towards Davie. 'He was stupid enough to bring a gun with him. His own gun of course. And as you know, whenever guns are around, people always get killed.'

Karen stared at Anderson in shock. 'I don't believe you. Why would he have a gun?'

'It is all foretold. All predestined. By me, of course.'

'What do you mean?' Karen said, now having nothing to lose.

'Davie will shoot John in a jealous rage. Oh, yes, my dear. You see I know all about his feelings for you. Now don't tell me you didn't guess?'

Karen shook her head in horror. 'No. That's complete rubbish.'

'And because you are foolish and brave, you will try to stop him and you will take John's bullet. That is bullet number one. He loaded three.'

'This is complete bullshit,' Karen shouted.

'John will try to stop him, and he too will be shot.' He turned to look at Davie.

'Then this one here will simply turn the gun on himself.'

Karen shook her head. 'No way.'

'He has issues. Suicidal tendencies. It's all in his files.'

'That's bollocks. Davie's the most down to earth man I've ever met. You can't make him do that.'

'Ah, but my dear, I can. I have been working on young Davie here for a while now. Not that he'd know it of course, but I have my ways and means.' He peered closely at her.

'And your Mr Binks has John entirely at his command, or had you not realised?'

Karen gulped. *I knew it. How could I let him get involved?*

'Yes, my dear. You are the only fly in the ointment as they say, or rather, in my web. Whatever is in your brain, you're not such a willing recipient of my directions. But to be frank, Karen, it doesn't much matter whether you play your part or not. A bullet hole is a bullet hole; however you look at it. And your best forensic man will be, shall we say, somewhat incapacitated.'

Karen fought against her restraints. 'It will never work. There are others who'll know the truth.'

'Oh, I doubt that. But in the meantime, I have to overpower you one way or another. We cannot have you giving the game away, can we?' He tied the scarf around her mouth once again then held up a phial. She struggled helplessly for a few moments until the chloroform took hold, and she fell back into unconsciousness.

44

John followed Mr Binks to his car. He was talking as he went. 'Now John, I must ask you to promise to do exactly what I tell you. Do you understand?'

'Yes, but you've got to tell me more than that,' said John. 'What's going on?'

Mr Binks carried on walking, talking casually as if he were merely talking about the weather. 'John, dear boy, your friend Karen has fallen into the clutches of the most evil being I have ever come across.'

John stopped in his tracks. 'What? Who? How do you know?'

'Well, actually I haven't exactly come across him in the flesh, so to speak, but shall I say that our paths have crossed, and we know of each other.'

'Who is it?' said John impatiently. 'Where is she?'

'I believe it might be, or was, the man you know of as Fergus Anderson. The one who wrote the book. The rambler. The one Karen suspected all along. Catch up, dear boy. We must be on our way.'

John paced alongside Mr Binks who continued to talk as if nothing had happened. 'He is a wretched tormented being who sold his soul many years ago. I have discovered, or rather I have inferred, that he was driven crazy by his experiences overseas in the army and somehow returned to England where it seems he sought solace in the black arts. He was a bit like a convert.' He turned to John to gauge his comprehension. 'And converts are almost always tiresome. They take things too seriously.'

'How do you mean?'

'I think he uncovered an ancient book and became obsessed with it. He followed footpaths and trails and somehow stumbled across some old magic almost forgotten by everybody else. He has spent his whole life ever since protecting it.'

'Magic?' John said in disbelief. 'You've got to be kidding me.'

Mr Binks stopped in his tracks. 'Well, that is my theory. Take it or leave it, but if you leave it, and I am right, you may never see Karen again.'

'But magic? You can't mean that. It's all rubbish, fantasy, nonsense.'

'Mock at your peril, young man,' said Mr Binks beginning to walk again. 'I am no magic maker myself, but I know their ways and everything is connected.'

They were now at John's car and Mr Binks turned to look at him, searching his face for scepticism.

'What can he do?' John asked.

'I believe he can harness people and machines to do his bidding.' Mr Binks replied. 'We are all driven by electrical impulses John. Our nervous system is electric. Think of the internet today. All those electronic communications, all those currents. It's only a small leap from one to the other.'

Mr Binks waited for John to unlock the car, then he sat inside and said quietly as John got in beside him, 'even I have dabbled a little.'

'How?' John asked. 'Did you really know Karen's father and what happened to him?'

'Now is not the time,' Mr Binks put on his seatbelt.

'Then what does he want with Karen? And where is she?'

'I believe that he thinks that Karen and her father before her were threatening his power. Of course, they didn't know that. They were just trying to find his victims. But if his victims were found, if they were brought up again, he thought it would destroy his power forever. At least that is what I believe he thought.'

John shook his head. 'This is all madness.'

'You believe what you will, John. My conclusion is that Fergus Anderson has used his powers to enslave his own son to do his bidding.'

John switched on the engine. 'I don't know what to think. But we've got to find Karen wherever she is, and yours is the only lead we have. If she's in danger and I didn't try to find her, I'd never forgive myself.'

'Sense at last,' Mr Binks replied. 'We must try to find her as soon as possible. I will direct you; we cannot get too close by car, but I believe I know where we are going.'

John drove as directed. The urban scenery gradually transformed into rural, and the fog began to appear.

'Another mile or so down this road,' said Mr Binks.

Where on earth are we heading? It feels like we're going round in circles. 'Where are we? Are we close?'

'Keep going.'

Finally, Mr Binks told him to stop. 'This is where it gets more difficult. Follow me, I think I have it right.'

'How can you see anything in this?'

'Oh, dear boy, I'm not seeing anything at all. I'm feeling my way.'

'Slow down!' Mr Binks was going so quickly John was beginning to lose sight of him in the fog. 'Mr Binks? 'Where are you? I can't see you!'

John tried to speed up but his feet stumbled along the rugged terrain. He slowed down to take a look around. *There. Is that him? It must be.* John increased his pace to catch up with the dark figure in front of him.

'John Steele I believe,' said an unfamiliar voice and John felt a blow to his head then saw no more.

***

Karen shivered with cold. *Now where am I?* Looking round she realised she had moved. No more cloying atmosphere, she was lying on the ground feeling wet fog on her face. *Must find a landmark.* She looked around. *There.* She saw stone walls. *A garden. I know this place. Davie's garden.*

She tried to get up but her legs failed her and she stumbled down again. *What the hell happened. Did I dream it all? This is where I was when I came back from seeing Hamish.* She looked at her watch. *But if it is, I've been out for hours.* She looked around again to find the tree.

What's that? Shit! She looked up to see a pair of legs seemingly dangling in the air, the toes of the feet scraping the earth. As her eyes travelled further up the body, she saw it was a man. John. His arms were tied to the branches of the tree like some sort of mock crucifixion.

'John!' She looked around for something to help him get down to the side and saw a dazed-looking Davie, on his feet but swaying badly. He was holding something.

'Oh my God!' she yelled, shocked as she saw what it was. A gun and it was pointing at John. *It's what he said would happen...*

'No Davie! NO!' she yelled and tried to get up again. 'This is all a setup. Don't do it! Don't shoot!'

Davie turned towards her and waved the gun in the air. 'I'm sorry, Karen. It's something I have to do. It's all his fault. Everything will be alright if...'

Karen half-got to her feet and started crawl-walking towards the unconscious John.

'Davie!' She shouted. 'You've been hypnotised or something. They can't make you do something against your will. You have to fight it.' She got closer until she was almost in front of John. She forced herself to her feet and stood in front of him, her head at the level of his chest.

'NO!' she screamed. She looked up to the sky and shouted, 'YOU CAN'T CONTROL US.'

Davie closed his eyes. *He's trying, I can see it.*

'Now, Davie!' said a voice coming from everywhere and nowhere.

'SHOOT!'

Davie held the gun in front of him and aimed straight at Karen's head.

Out of the corner of her eye, Karen caught the slight movement of someone to the right of her. *Who's that?*

Davie's eyes were now streaming with tears. His arm rigid he began to squeeze his finger on the trigger.

A voice. Davie froze. Concentrating. *What did it say?*

'Listen to me, my dear young man.' *A calm voice.* Davie swayed a little, his gun hand lowering.

'SHOOT NOW!'

Davie jerked to attention. He held the gun up again

'DAVIE' Karen wailed. 'DON'T DO IT!'

Another voice. The quiet one.

'Just a little to the left, my dear boy.'

Davie's whole body stiffened. He turned as if he was on a moving platform.

'SHOOT!'

He opened his eyes wide and pulled the trigger. The gunshot boomed in the silence of the garden, and Davie fell to his knees.

45

'Now, my dear,' Mr Binks said to a very bleary-eyed Karen who was sitting on Davie's armchair. 'The poison, curse, call it what you will, that was inflicted on you has left your mind in a very vulnerable state.'

Karen shook her head slowly. 'And why should I trust you? He said you had delivered us to him.'

'Because, dear girl, far from giving you up, I actually saved all your lives.'

'I definitely talked to him. I saw his face; I heard his voice. '

'Whoever or whatever it was out there, it is long gone now.'

Karen shook her head. 'I need to know what just happened to me. I saw him, this monster, hardly human. Was that Anderson?'

'I don't know what you saw, or what you think you saw. Fergus Anderson is dead is he not?'

Karen frowned. 'So I thought.'

'Then it cannot be him. I believe that *someone* is striving to maintain an ancient and, they believe, magic path of magnetic current.'

'What?'

'Try to imagine an electric current coursing through the ground but without the need for a cable. Think of the currents of the moon. The tidal flows, the earth's magnetic fields.'

'What?'

'These paths are the stuff of legend, my dear – if such paths existed and had the powers believed of them. They are never needed or used these days. Even back in 1964, very few people were aware of them.'

Karen sat up, her senses recovering. 'So what has this got to do with me? Or with the investigation?'

'We must take a step back to explain that,' Mr Binks said. 'I have ascertained that there was a belief, held by very few, that human sacrifice was necessary in order to protect the power of the paths.'

'You mean the girls?'

'I do. The idea would have been condemned by almost all but a tiny number of practitioners of the dark arts. If whoever it was had got it into his head that a new building, a road, a housing estate, whatever, would interfere with the current, that might have been enough of a catalyst to spur him into his despicable action. But it wasn't necessary, you see. The world of magic moves on like the rest of the world. There are always new ways and means.'

'That's good to hear. So who could it be?'

'Someone who believed in the sacrifice of innocents. The strength of the virgin sacrifice appears in many cultures and is believed to make very powerful magic. But his particular ritual seems to have relied on the sacrificed remaining at precise points in the path. I wonder even if they were buried immediately?'

'But why wait?'

'Because someone with a knowledge of local planning might speculate that by burying the bodies under new developments, like the road, or new housing estates, they would remain forever. It would also be a very clever way of concealing the evidence.'

Karen was now fully on board. A murderer who believed in magic was something very different from a monster. This she could relate to. 'All the developments? So the new buildings weren't a coincidence. They were a necessity. That makes sense.'

'Indeed. If I am right, it is someone who followed local newspapers obsessively to keep up to date with the latest housing and infrastructure developments. And of course, he tried everything he could to put the police off the scent.'

'Like Brian Appleby?'

'Oh, yes. I am certain that someone got to Brian Appleby. I'm also sure someone scared Sam Farnsworth to death. Who knows what happened to Mick Chatterton? Maybe that should be your next investigation.'

'You know he mimicked you, don't you? The... man who spoke to me in the cave. I almost thought it was you talking at first. And he mentioned his son. He called him obedient. What's that about?'

'How distasteful of him. On the other hand, politeness is a rare commodity these days. Now where was I? My dear, after what you just said I am wondering how much was imagined in your confused mind. Please do not think for a moment that I disbelieve you, but you were given exceptionally powerful drugs. I doubt that you were moved even an inch from where you were drugged. If there is a cave, I know not of its location.'

Karen shook her head. 'I know what I saw and heard.' *Do I?* 'But why do you care, Mr Binks? What has any of this got to do with you? And, while I think of it, how did you get here?'

'One thing at a time, young lady. I am very fond of John and I have the highest regard for you, too. And I take great pleasure in the idea that my hoard, my treasure trove of documents and papers could actually help to bring some relief to the poor families of the victims,' He paused to take a breath. 'Strange as it may seem, John and I were a mere stone's throw from this house when he was taken. I followed the sound of voices until I found you, as you were, in your — what do I call it? It was charmingly theatrical. No,' he changed his flow. 'Maybe that is to make light of it and it was extremely serious. Set piece, perhaps. Whatever. I could hardly stand back and let you both be murdered, could I?'

'So where is it, him, now? The thing that brought us all here? How do we know he's not still a threat?'

Mr Binks stared into Karen's eyes. 'Forget about him, Karen. Forget about the cave. I'll know what to do when the time comes.'

Karen blinked and looked around. She heard a groan coming from the sofa. *That's Davie. What happened?*

Karen scratched her head. 'Mr Binks, what I do remember, I think, is that it was you who told Davie to change the angle of his shot. Why did he act on your suggestion?'

'I see you remember that little scuffle. I think the young man was simply confused after his knock on the head. I merely steadied his nerves. I have some verbal skills, if I say so myself. But above all, I have the interests of all you, my young friends, in the very centre of my heart.' He patted Karen's hand. 'I won't pretend that the situation in which we find ourselves is anything other than tricky. But I also know you are compelled to follow your nose — I believe that is the saying?'

Karen nodded. *What a lovely man.* 'Thanks, Mr Binks. Knowing that you are on our side is very reassuring.'

'Good.' Mr Binks gave her his most charming smile then he leaned a little towards her. 'And please don't tell your companions what I said about that little business with the gun. It must be our little secret. The young male ego is a fragile thing and we can't be quite sure of the competence of their brains just yet. Do I have your assurance?'

Karen found herself nodding again. 'You do.'

'Good. Now let's see how Davie is doing. John should be back in the land of the living, too, very shortly.'

46

Upstairs, John was flat out on Davie's bed.

'John. John?' Mr Binks said, gently shaking his arm. 'Wake up now, we're at the cottage. You fell and hit your head. Do you remember?'

John slowly opened his eyes. He looked around at the unfamiliar surroundings.

'I thought we were out on the fields somewhere. Where are we?'

'We found our way to young Davie's cottage.'

'We did? I don't remember.'

'My dear boy. It was foggy. Don't you remember? You were driving me to see Karen and Davie when you slipped and fell. You couldn't reach her on the telephone so we came here.'

John registered Karen 'You're here? Are you all right?' He rubbed his head. 'Ah yes,' he smiled. 'I do remember now.'

'I'm fine,' Karen replied. 'How are you feeling?'

'I've been better.' He sat up. 'Where's Davie?'

'Downstairs.' *Hell, how do I explain what happened to him?* She looked at Mr Binks. He took her cue and hurried downstairs.

Karen gave John a loving hug. 'Come on. I bet you'd like a coffee or something.'

'And Aspirin,' he grinned. 'It's good to see you. I was so very worried.'

'Come down, when you're up to it. We should all talk.'

Downstairs, Davie was awake and gradually becoming alert. 'I just don't remember,' he said. 'And where did *you* come from?'

'It was clearly a slippery night,' Mr Binks explained. 'John fell and hit his head, too. There are quite a few rocks around here I noticed.'

Davie's eyes suddenly opened wide. 'Where's my gun?' He looked around.

'I put it safely back in the box it seemed to have been kept in. You discharged it when you fell.'

'Och, no. I could have killed someone.' He looked up as Karen came down the stairs, with John following. 'Karen. Where did you get to?'

'I was following ghosts,' she said.

Davie looked at his watch. 'Fuck. I've been out for ages.'

'I expect we're all tired and in need of refreshments,' Mr Binks said.

'Aye,' Davie got to his feet. 'How about coffee?'

Karen watched as John sat as far away from Davie as he could. 'Yes please,' John said.

'Tea for me. And after that, I will explain all,' said Mr Binks.

'And biscuits. I'm starving,' Karen added.

'No bother,' Davie said.

John was still rubbing his head and frowning as Davie left.

'What exactly have you found out Mr Binks?'

'Patience, dear boy,' He put his finger to his lips.

When they were all seated with their refreshments, Mr Binks sat up and beamed at all of them. 'It's all in here,' he said, taking a small ancient-looking hand bound book from his ample pocket. He held it up to show them.

'Semita Album,' Karen read. She looked at him. 'What does this add?'

'I believe it predates the book by Fergus Anderson.'

'How do you mean?' said John.

'Well, it is just a theory,' said Mr Binks, 'but I have looked at all the footpaths in this book very carefully, and I have found something very surprising.'

'What?' said Karen, excitedly.

'There were some very ancient paths, all networked around old Britain,' Mr Binks began. Most of them were disused many centuries ago, but Fergus Anderson's book is missing a few,' he paused and looked at them meaningfully.

'And?' John said.

Karen was ahead of them. 'Are you saying that Anderson deliberately excluded them from his book?' Karen said.

'To make sure they remained hidden?' John added.

Mr Binks beamed and nodded his assent.

'What's the order then? Did the first book come out before the murders?' Karen asked.

'1965. Precisely one year afterwards, ' Mr Binks said.

'So does this book prove anything?' she said. 'Maybe they were all built over by the time it came out?'

Davie had been listening intently to the conversation. 'It proves nothing. I think what Mr Binks is getting at, is that the book may, by accident, show us where the bodies of the wee lasses are. Am I right?'

Mr Binks nodded. 'I am no detective young man, just a humble keeper of maps. But I would suggest we compare the two editions and see if that gives us any further information. John? Do you have the copy by Anderson?'

'It's on my phone,' he searched his pockets. 'Must be in the car,' John stood up but wobbled a little.

'Give me the keys, dear boy. I'll fetch it.' Mr Binks went out. John looked puzzled.

'What?' Karen asked.

'Nothing. I just don't remember being anywhere near this cottage when I parked.'

'Quite a bump on your head then?' Davie said. 'I clearly remember coming here. But the fog was very thick.'

Karen remained silent. Thinking.

Mr Binks came in with John's phone and handed it to him. 'Could you find the images of the book, dear boy?'

John scrolled through his photos then handed the phone back to Mr Binks.

'Thank you, John,' he paused, looking. 'Comparing the list of contents,' he said, 'there are five more in the original.'

'So that doesn't work then,' John said. 'We're only looking for three. Unless there are more murders.'

'You have to compare them on an item for item basis,' Karen said. 'Some footpaths will have been closed, but he might have noted new ones. It's got to be worth checking.'

'Agreed,' John and Davie said together.

Mr Binks yawned, and within a few moments, they all followed suit. 'My dear young friends, we are all tired. I suggest we reconvene in the morning.'

The three looked at each other. This was indeed true, and once the idea had been planted, it became fact. Karen and Davie yawned simultaneously.

Mr Binks continued in a rather authoritative sort of way. 'You should concentrate on the matter at hand, and tomorrow I suggest you get the necessary paperwork together to exhume poor Caitlin McFee's body on the assumption that we will be able to locate it. There's no point in chasing ghosts. You must see if my theory is correct.' He turned to look at John. 'Are you fit to drive, my boy? It's very late and we must get back to the hotel.'

'Er, I think so.' John looked suspiciously at Davie and Karen.

'Don't be silly, man,' said Davie. 'I'm too knackered.'

'What?' John's hackles were visibly rising despite his fatigue.

'Och, it's a joke. Calm down.'

'You go, John.' Karen said. 'We'll see you bright and early tomorrow.'

Karen and Davie waved off John and Mr Binks, then looked quizzically at each other.

'Would you mind...?' Karen began

'I was hoping...' Davie replied.

'No funny stuff though,' said Karen firmly.

That night they slept like babies wrapped in each other's arms.

47

Thursday 14 November

Mr Binks was unable to sleep. His mind was in turmoil following the events that evening. *Did I manage to convince them? Did I make sure every angle was covered? Where the devil did Anderson get to? What unearthly power gave him that strength? Or was it Archibald? Yes, that would make more sense.*

And it was not over yet, he mused. *I still haven't located the manuscript. The cave. It must be nearby.* His instincts told him that Anderson would be weakened after using so much of his power, *but I must safeguard the youngsters. He will certainly recover...*

When he had decided precisely what he had to do, he fell into a brief sleep only to be awoken by the receptionist's call.

'Binks,' he said to himself. 'You chose not to go down that path for a reason. It is really not your sort of thing at all. And now you have more to do – if only to save these idiot young people from finding out the truth and maybe getting into more mischief.'

Then he remembered what he thought was likely to be the most powerful thing of all. *They'll find the bodies. And that's what matters the most to the rest of the happily ignorant and unknowing world. I just have to find it first.*

Tiredness overtook him, and he fell back asleep.

***

John had also slept well but was itching to get back over to the cottage, partly to make sure that everything was still as right as it could be between him and Karen. He also needed to satisfy himself that nothing was going on between her and Davie. There had been no opportunity for them to talk the night before. He was emotionally insecure yet physically wound up like a coiled spring about to burst. But he also knew that challenging Karen would be sure to be the end of their relationship. He would have to keep his emotions bottled a little longer.

He was up, washed and pacing in reception at the usual time. But Mr Binks was nowhere to be seen. Eventually, frustrated, John went to the reception desk and asked the girl to ring his room. The girl obliged and giggled when Mr Binks answered the phone.

'I'll tell him,' she said and she turned to John. She relayed what he'd said. 'A man needs his sleep. You carry on without him, he'll meet up with you when it suits him and not a moment before.'

'Good. That suits me, too.' John went into the restaurant, gulped down a couple of rolls and a cup of tea then went out to his car. He glanced up at the window of the hotel and wondered what Mr Binks was up to. It seemed most unusual for him to sleep in but then, John speculated, if he was right about the maps, maybe his role had now come to an end.

***

'Oh my god, we didn't, did we?' Karen leapt out of Davie's bed still wearing her underwear from the night before.

'No, of course we didn't. Your maidenhead is as intact as it was before.'

Karen ran to the spare bedroom, grabbed some clean clothes, and dashed downstairs to the bathroom. She stepped in the shower and began to sing loudly

'Oh, what a beautiful morning...'

John, Davie and Karen all arrived at the station at the same time. Karen, a little guiltily, gave John a small hug and a peck on the cheek. John, a little suspiciously kissed her back.

Davie took charge. 'Let's go to the office. I'll get the coffee and then we must get going. If yon man's right about the maps and we can all agree where we think the body is, I'll need to bring in my DCI. And he'll need to bring the high heads in if we're going to be digging up roads.'

They settled in the room and John held up his phone. 'We need to print out the book,' he said.

167

Karen held up the other book. 'And can we photocopy this too? Then I can scribble on the copies.'

'Aye,' Davie took John's phone and picked up the book. 'Play nicely,' he said as he left.

John waited for the door to shut before talking. 'Are you really all right, Karen?'

'I'm fine. Mr Binks is giving us such support. How are you feeling? Do you remember anything?'

John looked surprised. 'I'm pleased you see him like that now. Why do you ask?'

Karen stalled. *I can't tell him that Mr Binks saved all our lives.* 'Because you hit your head, and we don't know if you lost consciousness.'

John frowned. 'I'm confused about the driving I did last night. I'm sure I walked much further from the car than the distance the car was parked from the cottage.'

'You were probably walking round in circles in that fog.'

'Could be. And you know what else...'

'What?' Karen said, *Don't say...*

'You do know we're meant to be back at work on Monday, don't you?'

Phew! 'Of course I do. I'll sort it. For me, that is. As long as we find the body. If we do, everything will be a doddle after that.'

Davie held the door open while their coffee was brought in then handed Karen the copies and a red pen. While he and John studied their paperwork, Karen began cross-checking the pages.

'So, we know that there are five more in the original, but the names aren't the same.' John and Davie nodded their agreement.

It didn't take her long to work out what she needed to do. The contents page followed a similar order except that Anderson clearly used a different system from the older one. She found St Dunstan's Church Lane under S, not D. *I'll eliminate the saints first.* She crossed out all the corresponding paths on each map. 'OK. I can see the numbered ones, too,' she said out loud. 'Getting there.'

She carried on while Davie and John sipped at their drinks and tried hard not to catch each other's eyes.

Karen paused to take a long swallow of coffee before making an announcement. 'Right. In the Edinburgh area, there is one path I can't find in Anderson's book. This one.' She opened up the page. 'So how do we pinpoint it?'

Davie peered at the page. 'No idea.'

John looking smug – but not for long – also had to concede defeat.

Karen sat back, stumped. 'There's nothing obvious to look for. The maps are too small for any detail.'

'And the path is, what, five hundred yards long?' Davie said, calculating in his head.

'Mr Binks will know all the scales,' John said.

'But he's not here. Let's try York,' Karen said. 'We've got my father's map for that one. Damn. I mean we did have. Mr Binks has it now. I had a photo somewhere...' she reached for her phone.

'How about I look for the Lincoln one,' John suggested. 'I know all the footpaths – or I used to.'

Davie winked at Karen as they sat back and watched John compare the lists. He was slow but methodical.

'Here,' he said. 'There are three paths on this but nothing comparable in Anderson's book.'

'That could be our discrepancy,' Karen said. 'And do you know them?'

'No,' John admitted, trying to ignore Davie's sneer.

'OK. My turn.' Davie said with the photocopies in front of him. 'York. Easy. Got it in one.'

'It was the easiest one,' John replied.

'Let me see.' Karen peered at the map. 'Not enough detail again, but I think you're right. That curvy bit might be the same as Dad's map.' She looked at her phone. 'It's not a good image. John? You'd better get Mr Binks.'

'Did I hear my name being mentioned?' Mr Binks was escorted into the room. 'How far have you got?' he asked.

'Well hello Mr Binks,' Davie said sounding genuine. 'Great to see you again.'

'I was going to say that,' John said.

'Me too,' Karen added. 'I wanted to look at Dad's map.'

Mr Binks positively glowed. 'My dear friends, I have some exciting news. I think I know where Caitlin is buried,' he said.

'Excellent. Back in a jiffy,' Davie said as he left the room.

Mr Binks sat down and looked through the papers. 'It's like this...' he began.

48

Karen, John and Mr Binks looked up as DCI Stewart entered the room with Davie close behind him. Davie gave a tiny nod to show it was looking positive. He looked at Karen. She stepped forward and held out her hand. 'DS Karen Thorpe, I've been investigating three cold cases which we are convinced are related, and one of them happens to be Caitlin McFee.'

'Aye, my sergeant's told me that much. Out of curiosity, why are you doing it?'

'My father died while he was investigating one of the cases. I felt I owed it to him to finish the investigation.' *Wow. That definitely sank in. To me, too.*

'That's quite a reason. But we cannae get diggers up just on your say-so.'

'I understand. We believe that we have discovered who abducted Caitlin and two other girls. All three disappeared near ancient footpaths. Our prime suspect, who was at the scene of all three abductions, was also an expert on these footpaths.'

'So you think the wee one's near here?' DCI Stewart said.

'Yes,' Karen nodded. 'Mr Binks here has been able to identify a likely location. We're almost certain.'

'And what does Donald McTear have to say on the matter?'

'I haven't been able to contact him yet, he's away sick.' Karen crossed her fingers under the table. *There's definitely something dodgy about that man.*

'And I can confirm there have been sightings of the wee lassie in the same vicinity,' Davie said.

DCI Stewart peered at him with his eyebrows raised. 'Och I dinnae believe in that nonsense but there are many around here that do, and if nothing else it will put paid to all the rumours.'

'Are we on?' Karen said.

'I don't deny that if we resolved this case it would be a real boost for the force and the local community. But ye cannae dig up the whole path. Not without good evidence,' DCI Stewart said.

'And there I may be of assistance.' Mr Binks stood and gave a little bow. 'I have some information about the precise location. We won't need to dig up much at all.'

DCI Stewart stared at him. 'And what's your interest, sir?'

'I have been at the periphery of many an investigation. But thanks to my young friends here, I can be of some practical use in his instance.' Mr Binks smiled and the inspector's face lit up.

'I cannae argue with that,' he said. 'All right. You have my authorisation. But this is your only shot. If you're wrong, the case goes back into storage forever.'

'Och that's great,' said Davie.

'You won't regret it,' said Karen as he left the room. Shall I tell Peggy McFee?' she looked at Davie.

'No,' Davie shook his head. 'We can't raise her hopes. Not until we know for sure.' Karen nodded her agreement.

'Now Mr Binks. Where are we?' Davie looked at him.

Mr Binks pushed forward the open book together with a current map. He pointed to a road. 'There.'

Davie's eyebrows shot up. 'Aye. That's close to the new estate...'

'That Peggy took me to. It sounds likely.' Karen added.

'Let's get this show on the road then.' Davie picked up the phone as Mr Binks picked up the book. 'Can you get me through to Traffic Scotland?' He asked the switchboard operator. 'We need to dig up some of the East Lane bypass. See if you can find out who deals with it.' He sat drumming his fingers for a moment. 'Aye, it's DI Wallace here. We need to do some excavating; we believe there's a body under the road. It might be Caitlin McFee.'

The manager in charge was sympathetic. 'Och, what's a bit of digging compared to finding that wee lassie,' he said. 'We'll do what we can. I'll get the maintenance team on it right away. I'll ring you when we're ready for ye.'

Karen was amazed at the reaction. She looked at John. 'I bet it's not like that in England.'

'Not at all. But then most of England is much more populated than this. It is an easier scenario here.'

'And we're a tight-knit community, Davie said. 'Anyone here would want to find that bairn.'

'Talking of England,' Karen said, 'let's look at the Yorkshire maps.' She looked at Mr Binks.

Mr Binks, who had sat in silence, perked up. 'Yes, indeed. I have your father's map, my dear.' He passed it to Karen, and she smoothed it out on the table.

'Look here,' John pointed. 'This seems to correspond to the old map. But when we look at the new one, there's a whole new estate on it. I don't know how we would pinpoint it. There have been no sightings or anything there.'

'No, but we could talk to that chap Charlie Worthington,' Karen said. 'The journalist, Stanley Briggs told me he was wittering on about it. He might have an idea.'

John looked puzzled. He turned to Mr Binks. 'Did you mention that name? To me?'

'I did indeed. It was he who told me of the old volume.'

'Ah,' John said, looking visibly relieved. 'That makes sense.'

The phone rang, and Davie took the call. 'Och, that's great,' he said. 'We'll see you there.' He turned to the other three. 'All systems go,' he said. 'The digger's on its way.'

'That's impressive.' Karen said.

'That's community,' Davie replied.

'Please listen, my dear young people,' Mr Binks said. 'I am delighted to help you, naturally. But I, too, have my terms.'

'You do? You don't mean...' Karen began.

'Money? Gracious, no. I mean my identity. No one, but no one, must know my name or anything about me. Happenings such as this inevitably attract the attention of the press. If so much of a hint appears about me, I shall never offer any assistance again. Is that clear?'

Karen gulped. 'But we can't exactly hide you.'

'Those are my terms, do with them what you will.'

'Agreed,' Karen said. 'I'll take John. Davie, you'd better take Mr Binks and make sure everyone there understands Mr Binks' terms. We'll follow you.'

49

As they approached the section of road, Karen and John saw a large, parked truck with a digger already being driven down the back ramp.

Mr Binks was walking in the area ahead looking down at the road while Davie talked to the drivers. 'And if anything gets out about that wee man, I'll have your guts for garters.'

'What's he doing?' Karen pointed as Mr Binks took something out of his pocket.

'I don't know. Let's ask him.' John replied. They hurried to meet him.

'He seems to be walking around in circles,' Karen puffed.

Mr Binks looked up and gave them a little wave. He paced around and changed direction until he was satisfied.

'It looks like he's holding a compass,' John whispered to Karen.

'Here!' Mr Binks spoke as loudly as John had ever heard him, in Davie's direction. 'We start here.'

One of the men came over to him and began to lay out road cones. 'Poor wee lassie,' he said to Mr Binks. 'Let's hope we find her and can take her home to her mammy.'

Davie stood by the digger ready to guide the driver, when another car pulled up alongside. Two men in overalls got out. 'We heard about the lassie,' one said. 'We're here to help,' the other agreed.

Davie didn't question their presence. He'd guessed that the station grapevine would have been working. 'Och, that's just great,' he said. 'We'll need help shifting the soil and rubble.'

Karen, John, Davie, and Mr Binks stood by watching every move as the digger slowly began scraping off the surface bitumen with an excavator bucket. The next layers were harder, but the bucket filled more quickly with each dig.

Mr Binks was still pacing, looking at the instrument in his hand.

'Stop!' he shouted, standing immediately in front of the digger with his hand raised. 'I miscalculated.'

'Are you kidding me?' The digger operator climbed down to talk to him.

The three onlookers stood in hushed silence. Had Mr Binks blown the whole thing? Confidence in him was paramount for the entire operation.

Mr Binks gave the man his biggest, most charming smile. 'My very sincere apologies, young man. I'm afraid I misread the dial. It requires a minor adjustment.'

'And how big is minor?' The man looked him in the face.

'Oh, just back another three feet that way,' he pointed. 'And six inches to the left. I'm sure that will guarantee that we find the poor child.'

The man's expression softened immediately 'Och, nae bother. Nae bother at all.' He got back into his cab and began digging the new area.

'What was all that about?' Karen whispered.'

'No idea,' John replied. 'He probably failed to convert metric to imperial.'

Karen giggled and John squeezed her hand. They exchanged smiles.

Gradually an area of around six square meters was cleared. As the driver moved the digger away, the tension was mounting. Karen's heartbeat was increasing. John was holding his breath, and Davie paced up and down. Only Mr Binks seemed quiet and confident.

The two workmen and the other man grabbed shovels from the back of the truck. Gently they dipped into the softer ground below the road's surface. Karen, John and Davie stood as close as they could watching every shovelful.

'There,' pointed Karen as something black with a definite sheen was exposed.

'Aye. There's something here,' said a workman. 'Something plastic.'

'Do you want me to...' John stepped forward.

'It's his specialism,' Karen added but Davie shook his head.

'I've been here before an' all.' He went back to his car and took out a carrier bag. Taking out a brush, he went over to the hole and gently swept away some of the surface dirt to expose more of the black plastic.

One of the men got a tiny spade and dug carefully round the edges. It took ages but all eyes were transfixed on the spot. No one could look away for a second. When a small body bag was completely exposed, the outline of a small body was clearly visible.

Mr Binks stepped forward. 'Don't move it!'

'Why?' said Karen. 'We've got to take her to the mortuary.'

'We don't know it's her, Karen,' said Davie. 'Shall I take a look first?' Karen nodded.

'OK. Let's see.' The workmen also inched nearer to have a look. 'Sorry,' said Davie standing in front of Mr Binks and looking at the workmen. 'This is police business now. We must erect a tent.' He shooed them away and went to his car.

The workmen withdrew a little resentfully and went back to the digger. Mr Binks hovered as close as he could.

When the tent was erected, Davie, his head covered and his hands gloved, knelt beside the body bag giving a commentary as he examined it. 'It's not a police one. It's really stood the test of time. If, of course, it's fifty years old.' His hand moved towards the zipper pull. 'It's stiff...' he had to sit closer to open it. Slowly he began to unzip the bag. He had to pull it down a full twelve inches before he began to expose the red hair of the head.

'Stop!' Mr Binks, unable to hold back any longer, stepped forward. 'Don't open it!'

50

Davie, now visibly shaking, stood up to confront Mr Binks. 'No way,' he said. 'We've not come this far just to stop now.'

Mr Binks stood his ground. Karen and John watched nervously. Was Davie right to challenge him? Who knew for certain?

Karen stepped forward. 'Sir,' she said, being discreet. 'Whilst your assistance has been invaluable, there are certain procedures which must now be followed. Can you give me any reason, backed up by evidence, why we should not proceed?'

Mr Binks stood back. 'I implore you not to. I believe you may come to regret it,' he said, shaking his head.

Davie looked at Karen, who nodded as he knelt again. His hand shaking, he tugged at the zip pull and began to open the edges of the body bag. As he pulled the top open, the skies above began to darken.

Karen gasped. In the bag was the perfectly preserved body of Caitlin McFee. 'It's her,' she said, her voice quivering. 'That's what she was wearing when she disappeared. But it can't be. She looks like she only just died.'

John stepped up to see. 'Is it a different child?'

Davie shook his head. 'This doesn't make any sense.' He looked at John, the two united in confusion. The sky darkened even more.

Karen stared at the girl's face. It looked like she was trying to speak. *Jesus Christ! Did she say thank you?* She blinked. *That's impossible.*

Outside, the sky was now black. What had been a very weak sunlight disc behind the cloud had disappeared altogether. Instinctively they all looked up.

A sound began. It was unlike anything that Karen had ever heard before, but if she could imagine what a banshee sounded like, it would be that. It was a loud piercing cry that seemed to carry on for minutes before subsiding. Clutching her ears, she walked away. There was a loud rumbling, and she felt tremors under their feet.

Everything went quiet. The diluted sun reappeared through the cloud and light was restored to the tent. As one, they turned back to look at the body. Whatever they thought they had seen was now a mass of crumbling dust mingled in old clothes.

'What did we just see?' Karen yelled.

John scratched his head. 'It's possible the body was preserved so carefully that until it was exposed to air, it maintained an appearance of integrity.'

'But her lips moved,' Karen said.

'I didn't see that.' John looked at Davie. He shook his head.

Karen began walking away. 'We've got to tell her. I'm going to see Peggy. She has to know.'

Davie began to walk towards her as if to stop her, but John grabbed his arm. 'Let her go. She's good at this.' They watched as she went to her car and drove off.

Davie turned to John. 'So are you sure it was normal, what we saw? Did we actually see it?'

'It was a fleeting glimpse. The light was poor, and the clothes still held the shape of the body.' John replied. 'And it's definitely not typical, but probably not impossible that the face would be clear enough to make out. I'm going to check out the science when I get the time and resources.'

Davie shook his head. 'Maybe Karen *wanted* to see something.'

'Karen? No, she goes on fact and occasionally intuition. I suspect it was just the beginning of the decomposition.'

'Aye,' Davie agreed. 'And what about yon man there?'

John turned to see Mr Binks walking round and round the body. 'He warned us not to open the body bag. I wonder if he knew what would happen?' He turned his head. 'Is that for us?' He pointed at a van coming their way.

'Aye. It'll be to pick her up. I'm so grateful to Karen for this you know. She'll be a local hero now.'

'She'll love that, I'm sure,' John managed a weak smile.

Davie went to meet the van driver. 'She's just there, you can see. Do you need a hand?'

'Not for such a wee one,' he replied. 'We'll have her sorted fast enough. Are you sure it's young Caitlin?'

'Aye. As sure as we can be. I'll let you get on.'

Davie went to join John and the workmen who had settled on the ground enjoying a smoke. 'We'll need to keep the spot open for a wee while longer,' he said. 'Just in case forensics think it's necessary.'

'Nae bother,' said one of the men. 'We'll be taking this big bugger back though.' He nodded at the digger.

Davie walked back towards the tent where Mr Binks was still pacing. 'Can I help you?'

'No, dear boy. I'm set to go, whenever you're ready. If you don't mind dropping me off at the hotel.'

'Aye, not at all. And are you coming with me, too?' He looked at John who had followed him.

'I'd like to go back with the body if you don't mind. It could be very instructive regarding the other victims. I'll catch up with you later.'

'As you wish. Mr B?'

'I'm ready. But there's somebody I'd like to talk to if you have no objections. Something and nothing. I'll let you know if I uncover anything useful. Hamish Broad. Would you mind giving me his address?'

***

Karen drove straight to see Peggy McFee. She was barely out of the car when Peggy opened the door.

'You've found my wee Caitlin. I know. I just know,' she said. Karen nodded and was immediately gripped in a bear hug by the weeping old lady. 'Can I see her?' she asked when the tears had subsided enough for her to talk.

'She's been dead a very long time,' Karen began. 'There's not much left to see.'

'Och, she's my wee lassie, I want tae see her.'

Karen nodded. 'There are procedures to go through. I'll ring you as soon as possible. I'm sorry, but I have to go back to England very soon, so it won't be me. It'll most likely be DI Davie Wallace. But I promise I'll come up again to see you.'

Peggy suddenly looked worried, 'And you're sure it's her?'

The vision of Caitlin swamped Karen's head. It was imprinted on her brain, but no one else would know what she had seen. *Would it help to tell her? Probably not.*

'The body I saw was wearing a blue dress with an orange cardigan. That's all I could make out. There's hardly anything left, just a few scraps. '

Peggy's tears began again. 'Aye, I knitted that cardie myself.'

'I'll ring you as soon as I know what's happening,' Karen said.

As soon as she was in the safety of her car, the emotion hit her. She struggled to hold back the tears. 'We've found Caitlin, Dad. We'll find Katherine for you too.'

51

In the late afternoon, Karen, John, and Davie were reunited in the back room at the police station. A delighted DCI Stewart congratulated them. 'Aye, lads and lass. That's a grand result but we can't celebrate and share the news until we have confirmation from the pathologist.'

'Understood,' Davie said. 'But in the absence of any other missing child, and given her attire, I'd say we're ninety-nine-point-nine-nine per cent there.'

'I attended the autopsy,' John said. 'It's definitely a six or seven-year-old female. They're running the DNA tests now.'

'And Mr Binks needs some thanks, too.' Karen added.

'Aye. How did he know the exact location?' DCI Stewart asked.

'He understands underground magnetic currents,' John said. 'But that's as much as I know.'

'But he couldnae be the murderer? Or associated with whoever murdered that poor lassie, could he?'

John looked aghast. 'He's a bookshop owner from Lincoln. I don't know how old he is. But he'd have been very young fifty years ago.'

'He has hidden depths,' Karen added. 'But nothing murderous, I'm sure. Anyway, we're nearly done here. You can always run some background checks to satisfy any potential questions.'

'Aye.' DCI Stewart nodded. 'The job's not finished till the paperwork's done.' He eyeballed Davie as he left the room.

'I'll pass on some details about Mr Binks,' John said to Davie. 'If I can find anything. He is a bit mysterious.'

'So that's your DCI sorted. I'd better speak to mine,' Karen said. 'But first I'm going to put Macy out of her misery.' She took out her phone. 'Hey, Macy.'

'Tell me.'

'Yes, we've found Caitlin McFee!'

At the other end of the phone, Macy whooped. 'And where have you been Karen? I've been trying to reach you for ages.'

Karen guiltily looked at all the missed calls stacked up on her phone. 'Sorry, Mace. Thanks for all your info; it was really helpful.'

'So you found Andrew Ferguson aka Fergus Anderson, did you? And his sons?'

Karen stalled. She'd been putting her weird experiences to the back of her mind, and this was no time to bring them out. 'We're concentrating on the girls for now, but we'll get the bastard if he's still around. Did you say sons?'

'Yes,' said Macy. Archie Logan and Donald Anderson. Did John not tell you?'

Karen looked at John. 'Did you know Ferguson had two sons? Archie Logan and Donald Anderson?' she repeated.

'Er...' John was interrupted by Davie.

'Yes, he did. He told me.'

'I did?' John looked perplexed.

Karen rolled her eyes and went back to her phone. 'Sorry, Mace. We've had quite a hectic couple of days. How's the guv?'

'Same as. Are you back tomorrow?'

'Definitely not until Monday. I hope. I'll ring him now. See you.' She threw John a look.

'I had a bang on the head,' he said.

'Aye. I did too,' Davie sneered.

'Never mind, we all know now. I'd better ring the guv.' She punched in his number.

'Karen.'

'Guv, we've found a body. One of the missing girls. Caitlin McFee in Scotland.'

'And I'm meant to be pleased with that, am I Karen?'

Yes you bloody well are! 'I thought you might be. We're close to solving the other two cases in England, too.'

'Report back, in person. First thing Monday,' DCI Winter snapped. 'We'll then discuss whether I can let you continue.'

'Right guv.' Karen put the phone down. 'Mean old bastard.'

'What's the matter?' John asked.

'Nothing,' Karen forced a smile. 'But I'm starving now.'

'I've got paperwork to finish, but I know a great Indian,' Davie said. He looked at John.

'Fine by me,' John replied.

'Good.' But as Davie left, his face showed he didn't mean it.

John looked at Karen. 'I have felt very strange recently. I think I must be coming down with something.'

'It doesn't matter. It hasn't delayed anything, and we'd have got there as we did just now. But it does mean we've got someone else to look for. How about you carry on with the maps, and I'll get Macy on it. Now I know Donald's hardly unusual up here... but two in one case?'

She grabbed her phone. 'Macy? Donald Anderson again. Can you check him out? We've got another Donald. McTear. I'm just wondering...'

'On it.' Macy replied. 'Actually, I already made enquiries.'

'Brilliant Mace. Talk soon.'

Davie returned to a tidied room and two happy faces.

'Here are all the things which might be of use to you,' Karen said. 'I've got everything else. And I guess it's all your case now.'

'Aye,' said Davie. 'But you're the one that made it happen. I'll make sure your name gets written big in dispatches.'

Karen smiled. 'Some appreciation for once. Oh, and Peggy McFee; I said I'd ring her.'

'Talk to her Karen. But it's my job now. Here, I'll call her.'

Davie made the call, handing the phone over to Karen. Peggy answered.

'Hello, Peggy, it's me, DS Thorpe. I came to see you...'

'Can I see her yet?' Peggy jumped in.

'Not yet,' said Karen. 'We haven't got the DNA results. Peggy, I *do* have to go home tomorrow. DI Wallace will be taking over. He's very nice. He'd like to talk to you.'

She handed the phone back to Davie and smiled as she heard his lovely soothing tone. *So lovely. Not like...Stop it.* She listened while Davie comforted the old lady.

'Where's this restaurant then?' Karen asked.

'It's near the hotel where John's staying,' Davie said, his voice back to normal. 'I can meet you both there if you like.'

52

Mr Binks drummed his fingers on the reception desk until the receptionist handed him his key. He went straight up to his room mumbling 'Too soon. What to do, what to do?' What had Charlie told him? *In his father's footsteps. Archibald Logan.*

He opened his suitcase, took out all his books, then arranged them chronologically on the bed. One after another he leafed through pages looking for certain passages. Some he read out loud, others he read in silence but moving his lips. Finally, he put the last book down and looked at his pocket watch. He frowned.

'Time is running out. I will just have to do what I can with what I already know for now and see if that has any effect.'

He tidied the books away and locked his suitcase. He left the hotel, but this time he put his room key in his pocket. He hailed a cab and gave the driver Hamish Broad's address. *We'll sort it between us, I'm sure.*

He composed himself in the cab. When it pulled up outside Hamish Broad's house, he calmly got out, paid the driver then marched up the drive and knocked on Hamish's door.

'Who the fuck are ye?' said Hamish.

'Oh, we will be acquainted very shortly,' Mr Binks replied. 'We have a common enemy, and I think you may be able to help me.'

Hamish frowned. 'Ye'd better come in,' he said.

'Thank you.' Mr Binks followed him in and sat down in the living room. 'I am looking for the man you knew as Fergus Anderson. Please tell me where he is, it will save us both a lot of time.'

'I've nae idea,' said Hamish. 'I ken ye've found the wee lassie's body. Young Davie rang me but I didnae ken it was anything tae dae with Fergus Anderson.'

'And I am sure he is a murderer,' said Mr Binks. 'And I believe that your nephew, Archibald, is also implicated. He couldn't have had anything to do with the original murders, he was too young. But he is, at the very least, an accessory in covering them up.'

Hamish looked at him in surprise. 'How d'ye ken about Archie?'

'You mean you thought you had destroyed the evidence, don't you, Mr Broad? Please do not try to hide anything from me. I am not the police, but I do have a very important interest in this case.'

Hamish took a deep breath. 'I dinnae ken it all. But I've an awful feeling in my old copper's guts that somebody I ken knows something.'

'You refer of course, to Donald McTear. Formerly called Donald Anderson do you not?'

'Ye ken about Donald too?'

Mr Binks nodded, registering the shock on Hamish's face.

'Who are ye, and what do ye ken?'

'My name is Mr Binks, and I am a keeper of maps.'

'Whit the fuck has that got tae dae with anything...' but as soon as the words left his mouth, Hamish began to realise what that meant. 'We should get Donald over here.' He said compliantly.

'Tell him to bring Archibald, too,' instructed Mr Binks.

Hamish gave him a strange look. There was no point in arguing. 'Aye.' He rang Donald McTear and did not try to hide the conversation from Mr Binks. 'Donald. Git yir arse over here. And bring Archie.'

Mr Binks listened. There seemed to be some resistance.

'Just do it,' Hamish growled.

'How far away does Donald live?' asked Mr Binks.

'Pah, and there's me thinking ye know everything.'

'Mere details,' Mr Binks retorted. 'I could find out easily enough.'

A couple of minutes later there was a knock at the door. Hamish answered it and brought Donald and Archie into the room.

'Who the fuck's this?' Donald glared at Mr Binks.

Mr Binks took time to study both men. Donald, late fifties, still with all his wits about him, but Archie, although a few years younger had no spark of life in him. He walked with a stoop

185

making him look much shorter than his frame suggested. He wore a beard, and his eyes were dull. He addressed Archie.

'My name is Mr Binks. I am seeking something which I believe is in the possession of your father, Fergus Anderson.'

'You what?' Donald looked at Hamish who nodding, dropped his head.

'Mr McTear, the police are on the trail, and I have no doubt that they will find your father, if he is still alive, and will want to question your half-brother.'

'Och, that's just rubbish. He wouldn't hurt a fly. You can see that for yourself.'

'Please, answer me this. Is it possible that Archibald went to England, about a year or so ago?'

'Aye, it's possible. He's not been with me long. But ever since I took him in, he's had no ounce of sense in him.'

'How did he find you?'

'That I never knew. He just said he was my brother and had nowhere else to go. I knew him at once from the old man and I had the spare room.'

'Did you never try to find out where he came from?'

'From what I can gather, he's been a vagrant all his adult life.'

'Archie,' said Mr Binks, summoning up as much authority as he could. 'I want you to listen to me. This is very important. I need to find your father. Do you understand me?'

Archie turned to look at Mr Binks with glazed eyes. *This is going to take a while,* thought Mr Binks, *I'll have to get the manuals after all.*

53

Karen and John were waiting for Davie in the hotel restaurant. 'Are you sure you didn't hear a scream?' Karen said. 'It was piercing.'

'Where's Mr Binks got to?' John deftly changed the subject, almost immediately regretting his choice of subject matter.

'He's up to something, I can sense it,' Karen said. 'I wish he'd tell me what. I worry about him.'

'He'll be fine,' John sighed. 'Anyway, he's done his bit now. He can do what he likes.'

'I suppose. Ah, there's Davie.' She waved at him across the restaurant. 'What do you think about Mr Binks,' she said as he joined them.

'He's a strange wee man,' Davie said as he sat down. 'But I like him. I can't believe he's a murderer.'

'Me too,' Karen said. 'So. Back to business. This is a farewell dinner as well as a celebration.'

Davie looked thoughtful. 'Aye, of course. It's only been a couple of days, but it's felt like weeks.'

'It really has,' Karen agreed.

'For me, too,' John said to make his presence noticed.

'But what about the other cases?' said Davie. 'You'll have to see them through now.'

'Only if I can convince the guv,' Karen said. 'I'm sure he'll let me finish up, or at least put the wheels in motion. But I think it's not going to be so simple in York and Lincoln. Here, it was easy, just a road. There, well, there are new houses built all over the place. It could cause massive disruption, and the locals may not be so engaged as they are up here. Whatever, I can't see it happening quickly.'

'Aye,' Davie said. 'I hadn't thought about it like that.'

The waiter came and took their order and a few minutes later they were chinking glasses of red wine.

'Here's to the three of us.' Karen made the toast.

'Here's to the best-goddamned sergeant in the force,' said John. Karen and Davie looked at him.

'Er, OK. To the both of you then.' Karen and Davie laughed.

The good news of the day, helped by the wine, carried them through the meal, and for a while, there was no awkwardness between them.

'Och, and it's confirmed that the bairn was in an army issue body bag. So it was definitely a soldier – or someone with a strong connection to the army. My money's still on Anderson. We know he was killed in action so we'll never get the bastard, but we also know he has two sons, and I bet one of them knows something. I'll be speaking to Donald McTear, don't you worry.'

Karen registered what he said. It was bringing back fleeting recollections of something. But, as Mr Binks had said, it was probably down to the drugs she'd been given. It reminded her that she'd not mentioned the shooting. But now she was away from him, she wondered at the sense of that. She was jolted out of her thoughts by John.

'And I should be getting some useful evidence from Dr Moore. That will help the next two cases,' John said.

Karen's mind switched to focusing on the next day. 'We need to find this Charlie Worthington bloke,' she said. 'And update Stanley Briggs.'

'Let's just enjoy the evening for now,' said John. 'We can talk about it tomorrow.'

Karen was astonished. 'You? Not wanting to talk shop? Don't be silly.' She carried on. 'Then we'll have to head down to Lincoln. But not via your parents. Shit! Mr Binks. We still don't know where he is.'

John sighed. 'He'll turn up, he always does.'

'But we've got to find him soon...'

'Karen, will you please just shut up? Do we really have to do this now?' *What did he say?*

'Yes we do, you moron. We both have our cars, and you'll need to bring Mr Binks back with you.'

'Oh,' said John, turning crimson. 'You're right.'

Any remnants of good mood soon dissipated. The rest of their meal was eaten in silence – apart from necessary table behaviour. When they'd finished, Davie called for the tab.

'On me,' he said.

'Are you sure?' said John.

'Absolutely. The boss is pleased with me; I might be able to wangle it on my expenses. It's not a huge bill.'

Karen looked round awkwardly at John. *He's squirming now*. 'My stuff's still at Davie's,' she said.

John looked too uncomfortable to say anything. He looked at Davie and twitched his head sideways.

'Are you all right, John?' said Davie.

'I'd like to speak to Karen,' he replied.

'Ah, I get it,' said Davie. 'A domestic. I'll be off to use the facilities then.'

When Davie had gone, John looked at Karen. 'Are we OK, Karen? Because...'

'Your turn to shut up, John,' Karen said. 'This has been the strangest couple of weeks of my life. I just want to get things back to normal as soon as possible.'

John smiled at her nervously. 'Are you staying at mine tonight then?'

Karen laughed; not one of her generous hearty laughs but still a laugh. 'Yes. I'd like nothing better than to have a proper night's sleep in a proper bed in a place not surrounded by ghosts.'

John smiled so widely Karen thought his face might crack. 'I love you, Karen Thorpe,' he said. Karen smiled back at him but didn't reciprocate.

When Davie returned, he'd already settled the bill. 'I'll run you there and back here, Karen, if you like. Save us taking two cars. And I had only the one glass.'

'Thanks, Davie. That makes sense.' She turned to John. 'See you back at the hotel then. Is there a bar or something?'

'Yes. Don't be long,' he added.

Karen followed Davie to his car, and they drove back to his cottage in silence. When they got there, Karen opened the front door and gave Davie his keys back.

'I'll just be a minute,' she said and ran up the stairs to get her things. It didn't take long, there wasn't much anyway. She stood and stared at the little room with mixed emotions, then took her bag and went downstairs. Davie was waiting for her. He was silent at first. *He's going to say something he'll regret.* Karen thought. She could almost see something travel up his body. Then it burst out of his mouth.

'Stay with me, Karen.' He walked up to her and hugged her tight. She dropped her bag, and he kissed her passionately. *John's not like this. This passion. I like it. It's doing things to me.*

When the kiss finished she was as confused as she ever had been about anything. But Karen restored herself to pre-Davie settings. *Don't be stupid. If you can't deal with it, walk away.*

'I have to go back, Davie,' she said finally.

54

Karen and Davie arrived back at the hotel precisely the same time as Mr Binks arrived in his taxi. John appeared seconds later. The four of them stood there in silence until Mr Binks spoke.

'I shall be staying in Edinburgh just a while longer,' he said. 'John, may I ask that you also stay one more day, please? There are things I need to bring to a conclusion. I promise you it will be in all our interests for you to do so.'

'Oh,' said John, looking at Karen.

'I don't mind,' Karen said. 'We wouldn't have found Caitlin without Mr Binks' help so you should stay and help him.'

Mr Binks gave a little bow to Karen. 'I have said all I need to say, John. I bid you goodnight.'

'Goodnight, Mr Binks. See you in the morning then?' Mr Binks had already gone inside the hotel.

'What was that about?' said Davie. 'What's he staying for?'

'I expect he's looking for a book,' John said.

'A book? Yes, I remember,' Karen nodded. 'We've still got the other cases to solve. We need him back soon.'

John stood a little taller now. This was as clear a separation from Davie as he could possibly have wished for. 'I'll talk to him later,' he said confidently. He looked at Karen. 'There are a couple of things I'd like to talk about.'

Davie took his cue. 'OK guys. I'll leave you to your investigation. Good luck, Karen. I hope you keep in touch.'

'Let me know when Caitlin's funeral is. I'd like to be there.'

'Me, too,' said John just slightly too late.

'Och, I'll let you both know,' Davie put on a grin. 'Hopefully, the DNA tests will be out tomorrow.' He gave Karen a peck on the cheek and shook John's hand before going to his car.

***

Karen and John sat on stools in the small bar. John ordered more wine while Karen sat thinking.

191

'Don't you ever switch off?' John said.

'Don't be silly. I'm just thinking it through. Tomorrow I'll be miles away, but Davie still has to carry on the investigation into Ferguson.'

'And?'

'Damn,' she said. 'If Archie *is* his son, and he was the man in the clip, does Davie have a copy of that image? It might be useful. I'd love to know for sure if he was connected to Dad's death.'

'That's a good question,' John replied. 'But it's on my laptop.' He fumbled in his bag while Karen knocked back more wine.

'File not found,' he said, looking puzzled. 'You've got it haven't you?'

Karen frowned and pulled out her tablet from one of her bags. She searched her files and then her emails. 'That's weird. There's nothing resembling it here,' she said. 'And the emails are all missing, too. How could that happen?'

John shrugged. 'Some sort of date reactive coding I'd guess.'

Karen nodded. 'I'm sure I can get it from Jack in the morning if need be. Hey, we've got an image of Ferguson himself from the book. That's better than nothing.'

'Well remembered. Yes, I can send him that tomorrow.'

'Send it to me, too,' Karen said. And watch Mr Binks will you?' Karen said. 'It's strange, but I'm beginning to feel less sure about him now.'

'Why's that?'

Do I tell him what happened? Karen wavered until a massive yawn took over her body and forced itself out through her mouth. *Think about it tomorrow.*

'Let's leave it for now. I am actually knackered.' Karen knocked down the rest of her wine. 'By the way, where am I sleeping tonight? I didn't even think about it.'

'All sorted,' said John. 'It's not much more for two, and they've already put extra towels in the room.'

Karen laughed. 'Thank god for that then! Show me the way.'

John signed the bar tab and carried one of Karen's bags up to the room.

'Not bad,' Karen looked around, her eyes resting on the double bed. 'That looks comfortable. Better than Davie's sofa bed. I need a good night's sleep.' *There. Two birds with one stone. No, I didn't sleep with Davie, and no I'm not going to have sex with you either John.*

John too was tired and didn't need Karen's signalling. He avoided physical contact with her and when he got into bed, he turned his back to her. Almost instantly he began to snore.

Karen lay on her back thinking. She had a decision to make. Or a decision about a decision.

John and I are a team, doing different things. Complementary.

Davie and I are too similar. We couldn't work together; we'd fight the whole time.

John is clean and tidy and makes up for me being a slob.

Davie is a slob, too. We can be slobby together without feeling guilty. But think of the mess.

John is so sweet and caring.

Davie is so bloody sexy. Who knew?

At last, falling into that nether land between wakefulness and sleep, she had a visitor. A little girl.

'You're Karen the great detective,' Caitlin said to her, a big grin on her face. 'And all boys are horrid.'

'You're so right,' said Karen out loud as she finally drifted off into sleep.

55

Friday 15 November.

Mr Binks had risen early, breakfasted, and gone back to the old bookshop. The owner was happy to help in his quest, and the two men spent a few hours huddled over various books. Eventually, the bookseller spoke.

'I think that's the best we can do here,' he said. 'It has to be worth a go. If not, then you really do need to pull out that compulsion incantation. I've never seen it, but I know it's in the ancient opus. Alternatively, you may need to speak to Magda.'

Mr Binks shuddered at the name. 'It may come to that. But I do believe my aunt had the opus or a transcription of it. I just don't know if it was complete. I'll check before I consult Magda.'

'Aye, wise enough,' came the reply.

'Thank you so much for your time. I do hope I don't need to disturb you again, but it has been an absolute pleasure meeting you. You must come and visit me, whether you need to or not.'

The bookseller beamed at him. 'Aye. You're a true gentleman. I'll not say goodbye then, but till we meet again.'

The two men shook hands, and Mr Binks left the shop with almost a smile on his face. He would be better prepared now, *but is it enough*? He looked at his pocket watch, it was two o'clock. *Gracious* he thought to himself. *It's past lunchtime. I'd better find something to eat.* He strolled along the streets and back streets until he came to an old-fashioned tea shop with luscious looking sandwiches and cakes. 'Perfect,' he said out loud as he entered the shop smiling.

***

When John woke at ten the next morning, Karen had already gone but he found her text on his phone.
```
Sorry John, you looked so peaceful. See you
soon. K xx
```

Kisses? That's a good sign, isn't it? John got up relatively cheerfully until he remembered something. *I have to spend the day with Mr Binks again.* But when he was on his way to the restaurant the receptionist called out to him.

'Mr Steele? Your friend Mr Binks left a message for you.'

John walked up to her and took the proffered note.

'Dear boy. Amuse yourself until three o'clock precisely. I will be back then.'

I wonder what he's up to now? But the less time I spend with him the better 'Any chance of breakfast?' he asked the receptionist. She shook her head.

'Oh well, I'll go out for brunch then. Can you suggest anywhere?'

She winked at him. 'Aye, there's a nice place round the corner. Wee Jock's. They do an all-day haggis breakfast. Especially for visitors.'

'Sounds great,' said John, the humour bypassing his brain. He left the hotel. *I hope they have Starbucks up here.*

Reinvigorated by coffee, John headed for the mortuary to check on Dr Moore's progress. 'Good morning. How are you getting on?'

'Hello again, John. Very good progress. We have definitely identified Caitlin McFee.'

'Oh, that's good. And her family?'

'Yes, young Davie's on his way to see her mother. And I might have a little gem or two for you.'

'The killer's DNA?' John asked hopefully.

'Aye. We've definitely got traces from the bag. He was clearly careful, but of course, DNA was a world away in those days. Is there a suspect?'

'There is. Unfortunately, we think he died years ago. But there are two sons – if we can ever trace them.'

'That would be a good match. Keep me posted.'

'It'll be Davie Wallace, not me.' John clarified. 'I'll be heading back down south. Here.' He took out a card. 'Please email me anything you find, anything at all that might be of use. I've got access to some pretty good databases, too.'

'I will.'

John didn't have to think hard about what to do for the intervening time until he met up with Mr Binks. He was happy to spend time walking the white-walled streets of Edinburgh. His mind was still full of Karen. The more time he spent with her the more he loved her, but he was sure she didn't feel the same – and he didn't have a clue what to do about it. He looked at his watch. It was two forty-five. *What? It can't be! Mr Binks!* He ran back to the hotel as fast as he could.

***

Karen had a habit of bolting – but this time she had two good reasons – the second being that she wanted to get to York in time to catch Stanley Briggs at the local newspaper. *I have to find this Charlie Worthington before I run out of time*. By three o'clock she had made it to the Newspaper office.

'Stanley Briggs?' she said looking around. 'It's Karen Thorpe again.'

Stanley's head appeared from behind a screen. 'Well I never, lass. You look like the cat that's got the cream. You've got news, I take it.'

'Masses,' she said. 'Got any coffee?'

'Aye.'

Karen sat on a visitors' chair and looked around the office while she waited. No scoops, nothing major on his desk that she could see. *I'll make his day soon, I'm sure. Actually, I'll make his year.*

Stanley came back with two cups of coffee and sat at this desk. 'Out with it then.'

'I can't remember where we'd got to when I was last here, but we found a connection. The tall bearded man. He was mentioned in all the original cases. We think we know who he was, and we're almost certain he was the murderer.'

'You don't say,' Stanley's mouth dropped open.

'There's more,' said Karen, getting into the mood. 'We've actually found one of his victims. We've found her body, Stanley; another little girl just like Katherine.'

'Well I'll be fucked backwards!' Stanley said, swiftly followed by 'Sorry lass. Who is it?'

Karen stifled her giggles. 'It's a man called Fergus Anderson. He was a walker; ex-army and the girl was found in an army body bag.'

'So where is he now?'

'Missing, presumed killed in action in 1967. I'm sure that he suffocated the girls then carried them off in his rucksack.'

'The man, like a snail?' Mused Stanley. 'Why the heck didn't anybody think to search him?'

'Why would they?' said Karen. 'He was in full view and apparently kind and helpful. And the body was in a tough old army bag. There'd be no smell, nothing even a dog could detect.'

'What a rum do. Have papers got th'story yet?'

'No. It's early days. I'm telling you off the record. They still have to do the formal ID procedures.'

'Aye,' agreed Stanley.

'But it's given us a clue as to where Katherine's body is,' Karen added. 'I've got some maps, but you mentioned a man, Charlie Worthington. I think he might be able to help us pinpoint it. Do you know where I can see him?'

'Now, that I can. He's always in the pub on a Friday afternoon. We'll catch him soon. I take it you want me with you?'

'Yes, please,' said Karen. 'He won't know me at all. Better if someone he knows is there.'

'Aye,' said Stanley. 'Let's be going then.'

197

56

Charlie Worthington had already had a pint or two before Karen and Stanley reached him. Karen tactfully moved his half-full glass aside so she could spread out the maps while Stanley explained who she was.

'You told Stanley about the witches' path, I understand,' Karen said, looking intently at him. 'And that it had something to do with Katherine Engles' disappearance.'

'Aye,' Charlie went to reach for his pint.

'When you've told us what we need to know,' said Stanley, moving the glass to the end of the table.

Karen took out the rough map that her father had drawn. 'Does this mean anything to you, Charlie?'

Charlie's eyes widened but his response did not match his eyes. 'Nay. Never seen owt like that round here.'

'Charlie,' Stanley moved closer to him. 'That's a lie, isn't it?'

'But that chap were here t'other day. He told me...'

'What chap?' Karen was on alert. Stanley raised his hand in a stop gesture.

'Never mind him, Charlie. We need to know.'

'And I need my pint.'

Karen sighed and stood up to get his glass.

Stanley whispered in Charlie's ear. 'If you don't tell th'lass what you know, I promise I'll leak every little misdemeanour you've ever committed to th'paper. There'll not be a shop or a pub that'll let you in when I've finished wi' you.'

Charlie sat up and looked at Stanley in shock. 'But that other chap. He were a right scary bloke. He could curse me.'

Karen was all ears. *Mr Binks?* Karen wondered. *He's said Charlie had told him about a book.*

'Charlie, I promise you, I will be far scarier than you can ever imagine if you don't help us out here.' Stanley growled. 'Imagine no more beer, ever.'

Charlie gulped. 'Pr'aps I was wrong' he said pointing at the hand-drawn map. 'This here could be Pig Lane as was. All gone now see, but it weren't when yon lass disappeared.'

'And where was the witches' path?' Karen was now animated.

'Well, it were here,' said Charlie pointing. 'It crossed Pig lane right there. It were difficult enough to find at the best of times. But can't be done now there's all houses there now.'

Charlie began supping at his pint, and his eyes began to glaze over a little. Karen pulled out the new map and for the first time in ages, she wished John had been there. *He's so good at this sort of thing. So patient.* Trying to compare these two maps of different scales with completely different contents was almost impossible. The Scottish maps were much simpler.

Stanley looked at Karen. 'Have you not got a map from 1965?' he said.

'Yes, of course I bloody well have,' she said, banging the side of her head with her hand. She rummaged through her bag and pulled it out. 'OK, if we compare this one,' she placed her father's drawing over the map, 'with this, let's see.'

Stanley and Charlie both stood to look at it. 'Ey. That be Pig Lane there,' Charlie said pointing then falling back into his chair.

'Yes,' said Stanley. 'So we're looking for something here.' He looked at Karen. 'Can I mark this?' She nodded.

Stanley put a small cross on the map. 'Now lass, all we've got to do is find some permanent landmarks which cross both maps. See that church there. And look, yon school here. Almost in a line with the cross.'

Karen was getting excited. 'Yes, that's one coordinate,' she said. 'Any others?'

Stanley scratched his head. 'Ey, we want summat at ninety degrees ideally.' He said looking at the map. 'That crossroads there is still around. And look, the war memorial is there. Not quite right angles but close enough.'

Karen pulled out the new map and her eyes scanned the details. 'Here. Here's the church and the school' she looked around. 'Damn. No ruler. Do you think they'll have one at the bar?'

199

Stanley smiled. 'Not likely, but they'll have menus. Long tall thin ones.' He looked at Charlie who had sunk further back in his chair. 'I'll go.' He went to the dining area of the pub returning with the newest unused menu he could find. He placed it on the map and began to draw a line taking two attempts with a good overlap to make sure it was as straight as possible. While he drew, Karen was looking for the other landmarks.

'Here,' she said. 'And here.'

Stanley drew the line again as carefully as he could until it crossed the other.

'Briary Estate,' he said. 'But look. If we're right, that 'X', it might just miss houses. It might just be in a backyard.'

Karen sighed. 'This is where we need Mr Binks,' she said. At that Charlie's eyes opened, he sat up, stood up then waddled out of the pub as fast as his legs would take him.

'I knew it,' Karen said. 'He's met Mr Binks before. But why is he scared?'

'Can't help you there. What do you want to do now?' Stanley continued. 'We've damned near pinned it down. We need to get things moving.'

Karen sat back in her chair. 'I don't know,' she said. 'My contact name was Brian Appleby.'

'Leave it with me lass,' said Stanley. 'I'll do some stirring up.'

'I had one of his files. In the car.' Karen charged outside to the car park and returned with the envelope Mrs Appleby had given her. She tipped out the contents. 'Can you get hold of Elsie, Katherine's sister?'

'I can try.'

'And I can give you a photo of Fergus Anderson.'

'Aye. I'll get on to Old Mrs Engles. See if we can't get her daughter on Skype to identify him. Can you give me the picture then? Here's my email.'

Karen took out her tablet and emailed the picture. She thought for a moment. 'I'm running out of time, and we've only found the one girl.'

'Best thing you can do is prove you've found the Scottish lass and that it were that chap that killed the poor mite.'

'But we have to find his relatives first. To match the DNA.' She slumped in her chair.

'Ey, lass, you must be worn out.'

'I hadn't thought past today. I don't know what to do next. I don't know what I can do. Without enough evidence, we're not going to be able to dig up anywhere,'

'Ee, I can't help you there,' said Stanley kindly. 'Where's home?'

'Way down south.' She looked at her watch. It was four o'clock. She suddenly had a terrible yearning to be back in her pokey little flat. 'Home it is then,' she decided. 'Thanks so much, Stanley. The copper in Scotland is a good one. Davie Wallace. I'll make sure he keeps you posted. Then we'll need Mr Binks and his detector machine up here to pinpoint where the body is. If it's only in a backyard, that would be great. But life's never that easy, is it?'

'Nay, lass,' said Stanley. 'Safe journey. And I'll be in touch.'

57

'Where are we going Mr Binks?' puffed John as he arrived back at the hotel.

Mr Binks put away his pocket watch. 'Ah, dear boy. I will direct you.'

They walked to John's car and got in.

'Now, John,' Mr Binks said carefully and slowly. 'I'm going to meet somebody you've never met before. You don't need to say anything; all you need to do is to drive us wherever I tell you. Do you understand?'

'Yes, Mr Binks,' John replied mechanically. When he pulled up outside Donald McTear's house, Mr Binks spoke again.

'We're here now, John. Please wait in the car. I won't be long.'

Donald opened the front door and looked suspiciously at John, sitting in the car.

'Och, who's that bugger?'

'Never you mind, Donald. He's only the driver.'

'You'd better come in,' Donald stepped back.

'And where is Archie? I need to talk to him on my own this time.'

'He's upstairs in his pit. You're welcome to go up. Second on the right.'

Mr Binks went to the door and knocked lightly.

'Who's that?' said a flat voice.

'It's Mr Binks. I need to talk to you again.'

'Come in,' said the voice. Mr Binks opened the door. Stretched out on the bed was Archie Logan.

'Och, it's you,' he said sitting up. 'What do you want?'

'I need to see your father.'

'But I don't know where he is.'

'Oh, I think you do', said Mr Binks. 'And there are a few things I can ask you which will help you to tell me.'

'Do what you like,' said Archie.

'This time I think you will tell me,' said Mr Binks. He began to mutter strange words which Archie appeared not to notice. He tried a different order, he tried different words. He changed the order again; he changed the intonation and different sequences over and over again but nothing seemed to be getting through. After two hours he gave up with a sigh. 'That'll be all, Archie,' he said finally and went downstairs again where Donald was watching football.

'Tell me, Donald,' began Mr Binks again in a slow and deliberate manner. 'Does Archie still go out at night?'

'Aye,' Donald replied.

'And does he take food with him?'

'Aye,' said Donald again.

'And what time does he go out?' said Mr Binks.

'Eight o'clock. Regular as clockwork. I think he goes and sits somewhere on his own.'

Mr Binks looked at his pocket watch; it was only six pm.

'Is there anywhere to eat around here?' he asked.

'Aye. There's a pub round the corner of the block. On the right.'

'Thank you Donald. I will say goodbye for now.'

***

'We're going to have dinner now, John,' Mr Binks said as he got back in the now freezing car. 'Put the heater on, will you? It's not far but let's take the car anyway. It's chilly out there.'

'Yes, Mr Binks.' As instructed, John pulled up in the car park of The Thistle. When they went inside, Mr Binks ordered coffee and meals of steak and chips for both of them. It was easy for Mr Binks to make their dinner stretch for a couple of hours, and John seemed not to care one jot. He was in his own little world.

'Now, John, listen carefully.' Mr Binks walked with him to the car. 'There is a man in that house we were just in who is going to show us where a bad man lives. We must follow him, John. You are younger and fitter than I am. If I cannot keep up you must follow him all the way, but not let him see you.' John nodded. 'Do you have your mobile telephone with you?'

John nodded again. 'He will be finding the entrance to a cave, John. If he finds it and I am not there, you must film what he does for me. Do you understand?'

'Yes, Mr Binks.'

'Now then John, it is nearly time. Keep back and we will see where he goes.'

It was a very dark night. If the moon was there, it was well hidden. At eight o'clock precisely, Donald McTear's front door opened and Archie Logan appeared. He was holding a carrier bag and stared straight ahead. He turned right out of the front door, then right again onto a dirt track behind the row of houses. The track led into some fields with woodland further ahead. He walked slowly and methodically, and at first, both John and Mr Binks were able to keep up with him. When the track ran out and they found themselves walking on long grass it was harder going, and Mr Binks began to fall behind.

'Remember what I said, John,' he whispered.

'Yes, Mr Binks' John replied.

On and on they walked. Mr Binks now was way behind but John still doggedly followed until he came to a wooded rocky area. Archie stopped and raised his hands to the sky. Remembering his instructions, John took out his phone and began to record. John heard another voice say some words he did not recognise. A moment later Archie had disappeared. John looked around, confused. He waited and finally, a panting Mr Binks caught up with him.

'What happened John? Where did he go?'

John shrugged his shoulders and showed him what he had recorded. Mr Binks took the phone and watched the recording. His lips moved as he committed the strange words to memory. Then deleting John's film, he walked up to the spot where Archie had disappeared. He took out his current detector, studied it for a moment then turned round.

'Thank you, John,' he said. 'We must go home now.'

58

Saturday 16 November

Mr Binks woke early. Sleep had not settled his mind. He knew what had to be done but he simply wasn't skilled enough. *I must get that ancient opus, but I must take preventative action before all is lost.* He sat in his hotel room and started drawing a chart as he often did to help him sort out his thoughts. It was very similar to what logicians refer to as a critical path, but it was taught to him by his aunt long ago as a decision-making tool, which he adopted almost as his life path guidance in everything he did.

When it was finished, he sat back with a sigh. The results were clear; he would have to go back to Lincoln. He had already told John to prepare for a journey early that morning. All that was left to do was to rise properly and enjoy a hearty breakfast.

***

John had slept fitfully. Once again his brain had been muddled, and he was in a state of extreme confusion. At one point he woke, remembering something being filmed on his phone. But when he looked there was nothing on it.

He shook himself properly awake then looked round to see the time. It was seven o'clock and he'd promised to see Mr Binks at breakfast for seven-thirty. He hauled himself into the shower and felt the water beginning to work, refreshing him and washing away the dregs of his bad dreams. By the time he was dressed and downstairs in the reception area, he almost felt normal.

'Good morning, Mr Binks,' he said. 'Where to today?'
'Good morning, John. We should head home I think.'
'Not York then?' John frowned. 'Karen...' he began.
'Oh, I expect Karen will have already left York. Ring her, why don't you. After breakfast.'
'Yes,' said John, 'I will. Mr Binks?'
'Yes, John?'

'What did we do yesterday evening?'

'Gracious, dear boy. Have you forgotten already? We went out for a rather nice steak supper.'

'Ah, yes. I remember now,' John scratched his head.

Breakfast was about to become the usual regimented routine, so John ordered a coffee then asked for a continental breakfast. It was Saturday and he was sure his mother would fill him up at lunchtime. He shovelled everything down at a rate of knots, then made his excuses and left Mr Binks still enjoying his meal.

In reception, he was surprised to find Mr Binks had already settled up.

'Has he? OK. Thanks,' was John's astonished reply. *Why did he do that? There was nothing in it for him, was there?*

He bounded along the corridor and went into his room bundling everything in his rucksack. It was just past eight. *Too early to ring Karen?* He rang his mother instead.

'Hi, Mum. It's me. I'm coming back today, any chance of a late lunch? I'm not sure of Karen's movements yet.'

'Karen?' said his mother. 'I'm sure I can manage something.'

When he rang Karen, she answered almost immediately.

'Hi. I'm just about to leave Edinburgh to head home. More importantly, where are you?'

'Home,' said Karen. 'I needed to recharge a bit. Touch base. But I'm feeling great now.'

'I thought you were going to York?'

'I did. Got a lot sorted too,' Karen replied. 'But it's Saturday. I need to plan my next two days and get ready for a fight.'

'Oh, you're good at that. What happened in York then?'

'Finally got to meet Charlie Worthington, and we've got a very good idea of where Katherine's body might be.'

John stalled. *That name again. Why can't I remember it properly?* 'I was hoping you'd come to Lincoln on your way down from York. Lunch with Mummy and Daddy.' *She's gone quiet.*

'Tell me, John, who did you ring first? Me or your mother?'

'You, of course,' John lied. 'OK. I had to make sure it was all right with her. You could still come here. Amy Warren?'

'I'll think about it,' said Karen. 'The Katherine Engles case looks like it might be easier and quicker now. We might need Mr Binks again to pinpoint the grave. But it could be in a back garden, so it would be relatively easy to dig up.'

'I could come home too,' John said hopefully. 'I don't have to go back on Monday, either.'

'See how it goes,' said Karen. 'Is Mr Binks back with you?'

'OK,' said John sadly. 'Yes, we're just about to set off.'

When John's car boot was loaded he turned to Mr Binks.

'Are we ready then?' said John.

'Oh yes indeed,' said Mr Binks.

Mr Binks seemed to be back to his normal chatty self. The journey was spent regaling John with tales of journeys and footpaths of far-off climes and all sorts of places he wanted to see but knew he probably couldn't because he had problems with his eardrums and could never risk flying in an aeroplane.

'Besides,' he told a rather disinterested John, 'reading about travel is far better and much less expensive without all the side effects, tummy issues, and timing problems. Which reminds me. Stop at the next service station, will you please?'

They arrived back in Lincoln at two o'clock precisely. John resisted an urge to invite Mr Binks for lunch, but in any case, he seemed very keen to be getting back to his home. Before they'd quite arrived at his shop, John mentioned Karen's words to him.

'Karen said we'll probably need your help to track the bodies,' he said. 'They know roughly where they think Katherine Engles' body is but it's in a built-up area, so if you could pinpoint it...'

Mr Binks tutted. 'I don't know what you think I can do,' he said to John. 'I'm just an ordinary man of books and maps.'

'But...' John began. Too late, Mr Binks was out of the car and waiting by the boot for his suitcase. 'I'm sorry, John. I have too many other pressures now. You'll have to manage without me.'

What? After coming so far?

John handed him the suitcase. 'Thanks anyway Mr Binks. And thanks for settling the bill.'

Mr Binks looked at him strangely. 'Did I? Call it automobile fuel money.' He quickly disappeared through the shop door.

John's father opened the door as soon as John's car pulled up. 'Just in time, John,' he said.

John smelled the air. 'Fish and chips,' he said. 'Perfect.'

59

Mr Binks had not wasted a second coming back. Even his ever-expectant tummy was ignored. He'd gone straight into his house the back way, upstairs onto the landing, and was looking thoughtfully at the attic door. *If the transcript of the ancient opus was anywhere, it will be in Aunt Hermione's old travelling trunk. And it's either that or Magda.* He shuddered as he pulled down the loft ladder. Luckily, he'd had a light fitted a few years earlier. He mumbled some ancient words of gratitude when it worked.

It was a big and extremely dusty loft. Hermione Karnstein's trunk was right at the back near a wall to ensure it was properly supported. He approached the fabulously embellished wooden trunk with awe. His aunt had told him it used to belong to a pirate king. The original fastening was long gone and, being practical, he had affixed a modern padlock instead. He scrabbled for the key under his shirt; it never left the chain around his neck.

Gingerly, he unlocked it and with some effort, heaved up the lid of the old trunk displacing so much dust it made him choke. When the clouds had settled, Mr Binks took a deep breath and began very carefully to take out the items in the trunk. There were all sorts of artefacts mainly from Africa and India; a shrunken head, an elephant's foot, some strange carved creatures... but right at the bottom of the trunk was an old leather folder. Hermione's personal secret writings. He moved closer to the trap door where the light was better.

Slowly he looked at each page of her notebooks, his heart rate increasing at every turn of the page. He got to the very last book. It was dated the third of June 1966. That was three days before she died and was, like all her notes, in Latin. He turned each page, scanning them until he reached about halfway in. There was a transcript headed Vetus Veneficus OPUS. His heart was now beating faster than he thought possible. *This is it!*

He read each page, incantation by incantation. Finally, he found one headed Specus Porta. But he shook his head. Something didn't feel right. The rest of the pages were too close, undisturbed. He read what was written but it was a prelude, not the incantation. He turned the next page over and realised his worst fears. It was blank. 'Oh, Auntie! How could you do this?'

In a quite unusual display of abandonment, he went back down the loft ladder as fast as he could without even closing the hatch. He almost ran down the stairs and back into his shop. There he collected a local map which he unfolded and studied briefly. He looked at his pocket watch then nodded to himself. He picked up a telephone and ordered a minicab. 'To the Robin Estate as soon as possible please,' he said. 'Binks' Books,' He made his preparations then waited for the cab.

Mr Binks sat twiddling his thumbs the whole way there. When he arrived he spoke to the driver. 'Please wait there. I won't be long.' He took out his magnet device and began pacing around the estate, gradually homing in on one particular house. He knocked on the door. A young woman answered.

'Sorry, we're atheists,' she said.

'How perfectly apt,' Mr Binks replied with his most charming smile. 'So am I. I wonder if I may have a quick word with you?'

The woman looked back at him blankly. 'Of course. Please come in.' She was just as blank when he left.

'Goodbye, and thank you,' he said. 'Remember, nothing must be disturbed.'

'I will,' she replied, shaking her head in confusion.

An hour later Mr Binks had repacked his suitcase and taken another taxi to the station. He looked at his pocket watch while he sat in the back of the taxi. *If I got there in time for the quarter past three, I could be up in Penrith by eight thirty-five.* He arrived at the station in plenty of time to purchase his one-way ticket.

It wasn't a straightforward journey; he had to make three changes which meant at each one he had to pack away all his reading material. By the time he got the last connection, which was also the last train of the day, it was so crowded it wasn't worth opening his suitcase. Thankfully he had assuaged his appetite earlier while waiting at the intervening stations. *No point hurrying. I don't even know if she'll see me. I have to get the question absolutely perfectly correct first and I need help for that.*

At Penrith, he headed straight for the nearest B&B and checked in, ignoring the conversational niceties and asking to be shown directly to his room. There he unpacked. *Concentrate Binks. Your very survival depends on this.*

The instructions were very old and cryptic. His aunt had translated them herself, and he read them out loud.

'If Magda your needs must consult
Find red ring'd stones of her cult.
Go there when the god moon is slight
And the day be half of the night.
Your question must be good and true
If willing, she will come to you.'

Mr Binks tutted to himself. *You are an idiot Binks. That day will not be until the first minute of the twenty-third. And that's next week.*

'I wonder. I have to go to visit Long Meg and her Daughters anyway. There's no harm in having a look.' *After all, the rules were written a very long time ago and surely it wasn't only two days a year? But are you prepared, Binks?*

He steadied himself and looked at himself in the mirror. *Slightly portly but of good stock* he thought to himself. But he wasn't *really* of the blood. Would he even pass muster? And he didn't have his question properly formulated yet. *But I am sure and true of purpose.* And that would have to be good enough for her, he decided. He went downstairs and summoned a taxi from the receptionist.

'Where are you going?' she asked out of politeness. 'It's a bit cold and damp out there.'

'Long Meg and her Daughters,' Mr Binks replied.

'Thank you, sir. I'll call you a cab.' She disappeared into a small back room and rang a number. Mr Binks, whose hearing was exceptional, heard her say, 'Got another of those nutters here. Wants to go to Long Meg.' She paused listening for the response. 'Hang on.'

She reappeared at the desk. 'He says it's normally for midnight. Are you sure you want it now?'

Mr Binks was unusually flustered by her response. *Normally?* he wondered. *Do a lot of people go there?* 'This is just a practice run,' he said, smiling at her. That seemed to do the trick.

'OK, Sir,' The woman disappeared into the back room, again returning a few seconds later. 'He'll be here in five,' she said.

Mr Binks chose a small seat by the front door and looked scathingly at the rack of colourful pamphlets on display. *So uncouth*.

60

The taxi arrived before the five minutes were up and the driver repeated the destination as he got in. It was becoming foggy. By the time they got to the ancient stone circle, there was very little to be seen.

'Are you sure you want to get out here?' the driver said, turning his head back.

'Quite sure,' said Mr Binks. 'Would you mind leaving the engine running and the lights on pointing at the stones over there, please? I won't be very long.'

Mr Binks got out of the car and walked through the circle now skirted in mist. Outside the circle, the fog was even thicker. He came face to face with the largest stone. He had his quote ready, just in case it might help his cause and he began.

'A weight of awe not easy to be borne
Fell suddenly upon my spirit, cast
From the dread bosom of the unknown past,
When first I saw that sisterhood forlorn...'
He was stopped by a strange noise. No, a voice.

'Och save me from thy wretched utterings. Have I got tae listen tae Wordsworth unto eternity?'

Mr Binks whirled round. Was she already here? *Or is this some kind of joke?* He peered through the fog but could see nothing.

'All these years I serve those that walk the sinister path,' sneered a deep gravelly voice. 'And finally, an important question is asked. But it is by a paltry clerk.'

Mr Binks was petrified. It's her. Pull yourself together man.

'I am no clerk, I am a keeper of maps,' he said as firmly as he could manage.

'Och, ye're a miserable worm. Devoid o' powers. Aye, ye have skills but ye're no' true,' the voice responded.

'But I am at least preserving the ancient ways,' Mr Binks protested. 'And all your modern-day witch-folk, they are not interested in the old ways anymore.'

There was a hissing noise. 'So ye come before me tae ask a question when you know yir purpose is not true?'

'It is as good and true as any,' Mr Binks said bravely. 'If you do not help me, something important may be lost for eternity.'

'Quit yir babbling. I know what ye seek. The words may come tae ye they may not.'

Mr Binks looked around again; the voice seemed to be circling him. 'And what if they don't?' he asked in a tiny semblance of his normal voice.

'Then ye'll be flung intae hell with the lone walker.'

Mr Binks stood there a while longer. 'I have brought money.'

Shrieks of hellish laughter answered him. 'An' what could I do with your stinking money noo?'

The fog began to swirl around Mr Binks like a giant snake but as fast as a spinning top. He didn't want to look but he was transfixed. As the face of an old woman began to form out of the fog, he knew he was being tested. He stood still and firm as he felt the icy breath of old Magda on his face. He stared into her demonic ice-cold eyes.

'I had no idea...' he began

'That I was already a spirit? No, ye've nae idea at all. Ye're a mere worm o' a creature and yet what you seek is precious. The last volume. The other two long since destroyed. But what will ye dae with it when ye have it?'

'I will guard it with my life,' said Mr Binks.

The spectre rose up like a genie in a fantasy film. The huge wrinkled old face of Magda looked down upon him with an expression so disdainful he thought she had made her decision.

'Ye know the day,' she said. 'Ye must secure the manuscript afore then and whether ye dae or not, ye must know ye may die in the attempt. Its removal from the grotto may disrupt its power and that may take everything in its path as it subsides. Go to where ye felt the current. The words will come tae ye and ye'll meet your fate one way or another. Or go back tae your miserable books and bide a clerk till ye die.'

The shape dissipated back into the surrounding fog until there was nothing visible left. Mr Binks tripped several times as he actually ran to where the cab was waiting for him. He stumbled inside and gave the biggest sigh of his life.

'Are you OK sir?' the cabbie asked.

'I am absolutely fine, thank you for asking.' Mr Binks replied. 'Would you please take me back to the hotel now?'

'Och, on my way.'

***

After all the excitement of the last few days, Karen was feeling very disoriented and uncomfortable on her own in the flat. *Should I go up to Lincoln?* she wondered. *The last few days have been so momentous. It would be good to compare notes. And see him again.* She picked up her phone.

Simultaneously John was lying in his old bedroom thinking about Karen. *Should I go down to see her? I do miss her. It's been a difficult time, dangerous even. That does things to you. We need to reconnect. Share our experiences.* He reached for his mobile.

Line Busy. Both of them said to themselves.

Karen waited but John rang again. His heart leapt when she answered. 'Are you doing anything?' he asked as casually as he could manage.

'Of course. I'm going through the case,' she replied.

'Want a hand?'

'If you must,' Karen smiled to herself. 'You just want to get away from your parents, don't you?'

'Actually...' John tailed off. 'See you soon.'

Karen put the washing on and made a half-hearted attempt to tidy up. Then she pulled out all her papers again and started putting things into a semblance of order, but her brain wasn't working properly. Knowing that John would soon be with her displaced the discomfort but it brought new emotions to the fore. What state was their relationship in? But she knew that she wanted to see him more than not see him. By the time John arrived at her flat, she only had one thing on her mind.

'The Thai restaurant?'

215

'That's exactly what I was thinking,' John said, unconsciously tapping his still rather full stomach.

"We've got to be honest,' Karen said as they sat down. 'I can cope with anything related to my job, but this relationship thing is doing my head in.'

'I'm the same,' John replied at the same time as he felt his heart sink.

Over the food and the wine, all sorts of things came tumbling out. John's insecurities about Davie, Karen's grief at what happened to her father, how they had been kidnapped and drugged. Before long they were tapping into each other's experiences, both realising that far from pulling them apart, they were now closer than ever.

When they got back to Karen's flat, slightly inebriated, they reconnected. Karen looked at the case papers and looked back at John. 'This can wait till morning,' she said as she took John's hand and led him to the bedroom.

61

Sunday 17 November.

'Breakfast, sleepyhead.' John gently shook the snoring Karen's shoulder.

'*Mmm*. You cooked?'

'Yes, but first I had to go and buy something to cook. You never change, do you, Karen?'

'Nope and I never will. Give me five minutes,' she leapt out of bed and disappeared into the bathroom.

After breakfast, the serious conversation started. John took the lead and Karen, unusually, stepped back. *He's so logical*.

'OK, let's go through this one step at a time. What have we got from Caitlin McFee's case?'

'We've almost certainly got the murderer's DNA. We have identified the main suspect, Fergus Anderson. And he is the spitting image of the man who spoke to my father. At least two people identified him as such from that clip,' Karen stopped. 'No, three. And they are Matthew Warren, Stuart McFee and his mum, Peggy McFee, who also said he was the man that got Hamish's sister Gracie pregnant.'

'And the resulting child is Archie Logan – born Broad. Then there's Donald Anderson,' John said. 'The two sons from whom we can match his DNA.'

'But we don't have the video anymore. I'd better ask Jack to re-send it.' She picked up her phone. 'Jack? Remember that CCTV clip of Dad? I seem to have lost it. Can you send it to me? Thanks.'

'About that,' John said. 'I forgot to tell you. Or maybe I thought I shouldn't tell you.'

'What?' Karen said. John bit his lip. 'Tell me.'

'I showed it to Mr Binks. He was shocked when he saw it. I got the impression the man said something bad to your father.'

'What? Are you positive?'

'*Um*. To be honest, I'm getting pretty confused about a lot of things these days. But we can ask him.'

Karen's phone rang. 'Jack? Really? Damn. No, don't worry.' She looked at John. 'Guess what?'

'He hasn't got it either.'

'Yes, right. Hang on, how did you get it?'

John *umm*ed again. 'Someone sent it to me. Now who was it?'

'Floyd Cannon?' Karen suggested.

'Yes. That's it. How could I forget? I'll ring him now.'

Karen paced as he made the call, but she could tell by his face the story was the same. 'How can that happen?'

'Without investigating I can only speculate what I said before. If it's time-dated coding, it will delete all copies wherever it is,' John said. 'Or it could simply have been attacked by a virus, or was infected by one and destroyed by the firewall. There's nothing we can do about it now. I'm sure I can recover it from the actual recording device at the station.'

'What about going to see Mr Binks?'

John made the call. 'No answer.'

'Better get back to the rest then. Katherine Engles.'

'Yes,' John perked up. 'Tell me what you've got there.'

Monday 18 November

Karen arrived early at work. There was something placed on her desk. 'Now what?' *Not another file, surely?* She groaned but her colleagues began to clap. What's going on? *It's a newspaper.* She picked it up. The headline screamed **50 Year Abduction Mystery Body Recovered.**

'Wow!' she turned around and gave a little bow. *It's by Stanley Briggs. Clever man to get it on a national newspaper.* The article concentrated on the Caitlin McFee story but also linked it to the Katherine Engles case. And most importantly, she saw her name in print. *How cool is that?*

'My office, Karen. Now,' said a familiar voice. DCI Winter had just come in. She followed him into his room. There was no 'Did you have a nice break' stuff, it was straight into 'What the fuck are you playing at, Karen? Did you leak this? I've had my ear chewed off by the Chief Constable of Police Scotland.'

Karen looked curiously at her boss's face. Behind the anger, she saw something else in his eyes. *This is all for show, isn't it? You're pleased, very pleased. I can tell*.

'Sorry, Guv. I didn't endorse it, but it was a calculated risk Briggs would run the story. It puts pressure on the Yorkshire team to find the second body, then the third will be a walkover.'

'It's a fucking mess, Karen. That's what it is. I expect you to pull your finger out and bloody well sort it. And you'd better find the body, or you'll be back in uniform before I can say demotion.'

'Yes, Guv.' Karen walked out of his office and back to her desk wearing an enormous grin.

'Morning, Karen. Well done. We're all so proud of you.'

'Thanks, Mace, and guess what?

'He wants you to continue with it?' she said.

'Seems like it; before I bring disgrace on the team,' Karen replied, punching the air with her fist.

'Do you know what Mace?' Macy looked at Karen. 'Sometimes I fucking love my job.'

'Am I on the team too now?' asked Macy.

Karen looked back towards DCI Winter's office and just caught the smile on his face.

'You betcha,' Karen said. 'First stop York.'

Karen saw Macy's eyes wander over her shoulder. She turned round. John was walking towards her, smiling.

'Hi, Karen. I saw the paper. And I'm officially on the team.'

'Me, too,' Macy grinned.

'Yes,' said Karen. 'Let's nab an incident room. We've had a pretty good run-through already but we need to bring you up to speed Mace. Let's make it official now. It's still three murder investigations even if they're not on our patch. The locals will want our assistance and knowledge now.' She went down the corridor and found an empty room. John followed behind carrying his messenger bag, while Macy grabbed some papers from her desk and joined them.

Karen took gleeful charge of the big whiteboard.

219

62

1 CAITLIN MCFEE. EDINBURGH

'Murder suspect Fergus Anderson. He's been Identified by proxy as the man at the original scene of Caitlin McFee's murder. We have DNA but we can't match it with anything until we can find either of his sons. And that's Archie Logan, born Archibald Broad and Donald Anderson.'

'What do you mean by proxy?' Macy asked.

'I showed the victim's brother and mother a video of a man we believe to be the murderer's son. Also, Matthew Warren, Amy's brother, recognised him as the hiker they saw. Obviously, it couldn't have been, but unfortunately, I didn't have an actual photo of Fergus Anderson at the time. And even more unfortunately, since then we seem to have lost the clip from which the image was taken.'

'Do you mean these?' Macy pulled out two pieces of paper. 'John sent them to me. I printed them out.'

'Did I?' John frowned.

Karen stared at them, a smile creeping across her face. 'That's from the video we lost. Printing them out. How clever was that, Macy?' She pointed at one image. 'That's Fergus Anderson from the back of the book John found.' She pointed to the other one. 'And that man we think is his son. The likeness is very strong. And it's possible he's the man who killed my father.'

'What?!' Macy exclaimed.

Karen sighed. 'I might as well tell you. The other man in the picture – the back of his head. That's my dad. He died a few hours after he met that man. If it's Archie Logan, and we think it is, he said something to Dad which may have brought on his heart attack.'

'Oh, Karen. I'm so sorry.'

John broke the moment. 'I think I remember now,' he said. 'I took this still from the clip Floyd Cannon sent me. I don't know why it slipped my mind.'

'Well done you, too,' Karen said.

'But your father?' Macy asked.

'It's not our prime concern. But yes, I'd like to find out Mace.'

Macy nodded. 'Oh, and by the way, I don't know what it is with all these names changing, but Donald Anderson changed his name to Donald McTear.'

'What?' John and Karen said together. 'I knew it,' Karen said.

'You know him?' Macy asked.

'He's the semi-retired copper at Davie's station. He gave me the slip, and I never followed it up. Damn.' Karen kicked the table leg. 'Better tell Davie. She picked up her phone.

'Hi, Davie. An update. DC Dodds has been doing some great research.'

'Go on,' he said.

'Your copper Donald McTear....'

'Yes?'

'He's Fergus Anderson's older son.'

'Fucking hell,' said Davie. 'OK, Karen; I'm on it. I'll get what I can out of him. Are you coming back here?'

'Not yet. We're heading to York first; did you see the papers?'

'Aye. Quite a splash.'

'And hopefully, we'll get the next body shortly. I'll be in touch.'

She looked at Macy. 'Brilliant work, Mace. Now we're really motoring.' She turned to the next board and headed it up.

2 KATHERINE ENGLES. YORK

'OK. We're so close to this one I can almost feel it. Stanley's story will have revived interest and maybe some memories. I've asked him to contact Katherine's sister, Elsie. She's in New Zealand, but I've given him the original photo of Fergus Anderson from the book to show her for ID purposes. Also, we've made huge progress on the map – that is assuming the map my father had is accurate.'

Macy looked confused. 'Sorry, Karen. What?'

'Didn't I tell you my father was investigating Katherine Engles' death?' Macy gave a vague nod. 'Well anyway, I found this map in his wallet. It was there the day he died. John and I, and now

Stanley Briggs and this local chap Charlie Worthington, have all looked at various maps. This drawing seems to coincide with the nearest-aged map. The landmarks tie up. So we've projected lines onto the current map, and we think that it indicates where her body is.'

'Is that enough to get the authorities to dig there?' Macy asked.

'Good question.' Karen turned to John. 'I don't know how we're going to explain it, but we need Mr Binks to help us find the body.' She looked at Macy. 'Mr Binks is the funny guy who managed to locate Caitlin McFee's body,' Karen explained. 'The papers didn't name him because he wanted to keep his identity hidden. But the fact that he found Caitlin should be enough to convince whoever that he can do the same for Katherine's body. He's a very persuasive man.'

'I'll go and see him,' said John. 'Best to talk to him face to face.'

'Agreed. Now...' Karen headed up the third board.

3 AMY WARREN. LINCOLN

'John? You know more than me on this one.' She looked at Macy. 'He's from there.'

Macy looked surprised. 'You're a Midlander? You don't sound like one.'

'Mummy beat it out of me,' John quipped. 'OK, you've already mentioned Matthew Warren. He was Amy's little brother. He's seen the video, or was it the photo?' He looked at Karen who was having a lightbulb moment.

'Video! Make a note to chase him up. He's a journalist, he may have copied and saved it somewhere.'

'Will do. Then there's the police officer who reopened the case, Sam Farnsworth. He had a heart attack on a footpath.'

'Just like Dad,' Karen added.

John frowned. 'I need to contact Floyd Cannon. I'm pretty sure I know roughly the part of the footpath the body may be buried in. If I'm right, I think they're in close proximity.'

'We definitely need Mr Binks again for this one.' Karen looked at them both. 'OK, team, Macy and I are going up to York to get things moving ready for an exhumation. John, you track down Mr Binks and see if you can't pinpoint Amy's body before you bring him back to York.'

'I'll do my best.'

'Macy? We'll be up there at least a day or two. Go home and get some things together. Meet me back here, we'll take my car.'

'Will do,' said Macy, almost running out of the office in her excitement.

When she'd gone, John looked at Karen. 'Are we all right now?'

'We're absolutely fine, John. We're both on a case and there's nothing that makes me happier than that.'

John gave her as big a bear hug as a slim man can, then kissed her on the lips. 'See you in York then.'

63

Karen took Macy to Mrs Townend's B&B and booked two rooms for two nights. Mrs Townend was delighted and excited to see Karen again.

'Is it your doing? That what's in paper? Was it you found that poor lass in Edinburgh? Have you come to find our poor lass?'

'We have,' Mrs Townend. 'And this is detective constable Macy Dodds. She'll be helping, too.'

'Pleased to meet you. D'you know, I can't remember the last time we had such excitement in the village. Everyone's talking about it. Let me show you to your rooms.'

Karen waited in the little reception while Macy unpacked. 'What took you?' she said when Macy finally appeared.

'Pride in my appearance,' Macy replied, trying hard not to look at the creases in Karen's shirt.

'Ironing never solved murders, Macy. C'mon. Let's get going.'

They headed straight to Stanley Briggs' office. He was grinning from ear to ear when he saw Karen.

''Ello, lass. Sorry, I couldn't help it. Th'coppers are all wound up about it, and poor old Mrs Engles has been ringing me every hour to find out what's happening.'

Karen smiled back. 'It's good. Don't worry. Yes, there are a few feathers ruffled, but nothing that won't be a hell of a lot smoother when we find that poor girl's body. This is DC Macy Dodds. I wanted to introduce you to her.'

'Aye, pleased to meet you.' He shook hands with Macy. 'You've got a right good boss here, I hope you know that.'

'Yes,' Macy replied. 'She keeps us all on our toes.'

'That's grand.' He handed her a card. 'Now take my number, call me anytime. D'ye hear?'

'Thanks.'

'Have they made formal contact with Elsie yet?'

Stanley shook his head. 'Elsie Braddock as she is now. I've asked th'station to try on Skype. But first, someone's got to work out how to use it,' he laughed.

'Fair enough. We're just going there now. I suppose you know who's on the case?'

'Aye. Nowt gets past me. It's a chap called Tony Fox. And he's right clever, I hear.'

'Excellent,' Karen smiled. 'Foxes are cunning. See you later.'

'I want first go on th'story mind,' Stanley said after her.

'Of course,' Karen shouted back without looking round.

'I didn't go to the station last time,' Karen explained in the car. 'The original copper died, and the one who worked with my father had a stroke.'

'He was the one that tried to reopen the case?'

'Yes. Brian Appleby. Now the only possible witness we have is Katherine's sister, Elsie Braddock, in New Zealand. Let's hope they've made contact.'

They arrived at the police station shortly afterwards and after parking up, Karen and Macy were astonished to witness a sea of press photographers and journalists standing outside the station while a tall male officer read out a statement. They held back and listened.

'...And I am now in charge of the investigation. We will be looking back over the original case files and checking for new evidence emerging.'

'What about the body, Inspector Fox?!' someone shouted.

Karen took a good look at him this time. So did Macy. 'He's cute,' she said.

'Shush!'

Detective Inspector Fox continued. 'We will be making all possible efforts to locate the remains of Katherine Engles. That's all for now. Please. I have work to do.'

As the assembled press began to disperse, Karen and Macy walked towards the station. DI Fox came to meet them.

'You must be...'

'DS Karen Thorpe,' they shook hands. 'You don't sound local...'

Macy's hand shot out too. 'DC Macy Dodds. Pleased to meet you.'

'DI Tony Fox,' he replied as he took her hand. 'Relocated from London. Call me Tony. Coffee?'

'Drinkable?' Karen replied. Macy stifled a giggle.

'Barely. Have you eaten yet?'

'No!' said Karen and Macy in unison.

'There's a nice cafe round the corner; quite safe, we all use it from time to time. Let's go there and get some background before we get into the nitty-gritty.'

Karen agreed like a shot. *How cool is he?* She thought. *Is Macy actually drooling?*

Before they could get anywhere, Karen saw John's car pulling up. *No Mr Binks, I see.* She walked towards him.

'Hi. What happened?'

'There's no sign of him anywhere. I checked the bookshop, the house, even walked around it all. He wasn't there.'

'Hi, John.' Macy came over with Tony following.

Karen made the introductions. 'This is our head of forensics, John Steele.' The two men shook hands.

'Ah,' said Tony. 'You should join us. I'll introduce you to our team later, but we thought it would be good to get some basics sorted first.'

'Of course,' Karen said. 'John has been in this almost from the beginning, and most importantly he knows Mr Binks. Although it appears he's gone missing.'

'Damn. Is that the body-finder man?' Tony led the way to the coffee shop ignoring the dregs of the press who were snapping them all as they went.

'Yes,' John replied. 'He can be a bit mysterious. But he usually turns up when he's needed.'

'So you believe he can pinpoint the exact position of the body?'

'I think we can get pretty close without him,' Karen said. 'It's more the perception. He's been referred to in the papers, if he's not here, they may be less inclined to cooperate. I have no idea how he does it. John?'

'I think we should proceed without him if we can,' John replied. 'His means were not scientific; I'm sure there are modern technologies we can employ.'

Tony grunted in agreement. 'Yes, we are very up on things like that here, at least I am. Even if a body's been in concrete, we have specially trained dogs these days.'

Karen's head was suddenly filled with the memories of the discovery of Caitlin's body; Mr Binks' funny little machine, the body showing no signs of decomposition, all things which would never appear in an official version of events. She had enough nous to see where John was going on this.

'I agree,' she said. 'Yes, we are reasonably certain of where the body is; I would say within a radius of five metres.'

'I think we can work with that then,' Tony nodded. 'Now what are you all having? Lunch is on me.'

64

Mr Binks was in a terrible muddle. He had been scared half witless by Magda but needed more reassurance before he decided what to do. *There's a gatekeeper in Cumbria, I'm sure. I must consult again before I do anything rash. My life is even more precious than the manuscript.* Then he had another thought. Was there someone whose life was of no importance whatsoever? A man who can add no value to the world at large?

Someone like Archie Logan.

He wasn't a murderer. G*oodness no*. But Logan was little more than a living zombie, already in servitude to an evil being. *What was it Magda said? The words will come to you. But that doesn't necessarily mean I have to be the one to actually say them.* The Cumbrian gatekeeper will be able to advise me.

Nothing ever kept Mr Binks from his breakfast. After a particularly hearty one, he spent Monday morning researching his manuals and looking up old maps. The land had changed comparatively little in these regions; no thriving ever-changing cities here; the lands were, as far as possible, unchanged for many generations. Once he was certain he had located the correct destination, he called for a taxi to take him most of the way there. *I'll have to be off map for a short while,* he reasoned.

When he finally arrived at the tiny shop in a small, cobbled lane, he knocked on the door with the usual signal. The door opened. He was shocked. Standing before him was a lady. *A fine figure of a woman*. What happened to the old man? She was a little bit younger than him, he estimated, but very agreeable looking, and dressed in an elegant long gown over which hung her plaited grey hair As soon as she saw the surprise on his face, she spoke to him.

'You are clearly looking for my father. Sadly, he passed one year since. My name is Grizela; I am his daughter, and he passed his responsibilities to me.'

Mr Binks was both surprised and delighted; he had never come across a lady gatekeeper before.

'Well I never. So, modernity has, at last, come to gatekeeping,' he smiled. 'I bid you welcome, Grizela. I am here to discuss an interpretation, if I may.'

'Ooh yes,' said Grizela, her excitement showing. 'You'll be my first. Do come in. Would you like some tea?'

Within a few minutes, Mr Binks and Grizela were chatting away like old friends. Mr Binks was positively glowing with the pleasure of meeting her and almost forgot why he came.

'Now Mr Binks. What can I do for you?'

'Of course.' His face fell a little as he told her of his meeting with Magda. Grizela listened, her own face growing increasingly anxious as he talked.

'And so I am concerned whether or not Magda's words are true and that I might die in the attempt.'

'Oh, my poor man,' she said. 'Yes, she is deadly serious, pardon the pun. I have heard my father mention the volume you seek, and I understand your desires, but you must be very careful.'

'I was wondering whether it would be possible to *persuade* another to speak the words for me?' Mr Binks asked.

'No, it will not be possible,' Grizela replied. 'Magda will know your deceit. You must not even try to deceive her, for her punishment will be too severe.

Mr Binks began to blush. Forgive me, dear lady,' he said. 'It was uncharacteristically unbecoming of me even to suggest such a thing. I withdraw the suggestion immediately, and I promise you I will do what needs be done in person. I beg your forgiveness and your advice.'

'We will put our considering caps on and see whether we can devise a plan,' she replied, smiling sweetly.

The two became as thick as thieves for a while until finally, they were both smiling. 'I wonder,' Mr Binks asked a little apprehensively, 'whether you would care to partake of some luncheon with me?'

'I would be delighted,' said Grizela. 'I know a very nice little restaurant in the village. You can even get a taxicab back to the hotel from there.'

'That would be perfect,' said Mr Binks. *What a wonderful woman,* he thought. *Everything I could wish for in a companion.*

***

In Edinburgh, Davie was pursuing Donald McTear with enthusiasm. *I'll give him off sick, the scabby bastard.* He banged on the door. Donald's face appeared at the window.

'Go away,' he said. 'I'm bunged up with the flu.'

'You'll have more than that if you don't open the door,' Davie shouted. He waited until he heard bolts being undone and saw the door opening.

He walked in angrily. 'What the fuck's all this about, Donald?' he began. 'You're the son of a suspected murderer and you didn't think to tell me?'

Donald turned away sheepishly. 'Och, I didn't know him at all,' he replied. I only met him the once when we reopened the case. He gave me some sob story about not wanting to be court-martialled. Said he'd been a rotten father but asked me to let it go. He swore he had nothing to do with wee Caitlin and I believed him. I know a guilty man when I sees one and he wasnae guilty.'

'So why did you close the case? When did you stop looking?' said Davie impatiently.

'Och, it was all down to yon reporter, Mick Chatterton. He was the push behind it. One day he never turned up and I drifted back to the day job. That was it. Nothing sinister boss.'

There was a bumping noise overhead. 'Have you got company?' Davie asked. Donald went bright red. 'Don't dare lie to me.'

'Och it's my wee brother Archie,' he said. 'I took him in after he left home years ago. He's not all there poor soul. There's no harm in him.'

'You what?' Davie was on full alert. 'Do you mean Archie Logan? Your half-brother. Also known as Archie Ferguson?'

'Aye,' said Donald. 'What's it to you? He's done nothing. He's not capable.'

'I'll be the judge of that,' said Davie, and he charged upstairs. Scanning the few open doors, he made for the one that was closed and knocked on it not waiting for an answer. There, sitting on the floor he saw the grey-headed and bearded man. He held a child's console and looked up at Davie, smiling.

'Hello. Who are you?' he asked. 'Have you come to play with me?'

Davie stared at him in amazement. 'I just came to say hello.' He went back downstairs.

'I see what you mean Donald. But we're trying to find your father, and we may need you and Archie for a DNA match to what we've already found. I tell you now, Donald, if you're hiding him, you'll be up the Clyde without a paddle.'

Donald looked perplexed. 'But he died years ago.'

'You don't believe that and neither do I,' Davie shot back. 'And if you don't tell me, I'll have yon Archie taken into care.'

'I've not seen him, I swear.'

'OK, then I'm getting straight onto the Social,' Davie took out his phone.'

Donald crumbled. 'Alright, alright. I've never seen my father, but I don't know what Archie gets up to. He goes a-wandering at night. He takes food. I think he's going on a wee picnic for himself. But don't ask me where he goes. I don't know and I don't want to know.'

'Thank you, Donald,' said Davie. 'I'll be back.'

65

In York, all four detectives arrived on site. The forensics team had been briefed by John and were already surveying the area. They were also gathering a few bystanders.

'So, how does it work without Mr Binks?' Karen asked John.

'First, they've got to translate the map into land and see where the mark on your father's map is in reality. Then it depends. If it's concreted over, they'll drill small holes so that the dogs can pick up the scent – if there is any.'

One of the forensics team came up to Tony. 'It's looking easier than we thought,' he said. If – and it's a big if – that cross on the map really does indicate the position of a body.'

'We think it could have been deliberately placed before concrete was laid,' John said. 'So long as it coincided with the route of the old pathway.'

'That's what we're looking at,' the man pointed. 'See that long concrete walkway behind all the houses?' Four pairs of eyes followed to where his hand indicated. 'That's what we're looking at. It's concrete, but it looks like it's of a quality that hasn't over-hardened. Some of the stuff they used back then is nigh impenetrable after any length of time. We'll be putting up a tarpaulin covering for privacy, too.' He looked in the direction of the onlookers. 'We'll have it all marked out close of play today and we'll be ready to drill first thing.'

'Good,' Tony said. 'No need to hang around then, unless you have any questions?'

'Not me,' Karen said. She turned to John, 'I need to ask you something.' John and Karen took a few steps back to talk.

Macy watched them then spoke to Tony.

'I've got a question.'

'Fire away.'

'What's the nightlife like around here?' Macy said, grinning.

Tony's face broke into a smile. 'I do know a little place if you're interested.'

'Better than playing gooseberry to these two.' She nodded at John and Karen, their heads together.

***

Karen had stepped away for good reason. 'So what happens if the body is still un-decomposed? How will we explain it, or don't we have to? We *did* see it didn't we?' Karen said.

John nodded. 'We saw something odd. But it was all part of the decomposition process, Karen.'

'You're sure?'

'I'm positive. And it can't happen again. When they drill the holes, assuming there is a body there, the drills will allow the air in so decomposition will start straight away – if it hasn't already.'

'But only if the drills permeate the body bag,' Karen answered her own question.

John shook his head. 'It's extremely unlikely that it wouldn't have been damaged by now.'

'On Mummy's life?'

'Yes,' John replied, his fingers twitching but not crossing.

'Good. I don't want to see that again. What the heck are those two up to?' She nodded her head towards Macy and Tony.

'None of our business,' John replied.

'I need to check how Davie's getting on,' Karen said.

'OK. I'll chase Stanley Briggs. We can do both from the hotel.'

'Yes. Good idea. Let me talk to Macy.' She walked over to join Tony and Macy.

'We're heading back to the hotel now. Coming Mace?'

'Later. We're just discussing something about the case.'

Did she blush? 'See you later then.'

At the hotel, Karen managed to get through to Davie but the line kept breaking up.

'Talk tomorrow then. Ring me from the station.'

'Aye.'

'Any news?' John asked.

'Yes, he said something about finding Archie, but he's not much use. Anything from Briggs? Has he spoken to Elsie Braddock yet?'

'No. He's having problems working out the time zones to New Zealand. It's too early in the morning down under to ring or something. How about dinner?'

'You read my mind.'

Tuesday 19 November

Karen and John were already at their table and eating breakfast when Macy came down. She caught the waitress's eye to give her order then joined them.

'Morning. I've been dying to ask. What was it like when you found Caitlin's body?' Macy said.

Karen finished her mouthful. 'Completely different. Weird even. We thought it was on a road so they just got a digger out there and started digging. Then Mr Binks arrived with his machine, pointed, and hey presto, there was the body.'

'Wow! What sort of machine was it?'

'Some sort of current finder,' John cut in. 'Like a compass. No, maybe more like a water diviner.'

'And what state was the body in? I haven't seen many yet.'

'Until it was exposed to the air, it looked intact,' John said. 'The facial features seemed to be visible.'

'Then she tried to speak,' Karen jumped in. 'And she crumbled into dust like one of those old horror films.'

'Ugh. That sounds horrible,' Macy leaned back as her meal arrived. 'But not enough to put me off my breakfast.' She grinned and moved to let the waitress put the well-filled plate down. She began to eat.

'She didn't try to speak,' John corrected. 'It was simply the first place the decomposition began. And nothing like that can happen this time because of the process they're using.'

Macy swallowed. 'So where is this Mr Binks now?'

'AWOL.' Karen replied. 'I'm done. See you at the car in ten, Mace? John's off to meet Tony.'

Macy gave her a thumbs-up as John followed Karen out of the dining room.

***

'There's something different about you today Mace,' Karen said as the two of them got in her car. 'Can't put my finger on it.'

Macy gave a little cough in reply.

When they arrived at the site, they walked down the first part of the concrete walkway. The tarpaulin was almost completely erected.

'No reporters yet,' Karen remarked.

'A few onlookers still,' Macy nodded towards a small huddle of people behind the yellow and black barricade tape.

'And there,' Karen looked up to the facing windows of the houses behind the walkway. They heard a bark. 'And here come the dogs.'

They watched as the dog handlers unloaded the Labrador cadaver dogs from the van. Karen looked round to see John and Tony walking towards them. 'Oh, and here come the refreshments.'

Macy's face lit up. *Is that for Tony or the drinks?* Karen wondered.

Tony carried a big flask of coffee while John held a stack of paper cups. As they were filled and handed out, John began to speculate.

'I can't believe Mr Binks won't get here at some point.'

'I'm hoping he doesn't come. I'm *seriously* hoping that he's really not interested anymore and he's gone back to his shop,' Karen said.

'And who is this character?' Tony asked. Karen wandered up to the now complete tarpaulin leaving John to explain.

66

It was a long, slow, delicate process; the drill bits were very small – in order to cause the least damage – but fragile because of their size. While John watched every step, Karen and Macy made small talk with Tony; mainly discussing their respective careers and ambitions.

'So you'll be going for Inspector soon then?' Tony asked Karen.

'If the guv reckons so,' she replied.

'Oh, he so will,' added Macy enthusiastically. 'She's brilliant and he knows it.'

'But he hates me,' Karen said. 'Besides, you generally have to move sideways to go up.'

'After the exams,' Tony said. 'No reason to hold back taking them. It worked for me. And are you brilliant?'

'You've seen the headlines,' Macy said proudly.

Before Karen could take the compliment and comment they heard a bark, then a shout from one of the forensics team.

'Found something!' They hurried over to the site.

Karen glanced at her watch as they watched. It was nearly one o'clock.

'I'm going in a little deeper to gauge the hole,' said the man with the drill. He started it up and suddenly, like a whale's spout, a cloud whooshed up into the air. They all stood back in astonishment.

Jesus. What was that? Karen thought. *The shape of a little girl? Stop being so stupid!*

One of the forensics team got her camera out but it had gone before she could take a picture.

'What the fuck was that?' said the man with the drill.

'Excess body gases mixed with dust built up in an airtight body bag,' said John, sounding unperturbed. Nobody argued with him.

Karen looked round and up again at the distant faces in the window. *What did they see?* She turned to Macy. 'Did you see what I saw?'

'What, that puff of smoke, or whatever it was?' Macy replied.
'Yes, and anything in it?' Karen pressed.

'No,' Macy was curious. 'What did you see?'

'It doesn't matter,' said Karen. She looked over at John. He shook his head, but she was certain he had seen it too.

It took another hour before the body of Katherine Engles was eventually uncovered. It was in a similar condition to Caitlin McFee; almost skeletal remains but with slightly more clothing still intact. Karen was certain from the photographs it was her. *I wish I'd met her mother. Still, Stanley Briggs knows her, he'll want to put her mind at rest.*

She rang him. It sounded quite noisy wherever he was.

'Karen? I'm here. Behind the tape.'

'OK, I'm coming over.' She turned to Macy. 'Stanley Briggs is over there. I'm just going to have a word.' She walked over to join him.

'They've found her?' Stanley asked.

'They've definitely found some remains, and I'm as certain as I can be that it's Katherine.' Karen replied. 'The clothes – white T-shirt and blue shorts match the last sightings. Strictly off the record, I'd let her mother know if I were you. But warn her we can't be one hundred percent positive until the DNA's tested.'

'Ee. She'll be that pleased.'

'What about Elsie Braddock? Did you find her?'

'Aye. I did it meself in th'end. From th'office. Her mam were with me. They had a good natter after.'

'And the photo of the hiker?'

'Aye. She remembers him like it were yesterday.'

'Good. We'll need to formalise that at some point. Let her know, will you?'

'I will. Thanks again lass, I'll be going to see Mrs Engles now.'

Karen wandered back to the site. She was both pleased and unsettled. *At least we didn't hear that wretched screaming this time. I wonder what Davie's up to? Better ring him and tell him.*

'Hi, Karen. You found her then?'

'We did. How did you guess?'

'Was it at one o clock?' Karen blinked hard. *Was it?*

'Yes, how could you possibly...'

237

'I heard it again.'
'What?'
'That terrible shrieking.'

So he heard it last time, too. 'What the hell does that mean Davie? What's going on here?'

'Your guess is as good as mine. But I think it's all related, and I've finally made some progress.'

'What? Have you found Ferguson?'

'No. But I've confronted Donald McTear and I've met Archie. And I've set up the DNA tests, too, for both of them. I haven't collected the samples yet but I'm on it.'

'Archie? What's he like? Does he look like the man in the video?'

'Yes and no, but in his manner I can't say he does. He's like a little child. He's no bother to anyone. He's no threat. Donald says he hasn't seen his father for years. But he does say Archie goes a-wandering at night. With food.'

'So you're going to follow him?'
'Aye. I'll let you know what happens.'
'Damn. It doesn't sound very encouraging.'

'Karen, think about what you've done. You've practically solved two murders and brought peace to two families. That's a massive achievement.'

'I suppose.'

'And you'll be going after Amy Warren's body soon then?'

'Yes,' said Karen. 'As soon as we're tidied up here, but there's a problem with hers.'

'What is it?' asked Davie.

'With Caitlin and Katherine, we had a very good idea of where the body might be. But there are no clues yet with Amy. And Mr Binks seems to have disappeared.'

'Strange wee man,' said Davie. 'I'll keep a lookout for him.'

'Why? Do you think he might go up there again?' Karen asked.

'Aye. He didn't come up here just to help you, did he? He had another purpose, I'm sure.'

Karen thought for a moment and some more brain cells began to stir. *There was something else. What the hell was it?*

'Yes, please look out for him. And ring me if you find out anything more.'

'Will do, Karen. Catch you later.'

'Mr Binks,' Karen muttered. 'Where are you?' She went to find John.

'We have to get hold of that man,' she said as John's phone rang.

'That's easy,' he replied looking at his phone. 'It's him.'

67

Mr Binks was having fun for the first time in his life since he found his first book of spells. He'd found his true soul mate in Grizela. Not only was she beautiful to his eyes, she was even more knowledgeable than he was and just as keen as he to find the lost manuscript.

They spent the whole of Tuesday morning planning what they needed to do but Grizela had important gatekeeper duties to fulfil for the rest of the afternoon.

It wasn't until Mr Binks returned to his B&B he saw a copy of the local newspaper. There was a follow-up story outlining the attempt to find and recover the body of Katherine Engles. *Heavens*, he thought. *How naive it was of me to think that they would need my assistance again.*

Tuning into his television he was taken aback to hear that the body had been discovered. *Damnation.* He rarely swore even in his head but he was rattled. He had to find the manuscript before they found the last body, or literally, *all hell will break loose.* He rang John on his mobile.

'Mr Binks! Where on earth have you been? We need your help. We've found Katherine Engles, at least we think we have, but we'll have to look for Amy Warren soon, and we don't know where to start.'

'Thank you, John, for updating me. May I ask how you located the second body? I was rather expecting you would contact me before you arrived at that stage?'

'The map,' John replied. 'The map Karen's father had. It marked a possible location, and that's where we found the body. We don't have any leads like that for Amy Warren. We need you, Mr Binks.'

Thank heavens. I still have some time then. 'I will, of course, make myself available to you at the appropriate moment.'

He ended the call and immediately rang Grizela. 'My dear lady, they have already found the second body. We need to escalate our action. We must find the volume before they find the body. I shall call at nine tomorrow morning if that suits?'

***

'So what did Mr Binks have to say for himself?' Karen barked as John was left holding his phone. 'What the hell is he playing at? We've got to move on this now. Tomorrow's papers will be full of Katherine Engles and the pressure for us to find Amy will be momentous.'

'I know,' said John. 'He says he'll make himself available when the time comes.'

'And what the fuck does that mean? We're wasting time here.'

'Calm down,' said John, immediately regretting his words as Karen went from red to puce. 'There's something else,' he added hastily.

'What?'

'I've just remembered something which might be important.'

Karen glared at him. 'Are you joking me, John?'

'Didn't I tell you about Sam Farnsworth?'

'Yes, died of a heart attack on a footpath.'

'Floyd Cannon knows the exact location of his death.'

Karen drew back, taking it in. 'So you think it might be near where Amy was buried?' Karen said slowly.

'It has to be worth looking at,' John said. I'll call him.'

Karen nodded. 'You do that. I'll talk to Tony. I don't think he needs us to stay here now.'

'He's already headed back to base,' John said. 'With Macy.'

'Has he now? OK, see you there then.'

***

Karen walked into Tony's incident room where Tony and Macy were engrossed in a conversation. *Are they up to something?* She coughed to alert them. Macy looked up guiltily.

'Hi Karen.' Tony said as cool as anything 'Macy has been helping me with the details of our suspected murderer. I could really do with her help tomorrow too.'

Karen thought for a moment. *Macy's brilliant at paperwork and research; she doesn't quite have the 'nose' to help find a body yet. And god knows what John and I are in for when we get close to finding Amy's body – if we do.*

'That's fine, Tony,' she said. 'Let's exchange notes tonight, then tomorrow John and I will go back down to Lincoln to get the ball rolling there.' She gave Macy a *do you know what you're doing?* look.

Macy replied with a sly wink. 'That's great, Karen. There's lots I can do here.'

I bet there is,' thought Karen. 'OK, things to do. Tony, can I have use of a desk for John and me? Just for an hour or so?'

'Sure. You stay here. We can go to my room.'

'OK. See you two later.' *And what is going on?*

John joined her a few minutes later. 'Cannon's going to get the details ready for us tomorrow.'

'Good. I'm going to ring Matthew Warren to make sure he's around. We need to think of anything we should be doing while we're still up here. Like Archie.'

'I've been meaning to say something about him.' John said. 'I've got a really strange feeling that I've seen him somewhere.'

'And how is that possible?'

'I don't know. Maybe that bump on the head confused me.'

Karen decided it was time to open up, just a little. 'You're not the only one getting confused, John. I have some really weird recollections about a man in a cave. It was the night you banged your head. I think it was meant to be Anderson. But I'd been drugged and hallucinating. That's what Mr Binks said.'

'You were drugged? Why on earth didn't you tell me?'

Karen stumbled with her words. 'I wasn't hurt or anything. I came round pretty quickly outside the cottage.' *Do I tell him the whole thing? Not yet.* 'I'm fine now.'

'So it seems that when both of us are around Mr Binks, we get forgetful,' John said.

'But can we trust him or not?' Karen replied. 'We need him to find that body. What was it he said to you earlier?'

'That he'd be there at the right time or something like that.'

'OK. We'll deal with him when we have to. Let's hope we can manage without him again.'

'Agreed.'

'Is there anything else we need to do while we're up here? I'd better check where Davie is.' Karen picked up her phone. 'No answer. I'll try Matthew Warren.'

'At last,' Matthew sounded relieved. 'I've been waiting for you to call me. I read about the Scottish girl. Is it all connected? Are you trying to find Amy now?'

'Yes, I'm convinced it *is* the same murderer, and we have a good lead. I do want to get things started down with you. Where are you based?'

'I've nabbed a desk in the local newspaper office.' He sounded excited. 'I can't wait to find out what happened to her after all these years.'

'Don't get your hopes up,' Karen said. 'It's going to be the most difficult one to find, I think.'

'You'll do it,' Matthew replied. 'I just know you will.'

'Talk soon.' Karen looked at John. 'We might as well head back tonight. What do you think?'

'I agree. No point in wasting time. But where...'

'Anywhere but your parents' house.'

'They'll think that's very strange.' Karen looked at him. 'OK, OK, there's a small hotel I know. Let me ring ahead.'

'Good. And I'll ring Macy.'

Half an hour later they were back on the road to Lincoln.

'Supposing Mummy sees us?' Karen said.

'She won't,' John laughed. 'The hotel's in the cheap side of town.'

68

Wednesday 20 November.

John and Karen woke early. John's ordered newspaper was already poking under the door.

'Hey, look at this.' He showed Karen the headline. 'More missing girls reported.'

'Shit!' She grabbed the paper from him and began to read. 'Speculation mainly. An unidentified source has claimed that there could be ten more bodies yet to be uncovered. An unnamed source? Why does that make me think of Mr Binks?'

'Why him? Why not Stanley Briggs, keeping the story going?'

'Because I think Mr Binks is playing for time. But I don't know why.'

'Does it change anything?'

'It might. I'll be expected to follow up on them at least. It could take up all of our time. I'll have to phone the guv.'

'And there's an email from Tony.' John said looking at his laptop. 'They have unidentified DNA on Katherine's remains but haven't matched it with the DNA on Caitlin's yet. Could there be anyone else involved?'

'It's not something I've considered,' Karen said. 'But I should have done. If he was some sort of witch or whatever, don't they come in packs.'

'Covens,' John corrected.' But not all of them. And he was seen at all three scenes.'

Karen *hmmed.* 'Even so, we could crosscheck the names of all the searchers. But 'A', we don't have them all and 'B', they'd lie.'

'It might be worth getting Macy on it?' John suggested. 'Maybe she could field the so-called related cases.'

'John you're a genius. I'll get on to her as soon as we've had breakfast. I'll arrange to meet Matthew and Cannon. Maybe you should try to find Mr Binks again. It is his home ground after all.'

***

Karen headed straight to meet Matthew at the office.

'Nice to meet you at last,' he said. 'You're quite the celebrity. We even have use of the meeting room today.'

'Tomorrow's fish and chip wrapper,' Karen smiled. 'I don't do this for the recognition, which actually, rarely exists.'

'What's the plan? You seemed to find the other bodies incredibly quickly.'

'We had two very lucky breaks. We're not yet sure if we can narrow down the search for your sister, Amy. It'll be difficult, if not impossible, to get permission to excavate. Especially as we suspect she may have been buried under a major development.'

Matthew frowned. 'Then how were the others so easy?'

'To be honest, for the Scottish case we had help from someone who unfortunately seems to have gone missing now.'

Matthew looked thoughtful. 'I understand,' he said. 'There was mention of a body finder in one of the papers. Who was it?'

Karen breathed in between her teeth. *He's her brother. He has a right to know.*

'Matthew, I have to ask you to keep this entirely secret, which as a journalist, might be difficult for you to do. Do you agree?'

'Yes, but why?'

'Firstly, because he is a very unconventional man with methods most of us don't understand. Secondly, if his identity gets into the press, he will probably go into hiding forever. We have to keep him on side.'

'OK, so what do we have?' Matthew asked.

'You know Floyd Cannon, don't you? He should be here any minute. He has some information which may help. And our head of forensics, John Steele, should be joining us at some point. He's local to Lincoln, he's also a personal friend of the man in question.'

'Hey, it's not that weird old guy from the bookshop, is it?'

'Why do you say that?'

Her reaction gave Karen away. *Of course locals will know him.*

'It is, isn't it? I don't know him but I went into his shop once. He seemed very nice.'

'Please, please, please keep it to yourself in case it damages the investigation.'

'Of course.'

A head popped round the door. 'Morning both, ' Floyd Cannon announced himself. 'Where are we?'

'Just at introductions,' Karen said.

'And not mentioning Mr Binks.' Matthew added.

'Of course,' Floyd grinned. 'He has a price for his help.'

Karen gaped. 'You've worked with him too?'

'Oh, I've had the odd map from him in the past. In fact, this one is one of his.'

'And when did you get it?' Karen asked, surprising herself.

'It was in 1993 when the force tried to reopen the case.'

Karen breathed a sigh of relief, again, not really knowing why.

'I'm going to check it. Shall we have a look?'

Floyd began to unfold the map. There was another interruption. John appeared. The first thing he did was look at Karen and shake his head. She understood immediately. *Well, Mr Binks, we'll just have to manage without you.*

'We were about to look at the possible location,' she said. 'This is Matthew Warren.' John and Matthew shook hands while Floyd leaned over the opened map.

'This was where Sam Farnsworth died,' Floyd pointed to a dotted line indicating a footpath.

'Are you absolutely sure?' John said.

'No doubt about it. I attended the scene myself. Why?'

'Because I'd been working on a different assumption, from older maps we had. I thought we were looking somewhere here,' John pointed. 'There was an old grain storage facility put up in the war but it's now covered by the housing.

'It's known as the Robin Estate,' Floyd added.

Karen blinked and turned to John. 'It's the place I looked up when all this started.'

'What?' Floyd said.

'Sorry, just a coincidence. Carry on, John.'

John picked up again. 'It seemed to fit with the footpaths of the day and also with our theory that the bodies were buried under new developments.'

'I see,' Floyd frowned.

'What's the distance between the two points roughly?' Karen asked.

'About half a mile.'

'Could he have walked to the footpath from the grain place?' Karen said. 'To find help or a phone or something?'

'It depends on his health,' John said. 'I wouldn't rule it out. The grain storage looks as if it was the only building in the vicinity back then.'

'But if you're right, surely they'd have found Amy's body when they excavated the storage facility before demolishing it,' said Karen.

'Yes, unless somebody knew where it was and reburied it.'

'Sounds to me like you're clutching at straws a bit,' said Floyd. 'I can't see me getting any sort of permission to dig without something much more specific.' He stood up. 'Give me a call if you find anything.'

Karen sighed. 'I will.'

They watched him leave, then Matthew spoke. 'He's just not interested, is he?'

'Maybe not, Matthew. But John and I are committed.' Her phone rang. *Now what?* 'It's Davie.'

'Bad news, Karen.' *Of course it is.* 'The DNA we found doesn't match anything.'

'What? Neither Donald or Archie?'

'Aye, there's more news there. No, it doesn't match Donald because they don't know if it's even human.'

'What?'

'They're checking with the DNA on wee Katherine now, but interdepartmental labs an' all. It'll take a while.'

'Shit.'

'And Archie's gone missing. I haven't found hide nor hair of him.'

'Bloody hell, Davie. All I need is for my guv to ring and I've got the set. Hell, someone's trying to get through now.'

Karen's worst nightmares were confirmed. DCI Winter did not beat around the bush. Nor was he discreet. 'I have to have you back tomorrow, Karen.'

'But Guv...'

'Level with me. How close are you to finding that third body?'

'We've had a few issues.'

'That's it. See you tomorrow nice and early.' He hung up.

'Is that it then?' Matthew said 'He's called you back?'

'You heard?'

'The man in the next street heard. What's the score?'

'Without Floyd on board, and no hope of locating the body, there's not much I can do.'

'Then I'll have to work on Floyd,' Matthew said.

'Good. Keep in touch.' Karen looked at John. 'What now?'

'Now we go for a drive around the locale. We might or might not see something of interest. Then we try to find Mr Binks.' He got up. 'Coming?'

69

'So that was a waste of time,' Karen said as she sat down. 'This is a nice place.' She looked around the pub. 'Who did you say runs it?

'An old school friend of mine. He's very knowledgeable about the area, but sadly only recent events. But the food here is great.' John was just about to mention something else when he stopped in his tracks looking horrified.

'What's up?' said Karen, she turned to follow his gaze. John's parents had just walked into the restaurant part of the pub.

'I thought they didn't drink? Did you know they were coming here?'

'It's a restaurant, too,' John hissed back. 'And why they're here on a Wednesday I have no idea.'

Karen's question was about to be answered. Daphne came charging over leaving Big John standing just inside the door. She ignored Karen and spoke angrily to John.

'John-boy. What do you think you are doing? Why are you here? Why didn't you call us?'

John began to open his mouth but his mother was unstoppable. Big John walked up behind her looking aghast but Daphne was determined to have her say.

'Why on earth didn't you come home to see us? Don't tell me you think more of her,' she looked at Karen 'than you do of your own parents.'

Karen sat motionless. *What a bitch. John-boy? What are you going to do now?'*

John stood up and faced his mother eye to eye. He stuck his chest out and looked down on her sternly. Karen noticed that Big John had now put his hands to his head, screening his eyes as if he couldn't bear to watch.

'It's absolutely none of your business, Mother,' John said firmly. 'This is work. It is an extremely important case we are working on which you would know about if you'd looked at the papers. I can't just drop everything to suit you.'

Daphne took a pace back, stepping on Big John's toe. Karen saw the pain in his face but he put his hand over his mouth to stop himself yelping.

'Have you quite finished?' said Daphne, astonished but not ready to give up quite yet.

'No, I have not. And yes, Mother, frankly at this moment in time I do think more of Karen than you. I am in love with her, and you'd better get used to the idea.'

Karen stayed sitting trying to keep a straight face, but when Daphne looked down at her she choked with amusement.

'You'll regret this John-boy,' Daphne said with menace. 'Don't come running to me when it all goes wrong.' She whirled round and touched Big John on the shoulders to turn him round, too. 'Come along, Big John. I'm not staying here a minute longer.'

Big John stayed just quickly enough to wink at Karen. She smiled back at him then stood up and planted a smacker on John's lips.

'Come on, I'm starving' she said. 'Let's order.'

***

Mr Binks and Grizela were formulating a plan, and she was determined that he should take her with him on his quest.

'Dear Mr Binks,' she said. 'I believe we've grown quite close in the last couple of days, and it would be my utmost honour to join with you and if necessary, die in the attempt. But with two of us, there is more chance that at least one will save this precious writing.'

Mr Binks sighed loudly. 'My dear Grizela. We are undoubtedly kindred spirits. And I so value your knowledge and wisdom, but I could not possibly risk your life on such a venture.'

Grizela looked at him sternly. 'Mr Binks, before I say any more, I feel I must call you by your first name, and I don't even know it.'

Mr Binks shuffled uncomfortably on his chair. Small beads of sweat began to form on his brow. 'No one knows my name apart from some long-deceased relatives.' *And knowing a name is such a powerful thing. Do I trust this lady with the knowledge of my name? Do I dare give her that power over me?* He leaned towards her and looked her in the eyes. *These are the eyes of a true friend.*

'It is Gustav,' he replied. She smiled broadly at him.

'Then, Gustav, we are and must be a team. I believe that we were destined to meet, and now our paths are irrevocably intertwined.'

'I feel it too,' said Mr Binks, wiping his brow with relief.

'Then we must go to Scotland together. And we will stand at the entrance to the witches' cavern together, and as one we will say the words,' she paused. 'If that is what Magda wishes.'

'We will indeed,' said Mr Binks, suddenly feeling ridiculously light-hearted. 'When shall we leave?'

'Let us spend one more night on our research; we must leave no stone unturned, and I believe we should also consult with our brethren in Edinburgh. Three heads are better than our two.'

'Absolutely, my dear lady. You are correct yet again. We will leave in the morning. I will send a taxi to collect you at eight o'clock.'

'Or you could stay here,' Grizela smiled coyly at him. 'In my spare room of course.'

Mr Binks' face broke into a beaming smile. 'That would be exceptionally accommodating of you. I shall go back to the hotel and settle my account then return within the hour. May I use your telephone, please?'

'Of course, Gustav. And I will cook you a nice nourishing goulash for your return.'

Mr Binks' face froze. Grizela was taken aback. 'Have I said something out of place?'

'No, no, and again no my dear lady. Goulash is what my beloved aunt used to cook for me. How on earth did you know?'

'It is fate, Gustav. Fate'

'Indeed it is,' replied Mr Binks.

***

In Edinburgh, Davie was getting nowhere fast. The respective labs had confirmed a *no match* on the DNA samples of the two girls, and there was still no news of Archie. Frustrated, he decided to visit Donald again.

'Sorry it's so late,' he said at the door.

'Och, no bother,' Donald pulled the door open to let him in. 'Come in.'

'Is there still no sign of Archie?' Davie asked.

'Neither hide nor hair. I'm worried sick.'

'What about food? Has he been back at all?'

'Aye. This evening I thought I was missing a pan loaf and a big lump of cheese. I've not been eating that much.'

'He's got a key?

'Oh aye, he has. And I was out earlier.'

'Have you got any of his clothes? We can maybe get the dogs to sniff him out?'

'There's no other option,' Donald agreed. If he doesn't come home tonight, I'll give you a bell in the morning.'

'I'll get it set up. And can I get you to take a new DNA sample? You know what these labs are like. They couldn't spot a rabbit from a hen.'

'Aye, if you must,' Donald replied.

'And have you anything of Archie's that we could use? For the DNA and the dogs?'

'His manky pants? A dog would smell 'em a mile off.'

'That'd be perfect.' Davie nodded. 'Have you any idea at all where he might have gone?'

'Och, he wanders off along the path back there. It's a wilderness when you get to the trees. You've not got a snowball's chance in hell.'

Davie sighed and took out a test kit. 'Give us your sample then.'

'Aye.' Donald opened his mouth while Davie swabbed it.

'Cheers. And the keks?'

'Give us a sec.' Donald disappeared upstairs. Davie looked through the back window. It was pitch black outside. *Och, I've got my torch. Might as well have a wander*.

'Here y'are.' Donald flung some boxer shorts at Davie who pulled out a plastic bag from his pocket.

'Och, they're fair minging. Even I could follow that trail. I'm getting off now. Let us know if he turns up.'

'Aye, I will.'

'I'll see myself out,' said Davie.

Davie sat in his car for a while thinking it through. Where would a man like Archie go? *He's not with it but he must be going somewhere safe and warm in this weather. Where's my torch?*

He put on a jumper he'd brought in case it got too cold and decided to go out and investigate. *He must've gone out back. he'd have surely been seen if he went down the road. Unless Donald's lying to me.*

The ground was already frosty. Davie walked around the back of Donald's house. *Are they footprints?* He saw some indentations in the grass and began to follow them. But when he got to the wooded area, the trail ended. The ground was not so amenable to footprints. *But with the dogs, I reckon I'll find you, Archie.*

70

Thursday 21 November

Macy had been getting some excellent career experience in York and was enjoying the freedom of working away from her usual routine, but she was running out of things to do that had to be done in York. All the paperwork surrounding Katherine Engles was in top shape, all the reports were filed and signed off, and the body was ready to be released back to the family. Looking at all the other reports about missing children, she knew it could be done back at her own office.

She had initially enjoyed having a bit of a love life, too, but this was waning in a way that had become very uncomfortable. The women, in particular, had begun dropping comments in her direction.

'Ey, that Tony's wife, stuck at home with four kiddies to look after,' one woman had said.

'He's married?' I had no idea,' Macy had replied, to receive an eye-roll in return.

'Aye. He'll be going for the record for notches on the bedpost, that one,' said another.

The one that hurt her the most was. 'Tony loves a bit of the exotic – if you know what I mean.'

When he walked into the room she was using, she confronted him. 'You didn't tell me you were married. Have you just been playing with me? All that nonsense about finding the perfect woman?'

'Ah, yes. Sorry. But Macy, we had fun, didn't we? And I don't remember you actually asking if I was married.'

Macy suppressed a smile. *It was fun. I should have known. I'll rot in hell now.* 'You cheating bastard. I'm leaving now. I've done more than enough to help you here.'

'Yes, you have Macy. Your skills, in all departments, have been most appreciated.' He leaned forward to kiss her, instead, she slapped him as hard as she could. He rubbed his face with affection. 'Thank you, Macy. You're a great girl.' She still had the remnants of a smile when she left the office.

Halfway home, when she stopped to fill up, she rang Karen and left a message. 'I'm finished in York now; I'll be back in the office tomorrow.' When she arrived home, there was a reply. **Me too, see you there.**

***

'Oh good,' DCI Winter said as he walked into the office. 'We have the set. Karen my office in five please.'

Five minutes gave Karen and Macy time to catch up on their respective news. Then DCI Winter's door opened again. 'Now,' he said.

'Why did you need to call me back Guv?'

'Because, Sergeant Thorpe, we are seriously understaffed and we're getting into the season for RTAs again. Remember?'

'Yes, but I'm still owed holiday.'

He gave her a *really* look. 'I know about the two bodies you have helped to recover. I couldn't really miss the news coverage. What is the problem with the third, and where are we with the suspect?'

Here we go again Karen thought as she began to explain about Mr Binks and his ability to detect bodies.

'You'll be telling me next he has a magic wand, Karen.'

'And I could remind you about my theories with Stella Cary's case,' Karen shot back. 'Look, Guv, I acknowledge that at the moment I'm snookered, but you've got to let me back if we get more news.'

'And what news are you expecting that might precipitate that event?'

'Firstly, any definitive information or knowledge about the location of the body, and/or the reappearance of a willing Mr Binks.' DCI Winter nodded. 'The main suspect is assumed to be dead, but we have reason to believe that he has an accomplice and that he may actually be still alive somewhere. DI Wallace is searching for him now.' *Should I tell him about my dad?*

'What is it, Karen? You've got that weird look on your face, which means there's something else you probably shouldn't tell me.'

'OK. This is a tough one. The suspect accomplice looks very like another man.' She took a deep breath. 'I was sent a CCTV video clip of this man, dressed like a hiker, who spoke to my father when he was on the desk that time...'

DCI Winter looked shocked. 'You don't mean when Tommy died, do you?' Karen nodded. 'I want to see it. Can you send it to me?'

'Sorry. I don't have it anymore. It seems to have been wiped off the system.'

'Have you checked the station for back-ups?'

How bloody obvious is that? 'Not yet. I was going to do that today. But there's something else which you would definitely call weird.'

'Oh, I can't wait to hear this.'

'Apparently, the man spoke some sort of curse. It's possible it was meant to kill him, and it was just before he died.' DCI Winter shook his head. 'But there was a journalist, Sam Farnsworth, who also seems to have died the same way.'

'Karen, you know as well as I that we'd never be able to prove anything like that. But I do understand why you'd want to investigate it. Get on with your work here, but let me know of any developments and I'll reassess the situation.'

'Thanks.'

His phone rang. Karen went to get up, but DCI Winter flapped his hand down.

'Yes, sir.

I understand, sir.

What now? Well as it happens, she's right in front of me.' DCI Winter passed the phone to Karen and mouthed *Chief Constable Burns* at her.

Karen sat up straight. 'Sir.'

DCI Winter couldn't hear the conversation, but he knew the gist of what was being said. He also saw Karen's smile widen. 'Of course, sir,' she said. 'Three days? I'll do my very best sir.' She handed the phone back to DCI Winter, who put it to his ear.

'Yes sir.' He put the phone down and looked at Karen. 'Well, it seems you have a fan in high places. I'm sure it has absolutely nothing to do with the fact that he's retiring at the end of the month and wants to go out on a win.' Karen pouted. 'Do what you can. If you need more resources, come to me.'

'Thanks, Guv.' Karen boxer-danced her way back to her desk, sitting down with a thud. 'Now what do we do?'

'We have to go to Lincoln,' Macy said. 'We need to get closer to the area where Amy disappeared and walk the footpaths. Do you remember with Stella's case? That's how...'

Karen interrupted her. 'Macy, you're a genius.'

71

Karen, Macy, John, Matthew, and a somewhat reluctant Floyd Cannon sat round the meeting table at Matthew's office.

'We have three days,' Karen announced.

'Or what?' Floyd said.

'Or all resources are pulled off the case and it's closed again. The big boss is loving the publicity, but locally we're under pressure and he can't afford to have us out of action.'

'And he wants to retire on a high,' John added.

Karen nodded. 'I suggest that we all physically walk the footpath that Sam Farnsworth took and around the area where Amy was abducted. I know it's changed in fifty years, but we might just spot something, or make connections we couldn't get from simply looking at maps.'

'Makes sense to me,' Matthew said.

'It was Macy's idea,' Karen said. Macy beamed.

'And a very good one,' Floyd added, looking at Macy.

'Then let's go,' John said. 'Floyd, can you take us to the spot where Sam was found?'

'I can. Follow my car.' He stood up looking as cheerful as Karen had ever seen him.

He's engaged at last. He's found his purpose, she thought as they went outside and got in their cars.

It didn't take them long to get to the road where the footpath started. The small convoy parked, and the occupants got out, waiting for Floyd to lead the way.

'I used to cycle up here,' John whispered to Karen as they walked. 'And I got chased.'

'You were a hooligan? Who knew?' Karen grinned.

After walking about two hundred yards, Floyd stopped and turned to face them. 'OK. This is where he was found. There was a stile here back then, and here's the old post.' He kicked a stump of wood sticking out of the ground. 'That's how I know. Over there,' he pointed to a housing estate,' is where the old grain house was until those houses were built.'

'The Robin Estate.' Karen said.

'That's right. And the old footpath went straight down here. The first few yards are the original route, then as we get closer to the estate, it got built over. I'll lead the way.'

The five of them walked down the path, each one looking around to see if there were any visual clues.

'The first road built, according to the plans, was that one, right at the end of this central one,' Floyd pointed.

'Some of it crosses where we think the old footpath was,' John said to Karen.

'I just wish we had something more conclusive,' she replied. 'There's no way we'd be allowed to dig up any of this without proof. Even *with* Mr Binks and his compass.'

'True, but if we can narrow it down to a reasonable area, we can get the sniffer dogs out again.'

They'd nearly covered the whole estate when Floyd Cannon spoke again. 'It's no good. Even if we can pinpoint the location of the grain store, how the hell are we going to find which bit of it we need to dig up or knock down?'

'I agree. This isn't getting us anywhere,' Karen said. She looked at John. 'We'll have to go back to the maps and rethink. Maybe we can at least reduce the area we need to cover and get some sniffer dogs on the case.'

Matthew broke his silence. 'There's no way I'm letting any of you give up on this now. It's too important.'

While four of them exchanged glances, Macy was looking the other way. 'I think someone's seen us,' Macy said. 'I just saw a woman banging on the window of that house there.

The others turned to look. The front door opened, and a woman came running towards them. She was still wearing her slippers, and her hair was blowing in the wind making her look a bit unhinged.

'You go away,' she shouted at them. 'Leave me alone.'

'Who does she think we are?' John asked.

'Only one way to find out,' Karen said. She looked at Macy. 'You're good at this,' she said.

'Oh, thanks,' Macy rolled her eyes. She walked towards the woman and spoke soothingly. 'What is the matter? Are you all right? Is someone bothering you?'

The woman was clearly not all right. Her eyes were wild and unfocused. 'He told me I can't let anybody in,' she said. 'You're not digging up my house. Go away. Just go away. Leave us alone. You must leave everything as it is. Nothing must be disturbed.'

John and Karen had walked up behind Macy and heard what the woman had said.

Macy spoke to her again. 'Who is the man who told you this? What did he look like?' But the woman stood there shaking her head. Macy tried again, but the woman folded her lips into her mouth then turned round and went back into her house. John and Karen exchanged knowing glances.

'What was all that about?' Floyd joined them.

'Is it a lead?' Matthew asked, re-energised.

'It's impossible to explain,' Karen replied, 'But I'm fairly sure the body is under there somewhere. Under her house.'

Floyd's mouth fell open. 'And how in heaven's name do you reach that conclusion?'

'Let's just say that in a case full of mystery and confusion, what that woman said may actually give us a way forward.'

'You'll have to do better than that.' Floyd shook his head.

'I know,' Karen grimaced. 'I do realise that. We'll have to think about it.'

John and Karen talked as they walked back to the car. 'Why would he do that?' John said.

'I assume by him, you meant Mr Binks.'

'Yes.' He stopped walking. 'But we both had that thought. Why? It's a pretty wild assumption.'

'It was the phrase *nothing must be disturbed*. It's got Mr Binks' style all over it. But I agree. It's not enough to get an excavation authorised. We really have to find him.' Her phone rang. She looked at John. 'It's Davie.' She listened to him.

'Hi, Karen. I'm not sure why, but I think this is important. I've just seen that strange wee man of yours in Edinburgh. Do you know what he's doing up here?'

Karen looked meaningfully at John. 'No,' she said to Davie. 'But I think we're going to have to come up there to find out. Do you know where he's staying?'

'He was with a lady. I'll make it my business to find out. And I may be on to Archie at last. I've got a wee lead on where he's got to.'

'We'll be up there shortly. And hopefully, we'll have another colleague with us this time. DC Macy Dodds.'

'Aye,' said Davie. 'It'll be nice to meet the lady behind all the research.'

John waited for Karen to end the call. 'We will?' he said. 'Where's that?'

'Edinburgh, of course. Mr Binks has been spotted up there.' she paused for dramatic effect. 'With a lady.'

John's eyebrows shot up his head so fast Karen couldn't help laughing at him.

'Well, he is male,' she said.

When they got back to the cars, Karen addressed Macy, Matthew, and Floyd. 'I've just had some good news. Mr Binks, the man who helped us find Caitlin McFee, the first girl, has been seen in Edinburgh.'

'That's great news,' Matthew agreed. Floyd nodded.

'The three of us,' she looked at Macy, 'are going to head up there today. My colleague DI Wallace up there is on his trail.'

261

72

Mr Binks and Grizela were indeed together and had slipped into the little shop in Edinburgh to confer. The gatekeeper was, as ever, pleased to see Mr Binks and equally delighted to meet Grizela.

'My dear lady. I had, of course, heard tell of your sad loss and then of your appointment. But as you know, we servants are rarely obliged to travel far from our own fiefdoms. It was a delight to meet this gentleman here, and now I am almost beyond words at meeting the two of you together.'

'Call me Grizela. And thank you for your kind words. You know, do I rightly assume, the reason for our visit to you today?'

'Grizela. How fitting. You have something... something very spiritual about you, madam,' he bowed his head a trifle. 'I shall make a brew of my finest leaves and then, if you permit, we should talk of other things before drawing the sombre veil of your quest over us all.'

The three esoteric souls talked for an hour over tea: of books and maps and how so much better the olden days were.

'And now we should talk of your quest,' the gatekeeper said. He first looked at Grizela.

'Oh, I am here only to help my dear friend, Mr Binks. He fears the destruction of The Witches' Pathway.'

Mr Binks took his cue. 'Indeed, dear sir. There have been recent, how shall I say, disruptions to the pathways caused by a tragic and deluded individual.'

The gatekeeper nodded. 'I am aware of this. But the book lies elsewhere, does it not?'

'The individual concerned lives not far from this city. It is my intention to obtain it from him before the final disruption takes place,' Mr Binks replied.

'I assume you believe that the last disruption will destroy the book?'

'That is my fear,' Mr Binks nodded.

The gatekeeper's face paled. 'And I heard the shriek of the banshee, not once but twice. Have you have visited Magda?' Mr Binks nodded. 'I heard tell that she passed. Is that true?' He looked at Grizela.

'It's impossible to say for certain,' Grizela replied. 'I'm not sure she did quite die; she just became increasingly ethereal. The last time I saw her in her earthly form, she was so diaphanous you could see through her. That was about ten years ago.'

The gatekeeper nodded. 'This is why I think you should be there. You know her and she knows you. She will not lightly let your life be forgone. She will appreciate your skills and wisdom.' He turned to Mr Binks. 'She knows nothing of you, good sir. Forgive my brutal language but you are expendable. You are a mapkeeper only and have never adopted our ways, and I understand this. The world is moving on and you have great foresight. However, Magda would not wish harm to Grizela who has true and pure powers. Together I believe you will be protected.'

Mr Binks nodded and clasped Grizela's hand in his. 'So long as I am not putting this lady, who has become very dear to me, in any danger.'

Grizela smiled. 'None whatsoever,' she said. 'I feel completely safe, and I feel sure that Magda and the other spirits are looking after me. She leaned forward to the gatekeeper. 'I may even convert him,' she grinned.

'That would be a wonderful result,' the gatekeeper replied. 'When do you propose to undertake your mission? It must be soon. The date is approaching.'

'Tomorrow night at nine,' Mr Binks said. 'We know the portal is open about that time when his offspring tends to him. We still have one day in hand if we fail. I hope to take him by surprise and rescue the manuscript.'

The gatekeeper nodded. 'It should never have been in his possession. He stole it many years ago, it is only right it is restored to a trusted custodian. May the spirits be with you.'

'Thank you,' Mr Binks said. 'We will come to visit you the day after tomorrow and let you know how we fare.'

The gatekeeper laughed and Grizela joined him. 'I will know tomorrow,' he said. 'My hearing is exceptionally acute with regard to matters of the pathways. I wish you well.' He turned to Grizela. 'And especially you, Madam Grizela. I feel so fortunate to have met you and I look forward to you joining me for tea again soon.'

'The pleasure will be mine,' Grizela smiled back at him.

***

For Karen's team, the journey north was not a good one. The weather was cold and the traffic was bad all the way. They stopped several times for breaks and food.

'We're not going to make it before nine at this rate,' Karen said as they got back into her car.

'You're right,' John agreed. 'It's probably best we get booked in somewhere now, just in case we lose connectivity later. Shall I try the hotel I stayed at?'

'Yes, if it's the same one as Mr Binks was at. We might even catch him there.'

'I so want to meet this man,' Macy said from the back seat. 'I think he's a druid or something.'

John laughed. 'You'll be disappointed then. He's more like a civil servant.'

'I used to like him.' Karen said, 'But now I think he's borderline creepy. There's something extremely suspicious about him.'

'And what's this DI like?' Macy asked.

Karen looked back at her. 'Are you completely man mad?'

'Not completely.'

'I'm ringing him now to let him know what we're doing. I'm going to add a warning about you.'

Macy grinned. 'Tell him I'm a pussycat.'

They arrived at the hotel two hours later and went straight to their respective rooms. When they were tucked up in bed, John asked about Macy. 'Doesn't she have a boyfriend? She's very pretty.' Karen gaped. 'Not as pretty as you of course.'

'What? John, do you really think either of those comments is appropriate? Firstly, she's her own woman and does what she wants. Secondly, I don't give a stuff whether you think I'm pretty or not.'

'I can't say right for doing wrong, can I?' John replied. 'Did you or did you not imply that she...'

'Oh, sure she likes to have fun. She gave up trying to keep a boyfriend after our last case. And,' she prodded John in the chest, 'she's just as ambitious as I am and doesn't want to tie herself down to anyone. So be warned.'

'That's me told from your very own lips. Can I kiss them better?'

Karen puckered up and waited.

73

Friday 22 November

Macy was in for a surprise when she arrived at the station with Karen and John. As soon as Davie appeared, she peered at him and he at her.

'Don't I know you?' They both said to each other, then both laughed in unison.

'It's just that you look so familiar,' said Macy.

'You, too,' said Davie

'I used to get that all the time when I was in uniform. Do you know that saying? The only gay in the village? I'll tell you a secret. I'm not gay.'

Davie roared with laughter.

'Er, guys?' Karen said. 'We've got things to do when you're quite ready?'

'Sure,' Davie said. 'The room's all set up. You know the way. I'll get the coffees.' He left with a very definite twinkle in his eye.

Karen was keen to get on with business so as soon as they were seated around the table, she began. 'So, Davie, where exactly did you see Mr Binks and his lady friend?'

'It was a wee road, not far from John's hotel.'

'That makes sense. And you saw him with a woman?'

'Aye. And if I knew what a druid looked like with clothes, I'd have had her for one.'

'He's not at the hotel now, I checked. Maybe he's staying with her? I wonder why they came into town?'

'What does he do again? Books? Maybe there's a shop around there.'

John, who had been sitting looking somewhat dazed, joined in the conversation. 'That makes sense,' he rubbed his head. 'He does like to connect with other booksellers. Actually, I'm sure he mentioned a bookshop he wanted to visit. Maybe I should investigate?'

'That rings a bell with me, too. What about CCTV?' Karen asked Davie. 'You must have contacts in the central office?'

'Aye. That's worth a look. But there's something else I want to check out.'

'Archie?' Karen said.

'Aye. I followed a trail of sorts the other day in the frozen grass. Footsteps. I couldn't get far because as soon as it went towards the woods there was nothing to follow. But I'd like to have a look in daylight, just to get my bearings. We might just find something.'

Karen nodded. 'OK. Macy here is brilliant at CCTV. Why don't we split up? You and John follow the trail and if you can give us the name of someone to speak to, Macy, I can see if we can trace him.'

'Sounds good to me. I'll get right on it,' Davie said. 'Let's aim to meet back here at noon. There's a pub near Donald McTear's house. Does a grand steak pie. It's called The Thistle'

'Sorted,' said Karen.

'OK,' John agreed but he still looked puzzled.

'Great!' said Macy with genuine enthusiasm.

***

'Wow! This is such a beautiful city,' Macy said as she gazed out of Karen's car window. 'All that white stone.'

'If you say so,' Karen replied. 'We're here.'

'DS Thorpe and DC Dodds, here to check some CCTV,' Karen announced at the desk.

'Aye. Are you the copper who found wee Caitlin McFee? I recognise the name.'

'Yes.' Karen couldn't help smiling. 'But there's another girl still missing, and we think there may be some clues up here still.'

'Och, yes. We've set up a room for you. DI Wallace gave us the approximate area. Let me know if you need to delve further out. This way.' He led them to a well-prepared room.

Macy took to the viewer like a duck to water. Karen took out her map of the city. 'Here we go. We're looking for a turning off Leith Street, just here.'

'OK. I've got a camera fifty yards away. What time was it?'
'Around noon.'
'And what does he look like?'

'Good point,' Karen said. 'Did you ever see the film, Oliver?' Macy shook her head. 'If I said short, bald with side-whiskers, and very old-fashioned looking, would that help?'

'I'll try. But a proper image would be better.'

Karen was getting bored. *This really isn't my thing.* 'OK, you stay here, I'm going to walk to the hotel and see if they know anything about Mr Binks' whereabouts. They might be able to give me an image of him from the reception desk, if they have cameras. Ring me if you find anything.'

'Sure.'

Karen was a fast walker and soon got to the hotel. She waved her ID at the receptionist.

'I'm making enquiries about a man called Binks. I know he stayed here a couple of nights ago.'

'Aye, I remember him. Such a polite wee man. He checked out a couple of days ago I believe.'

'Do you know why he was here?'

'Och no. We don't ask our client's business here.'

'There wasn't a book convention or anything going on in the city?' she asked.

'No. But I believe he did ask for a map.'

Of course he did. Karen thought. 'Good. And did he leave anything behind in his room?'

'I'd have to ask housekeeping that. Give me a moment.' The receptionist picked up the phone. Her hand traced a line on her computer screen as she spoke. 'Room number eight. Can you tell me if the gentleman left anything behind?' She waited for an answer. 'Och, thanks.' She looked at Karen. 'I'm sorry, the room was spotless apparently. If only all our guests were like that.'

'Thanks.' *But no thanks* Karen thought. She looked around but saw no evidence of a camera. 'Do you have CCTV here at all?'

'Och, we do, but it's been down for a few days for maintenance.

Karen frowned and left the hotel. When she was outside she called Macy. 'Any luck?'

'Not really. I can see a bit of a man who might be him, but he seems to have been aware of cameras.'

'What about the woman? What did Davie say?'

'She looked like a druid.'

'I didn't see anyone in long flowing robes. But the man did turn into a small lane, I can't make out a name. There's nothing on the map but a dotted line.'

'OK, give me directions from the hotel and I'll have a look.'

Karen turned this way and that until she reached a break in the road. She walked into the area. She saw the sides of the buildings on the road she had just walked down and investigated a ramshackle building where the road changed into cobbles. She saw what looked like an old shop front but it looked like it hadn't been used for years. She banged on the door. No reply. *I wonder*, she thought as she walked back to the police station.

***

Davie drove John to Donald McTear's house and parked nearby. 'John? Are you OK? You look a bit disorientated.'

John scratched his head. 'I'm fine. This looks a bit familiar.'

'You've been here before?'

'No. But I sort of recognise it.'

'Come on. I'll show you how far I got.'

Davie led the way along the grassy path until he came to the outskirts of the woods. He stopped and looked around, shrugging.

'Go left,' John said. 'I don't know why, but I think it's that way.'

The two men carried on walking. John stopped every so often to look around. Finally, he too came to a stop. 'I'm sorry. I don't remember any more.'

'And I don't know how you could have got this far.' Davie replied.

'Neither do I. It doesn't make any sense at all. But I have felt like this before when I've been with Mr Binks.'

Davie shook his head. 'We'd better get going back to the pub. The girls will probably be there already.'

'No, wait a second,' John closed his eyes as if he was trying to force a memory. Without speaking he walked towards a large shrubby area full of green foliage and bright with berries.

Davie joined him. 'Well, there's nothing here.' He kicked at the shrub. 'Certainly not enough to hide a fully grown man.'

'Agreed,' John sighed. 'Let's get back.'

'And I'm going to phone Donald. I don't trust him.' Davie said.

74

At The Thistle, the four of them compared notes, and it was getting heated.

'We've got to follow him tonight. We know he's around there somewhere in the evening,' Davie said.

'What does Donald say? Has any more food gone missing?'

'Aye. And he says he hasn't heard from him. But he's lying, I'm sure, to protect him.'

'Only one way to find out,' Karen said.

John frowned. 'We must get back-up, I don't know what's going on up there, but I don't like it.'

'They'll never authorise it,' Davie said. 'And there's four of us. Against a man-sized child and an ancient man? We don't need any back up.'

'I'm game,' Macy piped up.

'OK. Where do we start? Davie?'

'Aye. John and I walked some of the route today. We can station ourselves at various points to look out for him.'

'That's settled then,' Karen said. 'Let's meet up back here at seven.'

'Eat well. Wrap up warm.' Davie warned. 'It's going to be a cold one. Minus two in the city so you can take a few more off for where we are. Dark clothes only. Luckily we're not expecting snow.'

That's sums up my wardrobe, Karen thought.

***

Over dinner, Macy had some questions for Karen and John. 'Tell me exactly what you think is going on here, Karen. What do you know, John? What do you think you remember? I'm cool with it all, I just want to get my head round it.'

Karen started. 'OK. The man missing, presumed killed in action, Fergus Anderson, aka, Andrew Ferguson – who is also the father of Donald McTear and Archie Logan – could, conceivably, be alive and well.'

Macy nodded. 'I got that much. And both his sons live here, too. But could he survive outside?'

'He was a hiker,' Karen said. 'A former soldier and, I'd guess, a survival expert.'

John nodded. 'He certainly walked all the paths of Great Britain, mountains and all.'

'But that was, what, fifty years ago?' Macy said.

'Yes,' Karen agreed. 'He's probably found himself a shelter or something. In fact...' she paused. *How weird does my so-called dream sound? Go for it.*

She took a deep breath. 'I had a weird experience, call it a dream, or a hallucination or whatever you like, but I was talking to this wizened old man about the murdered girls.'

'You what?' Macy gaped.

'Mr Binks said it was the drugs they gave me when I was knocked out,' Macy's eyebrows hit the roof. 'Yes, I haven't filled you in, I'm sorry.'

'And I have a bit of a memory,' John pitched in. 'I seem to remember following this very tall man on the route that Davie and I walked today.'

'Tall man? You didn't say that before, John.' Karen said.
'Didn't I?'

'No. But there is a common factor for both of us.'
'Mr Binks.' John said.

'He's at the centre of everything,' Karen added. 'John, can you remember anything else about the tall man?'

'John shook his head. 'I think we were following him, but we lost him. Anyway, what about your memory? I think you should tell us about that.'

'It was the night you and Davie and I were knocked out, or fell, or whatever happened.'

'Karen? I'm never letting you out of my sight again,' Macy said. 'What the fuck have you all been up to?'

'It is very strange Macy. But I was underground, I think. Talking to this horrible old creature. He knew my name, he knew about Dad and definitely Mr Binks. I think Davie was there, too, but I'm not sure. Mr Binks explained it all to me afterwards.' She shook her head. 'I'm sorry.'

'But who drugged you?' Macy asked.

'Anderson,' Karen surprised herself. 'Or someone acting for him. He was trying to kill all of us, but Mr Binks saved us.'

'And is that actually true or simply what he wants you to believe?' Macy asked. 'Sounds like I'm the only one who hasn't been screwed by this Mr Binks. I'll be ready for him when I meet him, don't you worry.'

***

At the appointed hour, Karen, John, and Macy met up with Davie outside the pub.

'Are you ready?' he asked. 'We might have a long wait.'

'We are,' Karen replied. 'What's the plan?

'I've been to see Donald and put the fear of God in him. He's in there,' Davie nodded his head back to the pub. 'He thinks food goes missing every day. So we go tonight.'

'So who's doing what?'

'This is my suggestion,' Davie said. 'Macy, you wait for him around the back of the house as near the path as we can risk without him seeing you. You'll tip us off if you see him.' Macy nodded.

'Karen, you'll be stationed in the entrance to the woods so you can see the path from the house and warn us if he doesn't follow the route we plotted earlier.'

'Got it,' Karen said.

'John and I will cover the wooded area. I've got torches for all of you, but don't use them unless it's essential. There'll not be much of a moon tonight.'

'And do we follow him?' Macy asked.

'So long as you're well behind. We don't want to spook him.'

'And this is so he'll lead us to his cave?' Karen said.

'What?' Davie looked at her frowning.

'It just came to me,' Karen said. 'I don't know why. Do you remember being in a cave?'

Davie scratched his head. 'I don't know.' He looked at his watch and his expression changed. 'Time's critical. Come on. Let's get in place. Donald says it could be around eight. We can't miss him.'

'Where was I then?' John said as they walked. 'That day. We all woke up together, didn't we? In Davie's house.'

It was Davie's turn to shake his head. 'No. OK, maybe. I don't remember.' His face froze and he stopped walking. 'I took the gun with me. I'm sure I did.' He looked at his watch. 'Seven-fifteen. I've just got time to get it.'

Karen shook her head. 'Whatever it is we're dealing with I don't think guns will help.'

John nodded his head in agreement. 'No guns.'

Macy was agitated. 'Look you're all freaking me out here. We've got a plan, can't we just stick to it?'

'Sorry, Mace. Weird stuff. We all seem to have lost our memory, or at least bits of it. Call it group hypnosis or something.'

'She's right. OK, no gun. Let's get going,' Davie said.

'Oh, yes, indeed,' said John. 'I might not remember words, but I have an infallible memory for routes. If he comes out, we'll definitely catch him.'

'OK, lads and lassies,' said Davie. 'We're off.'

The four of them walked to Donald McTear's road.

Davie talked as he walked. 'Macy, there's the house. Donald's not around, so you're looking for someone coming in the front door. He'll most likely not put the lights on. If you don't mind crouching a bit, you can hide behind the wheelie bin.'

'How glamorous,' Macy remarked as she got into place.

Davie led Karen and John to the beginning of the wooded area. 'Karen, if you can hide behind that tree, you can see him coming towards here.'

'I can do better than that,' Karen replied. She grabbed a branch and climbed ten feet into the tree. 'No one looks up into trees at night, and I can see for miles. Well not miles but you know what I mean.' She settled into the branches. 'And I've got a signal. I'm ringing Macy to check we're linked.'

'What a woman, ' John said.

'Aye,' Davie agreed. John glared at him. 'C'mon John. Let's get going. We're basically going north.'

75

Macy was beginning to get really bored when she heard a faint noise at the front. *That's definitely someone going in.* She ducked below the kitchen window and saw a light appear inside. *That's the fridge*, she thought. *Damn, he's coming out the back.* Creeping back behind the bin, she didn't dare look until everything was quiet again. Then popping her head up, she saw the tall bearded figure with a white bag walking up the path. She messaged Karen. 'He's heading your way.'

Karen was already watching him coming towards her. She couldn't see his face but even stooping, she recognised the slim man's frame from the video.

It was noisier where she was. The wind whistled through what was left of the autumn leaves and the crows cawed as they settled for the night crowding comfortably into the bare branches of the trees.

She could no longer see John and Davie, but she knew their direction and messaged them. When she was sure the man had passed far enough ahead, she waited for Macy to join her and they followed after him.

John chose his position behind a tree about fifty metres before the shrubs he'd identified earlier, while Davie paced the area in wide circles, stopping when John's hand signal indicated the man's approach. From their separate vantage points, they watched as he came closer. His eyes, shining in the half-light, looked blank and staring. The carrier bag he held swung in his hand. It was definitely Archie Logan.

Snap! Davie trod on a small branch but Archie carried on as if he'd heard nothing. Glancing at each other, John and Davie followed behind until they came to the shrubby area.

Archie stopped dead in his tracks. He suddenly looked around and pointed towards John, shouting something unintelligible. He ran at him, his hands held out in a strangling pose.

Davie sprang into action. Together they struggled with Archie, but he was too quick for them. He ran off into the woodlands with John and Davie running behind him.

Karen was way ahead of Macy as she ran towards the scene, but she spotted something else and held out her hand out to warn her. *What the fuck...*

Coming from their left-hand side were two bustling figures. Karen recognised one immediately.

Macy snuck up to Karen and whispered. 'Mr Binks'?

Karen nodded. 'And the woman,' she mouthed back.

They watched and listened as Mr Binks and Grizela walked up to the shrubs.

'This is the spot, my dear. Are you ready?' said Mr Binks.

'As I'll ever be,' smiled Grizela. 'Oh Magda, oh great one. Give us the words that we might recover and protect the ancient manuscript.' She looked at Mr Binks, and he looked back at her. They held hands and an expression of pure joy appeared on both their faces. In perfect unison, they said something out loud that neither Karen nor Macy understood. A moment later they had disappeared.

'What the hell?' Karen said. They were quickly joined by John and Davie.

'He was a decoy,' Davie said. 'Archie. We've left him up there, he fell into a dead faint when we caught him. This is where the real action happens. But where?'

'In there somewhere,' Karen pointed to the shrubs.

Davie waded in. 'There's something in here!' he yelled. A second later he was gone.

'I'm going, too. I think I know what this is.' Karen followed Davie into the shrubs.

John looked at Macy. 'Someone better stay here.' Macy shrugged. 'Fine by me.' She watched as John followed Karen into the void.

***

When she was in the cave, Karen brushed herself down a little and saw Davie was just ahead.

'This must've taken him years to build,' Davie said.

'Unless it was already here and he simply found it. Does it seem familiar to you? It does to me. That musty smell.'

'Aye,' Davie agreed. 'And that's a puzzle in itself.'

'How could we have got from here to your house?'

'Och, it's not that far from my place. It's the roads that make it seem farther.'

Karen frowned. 'Mr Binks and that woman clearly knew about it, too. I wonder what's so special about the place? Must be one of Mr Binks' footpath things. They said something before they disappeared inside, but I didn't hear it properly. Or it was in a different language.'

'Shush. I can hear talking,' Davie said. He saw John following behind and put his finger to his lips. They approached a fork in the path. Davie looked each way then back at Karen and John. Karen pointed at herself and John then tipped her head to the right. Davie nodded and went left.

Karen turned her phone light on and followed the right-hand wall of the cave where the headroom was the highest. *We're turning back in again,* she realised as she carried on. *There's a light ahead.* She stopped and looked back at John. Then she pointed onwards. He nodded.

At the next turn, they found themselves in a big, rounded area. Karen blinked, her eyes adjusting to the dim light of a single candle. There, cross-legged on the floor was a solitary figure. Karen recognised it immediately. This was no nightmare creature; it was a human being. A man. It was Fergus Anderson, but there was something different about him. This wasn't the vision floating in her head somewhere. This man was living, breathing flesh.

Opposite, Davie appeared from his tunnel. He took a deep breath and walked straight up to him. 'FergusAnderson; also known as Andrew Ferguson, I am arresting you on the suspicion of the murder of Caitlin McFee...'

Anderson stood up and with superhuman force threw his fist at Davie, knocking him flying. Karen had sidled up behind Anderson, but he turned in a flash and within seconds had her head in an arm lock. She struggled as she felt his rancid breath on her face. John crept up behind and rugby tackled Anderson's legs. As he fell, Davie threw his body onto Anderson and pinned him down.

'We've got him,' Karen said as she pulled out her handcuffs. Before she could cuff him, they were all made aware of more presences in the cave.

'Well, well, well,' said Mr Binks looking at Anderson. 'I see that which I seek before me now, and since it was stolen by you a long time ago, it is my duty to return it into safekeeping.'

Anderson snarled and lunged towards Mr Binks. John edged over to help Karen. Together they pinned him down.

Mr Binks stood firm, and behind him stood Grizela standing even more resolutely. Her eyes were fixed on something. Karen followed her gaze. There, on a small wooden stand at the back of the cave, she saw an old leather-bound tome. Grizela walked towards it.

Anderson shrieked in a voice that did not sound human. In that moment he transformed into the gnarled old monster of Karen's thoughts. 'Do not touch that. Leave well alone. You fools! You don't know what you are doing.'

Grizela was undaunted. She leant forward and grasped the book with both hands, holding it up so Anderson could see she had it.

Karen heard something before she could see it. Earth was falling from the ceiling. The ground was beginning to shake. The whole cave was beginning to disintegrate. Anderson wriggled free.

John held her Karen tight.

'We've got to get out!' Davie yelled. 'This way.'

Like blind mice, they held hands in a chain and tried to find a way out. Karen slipped, her mouth opened to yell, quickly filling with earth. Then everything went black.

76

Karen was falling. A small hand was outstretched towards her. She grasped the hand and saw the figure of Amy Warren in her party dress smiling at her. She heard the words. 'You can find me now, Karen.'

Karen was moving along the ground, but she didn't know how. There was another small figure ahead of her. Then she saw the smiling face of Katherine Engles.

Still moving, a grinning Caitlin McFee spoke to her. 'Tell those boys I still think they're horrid.'

'Where am I?' Karen was falling again. Falling through a dark nothingness.

'Karen!' Someone was shouting her name.

'Over here!'

Karen felt herself being pulled through something. She began to open her eyes. 'John?'

'Oh, thank god, Karen. I thought we'd lost you.'

Karen began coughing and spluttering, spitting out particles of mud. John rolled her onto her side.

Davie came up to them both. 'Any sign of Anderson?' John shook his head. 'And that wee man and his wifee?'

'No idea. I don't even know where we are. It's not the way we came in.'

'Macy? She might have seen something. MACY!' Davie yelled. There was no reply. 'I'm going to take a look around. You make sure Karen's OK.'

'I'm fine,' Karen muttered, still on the ground. 'Find Anderson. And Binks.'

'Aye, I'll do my best. And I will get back up. Damn.' He patted himself down.

'Now what?' John said.

'I've lost my phone.' Davie said.

'Mine's gone, too,' Karen said checking her pockets as she heaved herself to a sitting position.

'Take mine,' John handed it over. Davie saw the screensaver of Karen. 'Och, sweet.'

Davie paced due South until he picked up a signal. 'DI Wallace here. We need back-up. Can you pick the coordinates from the phone? Aye. We're looking for a murder suspect. He's very old, you can't miss him. And some witnesses. A dapper wee man with a fulsome woman. We were all in an underground tunnel with no structural supports as far as I can tell. They may still be underground. We'll need dogs and manual diggers.'

Karen was at last on her feet looking around. 'I think I know where we are. I remember seeing that massive fir tree over there. Follow me. It's this way.'

'How far did we walk?' Davie joined them. It couldn't have been this far, could it?'

Being underground is disorientating,' John said. 'And we followed a different tunnel out. What was that?'

The three of them stopped and heard a faint 'Karen!' in the distance.

'Macy,' they said together. 'Just coming,' Karen tried to shout but all she could do was squeak.

Two minutes later they were all reconciled, each receiving a mimed hug from Macy. 'I paid a fortune for this coat,' she explained. 'And you're all filthy. But it's good to see you all.'

'We're missing the main suspect. A very old man. Did you see him?'

Macy shook her head. 'When the ground shook, I ran out of the way. I could see the shrubs falling down and loads of branches fell, too. I was too busy hanging on to something to see anything. But I did think I saw a male figure weaving through the trees over there.' She paused.

'What?' Karen asked.

'I did see something else though. I caught a glimpse of what looked like a woman running through the trees ahead,' she pointed. 'But by then I was too busy looking for you guys to take proper notice.'

'No worry,' Davie said. 'It could be Anderson and the woman, going in different directions. And where's Mr Binks? Can't take any chances. We'll need to look for them all.'

'What happens now then?' Macy asked.

'I suggest you all get back to the pub. I'll wait for the back-up to arrive so I can show them where to go. If you see them, send them on up won't you?'

The cold was beginning to bite through the adrenaline. Karen led the way without question from John or Macy.

'This is where we came in,' she said. The others stopped to take in the scene. There was a clear dip in the ground but everything seemed to be covered with soil and broken branches.

'It doesn't look like it at all,' John said, looking at Macy.

'Everything caved in,' Macy said. 'All the shrubs were buried when the rest of the ground crumbled. I didn't hang around to watch the whole thing.'

They trudged through the woods back towards the grassy area in silence.

Macy grabbed John's arm. 'I saw something, just there,' she pointed.

'It moved, whatever it was,' Karen said. They hurried towards a dark shape lying on the ground.

'Dinnae hurt me,' the figure said.

'It's him, isn't it?' Karen said. 'Archie Logan. The man who killed my father.'

'I dinnae do anything,' Archie said. 'Who am I? And who are you?'

'Is he pretending?' Macy asked.

'What do you mean?' Archie said.

'There's no point,' Karen said. 'Davie said he wasn't right in the head. I'll call him now.'

'And there's the back-up arriving.' John pointed to a small convoy of two SUVs and an ambulance. 'They'll take him. They need something to do while they're waiting. I'm going to join Davie if you don't mind.'

'Oh, that's fine.' Karen said. 'I need a drink.'

'Me, too,' Macy agreed. 'See you later.'

John helped Archie up and took him to the ambulance. 'He's very confused. I don't think he's injured though. His brother lives just there. Donald McTear.'

77

Mr Binks didn't question how he and Grizela had emerged from the cave with the manuscript completely unscathed. *Fate*, he decided. *And the skill of a wonderful practitioner*. They had come through the woods a different way following a footpath no longer recorded in print but still serviceable. It led out to a different road where a taxi had set them down earlier and was due to pick them up again shortly. But now it was all over, he felt rather strange.

'Are you all right, Gustav?'

'I'm feeling a little under the weather actually. Do you mind if I sit?' He handed her the tome and settled down on the edge of the road. 'I expect it's all the excitement. And how foolish of me not to ask you, dear lady, are you unharmed?'

Grizela nodded. 'Not a scratch, Gustav. We were being looked after.'

'My thoughts precisely. So we did it! We actually recovered that precious book, and we both survived.' He looked up and around. 'Thank you, Magda, wherever you are. I will take great care of it for you.' His eye caught something strange. Grizela looked different somehow. 'My dear lady,' he began but she moved away from him. 'Where are you going?'

'There's somewhere I have to be.' She spoke clearly and firmly but her voice sounded different.

'Please explain. Have I done something to offend you?'

'I'm going back now to ma hame. I have all I need from you.'

'What do you mean, dear lady...'

'Ye dinnae need to call me that now. I'm no lady.'

Mr Binks was seriously worried now. 'Grizela? Is it you? You sound so different.'

'I have it and it's going to be safe wi me.' She cackled loudly and suddenly he remembered who she sounded like.

'You can't be!' he exclaimed, but as he tried to get up he was thrown back with a force that left him breathless. And scared. 'Who are you?' he said, his eyes as wide as saucers. As he looked, Grizela's features began to change. The friendly-faced woman became thin and bony, and her piercing blue eyes were not those of a friend, but of a fiend. He was terrified. 'You... you are...'

'Magda!' She gave a shriek which chilled him to the bone. 'You stupid wee scrote. Did ye really think I would leave that precious tome in the hands of a miserable clerk? Aye, I needed you to get it back for me, but now I have it you will never see it or me again.' The woman ran into the forest until Mr Binks had lost sight of her.

Mr Binks yelled out 'Grizela' in frustration. But by then, there was nobody alive to hear him.

Dejected, he sat down again and waited for the taxi to arrive.

***

It was eleven o'clock before a tired and weary John and Davie rejoined Karen and Macy in the pub.

'They've secured the site now,' John said. 'But there's no way they can start excavating until morning. They've had the dogs out there, and there's nothing living detected.'

'I can't see how Anderson would have got out of that, but it sounds like Mr Binks might have got away safely,' Karen said. 'We must interrogate him as soon as we find him.'

'Agreed.' Davie nodded. 'And I've had a word with Donald. Like as not Archie will be back with him by now. I suggest we meet up at the site in the morning bright and early.'

'Yes,' Karen said. 'Let's go.'

'In the car, while Karen drove, Macy was inquisitive. 'Why was Mr Binks even there?'

'Good question. John?'

'I know he was looking for a particular book.'

Karen's eyes lit up. 'That's it! It might explain a great deal.'

John nodded. 'I saw the woman pick up something just before the cave roof began to fall in. And yes, he's been acting extremely suspiciously lately. Like earlier today, I'm sure I recognised Archie, but I don't recall meeting him.'

'He was in the video clip, remember?' Karen said.

'No, I mean I saw him in person. Even now I can't quite connect him with the image from the clip. That man was tall and sturdy. Archie was, was... a shrivelled up wreck. A child, with a child's demeanour.'

'I recognised him at once,' Karen shot back. 'Face, beard, build... '

John ignored her. 'I also knew some of the route to the cave. It's like the time I thought I met Charlie Worthington, but I hadn't.'

'Do you think Mr Binks fiddles with your mind?'

'Don't be silly, Karen. I'm really not susceptible like that.'

'I bet you are.' Karen looked at Macy. She nodded.

'And why do you think that?' John retorted, suddenly engaged and a little offended.

'Because you're mild-mannered and logical. You take people at face value; you never challenge them.'

'That's because I was well brought up,' John said. He changed the subject. 'I wonder where Mr Binks is staying? He must still be with that woman.'

'Wherever he is, we have to find him. We need to find Amy's body urgently or we're off the case forever. And whatever else we find in that cave might just help us, too.'

'Anderson, dead or alive?' John said. 'You told me you had a dream about him. Was it him?'

'I wish you hadn't reminded me about that,' Karen said. 'Yes, he looked exactly like he did in my dream. Then I dreamt about the girls, too, while you were pulling me out. But I've seen their pictures. I've only seen that very old picture of him.'

As they pulled up at the hotel Macy looked out of the car window. 'There, in reception. I just caught sight of someone who looks very like your man.'

'On it,' John jumped out of the car and ran inside while Karen parked. By the time they got inside, neither man was visible.

Karen looked around. Her eyes followed the small pointed sign which read Bar. 'This way I think.'

There, sat at a corner table, they saw John and Mr Binks huddled together. Mr Binks looked up.

'Good evening Detective Sergeant Thorpe. I've just been explaining myself. The lady I was with, now has the precious volume in her possession.'

'Are you telling me, you came all this way just to find that book? Is that why you were helping us all along?'

'Good gracious no. My dear young lady, you do me a great disservice. I wanted to do my civic duty too.'

John threw Karen a *stop it* look. 'How did you get out of the cave?'

Mr Binks sighed. 'My companion was, how shall I say it?' He paused. 'She was someone with ancient ways and knowledge. She was familiar with the labyrinth and knew a way out. Indeed, it was her book in the very beginning, so all is well.'

'Then you'll help us find Amy Warren's body?'

'I give you my word. It's too late to go home tonight, but I shall be leaving early in the morning, and I will be at your disposal.'

'He can't do more than that,' John said looking at Karen. 'And I've asked him about the other things and it's fine. I imagined it all.'

'Did you indeed,' Karen looked suspiciously at Mr Binks. 'Anyway, there's nothing we can do tonight. Safe journey, Mr Binks. I'll see you later tomorrow.'

78

Saturday 23 November

Early in the morning, Davie was at the site when Karen, John, and Macy arrived.

'They've got something already,' Davie said. 'Over there in the tent. Human remains.' They followed him past the security tape to the tent. Karen was shocked to see a skeletal body laid out on a plastic sheet.

'A mummy?' Karen said. 'Anderson was scrawny, but he still had some life in him.'

'Aye. This body looks like it's been dead a good few years I'd say. But they're taking samples and testing. He fits the profile. About six foot six inches and in his eighties. There's a giant old army rucksack, too.'

'Strange,' Karen said. 'Could it be the man we wrestled with?'

'Karen, I've seen so many strange things since you came here, I'd believe anything.'

'Could there have been another family member?' Macy asked. 'Maybe another generation?'

'It's a thought,' Davie said. 'They'll be able to test all the DNA. And now Archie's back in the land of the living.'

'What do you mean?' John frowned.

'Och, he can't remember anything for the last two or so years. He claims he was under a spell. And Donald almost agrees with him. He says he wasn't like he is now when he came to stay, and he's certainly not the half-wit I spoke to. If he was pretending, he's done a bloody good job.'

The tent flap was pulled open as one of the forensics team came in. 'We've found another body,' he announced. 'This one had ID on him.' He handed a small flat object to Davie.

'It's a Press pass,' he said. 'Mick Chatterton.'

'The missing journalist,' Karen said. 'Poor man.'

'Last seen in Yorkshire. I remember searching the papers for him.' Macy said. 'Why this case?'

287

'He was a freelancer,' Karen said. 'Maybe he made the connection before we did, and someone didn't like it.'

'The forensics man took his mask off and looked at John. 'Hello again.'

'Hello, indeed. Last I heard you couldn't identify the DNA on Caitlin Mc Fee's remains as even human. Any update on that?'

'Och, it's a strange one. It looks like someone put something there to try to confuse us. But how, fifty years ago they could have foreseen DNA I cannae tell you. We've examined the inside of the body bag now and we think we've got something else. It's in the lab now.'

'Are there any other bodies back there?'

'No, we're pretty sure it's just the two. We'll do site testings of course, in case we find anything else, but we dinnae think it's likely.'

'We're still looking for an octogenarian then.' John looked at the mummy. 'I wonder who this man was?'

'I think we should be getting back to finding Amy now,' Karen said. 'There's nothing more we can do here, is there? And Mr Binks is ready and willing.'

'True. We could be there by lunchtime if we hurry.'

'Macy?'

'Oh, I was thinking of staying another day if you don't mind. It's such a lovely city, and I'd like to see more of it.'

'And I'd be delighted to show you,' Davie said. 'You can help me with the paperwork if you like and in return, I'll give you a night you'll never forget.'

Karen's eyes raced skywards.

'It is the weekend, Karen.' John said. 'And we know the routine now. I'll drive.'

'Sure,' Karen agreed. Suppressing the tiny bit of jealousy she felt, she added 'Have fun and let us know about the body.'

'Will do,' Davie said with a grin.

***

I'm going to call her Racy Macy,' Karen laughed as she and John drove home.

'What are you saying?'

'Never mind. She likes to have fun, that's all. Shit.'

'What now?'

'Voicemail from Floyd Cannon. Must've come through last night. I swear I didn't see it.'

'Saying what?'

'There's been some sort of earth tremor in Lincoln. The Robin Estate. Late last night. They want us down there as soon as possible.'

'Was it when the cave collapsed?'

'The voicemail was sent at midnight.'

'That's about right, isn't it?'

'It follows the others I suppose. Hearing the shrieking in Edinburgh. But a tremor of that magnitude. That's beyond weird.'

'Not if you follow through the logic,' John said. 'If these girls really did link together some sort of magnetic force, the destruction of the cave, or even the taking of the book, might have triggered it.'

'And we know that's bollocks, don't we?'

'Very true,' John said. 'I was getting carried away for a moment then. But whereabouts in the estate? Not that house where we saw the woman?'

'According to Floyd, that's exactly where.'

'It'll save on all the permissions then. And we might not need Mr Binks.'

'Let's get there first.'

They made good progress down to Lincoln, but stopped for a break halfway.

'I'm going to catch up with Matthew. To make sure he's in the loop.' She took out her phone.

'Matthew? It's Karen. Just wondering if you heard about the house.'

'Yes, I was about to ring you. Floyd told me. The site's not secure yet. Do you know the Dog and Hound?'

'Dog and Hound? John?'

'I know it.'

'OK, we'll meet you there. Should be around four PM.'

The rest of the drive Karen agonised over what to tell Matthew. *Does he need to know the whole thing? What would I do if I had the chance to see my mother again, as she was before she died?* 'I'd want to see it.' She said out loud.

'See what?'

'Nothing. Just thinking.'

'Karen, I know you. What?'

'I've made my decision. Just keep on going.'

It was five past four and already dark when they arrived at the pub. Matthew was already sitting inside with a bottle of wine on the go. He got up when he saw them. As they joined him they could see he was trembling with excitement, or nerves, or both.

'I've waited so long for this. Do you really think we're there? that we'll find her?'

'We can't be sure,' Karen said. 'But we think the earth tremor may be somehow linked to the discovery we made last night.'

'Which was?'

'Well, it's not definite yet but we may have found Fergus Anderson's body. It certainly matches his physical appearance and approximate age.'

'But physically linked? How could that happen?'

'There has been talk of pathways and magnetic currents. that's how we found Caitlin McFee's body. I know it all sounds a bit far-fetched. Supernatural even. But there's also something weirder that we've seen, possibly twice if we include last night.'

'What?'

'Look,' Karen began. 'This is going to sound really bizarre. But I think you might want to be there when we find the body.'

'Of course I do,' said Matthew, puzzled.

'No, I mean really close up.' Karen said.

Matthew scratched his head. 'I have tried for years to find my sister. Now I find someone who might just have done that, and she talks gibberish.' He sat back in his chair. 'I know there'll be nothing left of her. I'm happy not to see her, to be honest. They won't be able to tell straightway, will they?'

Karen took a deep breath and as she spoke realised that he would think her even more of an idiot. 'When we uncovered the body of Caitlin McFee for a second, just a second, she looked exactly as she did the day she went missing.'

Matthew took a slug of wine. 'You what?' he said.

'It was probably my brain playing tricks on me.' Karen said. 'But if there's a chance it happens again, I thought you or your mother might want to be there. If it does, that is, and I don't know if it will or even if it really happened last time or if it was in my head.'

Matthew sat silently for a moment. 'You said 'supernatural' before. Did you mean that?'

'I don't believe in the supernatural. But we've seen some really weird shit on this case. On the other hand, I am pretty screwed up, they tell me. You have to be in my line of work to understand.'

'You've been quiet,' he looked at John. 'What do you think?'

'Karen's right. We've seen some currently unexplained things. I don't know what I believe. But if you're not there, you may never know.'

'Mum's not up to that,' Matthew said. 'But yes, I wouldn't want to miss it.'

'I'll get you in. I'm going to the site. Floyd won't object. He knows you.'

'Can I come now?' Matthew asked.

'OK,' said Karen.' Let's go. I take it you're not driving?'

'Even if I were I wouldn't tell you that now would I?' Matthew joked.

'Don't worry about it,' John said. I'll drive us.

79

When they pulled up to the Robin Estate, Karen was shocked at what she saw. The whole area seemed to have become a building site with heavy plant and equipment and lorries all over the place.

'I'll park here. We can walk,' John said. 'It will be easier than navigating all this.'

They got out of the car and walked to the house from which the strange woman had emerged. It was all cordoned off but floodlit so they could see near the corner of the house itself. A huge crack had opened up in the brickwork, about a foot across at the widest point. The first floor was somehow intact apart from a big hole immediately above the crack. There were half a dozen hard-hatted builders busy on the site, and as Karen watched, a digger was reaching under the exposed floor to support it while Acro props were being manoeuvred underneath. Floyd was standing looking on. He turned round when he saw them approach.

'Karen, John, Matthew,' he said, looking at Karen for validation of Matthew's presence.

'I'd like Matthew to be here when we uncover the body, assuming we find one.' Karen said. Floyd raised an eyebrow.

'It's for ID purposes. When we found Caitlin McFee, the body was incredibly well preserved. We're not sure why. But it meant a visual ID was possible. This one, if it's here, may not be, but I'd like to be prepared.'

'If you say so. I've no objections,' Floyd said.

'Can we get in closer?' John asked.

'Not until it's fully secure. We haven't even thought about searching for the body yet. I've got no formal permission for that – unless you can give me some certainty.'

Karen shook her head. 'Nothing we can put on paper. I'm hoping that we'll find something. What happened to the woman living there?'

'She was in a right state,' Floyd replied. 'They had to bring a social worker in to calm her down. She's all right now though. The whole family have been put up in a swanky hotel until they can sort it all out. They reckon next door will be safe enough to move into later on today.'

As they watched, the builders eased a prop into position but then a large piece of brickwork broke completely away, crashing onto the concrete beneath. Already cracked it seemed to separate as more of the brick wall tilted outwards. The men ran to steady the prop and force the wall upright, but Karen's eyes were fixed on the concrete. She could see something.

'I can see plastic there!' she yelled at one of the builders. 'Be careful. It might be a body.'

The brick wall gave way, crashing down wrenching the foundations open even further. While the men tried to protect the rest of the building, John, Karen, and Matthew strained to look at the foundations. Floyd came running over. Karen pointed out the black plastic.

'That looks like what we found with the other two,' she said. 'Make sure they're careful.'

More masonry fell, and one of the builders shooed them away.

'We have to go slowly now. Best you get off. It'll take a while.'

'That black plastic could contain a body,' she said. 'Protect it at all costs.'

'Yes. I know about the missing lass. We won't let any more harm come to her.'

John sought out the forensics team leader and introduced himself. 'I think that black plastic is a body bag. You can carefully reveal it, but please don't touch it under any circumstances. Have you got a tent?'

'Yes, ready to erect as soon as the building is secured.'

'Good. We don't want a sideshow here. How long are you here for?'

'If we were positive there was a body, we'd be here all night. But we're only here as a precaution because of DS Cannon.'

'How about I guarantee it's a body bag? I have photos from another site.'

293

'With identification?'

John shook his head. 'But it is of a particular quality. Army, 1960 stock.'

'How sure are you?'

'As I'll ever be.'

Karen had wandered over and heard the end of the conversation. 'I'll talk to Floyd. He'll get authorisation. My DCI will intervene if necessary. The big boss wants this done.'

'If we can find him.' John muttered. 'From memory, he's not the most dedicated man ever.'

'Then I'll put the wind up him. Look, he's there.'

'Carrot not stick, Karen.'

'Karen took heed and spoke to Floyd.

'You what?' Floyd said, nearly dropping his flask of tea. 'My missus will have my guts for garters. I'm already ruining her Saturday and you want to carry on?'

'We're so close, Floyd,' Karen said. 'What harm is there if we at least look at the plastic. If it's not a body bag, we can all go home. But if it is, then think of the credit you'll get for helping to solve the case?'

'And you don't have to hang around all day,' John said. 'I'll liaise with your forensics team. And Karen's here for the duration.'

'All right, all right. Let's see if it's safe yet.'

Matthew joined them. 'Where are we?'

'We're just seeing if it's safe to look at the foundations. There's definitely something there, but they can't get to it until it's absolutely safe.'

As they approached the house, the forensics man held up his thumb. 'We've got the go-ahead,' he said. 'They're starting to clear around the plastic now.'

John, Karen, Matthew, and Floyd edged as close as they could to watch the operation. Painstakingly, the forensics team chipped away at the foundations and brushed away the dust until at last they had uncovered a body bag in the unmistakable shape of a small child. Almost immediately a small white tent was erected around the now floodlit scene.

'Are we ready?' Karen asked, her heart pounding as Matthew and John stood beside her.

'As we'll ever be,' said John.

'I've waited fifty years for this,' said Matthew. 'I'm ready.'

Inside the tent, they looked at the black body bag completely intact. 'It's identical to Caitlin McFee's,' Karen said. They were all awestruck, the tension palpable. The forensics man joined them. 'Who wants to do this? We're all friends here.'

Karen looked towards John. 'He's our head of forensics.'

'Fine by me. You'd better gear up.'

While John put on protective clothing, Matthew knelt next to the girl's head. Karen stood at her feet. Something caught her eye. A faint white figure. *Was that Caitlin McFee?* She shook her head and looked down at the body bag as John's gloved hand tentatively moved towards the zip. He shook his head, too, as if he'd seen something, but all he did was smile. Breathing heavily, he very slowly pulled down the zip on the body bag. First, the golden hair was revealed, then the perfect little face. Matthew gasped but did not move.

John continued pulling the zip down to expose a little silver necklace with a cat pendant around her neck then the pretty layered party dress that Karen had seen her in. Matthew was beginning to cry. Amy seemed to look straight at him. *Did her hand move?* He reached to touch her, and she smiled as for a split second they connected flesh to flesh.

A swirling wind whipped round the tent. Momentarily distracted, the three looked around. When they looked back, there was nothing there but dust rags and the skeletal remains of Amy Warren.

None of them spoke. Matthew was in floods of fifty years' worth of tears. Karen was nearly crying, and John was trying hard not to. Holding back her tears, Karen saw the glistening necklace lying in the dust. She looked at John. 'Can I?'

'No. But I will.' He carefully picked it up and handed it to her. She passed it to Matthew and closed the fingers of his outstretched hand tightly around it. 'Give this to your mother. So she knows.'

Matthew, still sobbing nodded and took a tissue from his pocket. Not for his face, but to wrap the necklace carefully so he could put it safely away. 'She loved cats. She had a little ginger and white one called Fudge.'

Karen and John, faces ashen, emerged first from the tent to an anxious waiting Floyd.

'It's her,' said Karen with authority.' We have an ID. It's Amy Warren'

'We'll have to do the DNA obviously,' added John hastily. 'But from her clothes, we are sure it's her.'

A moment later, a red-eyed Matthew emerged from the tent. 'Thank you so much, Karen, John. I'll go and see Mum now. I can tell her it's all over.'

Floyd went into the tent briefly then emerged stony-faced. 'I can confirm we have found the remains of a young girl,' he said. 'I'll arrange for a press conference to be held as soon as possible. Thank you, DS Thorpe. John. We'll arrange a formal statement at the station shortly. Probably tomorrow morning now. You will be advised of the time. Now I'd better get back to the wife.'

Karen and John walked back to the car together. 'Where are we staying tonight?'

'With Mummy and Daddy, of course.' Karen thumped him. 'OK, how about we treat ourselves to a nice little three-star hotel?

'Sounds perfect.'

'Can we just relax a little now? Please?'

'What? Without checking with Davie and Macy? No chance,' Karen said.

80

Sunday 24 November

Mr Binks woke up early with an empty stomach and a heavy heart. The loss of his soul mate was almost as hard to bear as the loss of the tome. *I'd better visit my friend*, he decided. *I can't even bear to think about breakfast.*

At the old bookshop, he was greeted with enthusiasm.

'Do you have it? Can I see it? I've waited so long...' The gatekeeper stopped in his tracks. Mr Binks' expression was not one of triumphant ownership. 'But I heard the currents break. What happened?'

Over a cup of tea, Mr Binks relayed the events of the night before. When he came to the part about Grizela, the gatekeeper was shocked.

'I knew by reputation that Magda was a crafty one. But I saw that lovely lady myself. Mr Binks, I'd have been taken in too. Don't distress yourself.'

'Could it have been...' Mr Binks began.

'Possession?' The gatekeeper finished. 'Aye. If she'd passed over, she'd need flesh and bones to take the book. A spectre can't pick things up.'

'The body of Fergus Anderson had been reanimated. By her do you think?'

'I think it likely. Until she knew the end was nigh.'

'But he was overpowered, and it was my dear lady who picked up the book.'

The gatekeeper nodded slowly at him.

'You mean she may have actually flitted from his bones to my beloved Grizela?' The gatekeeper nodded. 'I have heard such things before.'

'Why, yes. She was completely herself until we got to the road. How could I be so stupid?'

'Don't torment yourself, dear sir. You were dealing with an ancient and crafty being. But it is unlikely she will reside for too long in your dear lady friend. And the manuscript would be in the safest keeping of all now.'

Mr Binks smiled. 'So my dearest Grizela might be real and no longer possessed?'

'There's only one way to find out, my friend.'

'Thank you. You have given me true hope. I shall go and see her forthwith.'

Mr Binks returned to his hotel and packed his case for his long journey home. It would be even more complicated to go via Penrith, but heartened by the gatekeeper's words, he could not bear to miss the opportunity of seeing Grizela again.

Arriving at Penrith, he retraced his journey to Grizela's bookshop but his heart nearly stopped when he saw a written notice pressed to the glass from inside the shop.

Closed due to unforeseen circumstances.

Had Mr Binks been able to look past the curtains and the old opaque window, he would have seen Grizela, huddled in a corner, completely unable to remember what she had done for the past few days. The only thing she knew for sure was that she was now in possession of an extremely precious book, and that she would have to guard it for the rest of her life.

He knocked at the door and peered through the small dusty window but there was nothing. He wiped a small tear from his eye before turning around to continue his journey home. 'I tried, my love,' he said as he left.

By the time he arrived back at the station for the last leg of his journey, there was something else troubling him.

Good gracious. No breakfast. That will never do. I'd better book the buffet car.

***

'I can't believe I'm doing this on a Sunday,' Floyd's voice boomed from Karen's phone. 'But there's a first for everything I suppose.'

'C'mon, John.' Karen prodded the body lying next to her. 'We're on.'

'Ow! What about Macy and Davie?'

'Macy's getting here as soon as she can. She's finished with him.'

'Finished with Davie?' John stirred.

'Finished tidying up his paperwork.'

'That's a new one. Can I have a go at your paperwork?' He snuggled closer.

'No.' Karen sat up. 'This is my deadline and it looks like I've done it. Davie's managed to match Anderson's DNA to the body bags, so how his body shrank like that we'll never know. But I don't care now. I'm sure they can match Amy's DNA to Matthew. It's nearly all done. We just need to make an appearance then head back so the guv knows we've done it.'

'If you say so,' John hauled himself out of bed. 'Remind me to look up self-mummification,' he said idly. 'Monks used to do it in the olden days.'

'Please never say that to me ever again.' Karen said. 'Whatever the hell it is, I really, really do not want to know.'

John looked at his watch. 'Hey, it's still early. We've got hours yet. When does Floyd want us?'

'Don't you want breakfast?' Karen said. 'I'm starving.'

'And I know what will give us both a big appetite,' John inched towards her. Karen smiled. 'And then I've got something very important I want to ask you.'

'I know,' Karen smiled. 'But not today. Tomorrow maybe. Promise?'

'OK,' John smiled.'

81

Precisely three hours later, John and Karen were back at the Lincoln police station. Floyd stood outside ready to address the small gathering of the press and the public – who had either been alerted to the forthcoming announcement or had just stumbled across it.

'This reminds me a bit of the guv, when he had to talk about Stella's case,' Karen said. 'At least this is a happy sort of announcement.'

'It is,' John agreed. 'The family will have peace at last.'

Karen looked out of the door at the waiting crowd. 'That's not your dad is it?'

'Bound to be,' he replied. 'He called me yesterday and I told him what happened.'

'You never said.'

'It wasn't important.'

Floyd looked at his watch and beckoned them to come out and join him at the lectern. As he began to speak, Big John gave Karen a little wave.

'Ladies and gentlemen,' Floyd began. 'I can confirm that at six o'clock yesterday evening we found the remains of a young female.'

The crowd became visibly excited. 'Is it our Amy?' someone shouted out.

'From our initial findings,' Floyd continued. 'We have reason to believe, but cannot yet confirm definitely, that this is the body of Amy Warren.'

There were cheers from the crowd and flashes from the photographers' cameras.

He went on. 'Amy Warren was abducted from somewhere in this vicinity fifty years ago. All our investigations over the years and some identification of the clothes Amy was wearing at the time of her disappearance would indicate that we have indeed found her body.'

There were more cheers, mainly supportive, one very loud one was scathing.

'Fifty years? It's a bloody disgrace.'

'But we must clearly undertake due process to establish this beyond doubt.' DS Cannon carried on. 'It would be very unfair on Amy's family to give them false hope at this very difficult time.'

This seemed to settle the crowd a little.

'I would like to pass on my sincerest thanks to Detective Sergeant Thorpe for her work in helping us to locate this body.' Karen blushed a little and there were more photos taken. 'Any further announcements will be made in the usual way,' Floyd finished. He looked towards the few journalists there. 'OK, boys and girls. Fire away.'

The people watching began to disperse leaving just a couple of interested people who were trying to hear what Floyd was saying to the journalists. John's parents were both waiting, together with a couple of reporters who wanted a word with Karen. She was having none of it. She had spotted Matthew waiting, arm in arm with an elderly woman.

Karen walked towards them.

Mrs Warren embraced her tightly. 'You have brought me so much happiness today, love. I never thought I'd see this day.'

'I'm pleased I could help,' Karen replied, trying not to tear up.

'Thanks so much again, Karen,' said Matthew. 'Mum is overjoyed we've found Amy. We just want her back as soon as we can have it.'

'Of course,' Karen said. 'It's out of my hands, but you know Floyd Cannon; he'll keep you posted. They'll need to confirm the DNA. We think we have the murderer now, or at least his corpse. If it matches with his, then it's all over.'

Matthew nodded. 'I understand.' He looked at Karen and smiled. 'You will come to the funeral?' he asked.

'Of course,' Karen said. 'I'd love to.'

Waiting patiently, a very sheepish Daphne and a very proud looking Big John came forward when Matthew and his mother walked away.

'Well done, Karen. You are a hero locally now. Imagine that? My son, going out with a heroine.'

'Yes, well done,' said Daphne timidly. 'I know we haven't seen eye to eye. And I'm sorry.'

Is that it? thought Karen

'Will you come and have Sunday lunch with us?' Big John asked. 'We've organised a little something.'

John answered for both of them. 'Not today Dad. We have to get back home now. It's been a very long week.'

'There's someone else,' Karen nudged him and tilted her head backwards.

'I did wonder,' John replied. They turned away from John's parents to watch as Mr Binks, looking as dapper as ever, came to greet them.

'I'm sorry, my poor young friends. I had every intention of coming to help you with your quest, but I see that you have managed it without me.'

'There is one mystery still,' Karen said. 'Who sent me the files? You don't know anything about that do you, Mr Binks?'

Mr Binks smiled. 'I did promise your father that there was something I would never tell you. But since he is no longer with us, I sincerely doubt he would want me to leave you with unanswered questions.'

'What? You met him? You have to tell me!' Karen demanded

Mr Binks fiddled with his whiskers. 'As I'm sure dear John can tell you, I'm not very good with computers. But your father gave me the most precise directions.'

'Why would he do that? Explain.'

'He was worried about his health, and in the event something happened to him, he wanted these investigations to be concluded. You were the only person he could trust to do it.'

'Why didn't you tell me earlier?'

'As I said. I made him a promise.'

'I don't know what to say,' Karen said, shaking her head. She turned to John. 'Did you know anything about this? I know you were helping Mr Binks with setting up his email account...'

John blushed. 'I do remember Mr Binks asking me something... Now when was it?'

Mr Binks interrupted him. 'My dear young people, I will admit that the last few weeks have been full of some very, what shall I say, strange events. Not all of which will ever be fully explained.'

He looked at both of them together and spoke slowly and carefully. 'Now is the time to celebrate your achievements and look forward, not back. You do not need to remember everything you have been through. Just remember what you have achieved and how much joy you have brought to these unfortunate families. Do you both understand?'

'Yes, Mr Binks,' John and Karen said together.

Karen shook her head. 'What did you say again?'

Mr Binks smiled his sweetest smile. 'I asked you to promise that you will return to have tea with me again soon.'

'Of course,' John said.

'And there is a volume I seek. It's called The Lanes of Lucifer. A fascinating illustrated script I am told. And you, Karen, are an extraordinary detective.'

'I'll be pleased to help, Mr Binks.' Karen smiled.

'Karen? Karen!' Yelled a voice and in the instant it took Karen to spot Macy waving excitedly, Mr Binks slipped away.

Macy whooped when she reached Karen. 'I'm so proud of you. Even the boss will have to say something nice, too.' She gave Karen a bear hug.

'We're heading back home now,' Karen said. 'How about we catch up near mine for a little celebration?'

'Fine by me,' Macy grinned.

'At the Thai restaurant?'

'Where else. See you later, then.' They waved her off.

82

'This is turning into my favourite place,' Karen said as she clinked glasses of wine with John and Macy. 'It seems to be where the most important things in my life get celebrated.'

'Not all of them,' John said a little wistfully. His phone rang. 'Excuse me a minute,' he got up and went outside to take the call.

'Here's to you,' Macy raised her glass again. 'I so want to do my sergeants' exams now,' she said enthusiastically. 'They're bound to make you an inspector now.'

Karen laughed. 'There are exams for that too you know.'

'Easy peasy.'

Karen smiled. 'We'll see. By the way, did you ever find out where you first met Davie?'

'Yes, indeed.' Now it was Macy's turn to laugh. 'It was embarrassing really, for him at least. Not me.'

'Tell me more,' said Karen, intrigued.

'It was at a Take That concert,' Macy said, still giggling. Robbie threw a T-shirt into the audience and Davie and I fought for it.'

Karen guffawed. 'No! I didn't think he was like that,' she said. 'Who won?'

'He did, the git,' Macy said. 'But he's kept it, and he says he'll give it to me next time I go up there.'

'He's trying to tempt you up then?' Karen hinted. 'Would you?'

'Oh, I do like him,' Macy replied. 'But it's a long distance to have a relationship.'

'There's always transfers,' Karen winked at her.

'And it is a beautiful city,' Macy sighed. 'Anyway, tonight is all about you.'

John returned looking less than happy.

'What's up?' Karen asked. 'Not your parents again?'

'How did you guess? Mum was very upset that you wouldn't come for Sunday lunch.'

'Oh,' Karen said. 'Don't tell me she's had a change of heart at last?'

'Apparently, she'd told a few people about what we'd done. She had invited some of the local bigwigs over to meet you. It took her ages to organise it. Well, that's what she said.'

'Oh, dear.' Karen's expression changed. 'I almost feel sorry for her. If I'd known that I might have said yes. Was she very upset?'

John shook his head. 'She was absolutely bloody furious. She wants me to break up with you.'

John swore? Karen was shocked. 'And are you going to?'

Macy leaned forward, fascinated.

'Don't be so fucking stupid. I love you, you silly bitch.'

Karen beamed. Macy raised her glass. 'Here's to the both of you.'

A couple of hours later, Karen and John were back at Karen's flat. It was Sunday night, and all Karen wanted to do was chill out and watch the television. She turned it on with the remote. It was a rerun of the talent show which had started the whole adventure. 'I was watching this that night I picked up my tablet and saw Amy,' she said. 'I wonder...'

'Don't be silly,' said John, but Karen reached for her tablet anyway.

'Supposing I saw all three girls waving goodbye at me? Wouldn't that be the perfect end?'

'You know it's not going to happen, you nutter.'

'Let's just see.' Karen turned on her tablet and the first thing she saw was an image of three little girls grinning at the camera. She laughed. 'How about that then?'

John peered at the picture. 'Cute, but they're Chinese.'

'This tablet keeps sending me these things for screen savers. It's an odd coincidence though. I'm going to accept it as a sign.'

They cuddled together on the sofa watching TV and knocking back even more wine.

After polishing off the second bottle, John finally plucked up the courage to say something, 'Karen. You know what I said earlier?'

Karen giggled, but by the time he got down on one knee, nearly falling as he did so, she was crying with laughter. 'Don't be silly, John. Don't even think about asking me that. I can't get my head around it now. Or for ages. And how would Mummy like it?'

John struggled to his feet and flopped down beside her on the sofa, pouting.

'But I do love you,' Karen said, meaning to kiss him on the cheek but tipping forward and catching his shoulder instead. 'How about you move in with me and we see how it goes?'

John instantly perked up. 'I'll take that,' he said and for a reason he didn't understand, Karen collapsed into fits of unstoppable laughter.

Monday 25 November

Nothing could have prepared Karen for the welcome she got as she walked through the door to the office. The whole team stood waiting for her and at the front was Saskia.

Karen froze, momentarily as she looked her in the eye. Speaking slowly and carefully she said, 'Good morning, Saskia.'

Saskia smiled. 'Congratulations Sergeant.'

The whole team began to clap and cheer.

DCI Winter came straight out of his office and actually smiled for the first time since his team had won the cup.

'Well done Karen,' he said. 'You are quite the celebrity. For now,' he added. 'Enjoy it then I want you in my office in,' he looked at his watch, 'five minutes.'

Karen relished the praise and plaudits of her colleagues. She scanned the newspaper articles they had accumulated to show her and she scowled at some of the photos of herself.

Macy brought her a proper espresso coffee and a muffin from the Coffee Shop next door and Saskia brought in three bouquets of flowers. One from Edinburgh, one from York and one from Lincoln.

It was a good half an hour later she unapologetically walked into DCI Winter's office.

'Inspectors' exams,' DCI Winter said. 'Chief Constable Burns has been on to me to pass on his congratulations.'

'Thanks, Guv.'

'You'd better pass the first time or you'll be letting us all down. Now bugger off and get on with the job. Quite a bit for you to do I imagine.'

Karen, a little light-headedly, went back to her desk and logged into her computer. She noticed her phone, too, was blinking with voicemails. While she waited for her PC to start up, she listened to the calls. The first ones were calls of congratulations for her success. Then there was another, very different call. 'It's about my daughter...' It wasn't the only one.

When her emails finally came up the inbox was full. There were hundreds of emails from everywhere in the country and some around the world. All asking her to help with missing children. Karen stared at the screen, rigid with shock. When she could finally open her mouth it was to shout.

'Macy!' She yelled. 'Come and look at this. What the hell have I started now?'

THE END

Dear Reader, I hope you enjoyed Three Little Girls. If you did, you'll be pleased to know that the next title in the series, The Woman Who Knew Faces, will be out in 2022.

Three Little Girls was originally Karen Thorpe's first outing – written before Comatose. But somehow she nosed her way into that book too and that allowed me to introduce her character and back story more comprehensively.

The idea for the book was inspired by Jo Smith, an online friend for many years now, who wanted me to write a ghost story. In my youth, I was obsessed with the occult and it seemed to be a nice way to revisit old haunts!

I would like to thank my lovely beta readers Andrea, Sue, Lin, Dawn, Sarah and Shonagh for their invaluable help in tidying up the text and spotting errors. Also I'd like to thank all the people who volunteered to advance-read this book.

Special thanks go to Eoghan Egan for being, as always, great support to me. Fergus Martin for expert help with Scottish dialect. Kath Middleton for her wise words and great feedback and Shelagh Corker for her invaluable proofreading and editing.

Finally, I would like to wholeheartedly thank the whole team at QMP, past and present, for their continuing amazing help and support and especially Zoé O'Farrell for her excellent blog tours.

2021 QUESTION MARK PRESS NEW RELEASES

available at amazon

Stay tuned! More new releases this year coming soon...

Other books by Jane Badrock

The Shockalot box.
An assortment of dark and twisty short stories.

Sinister Sisterhood.
A dark comedy about a team of women taking on animal exploitation.

COMATOSE
The first story in the Karen Thorpe crime series.

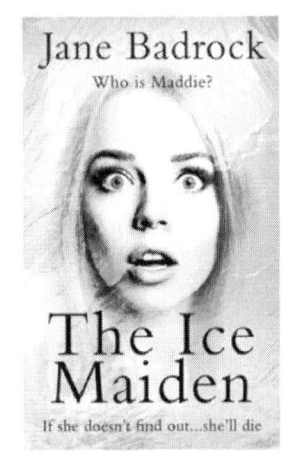

The Ice Maiden
A thriller. Maths student Maddie has to discover the truth about her identity